Overnight Delivery

The Douglas Files: Book One

Nathan Birr

Published by BEACON BOOKS, LLC

Beacon Books LLC

Cover Image Copyright ©
welcomia/iStock/Thinkstock

THE HOLY BIBLE, NEW INTERNATIONAL VERSION®, NIV®
Copyright © 1973, 1978, 1984, 2011 by Biblica, Inc.®
Used by permission. All rights reserved worldwide.

ISBN: 978-0-9967691-9-8 (hc)
ISBN: 978-0-9981813-0-1 (sc)
ISBN: 978-0-9981813-1-8 (e)

www.nathanbirr.com

To everyone who believed this day would come—
Thank you for your encouragement and for your prayers.

Chapter One

Five years ago . . .
Friday, May 25, 2007
4:14 p.m.

"FOR THE RECORD, this is totally your fault," Jackson Douglas said under his breath with a sideways glance at his brother.

"My fault?" Grant whispered. "You were the one who had to stop for some shrimp tacos."

"And you're the one who had to pull a John Wayne."

"I couldn't—"

"Shut up!" Dragon snapped, waving the Beretta M9 that punctuated his command. He pointed the gun briefly in Jackson's direction before returning it to waist level, still aimed vigilantly at the hostages. Of the two robbers, he was clearly the less stable. He was constantly in motion—if not pacing in what little space was available inside the trailer-turned-shrimp shack, then waving the gun, tapping his fingers, or fidgeting with something. Jackson was sure the same sweat that trickled down the back of the dragon tattooed on his arm was also beading under the black ski mask that obscured his face.

Sweat was the order of the day. Midday temperatures on Oahu had neared ninety and not cooled much since. There was a gentle trade wind blowing, but not down on the floor of the trailer where Jackson, Grant, and the other hostages were sequestered. The floor was sticky—where it wasn't littered with pieces of shrimp, fish, lettuce, tomatoes, and cheese—and the entire place smelled like a gym bag full of seafood. Combined with the high temperature outside and the heat of the grease fryers and grills—not to mention the heat of the moment—it was almost unbearable.

With nothing else to do, Jackson surveyed his fellow captives. Frank was calm, as if he'd been robbed before. His son's face was flushed, from heat or anger or more likely both. Surfer Guy looked dazed and his girlfriend looked ready to pass out or puke. Camo Girl just appeared bored. With Jackson and Grant and the two robbers turned hostage-takers, it made for nine people in what amounted to a galley kitchen.

"You have five minutes," Sergeant Keomalu announced over the megaphone, prompting several in the trailer to check their watches: Lefty, the other robber, who wore his watch on the inside of his right wrist, Hannibal-style; Grant, who was actually still concerned about punctuality; and Camo Girl, whose eyes flicked down in a casual glance.

"They're bluffing," Dragon said. It was almost a question.

"Either come out alone with your hands up, or we are coming in," Keomalu shouted.

"They wouldn't dare."

"Sooner or later they would," Jackson said.

Grant elbowed him. Lefty shot him a look but said nothing.

"They aren't going to just sit there forever," Jackson said.

"Shut up!" Dragon barked.

Jackson shrugged. "What, you think they'll just give up and go away? Tell me, when was the last time you heard a couple of thugs riding out a police siege? Maybe out here, but not on the mainland."

Dragon crouched down and stuck his Beretta in Jackson's face. "I've had about enough of your mouth."

"Look, there's three ways this goes," Jackson said, appealing with his eyes to Lefty. "You surrender, which I'm guessing isn't happening. The cops storm the place, which goes badly for you and probably most of us."

Surfer Girl whimpered, her main contribution to the situation.

"Or you guys leave with one hostage, and the rest of us go free."

"Why would we trade seven hostages for one?" Dragon asked.

"Because there aren't any nine-passenger vans in the parking lot," Jackson answered.

"Come here," Lefty said, motioning to Dragon with his gun. The two thugs whispered at one end of the trailer.

"What are you doing?" Grant asked, his voice barely more than moving lips.

"Being the hero," Jackson mouthed back.

"Isn't that why you're mad at me?"

"Yes, but I'm doing a better job than you."

"Are you crazy?"

"You know, this calm demeanor is really going to serve you well as a cop."

"You're going to get us all killed."

"Not all."

Grant frowned.

Jackson raised his voice. "I'm telling you, you slip out the door with a gun to a hostage's head, the cops will do whatever you say. Get in a car, tell them not to follow, and you're off."

"Whose side are you on?" Surfer Guy asked as Lefty and Dragon conferred for another moment.

"Whichever side gets me out of here the quickest."

"What about the rest of us?" Frank's son asked.

"Okay," Lefty said as he and Dragon separated. "I want everybody to slowly stand up and approach the counter."

Like all hostages, they hesitated for a moment out of fear.

"Now! Stand up and put your hands on the counter."

Jackson squinted as he stood and looked into the sun, just low enough in the sky to be a nuisance. He found himself in the middle of the group, his palms touching down on the trailer's serving counter, which was about as clean as the floor. Outside, forming a semi-circle in the parking lot, were half a dozen police vehicles, including a SWAT truck. Jackson had heard them arrive in increments from his position on the floor, but was surprised to see so many of them there, especially SWAT.

"If you approach us, we will kill the hostages!" Lefty shouted, his first communication with the cops. He and Dragon had remained in the end of the trailer, out of sight. But as he spoke, Lefty inched his way behind the captives until he was whispering in Jackson's ear.

"I like your plan, *haole*. And since it was your idea, you get to be our hostage."

"I'm honored, but take her," Jackson said with a slightly perceptible nod toward Camo Girl.

"Jack," Grant said.

"Listen," Jackson said, tilting his head to speak to Lefty. "She's a woman. She'll be a more sympathetic figure to the cops and easier for you to handle. She's calm; she's not going to make a scene. And she's a local. Half the women on the island look just like her. She'll blend in once you make your getaway."

"You're a coward!" Frank's son spat.

"Alternatively, you could take him."

Lefty stood back. Then he reached over and grabbed Camo Girl by the back of her collar. "You're coming with us," he said over her startled scream. He pulled her backwards, dragged her over, and shoved her in between Jackson and Grant. "We're coming out!" he shouted to the police. "If you make a move on us, we'll kill the girl!"

*   *   *

Forty minutes earlier . . .

"WE DON'T have time for this, Jack."

"Would you relax, dude? It's not a race. Everybody gets to eat."

"Yeah, a buffet. So why are we stopping here?"

Jackson turned into the gravel parking lot of Kolohe's Shrimp Shack. "Because I didn't come all the way to Hawaii to eat ham and pork. I want seafood."

"And this is the place you pick?"

"I did my research, bro. Best shrimp tacos on the island. The *kama'inas* swear by it."

Grant rolled his eyes. "*Kama'inas*," he muttered.

Jackson parked next to a Jeep with two surfboards bound to the roof.

"Best shrimp tacos on the island, huh?" Grant asked. "There's nobody here."

Jackson ran his eyes across the little promontory that was home to the humble shrimp shack, several picnic tables, and the small gravel parking area. There were only three other patrons.

"It's not a tourist place," Jackson said as he opened his door. "I'm buying, what do you want?"

"I'll wait," Grant replied as he got out.

"Suit yourself, dude."

Grant strolled behind Jackson to the counter of the small shack, where Jackson ordered three shrimp tacos and a lemonade. "Sure you don't want something?" he asked, digging out his wallet.

"Yeah."

Jackson handed a ten-dollar bill to the greasy-palmed, greasy-aproned owner—Frank, according to the patch embroidered on his shirt. Frank's spitting image filled a cup of lemonade for Jackson and tended the grease fryers while Frank made change. Jackson told him to keep it.

While waiting for his food, he glanced at Grant, who rubbed the back of his neck and stared out at the ocean. At six-two, two and a quarter, Jackson's younger brother was both taller and bigger—all of it muscle—than he was. He had inherited their dad's square jaw and brown hair, the latter of which was kept trimmed short. Wearing dorky board shorts, a cheap tee picked up in Waikiki, and his John Lennon sunglasses, Grant fit the bill of a tourist.

"Here you go," Frank announced through a mouth of gravel. Jackson nodded as he took the tacos, then headed for the precipice of a small cliff that overlooked the rolling blue waves. He bit into the first taco and savored the spicy shrimp, along with the breeze and the panorama in front of him.

"Any chance you could eat in the car?" Grant asked.

"You have no appreciation for ambiance," Jackson said, stuffing another quarter of a taco into his mouth. "You know how many meals I eat in a car?"

Grant sighed.

"Dude, relax. We're in Hawaii." Jackson gestured with the hand holding two tacos. "Look at this."

To the right, the beach curved around the greenish waters of Malaekahana Bay toward an uninhabited island. Left, the sea was pure blue, a few shades darker than the sky. Straight ahead, shelves of clouds lined the horizon, which was beginning to dim in anticipation of sunset. It was still several hours away, and for the moment, the entire peninsula was bathed in afternoon warmth.

Jackson bent to retrieve his lemonade, stashed in the grass at his feet. He took a long pull on the straw and looked over his shoulder as he heard wheels crunch on the gravel parking lot. They belonged to a blue pickup that rolled to within fifteen feet of the shack before skidding to a stop. The spray of gravel turned the heads of a couple of surfers at a picnic table, one male, one female. A local girl in camouflage pants and a plain black tee glanced up from the next table, checked her watch, then looked back at the cell phone in her hands.

Jackson faced the ocean again. "Just think, Mom and Dad are stuck on a bus full of overweight, middle-aged, white-legged tourists riding through the valley." He stuck the remainder of his first taco into his mouth, and had just started to chew when Grant lightly tapped his shoulder.

"Whub?"

Grant tugged on his sleeve, and Jackson turned his head. Two men got out of the pickup, both in jeans, tees, and black ski masks. Surfer Girl screamed. Camo Girl set down her phone, mid-text.

The pickup's passenger raised his gun and shouted. "Everybody over here, on the ground!"

Surfer Girl screamed again as the driver approached the counter of the shack. "Empty the register!" he shouted.

"On the ground!" the first man yelled again.

Jackson followed Grant toward the shack. On the way, he met the eyes of Camo Girl—blank—and of the surfers—frantic and possibly stoned. He had only a moment to look over the masked men. Both had darker skin, likely locals. The guy close to them had tattoos that entwined both of his arms—dragons or snakes or some multi-headed mutant lizard. The other was nondescript except that he held his gun in his left hand.

"Get down," Dragon yelled, pushing Jackson to his knees and shoving him off balance. He dropped his tacos as he collided into Grant.

"Nobody move," Dragon said, his eyes going back and forth from the five victims on the ground to the counter of the shack, where Lefty had produced a small bag that he thrust at Frank.

"Fill it."

6

Jackson glanced at his brother, whose eyes were aimed up the embankment at the main highway. It was far enough away that a casual passerby wouldn't be likely to notice anything amiss at Kolohe's Shrimp Shack.

Camo Girl looked toward the road too, her brown eyes flickering with the first signs of life, of concern. Beyond her, Surfer Guy was trying to console Surfer Girl, and in need of some consolation of his own.

Frank filled the bag and shoved it across the counter to Lefty.

"That's it?"

"That's it."

Lefty cursed and nodded at Dragon. "Let's go." He circled the pickup, and Dragon gave one last look at the group in the grass and turned to get his door. Jackson's eyes caught a flicker of movement to his left. Camo Girl had pushed up onto her palms. Was she nuts enough to try something?

Jackson's attention was diverted by more movement, this time to his right. Before he knew what was happening, Grant was on his feet, charging Dragon. In a blur, Grant hit the robber, driving him into the open pickup door. They grappled for a moment, and Jackson saw Lefty jump out his side of the pickup. He leveled his gun, ready to take a shot, and Jackson felt a scream freeze in his throat.

Before Lefty could fire, Dragon shoved Grant, creating enough separation and enough time for him to land a punch that knocked Grant onto his back. Both robbers trained their guns on him, and Jackson waited for the bullets.

Instead he heard sirens.

"Forget it, let's go!" Lefty shouted, and he and Dragon reached for their doors.

The sirens grew louder, and flashing red and blue lights appeared at the top of a small rise.

Lefty swore again.

"That's the only way out!" Dragon said.

Lefty paused a beat. "Everybody inside. Now!"

Camo Girl was first on her feet. Jackson helped Grant up, and they followed her into the shack where they joined Frank and his son.

7

"Everybody on the floor!" Lefty said, closing the door behind them.

"You all right?" Jackson whispered.

Grant rubbed his jaw and nodded.

The sirens whined and Jackson heard a car screech to a halt in the gravel. He shrugged. "At least we've got food."

*   *   *

4:51 p.m.

JACKSON LEANED against the side of a police car, munching on a taco he had made for himself while Frank and his son were being debriefed. He figured the combination of his earlier tip and having saved the day made up for it.

"I can't believe you're eating right now," Grant said.

"I dropped my tacos."

"I can't believe you helped them get away."

"I'm sure if you'd like to sit in the truck a while longer, Frank would let you. Provided you don't get in the way."

"You told them to take the girl? Gave them our car? I can't believe you."

Jackson reached for his lemonade on the hood. "Okay, first of all, I am hungry. We've been over this, and Dragon made me drop two of my tacos. Second, I would rather they get away than I get a posthumous medal for putting them in jail. And third, they're not getting away."

"What?"

Jackson turned as two police cars raced out of the lot. "Wow, that was even better timing than I hoped for." He bit down on his taco.

"What are you talking about?" Grant asked.

"I didn't tell you earlier, because I knew you'd flip, but I didn't get gas this afternoon."

"What?"

"I met Becky in the arcade for a few more rounds of air hockey. She is tough, dude."

"How much was left?"

"Empty light came on back before Kahaluu. I wasn't sure it'd start."

"That's great," Grant said. "So now you've created another hostage situation on a major highway, and they have the girl."

"Relax." He lifted the taco to his mouth. "She's in on it."

Before Grant could say anything, two very stern police officers approached Jackson and Grant. They were the last to be debriefed, which was how Jackson preferred it. He could set the record straight.

The shorter of the two, but clearly the lead officer, stopped in front of Jackson. He was white, no tan, arms of a weightlifter. He didn't mince words. "Why did you help them escape?"

Jackson swallowed his taco. "It was hot, and we're late for a luau."

"This a joke to you, son?"

Jackson bit his tongue before making a comment about jokes and the officer's haircut.

"He did get six of us out unharmed," Grant said.

The officer regarded him with a cursory glance. "Six of seven." He turned back to Jackson with a sigh. "Why the girl?"

"She wanted to be a hostage, so I figured I'd oblige."

"You're going to be a lot later for that luau if I run you in for obstructing justice."

"Or as an accomplice," his partner said. "The other hostages report you offered them your vehicle."

"I figured you'd have disabled theirs somehow. It's Hostage Situation 101."

"I say we run him in," the partner said.

Jackson laughed, then signed. "Let me ask you, how'd you guys know this place was being robbed?"

"Anonymous tip," the lead officer answered.

"By text?"

He swiveled his chin. "How'd you know that?"

Before Jackson could answer, the officer's radio squawked. "This is Heath," he said, unhooking the receiver from his shoulder.

The radio squawked some gibberish, and Jackson made out a few numbers.

"Where?" Heath asked.

"Waianae."

"Roger that."

"Sir!" a third officer shouted from just up the rise. Heath and his partner turned to face him. "Kalua and Rivers just apprehended two males in a blue Ford Fusion. Both taken injured but alive."

"What about the girl?"

"Unharmed."

"Where?"

"Just north of Kahana Bay."

Jackson made a face. "What about the car?"

All three officers ignored him.

"We have rental insurance?" Jackson whispered to Grant.

"Dispatch, we don't need SWAT anymore," Heath barked into his radio. "Send them to Waianae. We're rolling."

Heath's partner quickly took Jackson and Grant's names and contact information at their hotel in Honolulu, saying the police would be in touch with further questions.

"You're not going to confine us to an island paradise while you conduct a prolonged investigation, are you?" Jackson called after him as he got into the car.

It was too late. Heath was behind the wheel and whipped the car backwards, spinning the tires and spraying gravel—and sending Jackson's half-empty lemonade onto the ground. Heath hit the sirens and the car shot out of the lot. Only one police car remained on site, a last sentinel.

"I don't believe you," Grant said.

"So I hear."

"You act like this is your Xbox."

"We're free, aren't we?" Jackson asked. "They caught the baddies. The girl—whoever she is—is fine."

Grant exhaled.

"And," Jackson said, tapping his brother on the chest, "if we can get the Cowabungas over there to give us a lift, we can still make Waimea in time to see them dig dinner out of the sand."

Chapter Two

Monday, May 14, 2012
7:27 a.m.

JACKSON AWOKE WITH a start when his cell phone began playing Kiss's "Shout it Out Loud." He lifted his head off the pillow and squinted against the light streaming in through the blinds. It was morning already?

He reached for the nightstand and grabbed his phone, then rolled onto his back, bringing the tangled sheets with him. Even in his condition, he recognized the ringtone he had set for his neighbor Connie. He glanced at the clock and stifled a sigh. It figured.

"Yeah?" he said, his throat dry.

"Jackson, is that you?"

He seriously considered telling her no, it wasn't. But that would only get him in trouble later. So he confirmed and tried to blink the sleep and his headache away.

"It's Connie." He could have left the phone on the nightstand and heard her perfectly.

"Hi, Connie."

"I know it's a little early, but I need a favor."

Jackson lowered the phone from his mouth and nearly clapped it shut. But that too would lead to trouble. Instead, he cleared his throat before asking, "What kind of favor?" The lawn had just been mowed on Saturday, and he was pretty sure he had already washed her Mercedes this month.

Connie hesitated, and Jackson actually sat up in bed. "What is it?"

"Would you be able to come over? I'd rather talk about it in person."

"Um . . . sure. When?"

"As soon as possible."

11

"Well, I just woke up thirty seconds ago, so you'll have to give me a little while."

"Of course. Don't bother with breakfast. I made sticky buns."

"Right. I'll be over as soon as I can."

"Thanks, Jackson."

He nodded and collapsed his cell, then realized nods didn't translate too well through the phone. So be it.

Jackson closed his eyes and exhaled heavily, pinching the bridge of his nose. The headache remained.

With yet another sigh, he untangled the sheets and swung his freed legs off the bed. Looking down at his white T-shirt and rumpled blue jeans, he tried to remember where the headache had come from. Oh yes, the bottle of Scotch, a gift from a client.

He stood up slowly, wiping his face with his hand.

Wait a second. Jackson didn't drink and he was pretty sure he hadn't touched the Scotch. No, he had crashed on the couch with an old photo album and the unopened bottle, testing his willpower. It had passed, barely, and the Scotch was still sealed on the coffee table. He could use it to bribe Connie at some point in time.

So the headache had come from elsewhere, and as he trudged toward the bathroom, he remembered where. The same place all of them came from. But this time, the pain had been exacerbated by a stroll through a minefield of memories. And by the realization, as the clock had hit midnight, that it was his thirtieth birthday.

A dozen different thoughts swirled around Jackson's head, vying for his attention as he took care of the first issue of the day. He wanted nothing to do with any of them, and tried instead to think what Connie might possibly want. It was like guessing which Hollywood starlet would end up in rehab next.

Leaving his clothes in a pile on the floor, Jackson stepped into a warm shower and let the water pelt and massage his body for a few minutes. How was he going to get through the entire day now that his plan of sleeping till noon was shot?

There was always the Scotch.

After Old Spicing himself clean, Jackson shut off the water and toweled dry. Wiping the steam off the mirror, he decided to shave the stubble that had been growing all weekend. He also made plans to dump the Scotch down the drain before his willpower gave out once and for all. He could bribe Connie with name-brand doggy bites for Fluffy.

Jackson was halfway across his face with the razor when the phone rang, this time with a generic chirp instead of a customized tune. He trudged into the bedroom and picked the phone off his bed. Not recognizing the number, he held it up to the foamless side of his face.

"Jackson Douglas."

"Like, are you the private investigator?" The voice could have belonged to a thirteen-year-old girl. From Burbank.

"Yeah, I'm a private investigator."

"Great!"

Jackson rolled his eyes.

"I need to hire you," she said.

"I charge five hundred a day, plus expenses, with a thousand dollar retainer. Cash." Usually he brought up the money later, but if this were a sorority prank, maybe mentioning his fee would cut her off at the pass.

She laughed, a quick intake of air. "Money's no problem."

Jackson took a deep breath and watched a glop of shaving gel fall onto his towel. "What do you want to hire me for?"

"Uh, can we, like, meet somewhere?"

"We can meet, but that doesn't mean I'll take the case."

"Why not?"

"Because I'm selective."

"Oh." The disappointment was palpable. "Well, when can we meet?"

"Where do you live?"

"Beverly Hills."

Figured.

"You have wheels?"

"Yeah." It was two syllables. Yeah-uh.

"Can you meet me at Cameron's?"

"Cameron's?"

"Restaurant on the beach in Santa Monica, just west of the incline." He glanced at the clock and hoped Connie's favor explanation wouldn't take too long. "Say . . . eight-thirty?"

"Okay. Like, how will I find you?"

"They know me there. Just ask for me."

"Okay. Eight-thirty."

"Hey, what's your name?"

"Shay. Shay Carmichael."

Perfect.

Jackson forced a smile into his voice. "I'll see you at eight-thirty, Shay."

He closed his phone as another blob fell onto his arm. He returned to the bathroom to finish shaving and spent a moment making sure he hadn't missed any patches of stubble. He stared for a few seconds into hollow cobalt eyes, seeking a sparkle that wasn't there. And that wasn't likely to return today.

After brushing his teeth, he toweled off his dirty blond hair a little more. It was due for a trim, in that stage where it was about to assume a life of its own. For the moment it passed for tousled, and he let it go without another thought.

Still in his towel, Jackson returned to the bedroom and drew back the blinds. The view was fantastic, looking out at Pacific Palisades, Santa Monica, Malibu in the distance, and of course, the cerulean Pacific. He had gotten the property for a song, and had spent a year fixing up a condemned former crack house. Most of his life savings (such as it had been) was gone, but he had a killer pad to show for it. And killer taxes too.

Glad to see the typical morning marine layer was absent, Jackson slipped into a clean(ish) pair of jeans, the oldest and most comfortable he had, and a simple blue Dodgers T-shirt. It wasn't terribly professional, but if Magnum could wear a floral Hawaiian shirt and the male equivalent of hot pants, Jackson could rock a Dodger's tee and a shaggy mane.

Jackson jogged down the stairs and through the living room into the kitchen, where he quickly downed half a glass of orange juice. Then he laced up his sneakers, and exactly thirty minutes after Kiss had roused him from a tranquil slumber, he stepped out into the morning sunlight.

Connie's house was a mansion, at least by comparison to his. It boasted two full stories, four bedrooms, four baths, and a sprawling deck with a pool. Even her trees were bigger. She had lived there for almost twenty years, since the days of husband number two, and now lived off the dead man's money.

Jackson enjoyed the warm sunshine and the ocean breeze playing with his hair as he walked across the lawn to Connie's front door. Suddenly his mouth watered for sticky buns.

The doorbell hadn't worked since the days of husband number three, so Jackson clunked the heavy brass knocker on an ornate front door that was at least four feet wide. Like the entrance to a castle.

Jackson heard a female voice from the other side of the door, which was opened by a woman who was not Connie.

"Hey," she said, as if they were age-old friends.

She was average in size and appearance, except for spiky, dark brown hair and excessive makeup.

So she was a relative of Connie's.

She wore faded jeans and plain yellow shirt over a plain red one, all nicely accentuated by bright blue nail polish.

Yep, a relative of Connie's.

"Hey," he returned. "I'm Jackson. Connie called me."

"Come on in."

Before he could take a step, a shrill "Arf!" nearly stopped his heart and an orange ball of fur flew into his ankles. Fluffy, or "Wittle Fwuffkins," Connie's Pomeranian. The strongest counterargument to PETA in the animal kingdom.

"Fluffy, get out of here," Not Connie said. She kicked at the dog with her bare foot. Fluffy thought she was playing. "Fluff, move," she said, sliding the dog across the wood floor like a mop. She looked up at Jackson. "I'm Diane. Connie's niece."

Jackson nodded. There were three or four of them, and a couple of nephews, along with a daughter and three stepchildren. Connie's family tree was straight out of *The King's Stilts*.

15

He followed her through a wide-open front hall, dominated by a huge chandelier that hung from the second-floor ceiling. Tasteless artwork bought on Mediterranean cruises over the years adorned the walls and stood on end tables in every room, including the entryway. From the kitchen came the rich aromas of caramel and dark-roast coffee and the sound of Connie muttering to herself.

"We're in the dining room," Diane said, nodding toward the double doors that opened into the hexagonal room. Then she started down the hallway to the kitchen, leaving Jackson to wonder who "we" constituted. Connie hadn't mentioned anything about a family reunion.

With a shrug, Jackson pushed open the doors and stepped into the dining room, nearly tripping over Fluffy. She yelped and darted back out the door, and he quickly closed it.

Connie's dining room was impressive. Floor to ceiling windows looked out in three directions, providing views of the deck and the ocean in the distance and letting in plenty of sunlight. It reflected off a huge, teakwood table and momentarily blinded Jackson. When his eyes adjusted, they settled on a girl sitting at the far end of the table, cradling a steaming mug of tea.

She was slightly thinner than Diane, with black hair hanging to her shoulders. Her skin was darker and her eyes a lighter shade of blue, but she had the same aquiline nose and protruding ears as Diane. And the same eclectic taste in clothing—a navy long-sleeved tee with "Cal" stamped in yellow on the chest and pink pajama pants.

"Gina," Jackson said. "Diane's younger sister?"

She looked up and grinned, causing the mole at the left corner of her mouth to move. "You must be Jackson. You're good."

He nodded.

"Have a seat."

He walked around the table and pulled out a chair. Gina blew into her tea.

"If memory serves," Jackson said, "you have a brother too."

"Named?"

"Robert?"

"Albert," she said with another grin. "Robert was our father."

Right, the father who had died.

"Sorry."

She shrugged.

The double doors flew open and a sticky-bun carrying hurricane blustered through the door. Constance Marie DiMarco.

Red was the color of the day, from her bright pants to the spots on her leopard-patterned blouse to the nail polish on her long, curved fingernails to her freshly re-dyed auburn hair. It was short, but not quite as short as Diane's, and not quite as spiky either. It framed the upper half of a chubby yet angular face that had enough makeup for two. Especially garish was the abundant lipstick, covering abundant lips. The lipstick too, of course, was red.

"Hi, Jackson!"

"Connie."

One hand held a plate of sticky buns and the other a stack of small dessert plates. She clunked them all to the table and then stood back. Her hands rested, only for a moment, on her wide hips. Then she reached for a chair and pulled it back.

"I take it you've met Gina," she said.

Jackson nodded.

"She and Diane are visiting for a few days."

"I see."

On cue, Diane entered, carrying two mugs of coffee. "Connie says you take it black?"

"Yeah, thanks." He took the cup and smelled the brew. Connie made it stronger than the Colombians.

"Well don't just sit there. Eat!"

Jackson reached for a plate and helped himself to an appropriately labeled sticky bun. While the ladies DiMarco served themselves, he peeled off a bite. Connie was a gourmet-quality cook, and for all her attributes that drove Jackson nuts, she made amends by spoiling him with delicious treats and meals. The sticky buns were no exception.

He savored several bites before licking his fingers clean and perking up with a swig of coffee. Then he sat back. "So what's this favor you wanted to see me about?"

Connie broke off a big piece of her bun and chewed it most of the way before answering. "I want to hire you."

He sat up a little straighter. "Hire me?"

"Um-hmm. In a manner of speaking."

Uh-oh.

Jackson frowned. "To do what?"

Connie looked at Gina, who sighed before answering. "To scope out my date."

The frown intensified.

"Gina met a guy online," Connie explained. "His name's Brandon."

"Landon."

"Landon. He's from L.A., a student at USC, and they just met in a chat room about . . . what was it?"

"Urban social patterns."

"Seriously?" Jackson asked.

Gina nodded.

"Anyhow, since she was coming down for a visit, they made plans to go on a date." Connie looked at Diane. "We thought somebody should check this Landon guy out first, and I thought, why not you?"

Jackson stifled a sigh and hoped he hid a wince. He hadn't become a private investigator to play intercampus date police.

"I'm not crazy about the idea," Gina said, "but . . . I've had a few bad experiences with men."

And she was smirking?

"They convinced me it was a good idea."

"I wish I would have hired a P.I. to check out my husband," Diane said, tugging at nothing on her shirt. "Could have saved five grand in attorneys' fees."

"What do you think?" Connie asked.

Jackson reached for his sticky bun and broke off a hunk, buying him some time. Connie didn't respond terribly well to no's, and she held more and better cards than Jackson did. He would have to agree or face the consequences.

Unless he could hedge. "What exactly do you want me to find out?" he asked after a drink of coffee. "If you're looking to know if this guy's right for you, I'm not Neil Clark Warren."

"Who?" Gina asked.

"You know how it is with the internet," Connie said with a wave of her hand. It then reached for a second sticky bun. "We just want to know if he's some sort of creep or not."

Jackson took another drink. "If he tortures animals or keeps his aging parents locked in the basement, you mean?"

Connie made a face.

"Yeah," Diane said.

Jackson nodded.

"Will you do it?" Connie asked.

He sighed mentally. "Yeah."

"Have another sticky bun," she said, sliding the plate toward him.

Jackson helped himself. "So tell me everything you know about this Landon guy."

They turned to Gina, who ran a hand through her hair. She set down her mug. "His name's Landon Brower. He's going to be a senior at USC, majoring in social studies like me. He likes to sail, likes football, likes girls with dark hair."

It took great constraint for Jackson to keep from rolling his eyes.

"You know where he lives?" he asked.

"Um, no. On campus, maybe?"

"What else?"

Gina shrugged. "I don't know, not a whole lot. We really only chatted for like fifteen minutes."

Well, if that wasn't the making for a successful relationship.

"Sorry," she added.

"Do you think you can do it?" Diane asked.

Jackson took a deep breath and let it out slowly. "I'll do my best. When's the date?"

"Tonight," Gina said, scratching her head.

"Tonight?"

She nodded.

Jackson winced. "I'm not sure how much I can work on it today. I'm meeting with a client in a few minutes about another case." Potential client, but who was splitting hairs?

Gina made an "oh well" face. Connie frowned.

"Can't you squeeze them both in?" she asked.

"I don't know." He saw the dejected look in her eyes and, like a sucker, melted. "I'll see what I can do."

"Don't worry," Gina said. "You don't have to be picky." She winked. "I don't want him too perfect."

Chapter Three

8:18 a.m.

JACKSON DROVE WITH the windows down in his 1976 Ford Granada. The car had originally belonged to his grandparents but had been passed to Jackson when his grandmother died. Leroy Douglas had sold the house and car and bought a houseboat and a Vespa, and Jackson, at age sixteen, had had his own wheels. The car had been a classic already then; now it was a miracle of preservation.

The candy apple red paint still looked showroom fresh, the creamy white soft top was without a blemish, and the leather seats were free of stains or tears. Mechanically, the car was as good as new. Every part that hadn't been replaced by Leroy had been replaced by Jackson, some more than once. But it ran consistently, didn't burn oil or guzzle gas, and served Jackson as well as Leroy's Vespa served him.

As he drown down Chautauqua Boulevard toward the Pacific Coast Highway, Jackson wondered what he had gotten himself into with Connie. He had been afraid to broach the subject of his fee, knowing that she expected his favor to be just that. Fortunately Diane had announced that they (and by "they," he assumed she meant Connie) would pay his regular fee, whatever it was. Before Connie could balk, Jackson had said something about a half-price discount, and it was settled.

Finding out if Landon Brower was a convicted criminal shouldn't be too hard. Anything like that would be public record, and with a few well-placed inquiries, Jackson figured he could come up with a rough sketch for Gina. He just hoped Connie wouldn't hold him personally responsible for whatever happened on their date—or on any subsequent dates. With Gina, he figured that could be almost anything.

Jackson turned onto the PCH and headed south along the coast. The ocean breeze blew in off the beach, which at such an early hour, was almost deserted. His thoughts turned to Shay Carmichael and her unexplained case. In the half year that he had been working as a licensed private investigator, he'd had several clients who had preferred to meet with him before divulging any details of the task they wanted him to perform. That wasn't unusual. Having Nicole Richie as the client was.

After a mile of driving between the beachfront properties on his right and the bluffs on the left, Jackson turned into the freshly paved parking lot of Cameron's. He parked in the corner, made a quick check of his appearance in the rearview mirror, and manually rolled up the windows before getting out.

Cameron's was the brainchild of Jackson's best friend, Reggie Cameron. A former football star at the University of Nebraska, Reggie had moved to California and, after a failed marriage, invested everything he had in his own restaurant. Six years later, it was one of the more happening spots in Santa Monica and had become a franchise with locations in Newport Beach in southern Los Angeles and Mission Beach in San Diego.

Being actually two restaurants in one, Cameron's catered to everyone. The upstairs was a casual fine dining bistro, featuring linen tablecloths and centerpiece candles, four-star cuisine, and soft music in the background. Floor to ceiling windows looked out on the beach and the Pacific, making the bistro the perfect place for a romantic sunset dinner. The lower level was a beach bar with indoor and outdoor seating, a relaxed dress code, and cheaper but just as tasty food. The music ranged from Bob Marley to the Beach Boys, and customers could enter through the front door or straight off the beach.

The bistro didn't open till eleven, so Jackson headed downstairs from the main entrance. He was greeted by a pretty blond in a blue Cameron's polo and khaki shorts.

"Hi, Jackson."

"Katie," he replied with a nod. "You got an extra table . . . I'm supposed to meet somebody."

"A client or a date?"

"A date, for breakfast?"

She shrugged.

"Client."

Katie nodded at dual doorways opening to the dining room. "Take your pick."

"Thanks." Jackson sought out a booth in the corner, providing him a view of the other twenty indoor booths and tables, as well as both entrances. Turning over his shoulder, Jackson could also see the inside/outside bar and most of the tables on the beach through three massive windows. During inclement weather, glass panels could slide over to cover the openings, cutting off half of the bar and the beachside tables. Currently, they were all open, letting in the warm breeze.

"You want something to drink, man?" Esteban hollered from the bar.

"Coffee."

It was delivered thirty seconds later, piping hot, and Jackson let it cool as he scanned the room. There was a family several booths down, obviously tourists by their dress. Two old ladies shared a table—and a tube of lipstick—to his left. A single guy sat over his cup of coffee across the room, flipping through a newspaper and munching on toast. Then there was the hulking black dude coming his way, wearing baggy blue jeans and a double-X white, button-down shirt.

"You hate coffee, man," he said in a deep voice, sliding into the booth opposite Jackson.

"Hey, Reg."

The owner of Cameron's nodded at Jackson's cup.

"I hate the taste. I like drinking it."

"Better that then booze, I guess." He sat back. "Happy birthday, man."

"Thanks."

"You celebrating?"

"Meeting a potential client," Jackson answered. "How about you? Aren't you usually just hitting your second REM cycle about now?"

"I had two waitresses quit this weekend," he said, rubbing the stubble atop his head. "I've got interviews all morning, plus prep for a meeting with the accountant Wednesday. Life's rough for us small-business owners, man."

Jackson took a sip of the coffee. It was like water compared to Connie's concoction.

"So . . ." Reggie said. "How are you?"

Jackson looked up into his friend's deep, mahogany eyes. Capable of sparkling in carefree humor and good-natured ribbing, they also had the sincerity and understanding of a man who had gone through his own share of pain and sorrow. Six years ago, it had been Jackson providing a shoulder to lean on in a difficult time, and the friendship had only strengthened since.

"I'm okay," Jackson said, not having the time or energy to go any deeper.

Reggie let him off with a nod. "You got dinner plans?"

"Yeah. Going over to Grandpa's."

"Say hey, man."

Jackson nodded, and Reggie did too.

"I'll leave you to it, bro. Give me a call this weekend. We'll kick it."

"Yeah, sure."

Reggie stood and extended his fist. "Take care, man."

Jackson banged his knuckles against Reggie's, just hard enough to sting. "You too, big man."

Reggie winked as he walked away, and Jackson took another slug of coffee and sat back. When he looked up, Katie was pointing at him from the hostess desk. Standing beside her just had to be Shay.

She was exactly what Jackson had been picturing since she called. Bright blond hair—highlighted even brighter—that was perfectly styled as it dangled around her shoulders. A bright pink polo that snugly fit her petite body and designer denim shorts borrowed from Barbie. And bright sequins on the sides of periwinkle blue platform flip-flops that repeated their trademark sound as she strode toward him.

Her accessories were bright too. Silver string earrings, a matching necklace, and white gold rings lining her fingers and toes all sparkled as they caught the sunlight. Periwinkle fingernail polish to match the flip-flops and pink toenail polish to match the shirt were both traced with glitter. The small pink purse she carried under her arm had silver sequins and lettering. Even her makeup was bright.

But, Jackson recognized as he stood to greet her, regardless of all the glitz and bling, Shay was a very pretty girl. Her skin was smooth and tanned, her wide eyes the same color as the ocean in the late afternoon, her nose small and cute. Somewhere out there, a mall rat with a goatee and barbed wire tattooed around his biceps, wearing a stocking cap year round and listening to Eminem must be very happy.

"Are you Jackson?" she asked.

He nodded. "You must be Shay."

She nodded and offered a tiny, manicured hand.

Jackson shook it. "Have a seat. You want something to eat, something to drink?"

"No thanks." She flicked her hair out of her face and tucked a disobedient strand behind her ear.

Jackson pushed his cup to the side and rested his arms on the edge of the table. "What can I help you with?"

Shay huffed. "I should totally be on my way to Le Petite right now."

"If you're looking for a taxi, I'll do it, but I'm not cheap."

There was a quick flash as she raised her eyes to meet his. Then it was gone. "I need protection."

"Protection from what?"

"I don't know. Bad guys?"

Jackson fought off a sigh. Did competition for a sale at Dior constitute bad guys?

"Okay, why are these bad guys after you?"

"It's, like, kind of a long story."

"I've got the time if you do."

"Okay." She reached into her purse, but instead of pulling out some important clue, retrieved a stick of gum. She placed it on her tongue and chewed for several seconds before looking up at Jackson again. "So, my brother Blake, he works for this crazy, like, archaeologist guy, right? I mean, this guy goes all around the world looking for lost treasures, like he's Indiana Jones or something, you know? Only he doesn't find lost arks or crystal skulls; he finds woodcarvings and shrunken heads."

Jackson nodded, wishing very much that he had turned his phone to vibrate last night before going to bed.

"So anyhow, he finds, like, a million of these dumb woodcarvings, and then tries to sell them to people all around the world."

"And Blake makes the deliveries?"

"Yeah. How'd you know?"

Okay, so cute, but maybe not the brightest sequin on the proverbial flip-flop.

Shay flicked her hair again. "So Blake flies all over the world, right, delivering these trinkets. And I don't know why. I mean, seriously, it's not like he needs the money. But I'm like, whatevs, it's his life, right?"

She looked up, and Jackson figured she wanted a nod. So he gave one, wondering how long this would go on. Just listening to Shay was wearing him out.

She chomped hard on the gum, switching it to the other side of her mouth. "Then yesterday I get a call from Blake, who's in, like, Paris or Italy or France or somewhere, and he says he's going to be stuck there for another three days, and he needs me to make his deliveries for him. This is totally not cool. I mean, do I look like I work for FedEx?"

Or work, period? Ever?

Jackson shook his head.

"Anyhow, he e-mails me this list of addresses and tells me I have to make two deliveries today and another one tomorrow. Are you kidding me?"

"Delivering what, exactly? Woodcarvings?"

"He said they're Tahitian idols or something. And then he calls again last night and tells me they're worth fifty thousand dollars apiece."

Jackson's eyebrows shot up.

"Can you believe it?" Shay asked. "People pay fifty thousand dollars for a chunk of wood? It doesn't even give off Feng shui or anything."

Jackson shook his head appropriately.

"Then Blake tells me to be careful, because this boss of his just had some guy break into his hotel room, and some other delivery boy of his had four idols stolen in San Diego. And why can't this guy in San Diego make the deliveries in L.A.? Oh, and P.S., Blake says some tribal warlord may have put a curse on the idols. So now I've got that to worry about, and I really just want a good massage and a mani-pedi, you know?"

Jackson sat back and rubbed his chin. "Your brother didn't say anything about who exactly might want these idols?"

"He just told me to be careful. And I'm, like, freaking out because now he's probably got me involved in the mob or the Mafia or the al-Taliban or something. So I called Melissa, and she's like, 'Girlfriend, you should hire a bodyguard.' And I'm like, 'Where am I going to find a bodyguard?' You have to be, like, Lady Gaga to get a bodyguard. And then I said, 'Shay, duh, just hire a private eye.'"

Duh was two syllables. Duh-uh. Almost three, actually. Duh-uh-ah.

"So now I'm totally freaking, because I'm thinking all private eyes are going to wear tan suit coats and chain smoke and have a voice like Marlon Brando, and I keep thinking how I am so going to kill Blake when he gets back." She looked up. "Then I called you."

"Why me?" Jackson asked, hesitant to find out the answer.

Shay shrugged. "I had to pick somebody, and I so don't know any private eyes. I actually looked in the phonebook, and your name just stood out. I know, right. The phonebook?"

"Crazy," Jackson said.

"So will you do it? I've got seven hundred and fifty dollars in my purse, and I can get you another two-fifty before we make the first delivery."

"When do we have to make them?"

"Eleven and two today and ten a.m. tomorrow. And it's not like you have to babysit me all the time in between or anything. The carvings are in Blake's safe deposit box at the bank. I just, like, need somebody to go with me."

Jackson nodded. "Where are we delivering?"

Shay reached back into the purse and pulled out a folded up sheet of paper. She opened it and slid it across the table to Jackson. It contained three addresses, all in the northwestern corner of Los Angeles. That should leave him plenty of time to investigate Landon for Connie.

"Now, I know it's two days," Shay said, "but it's technically all within twenty-four hours. But I can pay for two days if I have to—Daddy left me plenty. Of course, I am so making Blake pay me back."

"We can count it as one day," Jackson said. "Five hundred, plus expenses. You can pay me the seven and a half, and I'll refund whatever's left."

"So you'll do it?" she said, physically perking up.

Something inside was nagging at Jackson, but he couldn't quite place it. He reviewed Shay's story, and although it was plenty quirky, he didn't spot any warning flags. Nor could he come up with any ulterior motives behind her desire for protection. And yet . . . that little voice kept repeating that something wasn't right.

All private investigators had gut instincts, Jackson had learned, both from TV and from real life experience. He'd spent the better part of two years working for MTR Investigative Services in San Diego, and although his work was largely as a gofer, he'd talked enough with the big boys to know they all listened to their hunches. And so too, now, did he.

Usually.

"Jackson?"

He looked up into Shay's baby blues, framed by long, diva-quality lashes. The perfect white smile that had no doubt persuaded Daddy to drop the AmEx on whatever she wanted and compelled high school boys to act like idiots at her whim was now working on Jackson. Mentally flicking Mr. Hunch off his shoulder, Jackson nodded. "I'll do it."

Shay beamed.

Jackson was still unsure. Tahitian totem poles selling for fifty G's each? Tribal warlords and unknown thugs who wanted them back? A, like, totally Valley Girl, like, delivering them for her, like, brother's boss? It was almost enough to make Jackson change his mind. But somehow he didn't think he could break it to Shay if he did. And that was scary.

The first carving had to be delivered at eleven to a location in West Hollywood. Jackson and Shay agreed to meet at the bank at ten-thirty and drive together from there. Shay determined she had time for a quick massage after all, and shortly before nine, she and Jackson parted company in Cameron's parking lot.

Jackson watched Shay ease into a navy blue convertible and tear out of her parking spot. She gave him a quick little finger wave through heavily tinted windows. Then, flinging her hair over her shoulder, she stepped on the gas and peeled out of the lot and into traffic on the PCH.

Jackson shook his head and started for his Granada. First Connie and now this. It was shaping up to be another doozy of a birthday.

Chapter Four

9:04 a.m.

WITH AN HOUR and a half before he had to meet Shay at the bank, Jackson decided to make a dent in Connie's case. His first task was to learn the basics about Landon Brower. With any luck, he had a criminal record and Jackson could write him off as a misfit right away. But knowing his luck, Gina probably would find a misfit with a few priors sexy, and he'd have to keep digging.

From Cameron's he took I-10 inland, then veered south on the 405 toward the Airport Courthouse. There he would have access to any and all public records, including births, marriages, land holdings, and arrests. If nothing else, it would give him a good starting point for the rest of his investigation.

As he merged with traffic on the San Diego Freeway, his cell phone began playing Creedence Clearwater Revival's "Bad Moon Rising." Jackson fished the phone out of his jeans and pried it open with his thumb.

"Hey, Maggie."

"Hey, yourself," she replied in a voice that was a touch husky. Demi Moore meets Jessica Biel.

"What's up?" Jackson asked. "You need an unidentified source for a story?"

"I need a story period," she answered. "I was hoping they'd let me do an op-ed on Mombassai—"

"Who?"

"Mombassai—the African dictator who was killed a few weeks ago."

Jackson had heard something about it, but he didn't spend a lot of time following current events.

"But now they've got me doing a three-parter on the ten-year-old eighth grader in Monrovia," Maggie continued.

"And for the paltry salary they give you at the *Times*?"

"Shut up."

Jackson grinned. "So to what do I owe the pleasure?"

"You got plans for tonight?"

"Actually, I do. Steaks with Grandpa."

"Ah."

"What'd you have in mind?" Jackson asked, glancing out his window as an irate suit in a shiny new Bentley wooshed by. Sixty miles per hour was about all the Granada was capable of, and that was pushing it.

"Oh nothing," she answered, and Jackson was sure her free hand had just gone into her jeans pocket. "I thought maybe I could buy you a birthday dinner."

"That's very '90s of you."

"Yeah well, my paltry salary is better than the peanuts you make, so it's the least I can do."

"Ouch, right in the male ego."

"Seriously, it's been what, since early April? I thought we could hang out, catch up."

Jackson nearly asked if her real motives were to babysit him on his birthday, but he let it pass. There was no need to insult a dinner offer, and it wasn't really Maggie's style anyhow. Odds were she just wanted to chill for a few hours.

"Any chance I could take a rain check?" he asked.

"Maybe."

"If I spring for dessert?"

"Last time you sprang it was for Dilly Bars."

"Peanuts, remember."

"What about lunch?" Maggie asked. "I don't have to interview the boy genius till this afternoon. Want to make it lunch instead?"

It was too bad alluring smiles couldn't be conveyed over the telephone. It was also too bad Jackson was double-booked already. "Um . . ."

"I'm a big girl, Jackson. You can say no."

"No, I'd love to . . . I've just got a case."

"On your birthday."

"Mmm. Two of them, actually."

"Wow. Forget I asked."

"No. What time's your interview?"

"I'm supposed to be there around two."

"I can fit an hour in for lunch," Jackson said, laying out the timeline in his head. "Noon?"

"Okay."

"You got a place in mind?"

"It's your birthday."

"Enterprise," he said, knowing Maggie loved seafood.

"Enterprise it is," she said, her voice rising an octave. "You sure you got the time?"

"I'm sure. See you at noon."

"Okay. Don't get shot."

"Don't spill ink on your pants."

Her phone clicked off and Jackson lowered his with a smile. He clapped it shut and tossed it onto the passenger seat of his car. He moved over a lane to pass a semi and took a glance toward downtown. It was a clear day, relatively speaking, but even so, a thin layer of smog hung over the city. That was the beauty of Santa Monica and Pacific Palisades—ocean breezes kept pollution to a minimum. That and the fact that everybody drove a hybrid and wore shoes made from recycled milk cartons.

Point of Grace's "By Heart" began playing from the passenger seat. Jackson scooped the phone up again. "Hey, Sam."

"Hey, Jackson. Happy birthday."

"Thanks."

"How are you doing?" she asked in a voice that was girlish compared to Maggie's. It perfectly portrayed her sweetness.

"I'm all right," he answered. Then quickly, "How about you?"

"I'm good."

"Working?" he asked, hearing hospital hubbub behind her.

"Yeah. I'm on a coffee break."

"I didn't think you drank."

"'Coffee break' being a manner of speaking."

Jackson heard a door close and the noise behind Sam quieted. It was replaced by the roar of a jet descending over the interstate to the south runway at LAX. "So what's up?" he asked when it subsided.

"I just wanted to check in on you," she said. "I didn't see you at church yesterday."

"Yeah, I missed. I was out pretty late Saturday." Out at Mouse's playing *Rainbow Six* until three a.m., but that was neither here nor there.

"But you're okay?"

"I'm fine, Sam," he said with a smile. It was very much *her* style to mother him, to make sure he was all right. But he didn't really mind when she did it. In fact, he almost craved it.

"I, um . . . I can't talk long," Sam said. "You want to grab dinner tonight? My treat."

"Ahh, I'd love to, but I'm going to Grandpa's tonight."

He hoped she didn't ask about lunch.

"That makes sense," she said. "Well, I have to work till four. Maybe dessert? Unless you were planning on staying at your grandpa's a while?"

"I think dessert would work."

"Great. Just tell me what you're in the mood for, and I'll take you wherever."

He toyed with the idea of cleverly suggesting she make the dessert herself. She loved to cook and was good at it, and he wouldn't mind a quiet bite on the loveseat in her apartment. But he didn't want to push, and it would be rude to ask her to cook for him.

"Can I get back to you?" he asked.

"Sure. Just give me a call."

"Will do."

"I have to work early, so if you find yourself not wanting to leave your grandpa's, don't feel you have to just for me. We can make it another time."

"I'll call you," Jackson said. "Grandpa can grill a steak, but his tiramisu needs work."

"I'd better get back to work."

"Okay." Jackson pulled into the parking lot adjacent to the courthouse and let the engine stall as he coasted into an empty spot. "You don't have to worry, Sam. Not anymore."

The bottle of Scotch flashed into Jackson's head, but he quickly shoved it aside.

"I'm not worried," she said with a confidence he wished he felt. "I'll talk to you later," she added.

"Yeah."

"Bye," she said, and the line went silent. Jackson pressed his phone against his cheek to close it and got out of the car.

The city of Los Angeles divided its various records departments into seven different locations from Van Nuys to East L.A. Since not every location contained a copy of every record, finding information could be a lengthy and frustrating process. Fortunately, Jackson had a system.

"Can I help you?" asked the female clerk. The nametag on her curve-hugging blue and white top introduced her as Chrissy. She had a flawless complexion, strong features, and perfect blond hair, not to mention a trace of flirtatiousness in her shining smile and vivid eyes. Or maybe she was just friendly.

"Is Brandon here?" Jackson asked, returning a level gaze and the slightest upturn at the corner of his mouth.

"No, he's off today."

So much for having a system.

"Is there something I can help you with?" Chrissy asked.

Jackson leaned on the counter, casually of course. "Maybe there is." He reached for his wallet and showed her his private investigator's license. "I need some information about a guy, and Brandon was usually able to help me out—cut through the red tape, you know?"

Chrissy leaned a little bit too, and her smile shaded toward a smirk. "Cut through the red tape, huh?"

"Yeah. Make a few calls, request a fax or two, maybe pull a few records."

"I see." She straightened up. "I take it you're a friend of Brandon's."

"He and my brother used to work together."

"And that earns you favors?"

"That and the occasional Lakers tickets."

"Ah, so you bribe him."

Jackson forced a charming smile as he made plans to run for the door. "More like trade favors."

Chrissy smiled, looked around, and leaned onto the counter, close enough for Jackson to smell her perfume. "So what favor would you be willing to trade me?"

"Courtside with Kobe not your thing?"

She slowly shook her head, crinkling her nose.

"Courtside with Blake Griffin?"

"I'm more of a theater girl. You think you could score a couple of tickets to *Wicked*? Then you might have a deal."

Jackson doubted he could bum a couple of theater tickets off Maggie like he could with Lakers tickets for Brandon. But whatever they cost, they would be less than Connie was paying him. They might even count as an expense, if he got creative with his billing.

"Okay," he said. "Tickets to *Wicked*."

Chrissy smiled. "Name?"

Jackson smiled back. "Landon Brower." He spelled the last name for her. "He's a student at SC, but that's about all I know."

"What do you need to know?"

"Anything you can get me," Jackson said.

"I'll see what I can do," she said. "Have a seat."

Jackson flipped through a back issue of *Sports Illustrated*, keeping an eye on the clock. Fortunately, there weren't many other patrons needing info, and Chrissy was able to focus on Landon. Shortly before ten, she summoned him back to the counter.

Holding a manila envelope in her hand, she leaned in on the counter again. "So, I've been wondering, what's to keep you from taking this envelope and never thinking about me again?"

"You're not an easy woman to forget."

"That's cute. So am I ever going to see my *Wicked* tickets?"

"Yeah. I never know when Brandon might be on vacation."

She smiled and slid the envelope across the counter. "I'm afraid there isn't much to it," she said. "Your Brower's a pretty boring guy."

"Makes my job easier," he said as he grabbed the envelope. "Thanks, Chrissy. Balcony okay?"

"Balcony would be fine."

"I don't get down to El Segundo too often. You got a mailing address?"

"Why don't you just meet me at the box office?"

Jackson regarded her coy smile and then shrugged to himself. Why not? He recorded her number on his cell phone, and as he walked to his car, wondered where he could get a ringtone for "Somewhere Over the Rainbow."

He had parked facing west, away from the sun, and the leather seat in the Granada wasn't too bad. Jackson undid the clasp on the envelope and pulled out a thin sheaf of papers. Chrissy was right, it was pretty boring.

Landon Lawrence Brower had been born October 13, 1990, in Anaheim. An only child, he had lost his mother to cancer when he was thirteen. His father still lived in L.A. Landon had never been married, never owned property or been part of any business ventures, and had no debt (aside from standard school loans) to speak of. He didn't own a gun, had never been in the military, and didn't have a criminal record other than for a pair of speeding tickets. He drove an old Plymouth Neon, licensed originally to his father. Since his eighteenth birthday, Landon had been a registered Democrat, as was everyone else in Los Angeles County.

There was nothing in the envelope to suggest that Landon was a creep or a pervert or any sort of danger to Gina. But there wasn't any proof that he wasn't either. Jackson wasn't surprised. Creeps and perverts weren't required to register with the county.

Returning the papers to the envelope and tossing it on the passenger seat, Jackson headed back to the freeway. Once in the flow of traffic (it flowed around him as he puttered along at fifty-eight miles per) he retrieved his cell and called Garrett Warren, a fellow P.I. acquaintance. Garrett got around L.A., particularly with the campus crowd, and Jackson figured it was worth a shot.

Garrett didn't answer, and Jackson left a message, asking for a call back if he knew anything about Landon. Then he punched in the number for Mouse. It was fifty-fifty if he would be home, and much worse odds that if he were, he'd be awake.

Mouse answered with a sleepy "Yeah?" after four rings.

"Hey, it's Jackson."

"Hey."

"You busy?"

"No."

"I need a favor."

Jackson heard crunching, probably Gardetto's, probably Mouse's breakfast.

"I'm investigating a student at SC, and I'm wondering if you can find him on Facebook or Twitter or whatever the kids are doing these days."

"What do you need to know?"

"It's a character study. I need to know if he's a perv."

"You think you'll find that from Facebook?" His question was followed by what sounded like a grenade explosion. Mouse was gaming.

"Not for sure, but you can get an idea. Who does he hang out with, what kind of photos does he post, what's he into, that sort of thing?"

"A student at SC?" Mouse asked.

"Yeah."

"Suggestive pics of co-eds with beer bongs and dirty jokes."

Now machine gun fire.

"You want to bother to look him up anyhow?"

Mouse huffed. "Whatever, man."

"And you can do it? You don't need to be the guy's BFF or have a space on his wall or something?"

"*I* don't," Mouse answered. "What's the dude's name?"

"Landon Brower. O-W-E-R."

"You got anything else on him?"

"Why?"

"There's more than social media I can access."

"Don't bother, Mouse. I just need to know if he's a safe date. And don't say it."

Mouse huffed again. "I'll see what I can come up with."

"You gonna be around this afternoon?"

Another grenade. "I'm off all day."

"I'll stop by later, see what you got."

"Don't expect much."

"Fair enough. Hey, take another crack at saving Vegas one of these days?"

"Yeah, if you want to stop shooting civilians this time."

"Sure. See you later."

"Later."

Jackson closed the phone. Depending on what Mouse found, he might have enough to satisfy Connie. But the last thing he wanted was to okay Landon and have him date-rape Gina. He should have time between the second delivery with Shay and dinner with his grandpa to run out to campus and ask around. There had to be enough professors and summer schoolers who knew Landon to give him some info. If not, well then, there wasn't much else he could do on short notice.

As he neared the Santa Monica Boulevard exit, his phone rang again. This time it was Relient K's "Therapy," and he toyed with letting it go to his voicemail. With a sigh, he snapped his phone open.

"Hello."

"Is this Jackson?" asked a female voice.

"It is."

"Jackson, this is Alaina from Dr. Zachary's office calling to confirm your appointment tomorrow. I have you down for eleven-thirty."

Jackson winced. It was the third Tuesday already?

"That sounds right," he said. The third delivery with Shay was scheduled for ten. He shouldn't have trouble making it to Malibu by eleven-thirty.

"Okay then. We'll see you tomorrow at eleven-thirty."

"Right."

He had yet to figure out if Alaina faked her perkiness or if she really did have that much zest for life. She was a former patient, as she proudly told all newcomers. A walking, talking, peppy advertisement. Jackson was still a few sessions from perky.

Shay's bank was a block south of Sunset, and obviously catered to the wealthy. A ten-foot-high block of granite engraved with the bank's name floated on the top of a reflecting pool at the corner of the property. Towering palm trees lined the ample lawns around the parking lot and the sidewalk to the front door. The building itself was reflective glass, almost blinding in the morning sun. The drive-up windows probably featured complimentary beverage service and flat screens displaying the latest stock prices.

Jackson parked the Granada in the corner, wondering if security would ask him to remove such an eyesore from their property. They didn't, and within two minutes, he saw Shay's convertible whip into the lot. She careened into a parking stall across from his and, before the car had finished lurching to a stop, threw open her door.

Brown butterfly sunglasses blocked half of her face, but she quickly flipped them up into her golden hair. "Jackson, hi," (Jack-son, hi-ee) she called, as if they were former roomies who now needed to kiss cheeks. He fought the urge to roll his eyes.

Shay wrapped her purse around her arm and, using her hips far more than necessary, pushed her door shut. Then she sashayed to him. "So, are you ready?"

Jackson nodded. "After you."

There was a hint of flirt in her smile as she turned, hair flicking as she did so, and strode across the parking lot. Jackson followed, wondering which female would get him into the most trouble. Like, Shay, and her wooden idol deliveries? Connie, if Landon was anything less than the perfect date? Or "wicked" Chrissy?

Chapter Five

10:32 a.m.

SHAY'S FLIP-FLOPS echoed through the cavernous interior of the bank like an approaching cavalry charge. Jackson noticed several heads turn in their direction, and he wasn't sure if they were looking at Shay because she was cute or because she was a perfect stereotype. Or because she and Jackson were both underdressed, judging by the tailored suits worn by all the employees. No polos and khakis like at Jackson's bank.

They were greeted and seated by Mr. Everett, a middle-aged man with hair graying at the temples. He wore an impeccable navy suit and the thinnest of framed glasses, which served only a cosmetic purpose since he looked over them at everything. Maybe—but Jackson didn't think so—that was why he got the feeling that he and Shay were being looked down upon.

Almost immediately, Everett excused himself to take an urgent phone call. He turned away and spoke in a hushed voice, and Jackson let his eyes wander around the bank while they waited. Black and gray marble in the floors, support columns, and countertops gave the bank a chilled feel. Natural sunlight filtering in through muted skylights offset that sentiment. Seemingly unsupported wooden stairs led to the second floor, which ringed the first on three sides, providing office space for the V.P.s and department officers.

Jackson's eyes settled back on Shay, who had gone to her purse in search of gum. He felt a tugging in the back of his brain again, triggered by Shay. Maybe it was something with her case, or maybe it was the fact that despite Shay's Valspeak and apparently limited IQ, he had to work not to stare at her diminutive but attractive figure.

All the TV private eyes had strict policy about never dating their clients, and then they always ended up dining by candlelight and kissing—or more—

by the fireplace. And while Jackson had no formal policy, he'd never needed one. From middle school on, he'd always known when and where to draw the line—especially the ultimate line, which had never even been approached. Perhaps that explained the tugging.

Or maybe it was her brother Blake and his Indiana Jones-ish boss and their idols of doom after all.

"You want some gum?" Shay asked in a loud whisper.

"No thanks."

She returned her wrapper and the rest of the pack to her purse and tucked it under her arm. Then she re-crossed her legs, bouncing the left on top of the right, so that even while sitting, her flip-flops still flip-flopped.

Fortunately, Everett wasn't much longer. He apologized with a perfunctory smile and then got down to business. "What can I do for you?"

"I need to get into my safe deposit box," Shay answered.

He frowned. "Your name?"

"Shay Carmichael," she said with a rise of the shoulders and a pitch increase in her voice. What '80s movie was to blame for this dialect?

Everett made a few mouse clicks and typed in her name. A few more clicks. "Box number?"

"Um . . ." Shay dug into her purse and retrieved a small card. "Three-forty-four. It's actually my brother's box, but I'm on the card."

"What is your brother's name?"

"Blake."

More clicking.

"And do you have your key?" Everett asked.

She held it up.

"All right, come with me."

They followed Everett around his desk and back into the vault. Using his and Shay's keys, he pulled out one of the largest safe deposit boxes Jackson had ever seen and carried it to a small room off the main chamber of the vault. He set it on a table, unlocked the lid, and stepped back. "Just let me know when you're ready to leave," he said. He drew a curtain shut, and Jackson and Shay were relatively alone.

41

"This is, like, totally freaky."

"What is?"

"It's like opening a grave or something."

"They're just blocks of wood," Jackson said.

"Yeah, with a totally evil curse on them."

As opposed to those only semi-evil curses.

"Want me to do it?" Jackson asked.

Shay stepped back and nodded, and Jackson slid back the lid of the box.

Freaky was not the word to describe the idols. They were hideous. The wood was almost black, and the faces on each of the idols were contorted as if in agony. Jackson had been expecting quality work with realistic faces. Instead they looked like totem poles that had gone fifteen rounds with an angry Ali.

"Who carved these things, Picasso?"

"They're old," Shay said. "They, like, probably only had hand tools."

"Safe bet."

"I don't even want to touch them," she said. "Will you do it?"

Jackson picked up one of the idols, about eighteen inches tall and six inches in diameter, and was surprised at how light it was. For some reason, he equated dark wood with heavy wood, stone-like in weight. Not the case.

He reached for another with his other hand and compared the two carvings. They were similar in design but obviously not perfectly equal. Several of the features were off in size and shape, but the right eyes of both were closed, and the mouths of both sloped from left to right and widened.

"The god of winking or of Elvis impersonating."

"That's not funny."

"What's not funny is I could do this with a chisel while watching *The New Yankee Workshop.*"

"The New York Yankees what?"

"Never mind." He looked down at the box. "There are six."

"They, like, go in pairs or something," she said.

Jackson replaced the two idols and scoped out the others. It took some imagination, but he was able to match them in pairs: Eyes open or shut. Noses crooked this way or that. Mouths big or small, wide or sloped.

"Why two?" he asked.

"Like I know."

"Okay, so which two go first?"

Shay's face momentarily went blank. "Um . . ." She closed her eyes for several seconds and Jackson wondered if anybody could really care if their carving had a closed right eye and a straight nose as opposed to a narrowed left eye and a J-shaped nose. Maybe so. The wrong facial feature would totally give off the wrong vibe.

"These two," she said, pointing at the middle set of idols. "They go to the first address. I think."

"Great. Should we take them all?"

"Why?"

"Save us trips back here every time."

"I so do not want to have to carry them around," she said. "Besides, if the idols are here, I'm safe."

Jackson looked her in the eye and wanted to tell her he was almost positive that no Ninjas were going to jump out of nowhere while she was stopped at a red light and try to steal the carvings. But he didn't. Instead, he said, "I can keep them."

"Where?"

"In my car. Or at Cameron's. They've got a safe."

"For you?"

"The owner's a friend," Jackson said. "It'll be a lot easier than having to come back here and go through the rigmarole two more times."

Shay sighed and switched her weight to the other foot. "I don't know."

"Hey, it's your firewood, but the two of us coming in here three times is probably going to raise some red flags."

"Seriously?"

"They're probably already on high alert because we're wearing denim."

Shay frowned, switched her weight back, and then shrugged. "Whatever."

Jackson opened one of the provided totes and began loading the idols.

"Careful!"

"Like it matters if they get dented," Jackson said. "Who would notice?"

Four fit in one bag, and he dropped the two to be delivered right away into the other. "Anything else?" Jackson asked. Shay shook her head.

"Then let's go."

They closed the box back up, thanked Everett, and left the bank.

"My car or yours?" Jackson asked. He shifted the bags to one hand and retrieved his phone with the other. It was ten-forty-four.

"Mine," Shay answered.

Jackson nodded as she beeped open her doors. They stowed the extra idols in the trunk, and Jackson kept the third pair on his lap. Then he braced himself as Shay started the car.

She flipped her shades down and away they went, tearing out of the bank parking lot as if the building were about to blow.

"What's the address again?" Jackson asked.

"Um, I don't remember. It's in my purse."

"Is that an invitation?"

"No," she said as if disgusted. She reached down for her purse, set it on her lap, and began rifling through it, oblivious to traffic on Sunset Boulevard. She came up with a slip of paper and extended it to Jackson.

"Longhorn Avenue," he said. "You know where that is?"

"Um, I think so. Here, I have GPS."

"Let me," Jackson said, reaching over to activate the car's global positioning system. In seconds, directions to 414 Longhorn Avenue appeared on the screen. Jackson sat back and tried to enjoy the ride. Work and crazy clients and birthday memories aside, it was a beautiful day.

"Can I, like, ask you something?" Shay asked a moment later.

"Yeah."

"Why did you become a private investigator?"

It was a common question, and Jackson nearly trotted out the common answer, the one he could give without even thinking. But something in Shay's voice made him change his mind. For a moment, he saw vulnerability behind the Valley Girl façade, and it drew the same from him.

"It was three years ago, on my birthday. I was sitting there, twenty-seven years old, and still going from job to job, to college twice, the Army once. I didn't feel like anything I did mattered."

She glanced at him.

"I worked forty hours a week, not accomplishing anything but earning a living. It seemed like a waste. I wanted to do something with a purpose; God didn't put me here just to kill time. And I'd worked for a few years at a P.I. firm in San Diego, got a taste of the job. I thought why not. I could take only the cases I wanted, work the hours I wanted, and actually do some good. Help people out."

"So it's like a ministry or something?"

"I guess, in a manner of speaking."

"That's why you said you were selective."

Jackson nodded.

"But . . ."

"But what?"

"Nothing. So you've been a private investigator for three years?"

"No. I worked for an insurance company for a year and a half, as a claims adjustor."

"Why?"

"Because I needed three years experience to get a license. That, combined with what I did at MTR, put me over the top."

"Oh." She chomped on her gum for a while.

"What about you, Shay? What's your story?"

"Like, how do you mean?"

"I mean, you haven't told me very much about you. Who are you, what do you do, what's your brother like?"

She wrinkled her brow. "Blake? He's a loser. This is his fourth job in the last two years, all of them crazier than the one before. He's got, like, ADHD or something with jobs. And he totally thinks he's about to become the next zillionaire. Like Daddy's money isn't good enough for him or something?" She huffed. "I mean, why make your own?"

"This archaeologist, what's his name?"

Shay turned. "Figueroa. No. Figaro. No . . ." She closed her eyes—for far too long considering she was driving through L.A. "Ferragamo? I don't remember. Something like that."

"So Mr. F, he pays Blake well?"

"The way Blake runs around for him he must."

"What about you?" Jackson asked. "You work somewhere?"

"Me?"

Jackson accepted the condemnation in her voice. It was the dumbest question ever. He shrugged. "So you're totally dependent on your parents?"

"On their money. They died three years ago."

Jackson looked down. "I'm sorry."

"Thanks," she said softly.

They were at a stoplight, and for a moment, each lost in their own thoughts. Then the light turned, and out of the corner of his eye, Jackson saw Shay flip her hair over her shoulder. "It so wasn't fair," she said. "They crash in a car accident, and I'm left alone to deal with Blake. He was normal enough then, and then he goes way postal."

Jackson raised his head. "Postal? How so?"

"He quit school and, like, opened his own business, which totally flopped. Then he started taking all these classes online thinking he'd try again or something. And I'm like, whatever. I mean, Blake's not an idiot, but he's not a magma cum laude either."

"Few people are," Jackson said, managing a straight face.

"Yeah well, after a few semesters he quit school again and started taking all these crazy jobs."

"Like?"

She sighed. "Like being the personal assistant to this Hollywood producer. He, like, ran his errands or something. I mean, why not just be a butler? And then he worked for one of the movie studios as a paid date for out-of-town actresses."

Jackson frowned. "Really?"

"Really. And then he hooked up with Figueroa or whatever his name is."

Jackson looked out the window. Shay had steered the conversation back to Blake again. Or maybe he had. Either way.

"There it is," she said, turning onto a side street. Longhorn Avenue. It ran south from Santa Monica Boulevard, into a neighborhood of properties lined by fences and head-high hedgerows. They counted off the addresses to 414, and Shay whipped into a short driveway that led to a single story, white-sided house that seemed to flow in every direction across the expansive grounds.

Shay ripped off her sunglasses and just as violently pulled down her visor. She reached for her purse and came out with a small makeup kit and began administering a few touchups. Shockingly, Jackson realized, it was the first time he had seen her do so. He would have thought she would have stopped every few minutes to add more blush and freshen her lipstick.

Satisfied, she fumbled with the kit as she returned it to her purse, then dropped the keys as she removed them from the console.

"You all right?" Jackson asked.

Shay moaned. "I wish Blake were here, that's all."

"Anything I need to know?"

"Let's just get this over with." She fluffed her hair, double-checked her appearance in the mirror, and opened the door. Jackson got out slowly, stretching and wondering what a house in this neighborhood went for. Depended if the previous owner had hidden coke in the walls.

"Maybe you should wait out here," Shay said as Jackson handed her the bag with the idols in it. "Guard the car and the other idols."

"I don't think this neighborhood gets a lot of daytime burglaries," he said. "Besides, if anything is going to happen, it's probably going to happen during the exchange."

"Are you sure?"

He nodded. "Reasonably."

"Okay, let's go."

Chapter Six

JACKSON FOLLOWED SHAY along a cobblestone path that wound around the side of the garage and into the shaded side/back lawn. The grass was perfectly kept, the hedges scrupulously trimmed. Tulips and daffodils lined the walkway. Even the large shade trees looked straight out of a fairy tale . . . the sunshiny flowery meadow in the woods kind of fairy tale.

Shay rang the doorbell beside a pair of intricate wooden doors and then stepped back. She met Jackson's eye with a nervous look and bit down on her freshly glossed lip.

He touched her elbow. "It'll be fine."

That drew a thin smile as the door opened.

Jackson looked down at a gaunt, pale man in a wheelchair. His receding forehead comprised half his face, which was otherwise marked by sunken eyes hidden behind wire-rimmed glasses and a long, prissy nose. With tweed brown pants and a lavender turtleneck, he was a figure fit for a comic book. *Unbreakable*, maybe.

"Hi," Shay said, again in three syllables.

"Hello," the man answered with a frown. The voice fit the nose.

"I'm Shay Carmichael, making the delivery for Blake." She held up the bag as evidence.

His wheelchair blocked the entire doorway and he made no move to change things. Instead, he studied Shay with narrow eyes for several seconds, his head tilted slightly to one side. Then he removed his glasses and began wiping them with the bottom of his shirt. "I'm Adam Jones," he said, returning the glasses to his nose. He extended a sickly hand to Shay, who forced a smile and shook it.

Jones cocked his head to look at Jackson. "Who's he?"

48

"He's my bodyguard," Shay said. "Can't be too careful."

Adam Jones apparently regarded every remark for several seconds before responding. Finally, he wheeled back slightly. "Come in."

Nice to meet you too.

Jones spun his wheelchair around, and Jackson and Shay followed him into a pristine, minimally decorated entryway. There were two mirrors, one on each wall, and a coat hanger—the old-fashioned kind, a pole with hooks. Nothing else.

Jones veered through a doorway into a large living room that was void of color. It had white walls, white carpet, white furniture, and white bricks around the fireplace. The soot was probably even white. It looked like a photo shoot for skin care products, sans the reptile and a woman in a towel.

Jones stopped in the center of the living room next to a glass table with a single book on its surface. "I was told it would just be you coming," Jones said, his voice colder than his decorating taste. "I prefer to keep this private."

Dude, they're blocks of wood.

"He can, like, wait outside," Shay said.

He could, like, have waited back at home, staring at the ocean.

"That won't be necessary," Jones said. "We can adjourn to my library. Please," he added, cocking his head toward Jackson again, "make yourself comfortable."

If that were really possible in this hyperbaric chamber.

Jackson eyed Shay. She flashed a beaming smile back at him and followed Jones through a pair of translucent French doors. At his request, she closed them behind her, and Jackson was alone with the whiteness, unable to see through the glazed panes in the doors.

The private investigator side of him wanted to snoop around and see if there was any color in Jones' house. But there could be a "Mrs. Jones"— probably in the midst of a yoga routine—or the customary Spanish-speaking maid lurking about. And while Jones certainly was creepy enough, Jackson doubted he posed any real threat to Shay. Unless this really was *Unbreakable*.

So Jackson waited, straining to hear anything through the French doors but unable to pick up a sound. He checked out the book on the coffee table—a picture book of various cloud formations. Fascinating. There was a bookshelf on the wall adjacent to the study—also white—and Jackson perused the titles. Mostly non-fiction, the topics ranging from abstract philosophy to biographies of dead artists. Doubly fascinating.

Jackson strayed as far as the doorways of the living room. A hallway ran one direction, leading, it appeared, to bedrooms and a bathroom. A door in an adjacent wall led to a small study, the white broken only by the occasional light oak in a computer desk and a wall bookshelf. Jackson read a few spines, more of the same. And Jones still had a library too?

Jackson returned to the entryway, off which sprung another wing of the house. He could see what looked like a breakfast nook, and beyond that, surely a kitchen, dining room, solarium, and who knew what else.

The clock on the wall—twelve large numbers and two hands built right into the wall—indicated it had been less than three minutes since Shay had gone into the library with Jones. Still, how long did it take to hand two idols to somebody? Jackson put his ear to the door again. Again he heard nothing.

Jackson's curiosity got the best of him and he decided to do a little more exploring. He started down the bedroom wing, which was also completely white. There were no decorations on the walls, save for a full-body mirror at the end of the hall. If Jackson looked like—and dressed like—Jones, the last thing he would do was put up a bunch of mirrors.

He peeked into one bedroom, saw nothing but white in what he surmised was a guest room. Two other doors both were closed, so he returned to the bathroom and shut the door behind him. Everything was white—even the fixtures and hardware on the cabinets—except for a big mirrored medicine cabinet. Jackson opened the door and saw the standard items—toothbrush and toothpaste, razor and shaving gel, deodorant, and three bottles of the same cologne. On the other side of the cabinet were half a dozen prescription meds, in addition to the expected antacids, pain relievers, and allergy relief products. None of the prescription names rang a bell, nor were any of them pronounceable. Jackson closed the cabinet, flushed the toilet, ran the water in the sink for a few seconds, and returned to the living room.

He was just in time, dropping to the couch and flipping open the cloud book from the coffee table as the library doors opened. Shay emerged, followed closely by Jones in his wheelchair.

"All set?" Jackson asked.

Shay nodded and smiled cheerfully. Jones decided to clean his glasses again. This was ridiculous. Shay needed a bodyguard like Kobe needed a confidence boost.

Jackson stood up and took the empty tote bag from her. "Okay. Let's roll."

Jones returned his glasses to his nose and rolled ahead of them to the door. He ushered them through it with a quiet, "Goodbye," and closed it behind them without another word.

Jackson eyed the house over his shoulder as they returned to the car. "Was Pacman as friendly with you?" he asked.

"I know, right. He hardly said a word. I hope you weren't, like, offended."

"Don't worry about it," he said, opening Shay's car door. It earned another smile. "If I was dropping a hundred large on a couple of third-grade art projects, I'd want as few people as possible around too. He'll probably just paint them white."

He walked around the car and got in.

"Blake mentioned some of the people are kind of like that," Shay said. "I think they're afraid of the curse."

"You really buy into that?"

"Like, totally."

Jackson shook his head. "You buy the name he trotted out? Adam Jones."

"It could be real."

"Yeah, if he hadn't thought about it for several seconds first. Look downs, wipes the glasses, and Adam Jones is the best he can do?"

Shay shrugged. "He's probably just embarrassed. And caught off guard. I mean, I'm already filling in for Blake, and then you show up too. Don't take it personal," she said, turning on the car.

"I won't."

Shay shifted into reverse, then looked at Jackson. "P.S., he was like a total weirdo. I mean, I thought his head was going to fall off his shoulders. And did you see those glasses? Hello, they make contact lenses."

If that wasn't the tagline for the next Dove commercial.

They drove back toward Beverly Hills in silence. Shay seemed occupied with her thoughts—probably debating between spa treatments—and Jackson wasn't in the chatting mood. That nagging feeling was still there . . . something, although he couldn't place it, was off with this whole deal.

"So do you get scared?" Shay asked as they neared the bank.

"Scared?"

"Yeah. I mean, like of dying or something? Isn't being a private investigator totally dangerous?"

Jackson thought for a moment, then shrugged. "I guess it can be. But I'm careful. And I'm prepared."

"Prepared how? Do you, like, have a gun?"

He smiled. "Not on me, but yeah. And I've got a cousin who was a Marine; he showed me how to kick some butt."

Shay looked at him. "But still, aren't you afraid to die?"

Jackson looked out the window and uttered a soft, "No."

Not anymore.

Back at the bank, Jackson assured Shay that she and the idols would be safe without him riding in the car beside her. Then they each got into their respective cars, and he followed her back to Cameron's. He called ahead, and when they arrived, Reggie was waiting for them. He locked the four remaining carvings in the safe in his downstairs office and agreed to meet Jackson and Shay that afternoon to unlock them.

Back in the parking lot Shay asked, "So, I'll meet you here at one-thirty?"

Jackson nodded. "I'll be here."

"Great." She wiggled her fingers at Reggie, smiled at Jackson, and strode to her car. For the second time that morning, Jackson watched her drive away.

"She for real, man?" Reggie asked.

"Like, totally."

"Man, the things you do for money."

"Tell me about it."

Reggie backhanded Jackson's shoulder. "You want some lunch?"

"I've got a date."

"Of course you do. Sam?"

"Maggie."

"You're something else."

"That reminds me, you know where I can score some cheap tickets to *Wicked*? I've got to take Chrissy."

"Who?"

"The girl at the courthouse. I had to bribe her to get a background check."

Reggie shook his head. Jackson grinned.

"You'll hate theatre, man."

Jackson shrugged.

"And you'll have to wear a tie."

He shrugged again. "Yeah, but I get to see Chrissy all decked out."

"Go on your date."

Jackson grinned again. "Later."

Chapter Seven

11:50 a.m.

THE ENTERPRISE FISH Company was located just down the beach a few miles from Cameron's, and the drive took Jackson less than five minutes. As he turned into the parking lot across the street from the brick building, his cell rang. The caller ID said it was Garrett Warren, who did not merit his own ringtone.

"Hey, Garrett."

"Douglas. How ya been?"

"I've been. Yourself?" Jackson asked, looking for an open spot.

"Fabulous. Got your message. You need the dope on a Landon Brower?"

"That's right. You know him?"

"Name's not in my files anywhere and it doesn't ring a bell. What else can you tell me?"

Jackson sighed and gave Garrett everything he knew about Landon. "That do anything for you?" he asked, finally parking the car.

"I don't know him, but I can bet I know the type," Garrett said. "Likes to party, likes to drink, probably likes to blow a few, but I doubt he's into anything serious. No criminal record?"

"Nope."

"Yeah. What do you need on this guy anyhow?"

Jackson sighed again and got out of the car. "Promise not to laugh."

"Yes."

"I'm supposed to make sure he's a safe date."

Garrett laughed.

"Hey, man, it pays."

"Sure," Garrett said. "If you're that hard up, I got some legwork I can source out."

Jackson crossed the street, letting Garrett get it out of his system.

"Seriously, this for a kid sister or something?"

"Close. A friend."

"Yeah well, my guess is he's not searching for a serious relationship, you know what I mean?"

Well that was good, because Jackson doubted Gina was either. "Yeah, I know what you mean."

"Hey, I gotta go, man. Paying client on the other line."

"No problem."

"I'll ask around a little and hit you back if I hear anything."

"Thanks, G."

Jackson set his phone to vibrate and slipped it into his pocket. He scanned the outdoor tables, but didn't see Maggie. So he went to the front door and opened it to the smells of freshly cooked salmon, shrimp, lobster, and grouper. He waited for his eyes to adjust from the California sunlight, and when they did, he spotted Maggie, bent down, inspecting fish in an aquarium. He walked over and stood beside her, just waiting. After a moment she turned her head, causing chestnut brown hair to tumble off her shoulders. "Hey." She reached up and pulled on his wrist. "Check this out."

He dropped to the catcher's position. ·

"See him," she said, pointing at an eight-inch fish that was ashen blue with white spots all over it. The fish was almost see-through, like a jellyfish. Maggie said as much, staring at the creature in awe.

"What is it?" Jackson asked.

"A blue puffer."

"He on the menu?"

Maggie backhanded him in the shoulder, then stood up. So did Jackson.

"Hey," she said again, giving him a quick hug. "Happy birthday."

"Thanks. You already see about a table?"

"Yeah, I was just waiting for you. Right over here."

He followed her to a two-person booth near another aquarium and slid in opposite her. Sun filtered in from a skylight almost directly overhead and seemed to center on Maggie.

As always, she was dressed casually. Today that consisted of a mauve polo and blue jeans. Her tan face contained a slight trace of makeup, and then again, maybe it didn't. Energetic gray-blue eyes, an enticing smile, and pronounced dimples in each cheek made cosmetics unnecessary. There was no jewelry, no nail polish, no frills of any kind. She and Shay would make great pals.

Almost immediately a waiter in all black delivered menus and took drink orders.

"So how's your story on the eight-year-old tenth grader?" Jackson asked when he was gone.

"Other way around," Maggie said, opening her menu. "And it's been written a dozen times by a dozen papers. The name, age, and grade just change with each writing."

"Child genius wows teachers, parents," Jackson said. "Plans to attend Stanford, become a doctor, cure cancer?"

"Something like that. Occasionally they play the violin by ear or something."

"What's this kid do?"

"Read encyclopedias."

"Popular, I bet."

"I'm sure."

The waiter returned with a pair of iced teas, and for a few minutes, Jackson turned his attention to his menu. Everything looked pretty good, but he eventually settled on fish tacos. It almost seemed sacrilegious to get a burger or a chicken sandwich. Maggie ordered the Cajun jambalaya and asked for extra seasoning. And more iced tea.

"So," she said, resting her arms on the table, "how are your two cases going?"

"Thrillingly," Jackson answered. He gulped a third of his tea and told her about Shay and the woodcarvings, sparing enough details so that he wasn't breaching any confidentiality. Then he delved into Connie's case, figuring that if she wanted to consider it a favor, he could too. Favors weren't covered by confidentiality agreements.

Maggie, for genuine interest, or because it beat the Monrovian mastermind, hung on every word. Jackson briefed her on his research so far, from his findings at the courthouse to putting Mouse on the social media trail to Garrett's theories about Landon.

"Hey," he said when he was finished, "you think you might be able to dig something up on Brower for me? If the whiz kid doesn't eat up your whole afternoon?"

"Maybe. What do you need to know?"

"Anything you got. Run his name, see if he's ever been in the news for anything. So far all I've got is he speeds."

She shrugged. "Sure."

Jackson sat back. "So what else is new? How are your Yankees shaping up?"

Maggie fiddled with her straw. "Better than your Dodgers," she said. She took a sip.

"Speaking of," Jackson said, "the Giants are in town next weekend . . ."

"If there should happen to be some extra tickets? Whatever happened to 'Hey, Maggie, want to go to a ballgame?'"

"Actually, I was thinking of taking Grandpa."

She found his shin under the table and kicked it.

"Ah—taking Grandpa to the senior center to play Bingo while we went to the game."

"Yeah, well, now I'm thinking of taking Bill."

"Bill Plaschke?"

"Yeah. I'll go to the Dodgers game with Bill Plaschke." She took another sip of tea. "Bill's a guy in Entertainment. We went out a few times last year."

Jackson nodded. "Wow, you take my tickets, throw your boyfriends in my face. Want to kick my other shin?"

"Your tickets?" She shook her head, then leaned a little closer. "It just so happens, your present was going to be tickets to Friday's game. First base, four rows up."

"And now?"

"Now it depends," she said, tilting her head to the side. She grinned. "You taking me or your grandpa?"

Jackson took a drink before answering. "You," he said. "Grandpa can't smile like that."

Maggie's eyes locked with his while her fingers continued to play with the end of the straw.

Her house salad arrived.

She sat back and Jackson scanned the hubbub around them while she poured out her dressing and tossed the salad. The Enterprise Fish Company didn't really get swinging until happy hour, but even the lunch crowd nearly filled the place. Combined with the background music and the various sports programs on the overhead TVs, they made enough noise to create an edgy but fun atmosphere.

The salad was good judging by how quickly Maggie polished it off. It was a good thing too, because moments after she finished, their entrées arrived. Connie's sticky buns had been delicious, but they had worn off, and Jackson attacked his fish tacos and double order of fries with delight. Maggie plowed into her jambalaya and cornbread with equal relish, and for several minutes, their conversation centered on the flavor of the tacos and the spiciness of the jambalaya.

By her third glass of tea, Maggie started to slow down on her meal. "You want some?" she asked, sliding her bowl of jambalaya to the middle of the table. Jackson singled out some of the meat and stuffed it into his final taco.

She continued to pick at the bowl for several minutes before shoving it aside for good.

"You gonna finish that cornbread?" Jackson asked.

"All yours."

He grabbed the plate and slid it to his side of the table.

"So be serious with me for a minute, Jackson," she said, leaning on the table where her bowl and plate had been.

Jackson looked up as he took a bite of his taco.

"How have you been doing?"

"Fine."

"We're not old guys in the hardware store, Jackson. How are you really doing?"

He set down the taco. "April was rough. No late-night construction projects to keep me busy, no repeated trips to Home Depot. I spent a lot of time shooting baddies with Mouse."

"I guess that's therapeutic."

"It occupies the mind."

She nodded. "So that's it? Keeping busy?"

"One day at a time."

"Like Tom Hanks in *Sleepless in Seattle*."

"Sure."

"Or at the end of *Cast Away*."

"Is this going to be a complete filmography?"

She made the woman face, and he reached for some fries. "Maggie, last night I was this close to seeing how far I could go into a bottle of ten-year-old Glenmorangie."

"You don't drink."

"Never a drop. That's the scary part."

"Why didn't you call someone? Call me. Or your grandpa."

He shrugged. "I wanted to be alone. Part of me wanted to get wasted."

"But you didn't."

"It was this close."

"But you didn't." She smiled.

He downed a pair of fries. "No, I didn't."

"You can call me, Jackson."

"Yeah."

"I mean it."

"Yeah."

She leaned back, her eyes still searching him. "So how are you . . . today?"

"Occupied."

"And tomorrow?"

"Daddy's Little Princess and I have a delivery to make."

"Wednesday?"

"Should I have brought my calendar?"

"I'm concerned about you, Jackson."

"Join the club. I'm thinking of sending out a mailer."

She made the face again. Jackson finished his taco and started on the cornbread.

Maggie leaned over the table. "Look, far be it from me to play psychologist. I just want to know that you're going to be all right."

"So do I."

She reached across the table and took his wrist.

"You're making it hard to eat my cornbread."

She smiled tongue-in-cheek and let go. "You're not going to just bat me aside with humor."

"Did you just split an infinitive, Miss Newspaper Reporter?"

"Jackson."

"Sorry. It's a habit." He smirked.

She leveled her eyes at him.

"I'm sorry, Maggie. Really." He shrugged. "But I don't know what's going to happen. I just try to find a way to go five minutes without pain. First it was fixing up my place, then it was killing terrorists with Mouse, and today it's babysitting Paris Hilton."

She nodded.

"You want to hold my wrist again?"

Maggie smiled but sat back. "You need distractions, is that right?"

Jackson nodded and ate the last bite of cornbread.

"So let's do something," she said. "Let's get away for the weekend. Hit Vegas or Carmel or just get out and ride. I could get vacation, and you can always leave."

Six months ago, it would have been tempting. In fact, it was tempting now. But six months ago, he might not have had the willpower or the resolve to resist.

Jackson leaned back slowly. "We talked about this before, remember?"

"I didn't say shack up for the weekend. Just hang out. Separate rooms."

He shook his head.

"You Christians are fuddy-duddies, you know that?"

"Yeah well, you're a licentious temptress."

"Licentious?"

"It's King James, I think."

"I just want to help, Jackson. Occupy your mind."

"You already do."

That brought an expected smile to her face.

"And I appreciate it, Maggie. I've got nothing this weekend. We'll do something, and I'll even pay."

"So what, a round of putt-putt?"

"Hey, if you don't like it, you can call Bill and I'll just sit at home with my Glenmorangie."

"And blame your fall from grace on me? I don't think so."

Jackson smiled and drained his tea.

"This weekend then?" Maggie asked.

"Absolutely."

They paid and stopped once more to examine the fish before heading outside.

"Where'd you park?" Jackson asked.

"Around the corner."

"I'll walk you."

They started to stroll, and Jackson wished he could blow off Shay and Connie and spend the afternoon with Maggie. Judging by her posture, she wished it too.

"You're going to your grandpa's tonight?" she asked.

"Yeah."

"How is he doing?"

"Pretty well," Jackson answered. "The guy's amazing."

"Is he like most grandpas, falls asleep watching the news every night?"

"Not every night," Jackson said, smelling trouble. "Why?"

She gave a half-shrug. "I'll just be sitting at home trying to figure out how to spin the boy genius. If you need somebody to talk to, I'll be there."

He couldn't picture himself having one of those long "you hang up first" phone conversations with Maggie (especially since he'd be having dessert with Sam) but the sentiment was nice. "I'll keep that in mind," he said.

Maggie stopped. "Take care of yourself, Jackson."

"I will."

She leaned in and gave him a quick peck on the cheek. "Bye."

"Bye. Thanks for lunch."

With a smile, she tipped her head back, then pushed her helmet down over her hair. She lifted up the visor and made eye contact. "This weekend."

"This weekend."

She swung her leg over the body of her black and silver Yamaha motorcycle and fired it up. She winked, lowered the visor on her helmet, and roared away. Jackson watched her go, picturing the two of them on her bike, cruising across the California backcountry away from the setting sun. He smiled to himself, feeling the least bit of coolness as the breeze brushed against the spot on his cheek where she had kissed him.

Then he turned and walked back to his car.

Chapter Eight

12:58 p.m.

IT TOOK A little more than ten minutes to drive from the restaurant to Mouse's house in Culver City. Jackson used the time to try to figure out just what the nagging voice in his head was nagging about. That was the problem . . . nagging voices often sounded like the adults in a *Peanuts* holiday special.

Mouse's house was not actually a house but a duplex, the left side of which belonged to Mouse and his sister Pam. As Jackson pulled to the curb, he recognized her white Honda Civic parked with one tire scraping the curb, one tire a foot away from the curb. A bumper sticker with tiny print made several crude anatomical references about following too closely. That was Pam.

Jackson sighed and got out, locking his doors and hoping that she was out back working on her tan. On second thought, the duplex had rear-facing windows. In her room reading a trashy paperback (with mostly small words) would be better. Her tan came from a bottle anyhow.

Hands in his pockets, Jackson walked across the cracked sidewalk leading to the front door. The grass needed mowing and the shrubs in front of the building were nearly dead. As far as Jackson knew, Mouse and Pam had ignored them since moving in. In other words, they kept up with the neighboring Joneses.

Pam answered the door on Jackson's second ring of the bell. Ideally, a friend's older sister was supposed to be hot and perhaps a little bit of a tease. Pam was not ideal. She was tall and pudgy and looked down a hawk nose from gray-brown eyes. Clumsy physically and mentally, she was almost always crabby, convinced that the world owed her.

63

"What do you want?" she grunted.

"Nice to see you too, Pam." Her eyes narrowed. "Mouse here?" Jackson asked.

"I suppose you're here to play video games for eight hours again."

"Nope."

"You want another favor?"

"Should I have made an appointment with you?"

Few women had the combined physical prowess and temperament to scare Jackson. Pam was close, but he couldn't help himself.

"I'm missing *Days of Our Lives*. He's in his room." She turned back to the television set in the living room. A stiff and a tramp were arguing. About time for a slap, a stare, and then a passionate kiss.

Jackson let himself in and closed the door. "Shouldn't you be working?"

"Shouldn't you?"

"I am."

She grunted again as Jackson started down the hallway. Mouse's room was last on the left, and Jackson rapped on the open door just as something otherworldly was decimated by a laser beam on Mouse's computer screen. The resulting shriek of death was amplified by the subwoofer beneath the desk, causing Pam to holler from the living room.

"Blah, blah, blah," Mouse muttered, not turning from the screen.

"To be fair," Jackson said, "alien death screams do ruin a good kissing scene."

Kyle Joshua Polinski slowly swiveled around in his chair. His nickname, which he had earned long before meeting Jackson, had nothing to do with his appearance, although it easily could have. Mouse was thin and his constant slouched posture made him appear short. Shaggy brown hair covered a face that was marked by equally dark eyes and a long, hawk nose. And by a one-inch scar on his forehead where it had cracked the countertop when his father—a deadbeat who had run out when Mouse was eleven—had hit him. His mother had turned to drugs shortly thereafter and had overdosed on heroin six years later. Pam had become . . . well, Pam. Mouse had withdrawn into a shell.

Except around computers. He could do almost anything with a keyboard and a mouse. Hence the nickname. Without ever taking a class, he'd become an expert at finding any kind of information on the internet, creating and cracking computer code, and killing everything from terrorists to aliens in video games. In front of a computer, Mouse was in his element. Away from it, he was . . . mouse-like.

"Hey, man," Mouse said. He lifted a bag of Chex Mix from off his stomach and tossed it to an empty spot on his desk.

"Hey. I catch you at a bad time?" Jackson asked.

Mouse brushed some crumbs off his T-shirt. "No. What's up?"

"You got anything on Brower?"

"Who? Oh, yeah. Check this out," he said, wheeling back around and exiting his game. Jackson grabbed the spare chair from the corner and pulled it beside his friend.

"I checked Twitter, YouTube, Flickr, a handful of other sites I'm sure you've never heard of, and hacked into his Facebook page. Pretty much what I thought."

"Girls, beer, and more girls?"

"Yeah." Mouse's fingers raced over the keys, and in seconds, Jackson was looking at Brower's page.

"Is that him?" Jackson asked.

Mouse nodded. Landon was what Jackson expected. Tall, muscular, tan, short brown hair with fading blond highlights. He was good-looking, but not a heartthrob. Perfect for Gina.

Mouse clicked through a handful of photos. Landon at a bar with two girls, all three of them with full glasses. Landon with some girl on his lap on somebody's basement couch. Drinking again. Landon at the beach with nearly naked girls. No beer involved. Landon and a buddy at Hooters. More beer. The girls were all pretty, in a tacky sort of way—always laughing, bubbly, half-drunk. Gina's sorority sisters.

"Can you go back to the ones at the beach?" Jackson asked.

"Yeah, can't blame you."

Jackson rolled his eyes as Mouse accessed the album. "Any photo in particular?"

Jackson scanned the thumbnails. "That one."

Mouse clicked on a photo of Landon and a brunette standing ankle deep in the ocean, playfully wrestling over a football. Both were laughing like they were in a beer commercial.

"Can you zoom in?"

Mouse clicked and tapped a few times, opening his photo-viewing software. "Anywhere in particular?"

Jackson pointed at the screen, and Mouse highlighted the area with his mouse and tapped the keyboard. The selected portion of the image doubled in size.

"The tattoo," Jackson said, looking at Landon's left biceps. "Can you make that out?"

Mouse zoomed again, then resampled the image.

Jackson sat back and sighed. It was Tommy Trojan, the USC mascot.

"I could have told you," Mouse said. "He has USC stuff everywhere."

"Well, the tat says he's probably not a bandwagon fan."

"Or he was drunk."

Jackson assented. "Okay, what else? Can we poke him or something?"

Mouse led him on a tour of Landon's page, highlighting various characteristics he had discovered. Landon played the drums, was a "guy movie" buff, listened to Green Day and The All-American Rejects, flirted and received flirts, and preferred Miller Genuine Draft. Landon liked seafood and chocolate chip cookies, quoted *Wedding Crashers* and *The Hangover* a lot, and enjoyed sailing. He complained about pollution, disagreed with every military involvement since World War II, and lamented the lack of social equality in the world. And he did it all with a frat boy's lethargic detachment.

Jackson sat back and rubbed his head. Mouse, as he often did, rocked slightly in place. He claimed it was a coping mechanism he had developed as a child. Pam claimed he was just a freak.

"Okay, did you find anything on Myspace or Twitter or anywhere else?"

"He's not on Myspace, but who is anymore," Mouse said, leaning forward and taking control of the computer mouse. "He is on Twitter, but doesn't say much."

"Who's he follow?"

"Charlie Sheen, Owen Wilson, Megan Fox, a couple of classmates, and some guy named Mark Sanchez?"

"Former USC quarterback. Anything interesting there?"

"It's Twitter." Mouse shrugged, then pulled up several tweets for Jackson to look at. They were all variants of the same strain—crass humor and vulgar flirting. And beer references.

"You see anything anywhere about drugs?" Jackson asked. "He smoke pot, take speed, anything?"

Mouse shook his head. "Didn't see anything."

"Did you check out any of his friends?"

"There's like a million. Every picture was a different girl. I started making a list; there were at least a dozen."

"Poke any of them?"

Mouse rolled his eyes. "Poking doesn't do anything."

"Whatever. Did you check any of them out?"

He shook his head.

"Could you?"

"All of them?"

"Just pick a few."

"Looking for what?"

"Any complaints about Landon. He treated them bad, got physical, cheated."

Mouse sat back. "He going out with one of your girlfriends, or something? You want to find dirt on him?"

"Neighbor's niece. I need to make sure he's safe."

"You mean . . ."

"No, not like that, although that might be good to know."

"You're asking a lot, man."

"Just check out a few of the girls, see if they complain about him. You can be Bond next time we play *Nightfire*."

"Whatever, man."

"You want me to swing by Starbucks and nominate you for employee of the month."

"No, they'd know it was bogus."

Jackson grinned and glanced at the clock above the desk. He had a few minutes. "So, you on the mother ship yet?"

Mouse spent five minutes showing him around the final level of the video game he'd been trying to conquer for almost two months. (Conquer, that was, with a perfect score. He'd beaten the game in six hours.) Then he promised to call Jackson when he had anything. Jackson thanked him and got up to leave, hoping that poking strange women on Facebook would outrank killing aliens in Mouse's mind. He knew his friend would call, just not necessarily before Gina's date with Landon.

Pam was curled up on the couch, a bag of Cheetos in one hand and a box of tissues in the other. On the television, two twenty-something girls were arguing over a guy not in the picture.

"Don't worry, they'll both get him."

"Leaving already?" Pam said.

"Just running out to get some tacos," Jackson said. "We've got aliens to kill."

Her sigh was audible, and he grinned as he headed for his car. Pam would accurately be described by those in the Christian circle as "searching," and Jackson knew he really should try to reach out to her. But taunting and tormenting her was just so much fun.

Shay's convertible was not in the parking lot when he returned to Cameron's a minute ahead of their scheduled one-thirty meeting. Jackson quickly used the downstairs restroom, and was met at the bar by Reggie when he came out.

"Hey, man, your girlfriend called."

"Which one?"

"The one who's still in junior high."

"Shay?"

"Yeah. Said she's running late."

"Oh man, I sure hope those bookends aren't going to get delivered behind schedule."

Reggie smirked, and Jackson briefed him on the case, acceptable since Reggie was sort of an associate. By Jackson's standards, half of Greater Los Angeles was privy to case details under the "associate" clause.

"So let me get this straight, man, you just tag along while this girl delivers those nasty looking things we locked in the safe?"

"Yeah."

"And she says they're worth fifty grand each?"

"That's what she says."

Reggie rubbed his head. "Man, we have two hundred thousand dollars a' wood sitting in that safe?"

"Same as in your fireplace."

"Two hundred thousand," he repeated, then frowned. "Man, anything about this seem off to you?"

"Yeah, and it's bugging me. I don't know what it is, but ever since I heard her story, something's been nagging at me. You see any holes in it?"

"Not really. It's too crazy to be made up."

"That's what I thought. I don't know."

The bartender—not Esteban—put down the phone and signaled for Jackson's attention. "There's a woman upstairs for you."

"High-pitched, excited?" Jackson asked.

The bartender nodded.

"Duty calls," Jackson said. Reggie thanked the bartender and they hurried to meet Shay, who was waiting in the curved vestibule between the two levels of the restaurant.

"Sorry I'm late," she said. "Traffic on the 405 was, like, terrible."

"What were you doing on the 405?" Jackson asked.

"Lunch," she said, as if it were obvious.

Reggie exchanged looks with Jackson and led them back down to his office.

"It matter which two?" Jackson asked as Reggie opened the safe.

Shay peered at the four remaining idols. "These two."

Jackson dropped them into the extra tote. "Ready to ride?"

"Yeah, we're late."

Reggie closed the safe and pulled on Jackson's arm.

"Hey, man, there's something about this girl."

"What do you mean?"

"I mean, have you seen the way she looks at you?"

There had been a few glances that had made Jackson curious, but nothing concrete. He shook his head. "No, how?"

"I don't know exactly, but . . . it's like she wants to make sure you like her or something."

"You think she's feeling me?"

"I don't know, man. Just keep an eye out."

"Great," Jackson said as they turned to follow Shay. "An ominous warning from the big black dude. The plot has thickened."

Chapter Nine

"LIKE, WHAT WAS that about?" Shay asked as they walked briskly across the parking lot.

"Reggie?"

She nodded.

"Nothing."

Shay frowned but didn't press the issue. Jackson, carrying the carvings, got into the passenger seat and buckled up. Shay floored the accelerator and didn't bother with her seatbelt until they were on the freeway headed east, ultimately to Beverly Hills.

She seemed a little out of sorts, and not talkative. Jackson didn't mind. He could use the time to think. If Reggie was right and Shay was up to something, it would explain the nagging feeling. Maybe something tucked away in his subconscious had picked up whatever Reggie had observed. A look in Shay's eye, an expression, something that wasn't quite right.

But what? Was she manufacturing this entire story to have an excuse to hire a private investigator, to fulfill some damsel in distress complex? Did that mean she had also set up fake deliveries? No, that didn't wash.

So maybe the deliveries were legit, but she still had a complex. Or maybe Little Miss Perfect had ostracized all of her friends and was desperate to be liked. Or maybe it was as simple as that look in her eye being *that* look. Maybe she was coming on to him.

Jackson hoped not. It was dangerous enough to be working for a woman that he found attractive. If the feeling was mutual, well, that's how the TV private investigators usually ended up tied to a chair in a building about to go up in flames after alienating their best friends.

Or maybe it was nothing at all. Maybe Reggie had spent too much time on paperwork and Jackson was just having trouble reading a Valley Girl. He wouldn't be the first guy. At any rate, he wasn't about to sit around analyzing every one of Shay's facial expressions, looking for hidden meaning. That wasn't how he rolled. If there was something to sniff out, he'd find it soon enough.

Shay drove to make up for lost time, and soon they were winding through posh neighborhoods that made Adam Jones' environs look like slums. Enormous mansions were splayed out across acres of perfectly clipped lawns, with meticulously manicured hedges and flower gardens surrounding them, all beneath the shade of ridiculously tall palm trees.

"So what do you know about this buyer?" Jackson asked. He and Shay had said almost nothing on the trip, and he was starting to wonder if she was mad.

"Nothing. Just the address."

"Does Blake know these people?"

"I doubt it."

"Just the boss man?"

She shrugged.

They drove a few blocks.

"How long's Blake been working for him?"

"Six months. Why?"

"Curious. He doesn't talk much about his work?"

"Like, hardly at all before he calls me out of the blue to do his errands for him."

"You don't know anything else about his boss?" Jackson asked. "First name, maybe where he went to school, companies he's associated with, anything?"

"Hi, do I look like 4-1-1?"

"Sorry."

They drove two more blocks.

"So, like, what's with the sudden third degree?"

"I'm a private investigator. I'm investigating."

72

"Me?"

"Pays to know who you're working for."

"I've told you everything I know," Shay said, veering left in front of traffic. "What, you, like, think I'm making this up?"

"No," Jackson said. "Not really."

"Well I'm not. Seriously."

"I believe you."

She turned her head, and looked at him for the first time in the conversation. "You do?"

"Yeah. If you were making up a story, you could do a lot better than this."

Shay smiled and slammed on the brakes. "We're here." She made a left turn into a long driveway that was blocked immediately by an iron gate. She lowered her window and leaned toward a speaker mounted on a small stand beside the driveway.

Jackson heard a muffled voice through the speaker.

"Shay Carmichael."

The muffled voice said something about business.

"I'm, like, supposed to be here at two o'clock, in place of my brother Blake."

Jackson heard a, "One moment," and then silence. The moment was several minutes long, and ended when the gate in front of them began to squeak open. Shay vroomed through, her mirrors just clearing the gate, and tore up the driveway. She skidded to a stop in front of a two-story mansion that looked like the Fresh Prince's palace. White siding met with a three-foot high brick façade that lined the entire front of the building. There was a covered portico, framed on both sides by massive picture windows. The roof had more slants and peaks than a mountain range, and the garage off in the distance to the right was the size of a downtown parking structure.

"So," Jackson said as they got out of the car, "your buyer's Rockefeller."

"Who?"

"Never mind."

The front door was eight feet tall and half that wide, a dark green to match the shutters and shingles. It swung open before they could ring the bell or knock, and Jackson expected to see a stooped old man in a tuxedo, wispy white hair and all. He could not have been more wrong.

The man was young, in his late twenties or early thirties at most, with jet-black hair and a movie star's face. He wore a white dress shirt, brighter than the sun, and crisp black pants. No tie. No vest. No jacket. Perfect posture. And perfect teeth, which he flashed as he greeted them in an Italian accent.

"Mr. and Mrs. Carmichael? I'm Ricardo."

"Uh, it's just miss," Shay said as if gravely insulted.

"Oh, I'm terribly sorry."

Shay waved him off. "This is Jackson Douglas."

"A pleasure. Miss Delacroix is waiting for you on the terrace."

"Delacroix," Jackson said. "Emmanuelle Delacroix?"

"Yes," Ricardo answered with the proper bewilderment. He covered with a smile. "This way, please." He led them down a long, wide hallway, adorned with impressive landscape paintings and photographs.

"Who's Emmanuelle Dela-whatever?" Shay asked.

"She's a world-famous painter," Jackson said. "Photographer too, I think," he said, admiring a panoramic shot of some mountain range. It reminded him of the single file prancing scene at the end of *The Sound of Music*.

"Can I get either of you something to drink?" Ricardo asked, gesturing at a wet bar to their right. The hallway had opened into a small seating area that Jackson deduced served as a waiting room for Emmanuelle Delacroix's guests. Additional hallways branched out both left and right while French doors directly ahead opened onto the back patio.

Jackson and Shay declined beverages, Ricardo smiled as if this pleased him more than anything, and the trio proceeded onto the patio. It was expansive, made of cobbled stone that matched the brick façade on the house. Beds of flowers lined the patio on every side, creating a private, secluded courtyard. In the middle, several steps down and ringed by a concrete patio of its own, was a large, rectangular swimming pool. The water beckoned seductively on a warm afternoon.

But the best feature of all was the view. The entire backyard looked out over the neighborhood, Los Angeles suburbs in the distance, and ultimately the Pacific Ocean. From where they stood on the patio, the view was framed by elevated rows of birds of paradise on the right and a small strand of palm trees on the left. Jackson suddenly craved a chaise lounge and a frosty glass of lemonade.

Ricardo offered Jackson and Shay another dentist-office-poster smile and led them across the patio. Emmanuelle Delacroix was in the back corner, alternating between staring at the view and staring at her easel.

"Em?" Ricardo said quietly.

Em? Was Ricardo her manservant or boy toy?

"Miss Shay Carmichael and Mr. Jackson Douglas to see you."

With appropriate disinterest, Delacroix ignored him for several seconds, paintbrush in hand, her eyes fixed on the canvas. So far the sky was filled in, a blue that matched the real thing.

"Thank you, Ricardo," she said after several more awkward seconds. She set the brush on her stand, wiped her hands on a towel, and finally turned to acknowledge her guests.

Emmanuelle Delacroix could have been a world-famous supermodel as well. Not even the paint-splattered denim overalls worn over a white sleeveless tee could hide her tall, lithe figure or take away from her alabaster skin and perfect complexion. Long, silky, ebony hair that could stop traffic was loosely bundled in the back of her head and held there by . . . yes, a thin paintbrush. The rest of it hung in wisps beside her cheeks and in front of piercing green eyes. Even in her scrubs, Jackson thought, she could walk the runway right now. Disheveled was in this year in Europe, wasn't it?

"Please excuse my appearance," she said in an accent that would cause most men to melt. Jackson disliked all things French (except for fries and toast) and therefore wasn't impressed. Delacroix continued. "You are Blake's sister?"

Shay nodded. "This is . . ."

"Jackson Douglas, her associate."

"It is nice to meet you." She didn't smile to prove it. "You have . . ." She stopped as she saw the bag in Jackson's hand.

"Maybe we could, like, talk inside," Shay said.

The green eyes scrutinized her, and then Delacroix nodded. "Very well."

Shay beamed as the artist removed the paintbrush from her hair and tossed it on the stand. She pulled her hair through her hands and let it fall on her back, then ran her fingers through it.

Steady.

"Come with me," Delacroix said, starting past them toward the house.

Shay grabbed Jackson's arm. "Maybe you should just wait out here."

He frowned.

"Remember last time?"

Jackson thought about arguing, but didn't want to make a scene. So he shrugged. "It's your show."

Shay smiled again, took the bag from Jackson's fingers, and followed Delacroix toward the house. There were chairs on the other side of the pool, and Jackson wandered over and sat down. He thought of Reggie's comment about the look in Shay's eyes, then pictured her baby blues as she had suggested he wait outside? Was there something more there?

He sighed and told himself to quit worrying. He was getting paid to drive Shay to the Beverly Hills home of a renowned artist and sit and stare at a million-dollar view while they exchanged Tahitian treats. What did he care what look was in her eyes?

That sentiment lasted for a couple of minutes before the nagging came back. The voice was starting to get some cadence. Now if only it would take the marbles out of its mouth so Jackson could understand it.

He got up and started for the house. He had no idea where Delacroix had taken Shay, no idea where Ricardo was lurking, and no idea who else might inhabit the house with them. But curiosity had again gotten the best of him.

The waiting room was empty and quiet and Jackson stopped to listen for distant sounds. Nothing. He started down the first hallway, which led to the kitchen. Jackson paused for a moment. Hearing nothing, he retraced his steps.

Down the opposite hallway, Jackson found a powder room and a massive living room, the focal point of which was a two-story stone fireplace. It was surrounded by fancy furniture, elegant décor, and a small forest of potted plants. But it was vacant. Several doorways opened off the far end of the room, but Jackson decided that instead of venturing off into one of the house's many wings he would retreat down the main hallway toward the front door. They had passed a small den on the way in, and he guessed it was where Delacroix and Shay were doing whatever they were doing.

He stopped at the doorway to the den and listened. He heard voices, one of them carrying the unmistakable shrillness of Shay's. But they weren't close enough to make out and weren't coming from the den. The voices were soon drowned out by another noise. Clip-clop, clip-clop. Clip-clop, clip-clop. Shay's flip-flops.

Jackson turned around, toward the massive marble staircase leading to the second floor. He was just in time to see the two women appear atop it. He quickly pretended to be examining one of the paintings on the wall, a seascape between two sand dunes. It was the type of thing you saw at every art gallery and on every calendar in the world, and yet this one was somehow captivating. It must have been the genius of Emmanuelle Delacroix.

"I'm, like, just the delivery girl," Shay said. "You'd totally have to ask him."

"Do you have his phone number?"

"Yeah, in my purse."

Jackson turned around as they reached the bottom of the stairs. "Hope you don't mind, I let myself in."

"Not at all," Delacroix said, walking over and standing beside him. Being French, he expected her to smell like pricey perfume or armpit sweat. She smelled instead like turpentine. Irresistible.

"That was my first seascape," she said.

"Your first?"

"I was twelve."

"At twelve I was still mastering Legos."

Delacroix grimaced, but managed to do so in a way that manifested itself as a cursory smile. All celebrities could do it.

"Here," Shay said, handing Delacroix a business card. Jackson tried to see what was written on it, but it was quickly tucked into the artist's overalls.

Shay smiled beatifically. "We won't take up any more of your time."

Delacroix showed them to the door. "It was nice meeting you."

"You too," Jackson and Shay said at the same time. She giggled, he didn't, and the door closed behind them.

"Mind if I drive?" Jackson asked.

"Why?"

"It's a convertible."

Shay shrugged and reached for her purse. She tossed him the keys.

After adjusting the seat and the mirrors, Jackson started up the car, took one last look at Delacroix's mansion, and pressed on the gas. The gate swung open before they got there, and as Jackson turned back onto the street, his brush with fame was over.

"Emmanuelle wasn't too put off by my being there?" he asked.

"No."

He nodded.

"What, are you, like, mad because I made you wait outside?" Shay asked.

"It's your money," Jackson said. "So what'd she want to know?"

"Huh?"

"You told her as you were coming down the steps that she'd have to ask him. Blake or his boss?"

Shay frowned at him for a second, then snapped to. "Oh, Blake. She had some question about the tribe they came from or something, I don't know."

Jackson turned west onto Sunset. "What'd you think of her?" he asked.

"How do you mean?"

"I'm just trying to figure out the people who would buy these things," Jackson said. "You were around her more."

Shay shrugged. "She's, like, an artist. They're kind of strange."

"She didn't strike me as the 'collects tribal idols' kind," Jackson said.

"What are you, like, star-struck?" Shay asked. "How'd you know who she was anyway? I've totally never heard of her."

"I just know . . . the name," Jackson said.

"What is it?"

"I don't know. Something . . ." He shrugged it off. "My friend Sam likes her work, and I knew she lived in the Hills. I put two and two together."

Shay sat back and they cruised west until hitting the 405. Traffic was light, and they were back at Cameron's an hour after they left. Jackson pulled into a parking spot by the Granada and put the gearshift into park.

"Are you, like, busy tonight?" Shay asked.

"Why?"

"I just don't feel like . . . being alone."

He unbuckled his seatbelt. "'Afraid of Tahitian baddies' don't want to be alone or should I be flattered?"

"Huh? I just . . . Never mind."

"Shay, I do have plans tonight. And I don't think you're in any danger, not with the idols here. But if you're worried, we can make sure you're protected."

"Whatever. I'll be fine. If not, Blake will pay."

"You sure?"

"Yeah." She unstrapped her seatbelt too, and they got out.

"Nine-thirty tomorrow?" Shay asked as they met behind the car.

Jackson nodded. "You've got my number. If you need anything, give me a call."

"Thanks."

"No problem."

They got into their respective cars. As Shay left rubber on the asphalt, Jackson rolled down his windows to let some cooler air into his car. He gave the leather seats five minutes to cool down, enough time for him to reminisce about meeting Emmanuelle Delacroix. And to wonder why that nagging voice was suddenly shouting.

Chapter Ten

2:47 p.m.

JACKSON COULDN'T SHAKE the feeling as he got into the car and headed back to the highway. Something about Emmanuelle Delacroix was setting off alarm bells in his brain, but they weren't playing a tune he recognized.

He didn't have long to think about it. The bells were replaced by "Bad Moon Rising."

"Hey, Maggie."

"Hey, this a good time?"

"Good as any."

"I did some checking, ran Brower through the system like you asked."

"Find anything?"

"Yeah. Turns out he's the great-great-grandson of Rasputin."

"That's very clever. Is your strip a daily or just in the Sunday funnies?"

"Ha, ha. Hey, I did find something though."

"What's that?"

"About six months ago he wrote a letter to the editor. There was this big deal about homeless shelters and soup kitchens in the inner city having to turn people away because they didn't have enough room or food. He wrote and complained."

"Not enough room or food, isn't that normal?"

"To an extent, maybe, but this was pretty widespread. It was on the news and in the paper for a while, until it tired out."

"Hmm. He complained?"

"Yeah?"

"What'd he want them to do?"

"Well that was just it. I read his article, and it was pretty well written, but it was just a diatribe. Blamed the mayor, blamed the bureaucrats, blamed the Republicans. It was everybody's fault, but he didn't have any solutions for anything. Just ranted for three hundred words. He's a bleeding heart malcontent."

"He'll be pushing for your job soon. Anything else?"

She paused a beat, letting his barb pass. "Yeah. A year before that, he wrote another letter that didn't get published, but I found it on the slush pile."

"Ranting against traffic?"

"Close. It was another tirade, a little more passionate, about free healthcare. It read like an ode to Canada."

"You're sure this is the right Landon Brower?"

"Age twenty-one, student at USC?"

"That's him," Jackson said. "He's awfully social minded for a beer-chugging, skirt-chasing frat boy."

"It's not much," she agreed, "but it's all I could find."

"Thanks, Maggie. I owe you one."

"You owe me half a dozen."

"You got an ex you want me to tail?"

"Hmm, is that thinly veiled jealousy I hear in your voice?"

"I thought it was a pretty thick veil."

"Well, I'd love to continue this banter, but it's almost three."

"What happens at three?"

"My interview."

"I thought it was two?"

"Got pushed back. I'm at the phenom's house now, and I still don't know what to ask him."

"Didn't they teach you that at LBSU? Maybe you should transfer to comics."

"Shut up."

Jackson grinned. "Ask him what his favorite word is. Or what's the middle word in the dictionary."

"He reads encyclopedias."

"Well see if he can go chapter-verse with you. Maybe he's like those Indian programmers."

"The Navajos?"

"No, those guys from India—maharajas or whatever—the guys who can read a string of eight thousand letters and repeat it back to you verbatim. This might be a gold mine, Maggie. 'Stupid Human Tricks' or something."

"Great. I'll call Letterman."

"Yeah, and tell him some of your jokes too."

"Shut up."

"See ya." He started to lower the phone, but stopped. "Hey, Maggie, what do you know about Emmanuelle Delacroix?" It was too late; she had already hung up.

Jackson tossed his phone onto the passenger seat and spent a few more minutes picking his brain. Nothing. He gave up as he neared his exit, Vermont Avenue. It took him south to the campus of the University of Southern California. The old stomping grounds.

Fresh out of high school, Jackson had enrolled at USC with high expectations. He would watch football games in the Coliseum on Saturdays, get a quality education leading to a high-paying job, and marry a song girl. Four semesters later, he had been in debt without direction regarding a major and had never met a song girl (although the football team had been on the uptake). So he had dropped out, and a pattern had been born.

Jackson made his first stop the Bovard Administration Building. He wasn't likely to get any information out of "the man," but it couldn't hurt to try. On summer hours, maybe the man would be a pretty girl who liked Lakers tickets.

The man was middle-aged, frumpy, and had librarian's glasses perched on the tip of her nose. "Can I help you?" she asked in a voice that sounded as if it wouldn't hold out for more than a minute's worth of conversation. It was as long as Jackson wanted to spend with her.

"I need to find a friend of mine," Jackson said. "He's a student here."

"Um-hmm."

He wasn't sure if she didn't believe him or was just acknowledging that his comment had pierced the coifs of hair that hung over each ear.

"His name's Landon Brower."

"Um-hmm. Why do you need to find him?"

"We're supposed to go to the Dodger game tonight," Jackson said, figuring it was safe ground.

She finally turned her attention to him fully, sliding aside a form she had been studying since he walked in. She laid her pen down on top of the paper and cleared her throat. "Aren't the Dodgers in San Diego this week?"

He blinked. "That's why I need to find him. He's got the tickets, and you know traffic on the 5."

"Um-hmm." She was gaining rhythm. "Well, did you try his apartment?"

"I can't remember the address."

"The two of you are close then, huh?"

Jackson leaned on the desk, hoping that his charm was working on old and young today. "Can I be honest with you?" he asked.

"I wonder."

"I'm a detective, investigating Landon Brower. I just need some information on him."

"A detective. Plainclothes division, I take it?"

Jackson grinned. "That's very good."

"Can I see your badge?"

Jackson reached for his wallet and pulled out his private investigator's license. He set it on the desk.

"In my day these used to come in gold."

"No, ma'am, I'm a private detective."

She harrumphed.

"It's really more of a character study. I'm hoping to talk to friends of his, professors, anyone who can vouch for his character. But, I don't know who to talk to. I was hoping you could . . . direct me."

She didn't answer, instead picking up and examining his license. "Did you have to go to school for this?" she asked finally.

"In a manner of speaking."

"Was this school accredited?"

Jackson frowned. This wasn't going in a good direction. He decided to up the charm. "Ma'am?"

"I can't give out that kind of information," she said as she handed his license back. "Unless you've got a warrant in that billfold of yours."

"I'm afraid not."

"Um-hmm. Then it looks like you'll have to pound the pavement," she said, a grin tugging at the corner of her mouth.

Jackson nodded. "Thank you, anyway."

"Don't mention it," she mumbled as he retreated. Back outside, he went to Plan B and pulled out his phone.

"Yeah?" a sleepy voice answered.

"Mouse, it's Jackson."

"Hey. Long time."

"Hey, I'm hitting a brick wall. Any way you can find out which professors Brower has had?"

"Legally?"

"Preferably."

"Give me five."

"Call me."

Mouse clicked off and Jackson found a park bench. Officially on summer break, the USC campus was emptier than Jackson had ever seen it. A few students still crisscrossed the campus as they headed to summer school, jobs, or the newest hotspot. But most of the activity was from a construction crew fixing the parking lot outside the Trojan Bookstore and a guy with a weed whacker edging the sidewalks.

The scenery improved as two song girl candidates approached, talking and smiling and sneaking glances at the guy parked casually on the bench. Mouse picked that moment to call back, sending Jackson's phone into its rendition of the James Bond theme. He broke eye contact and fished it from his pocket.

"Hey."

"I've got a few classes here, and profs."

Mouse read off the names, and Jackson committed them to memory. "What about the girlfriends?" he asked. "Making any progress?"

"Just about to start," Mouse said.

"Let me know."

"Yeah."

Jackson closed his phone and got up. Back inside, the clerk reluctantly gave him phone numbers, office locations, and hours for the professors Mouse had given him. Jackson borrowed her pen to write them down, thanked her, and headed back outside to make calls. He got two voicemails, passed on each, and then got a live person. Landon's American Social History teacher, a bombastic woman who made it quite clear she was too important and didn't have the time for Jackson's questions.

After another voicemail, Jackson reached a Dr. Lamar, a Professor Emeritus who taught an occasional history class. The previous fall, Landon had taken his Ancient European Civilizations course, and according to a comment buried deep on his Facebook page, earned a B-minus. Lamar was working in his office till four, and he agreed to meet with Jackson and gave him directions.

It was a short walk, away from road construction and weed whacking, and it caused Jackson to reminisce about the good old days. Autumn mornings, when a chill found its way into the Southern California air. Breezy spring afternoons when you couldn't walk a dozen feet without seeing a girl dressed to the nines. "Fight On" ringing through the air during a football pep rally. Algebra homework. Fussy profs who wanted their answer more than the right answer. Ninety-eight-dollar checks each month to pay off student loans. So it wasn't all perfect.

Dr. Lamar had stepped out when Jackson arrived, but the secretary who served his and two other offices at the same end of the building told Jackson he could go in. The office was simple and old, and half-abandoned. The bookshelves that lined two walls were sparsely populated, the United States map on the wall was yellowed, and there was only one picture on the desk. It was of a black woman in her sixties or seventies, not terribly photogenic, the kind of picture a guy would only display prominently if he really cared for the person and didn't care what anyone else thought. It made Jackson respect Dr. Lamar.

So too did the sheepskins on the walls. Bachelors from Auburn. Masters at Cal-Berkely. Ph.D. from Stanford. A second Ph.D. from Texas. All history majors, except the Masters from Cal, which was a combined History and Religious Studies major. What must Dr. Lamar's student loans have been like?

Jackson turned his head as the doctor announced himself with a clearing of the throat. He was tall, stood even taller, and walked with a cane that he didn't need. His hair and beard were white, in stark contrast to his aged, brown skin. Even though it was practically summer, Lamar wore a long-sleeved shirt under a vest that was perfectly coordinated with his navy slacks. When he invited Jackson to sit down, he did so with a deep voice that Jackson could picture carrying throughout a lecture hall, or more accurately, it seemed, from the pulpit of an old, gothic church.

"Thank you for seeing me, Dr. Lamar," Jackson said.

"You have questions about a student," Lamar said as he eased himself with a slight grimace into his own chair. Between them was a solid oak desk, void of a computer or any clutter. Just a nameplate, phone, and the photo—presumably of Dr. Lamar's wife.

"That's right, sir. Landon Brower."

"Mr. Brower," Lamar said, searching his brain for the memory. "Ah, yes." He leaned slightly forward. "Mr. Douglas, you can ask any question you like, but I can't promise an answer if it would violate Mr. Brower's privacy."

"I understand," Jackson said. Then, because he respected the doctor too much to play games, he told him the truth. Very nearly. He left out the names and the reason for the inquiry, but said he had a client who wanted to know Landon's character.

"I'm afraid I can't vouch for or against Mr. Brower's character," Lamar said after a good throat-clearing. "I only had him as a pupil for one semester. You know, I find it harder and harder to relate to young people these days. Your generation," he said, but with a twinkle in his eye.

"Yes, sir." Great, lumped together with all the wackadoos of Generation Next or the Millennials or whatever the buzzword for them was this week.

"And if I recall correctly, there were fifty-four pupils in that class, so you can appreciate the difficulty of forming any real relationships with many of them."

"Yes, sir." Jackson twisted in his chair. "Anything at all might be helpful."

Lamar scratched his head. "Well, I can tell you that Mr. Brower was a good student. Mind, that doesn't imply the grades he did or didn't receive. But he applied himself. And he was a thinker."

"How so?"

"His essays had original ideas. So many students just regurgitate what they hear in class or what's in their textbooks. You can't really blame them; it's largely what they're asked to do. But Mr. Brower came up with his own ideas. In fact, I remember one particular essay on the fall of the Roman Empire. He equated the ills of their society to the various problems of the twenty-first century. Not many young folks today see the corollaries with the past like that." Lamar smiled. "I can't say how accurate his conclusions were, but they were thought out."

"Was there a pronounced social theme?"

"Mr. Brower was a sociology major, if I recall."

"That's right."

"Did it permeate to other areas, you mean? Did I see it in my class?"

Jackson nodded. "Yes, sir."

"To a degree, perhaps. Not to the point of singling him out more than anyone else."

Time for another tack. "I'm sure you observe a lot of social interaction," Jackson said.

"Is that what they're calling it these days?"

Jackson grinned. "Any comments on Landon's relationships with women? Anything jump out at you?"

"Mr. Douglas, I've been married to Henrietta here for fifty-one years. I like to think we're more in love than when we first met, but if I had to, I wouldn't have the slightest idea how to woo a woman. As for my students, I honestly can't tell what they are thinking. I don't know if they are seeking a relationship or seeking to avoid one forever."

Jackson grinned again.

"I'll say this, Mr. Douglas. Mr. Brower was often in the company of young ladies, but that doesn't differentiate him from many of the young men around this campus."

"No, sir."

Lamar sat forward. "I'm not providing you much help, am I?"

"Maybe. Do you happen to know any of his friends? Male or female, anyone he hung around with frequently?"

"I only saw him in class, you understand. But he did seem to have a good rapport with one girl, Mindy Brandt."

"Rapport. That doesn't sound romantic."

"I don't think so, but I'm an old man remember." Lamar smiled. "They sat next to each other, seemed quite friendly."

Dr. Lamar described Mindy, and said he was pretty sure she worked at The Coffee Bean and Tea Leaf on the northwest side of the campus. Whether she would be there during the break was uncertain, but it was a lead.

"Is there anything else I can do for you?" Lamar asked.

"I think that's it," Jackson said, rising from his chair. Lamar did as well. "Thank you, for your time, Doctor."

"Certainly. I hope I was able to help."

They shook hands, and Jackson left the doctor's office, feeling somehow enriched. But not much more informed. Landon was a socially aware college kid. He and Gina could toast the plight of the poor as they got plastered.

Chapter Eleven

3:38 p.m.

LEAVING LAMAR'S OFFICE, Jackson headed for the café. A guy with a metal bar through his eyebrow told him that Mindy's shift had ended at three and that she had said something about going to play tennis.

"By Brooks?"

The guy shrugged, and Jackson thanked him and headed for the Trojan baseball team's stadium on the west edge of the campus. It was surrounded by tennis courts, and on the near court on the south side of the stadium, Jackson found Mindy. He assumed.

She was exactly as Lamar had said she would be. Five-six, medium build, blond hair styled short. She wasn't terribly pretty (Jackson's opinion, not Lamar's) and seemed to lack the flashy quality of the girls on Landon's Facebook page. Then again, maybe his judgment was based on the fact that she was sweating and grunting as she practiced her serve. Alone. He watched her hit a few balls and determined she wasn't bad.

Out of balls, she took a few steps over to the deuce court and plucked three out of a wire bucket containing half a hundred. When she looked up, she saw Jackson.

"Are you Mindy Brandt?" he asked.

She tested one of the balls by bouncing it at her feet a few times. She slipped it into a pocket in her shorts. "Yeah. Who are you?"

"My name's Jackson Douglas. The guy over at the café said I might be able to find you here."

"And so you have." She turned her back, lined her toe up with the baseline, and bounced the first ball twice. Then she tossed it into the air, arched her back, and with a scream befitting a woman in day two of labor, swung her racquet. The ball clipped the net and skittered to the corner.

She wiped her forehead on a wristband and retrieved a second ball from her pocket.

"Do you know a Landon Brower?" Jackson asked.

She stopped mid-bounce and turned toward him. "Who wants to know?"

It was the moment of truth again. Shoot straight, charm, or deceive. Jackson split the difference. "My sister's supposed to go on a date with him this weekend. I just want to make sure he's a decent guy."

Mindy's smile indicated she was impressed. "That's sweet. Is she a student here?" She turned and served ball two.

"No, at Cal actually."

"Don't tell me you came all the way here from Berkeley."

Jackson smiled. "No. I, uh, live here in town."

Mindy served ball three, then walked toward him. She nodded at a bench against the chain-link fence. "What do you want to know?"

Jackson followed her to the bench. She sat down, the racquet on her lap, and wiped her face on a towel from her bag. "This might sound a little weird," Jackson said, still standing, "but are you and Landon . . . involved?"

Mindy shook her head and dropped the towel. "We're friends, sort of."

"Sort of?"

"We talk in class, if we see each other around." She chuckled. "But we've never dated."

"Is there a reason?"

"Yeah. I'm not glitzy enough for him."

Jackson stayed out of the water, offering just a frown. "How do you mean?"

"Landon's like a lot of professors. He grades on the curves."

"I see."

"I'm too short and too . . . you get the idea."

Jackson let an appropriate few seconds pass. "Do you know any of his girlfriends?"

"Girlfriend is a little strong."

"Oh?"

"Girlfriend implies a relationship, or at least multiple dates. Landon is more of a one-and-done sort of a guy. If your sister's looking for a good time, he's her man. If she has prospects for a long relationship, she might want to try some Berkeley boys."

Jackson nodded. "So what do his dates say about him, do you know?"

"He gets mixed reviews."

Jackson waited.

"Party girls get what they want. Serious girls get hurt." Mindy wiped her face again, then stood up. "I really should get back at it."

"I won't keep you. Thanks for the info."

"I really don't know him all that well. We've had a few classes together, and Brandt and Brower, we get seated together. And I know a few of the girls he dated so I've heard some things. But if you want to know if there are any skeletons in his closet, talk to Barney."

"Barney?"

"That's what everybody calls him . . . I don't know his real name. He and Landon roomed together freshman year."

"It not go well?"

"Landon broke his jaw in a fight. He was suspended for a week or two."

"No criminal charges?"

Mindy shrugged.

None that had made it to the Airport Courthouse anyhow.

"Any idea where I can find Barney?" Jackson asked.

"He works at the bookstore. Big guy, orange beard."

He sounded like a Barney.

"Or you could go to the horse's mouth."

"How's that?"

"Talk to Landon."

"Is he on campus?"

"I don't know where he lives. But his dad tends bar at a little place down in Manhattan Beach. Landon spends a lot of free time there."

"You know the name of the place?"

"Snappy's. Snapper's? Something like that."

Jackson thanked Mindy and left her to her serving. He strolled toward the bookstore, identifiable by the sound of the construction. As he mounted the front steps, Mouse called back.

"Yeah?" Jackson said, plugging his free ear.

"I've been checking out these girlfriends," Mouse said.

"Yeah."

"They're hot."

"Lucky you. Find anything?"

"Not really. None of them Tweeting that he abused them or anything."

"Any of them talk about him?"

"He was tagged in some photos, mentioned on a survey for having the best bod, that sort of a thing. But no 'he's such a jerk' comments."

"Fair enough. Thanks, man."

"Forget it. I enjoyed it."

Jackson closed the phone, went inside, and sought out Barney. He was working the front desk and was easy to spot. Orange stubble on his head to match the beard made him look like a Nerf ball. He was with a customer, and Jackson waited until he was finished.

"You Barney?" he asked.

"That's right."

Jackson introduced himself and displayed his ID. "I'm investigating Landon Brower and was told you might be able to give me some info."

"He slug somebody again?"

"Not that I'm aware of," Jackson replied.

Barney cussed under his breath. "What do you want to know?"

"I need to know if he's just a playboy or something worse. I heard about your fight—"

Barney cussed again. "It wasn't a fight, brother. It was a sucker punch."

"What happened?"

"We both had it for the same girl, some freshman. Rebecca. A real hot blond number. Anyhow, she picked him, and after one date, dumped him. Said she'd heard stories. He comes back, accuses me of lying about him, and when I deny it, he breaks my face."

"Did you?" Jackson asked. "Tell her stuff about him?"

"Yeah, but it wasn't a lie."

"What'd you say?"

Barney grinned. "I mentioned that she was the fourth girl he had gone out with that semester."

"Four's not that many."

"It was early February."

Jackson grinned.

"I may have also implied that he had an unpleasant disease."

"Does he?"

Barney shrugged. "The way he goes around, I wouldn't doubt it."

"But you don't know of anything?"

"All I know is the guy's a punk. They suspended him for a month, moved him to a different dorm. He lives off campus now, I think." He shrugged.

"So other than being a player, is there anything else I should know about him?"

"Yeah, he thinks he's cooler than he is. He does this dorky little finger salute, like he's in the Navy or something. And he winks a lot, like there's something in his eye. I don't know, bro. He's a punk."

Jackson thanked Barney and headed back outside. The construction crew was knocking off, and Jackson checked the time on his phone. He had told Leroy he'd be over late afternoon, and determined he still had some time. If he really wanted to do right by Connie and Gina (and do everything he could to keep his butt out of the frying pan) he should leave no stone uncovered.

And the only stone left was Landon himself. So Jackson headed for his car, wondering what it was that Barney had said that had turned his mind reeling. It wasn't anything to do with Landon, so what was it? It had been a two-minute conversation.

Jackson reached the Granada and unlocked the door. Then he stopped. That was it.

"We both had it for the same girl, some freshman. Rebecca. A real hot blond number."

Rebecca.

*   *   *

Five years ago . . .
Friday, May 25
5:38 p.m.

"YOU SEE," Jackson said to Grant, extending his hand. In front of them, half a dozen barrel-chested men in scant Hawaiian costume danced to the rhythm of a single drum. "All we missed were some sumo wrestlers in loincloths trying to create a tsunami."

"That's a lovely interpretation of Hawaiian culture, Son."

Both brothers turned to see David Douglas standing behind them. He placed a hand on each of their shoulders. "How was the drive over? You get lost looking for Robin's Nest?"

"As a matter of fact, yes, but that's on the hotel guide," Jackson said as they turned to face their father.

"We also ran into a little trouble," Grant said.

"What kind of trouble?" David asked, the wrinkles on his forehead deepening and his dark blue eyes narrowing slightly. Fear, uncertainty, the onset of anger, and general musing always produced the same sort of frown on David's face. More than a few mixed signals had resulted from "the frown" during Jackson's teenage years.

"We stopped off for some tacos," Grant said, shooting a look at Jackson. "And a couple of guys held up the shrimp shack."

"You guys were witness to a robbery?"

"Would have been just a robbery," Jackson said. "But baby brother here went all Steve McGarrett and tried to book 'em."

The frown and the brow furrow both intensified as Jackson and Grant explained how the robbery had turned into a hostage situation. David listened, eyes darting back and forth, until their tale was finished.

"So let me get this straight . . . you tried to tackle an armed robber, and you wisecracked them into taking a young lady as a solo hostage?"

"Yeah, but she wasn't exactly a damsel in distress," Jackson said.

David crossed his arms. "How do you mean?"

"She was in on it."

David looked to Grant, who shrugged, and back to Jackson.

"She was waiting for them to arrive," Jackson continued. "When the pickup rolled in, she was doing something with her phone, and she checked her watch."

"So?" Grant asked.

"So, do you often check your watch when cars arrive at a restaurant? She was also texting when they jumped out of the pickup with masks and guns. And the cops were there in like two minutes."

"Maybe Frank called them."

"He wouldn't have had time unless he had already dialed, and the cops said it was a text."

"Okay, so maybe he or his son texted them."

"Neither of them had a cell phone. By the way, did you pick yours back up?"

Grant groaned.

"They made us unload," Jackson said to David.

"So she was waiting for them to arrive," David said, "and texted the cops right away?"

"And before 'My Brother the Hero' jumped up to get shot, she was about to make a move. I'm telling you, she didn't want them to get away, and not because she was a model citizen. I think she wanted that to turn into a hostage situation. The only time she was anxious was when they were about to get away. Once the cops showed up, she was calm and relaxed . . . almost bored."

Grant shook his head. David continued to frown, but more in the musing sense, Jackson thought. "I don't know, Son. It's rather thin. Why would she want a hostage situation?"

"Beats me. I just know what I saw. I went with my gut, and here we are."

"And you're both all right?"

Grant huffed. "Other than Jack being miffed that he didn't get a reward."

"Or at least a commendation or something. I did save the day."

David shook his head. "Wait until your mother hears this."

"Where is she anyway?" Grant asked.

David turned and looked over his shoulder into the throng of people. Open to the public—and with a special discount for residents at the Douglas family's hotel—the Ono Ono Luau was a tourist hotspot. A night on the beach with authentic Hawaiian food, music, and entertainment was the perfect "aloha" to an island visit, the organizers claimed. Judging by the turnout, tourists agreed.

"She's somewhere over there," David said, giving up on pinpointing a location. "Making leis."

"Buffets open yet?" Jackson asked.

"Are you kidding me?" Grant said. "I thought you didn't want a Hawaiian spread?"

"I dropped my tacos when we hit the deck. I'm hungry."

"It think it's just hors d'oeuvres right now," David said.

"I'm going to check it out. Get you guys something?"

They shook their heads, and Jackson struck out into the crowd. He recognized a few of the faces, familiar ones from the hotel who had been on several of the same excursions as the Douglas family. Diamondhead at dawn, a helicopter tour of the volcanoes on the Big Island, surf lessons off Ala Moana, a trip to the *Arizona* Memorial—they had packed in as much excitement as possible in a week. David had even taken them sightseeing to Pearl Harbor, where he had been stationed shortly after he and Hannah were married. He showed them the tiny house off base where they had lived right up until the moment Grant was born, when they had relocated to San Diego.

That drive had made Jackson's parents a little nostalgic, and reminiscing on the week now was making Jackson a touch melancholy. Or maybe it wasn't end-of-vacation blues. Maybe it was the feeling in his gut that something about the afternoon's events still wasn't right. Or maybe he was just second-guessing himself. Now that the adrenaline was gone, he had to admit, his hunch had been a little weak. But, it had worked out.

The appetizers were largely dubious, so Jackson settled for some pineapple wedges and surveyed the scene. On the plateau of grass to his right, a reenactment of a chieftain's daughter's kidnapping or some such incident was taking place, with all the color and pageantry typical of the Polynesian islands. Those not watching the performance kept busy by stringing leis, crafting origami trinkets, having their face painted, playing lawn games, or flirting with hula girls.

Jackson took all the activity in, but his eyes came to rest on a lone individual at the edge of the property, her tall, toned figure half-silhouetted against the late afternoon glow. The sun colored her skin a burnished bronze and glinted off blond hair that curled up just above her shoulders. Grabbing a few more slices of pineapple, Jackson headed her way.

She stood a few paces onto the beach, bare feet dug into the sand, a pair of flip-flops cast a few feet off to the side. A denim skirt cut at the top of the knee and a frilly, orange, baby doll top played brilliantly in the sunlight, and Jackson couldn't wait to see her face in the soft glow.

He ignored the cheesy lines that ran through his head and, sticking a wedge into his mouth, just walked up and stood beside her, eyes out to the sea. The waves off Oahu's North Shore were a subdued thunderous, like harbingers of an approaching storm. But the sky above was clear, save for a few delicate wisps.

"You finally made it," Becky said after a few moments.

"We got held up getting something to eat."

She nodded, and Jackson turned his head. Her lighthearted, somewhat impish smile was gone. "Trouble?" he asked.

"I can't get a hold of Dad." She slid open her cell phone and studied the display.

"He's not here?"

"Senator Dennis had a last-minute schedule change."

"The life of an aide," Jackson said. Becky's dad staffed the senator, but that was about all he knew. Their only meeting had been a thirty-second introduction and handshake in passing.

"Still, I thought he'd have time to return my call by now," she said.

"When'd you last talk to him?"

"Little before four."

Jackson nodded and took a glance down the beach, toward where dinner was smoking in an underground pit, an *imu*. "Take a walk?" he asked. "Take your mind off it?"

She shut her phone. "Yeah, why not."

Becky bent to pick up her sandals. She clutched them in one hand and tucked her hair behind her ears with the other. They started down the beach, and Jackson tried to ignore an odd sensation in his gut. It wasn't the fluttering that being around Becky had caused throughout the vacation, nor was it aftereffects of the shrimp. That nagging feeling was back, and suddenly stronger.

"When's your flight?" Becky asked a hundred feet down the beach.

"Eight-something."

"We're off at six-twenty," she said.

"Hardly worth going to bed."

"Arcade's open 24/7," she said with a grin.

"After this afternoon, I'm running a little low on coin."

Becky smirked as they meandered toward the *imu* oven. Her smile dissipated like the smoke wafting into the air. "So what's waiting for you back home?"

"Paperwork," Jackson answered. "Nine-to-five humdrum. You?"

"If I'm lucky, an internship on a presidential campaign."

"Dennis running?"

"That's the scuttlebutt."

"If I post that on my blog, do I just call you an 'unnamed source'?"

"I didn't take you for the blogging type."

"I'm more than just a quick air hockey paddle."

"Good, because you're not that quick."

He clenched his teeth.

"It's the worst kept secret out there anyhow," she said. "If not this election, the next one."

A ululating scream interrupted them, and they turned back to see more dancers taking the sod "stage." Jackson and Becky continued to walk, talking about nothing, reminiscing about some of the fun they'd had over the last week. Jackson and Grant had met Becky during a late-night swim in the hotel pool their first night in Hawaii, and had gotten to know her on several shared excursions. They'd scheduled surfing lessons together, hung out when their parents were busy, and rendezvoused by the pool most nights to relax, unwind, and brief each other on the day's events.

Gradually, Jackson and Becky circled around the far end of the luau property, back toward the main crowd. Grant met them, a glass of punch in his hand. "Hey, Becky."

"Hey, Grant," she said with a wink and a smile. Becky was an equal-opportunity flirt.

"How was your afternoon?" he asked.

"Boring. I should have come with you guys."

Jackson shook his head. "What did I tell you?"

She threw down her flip-flops and stepped into them. "How about you guys? See any more sites?"

"Jack didn't tell you?"

Becky glanced at him. "Tell me what?"

"We witnessed a robbery," Grant said.

"What?"

"Actually, we were taken hostage."

"What?" She looked Jackson's way again.

"I told you, we were held up getting something to eat."

Becky backhanded him in the chest. "What happened?"

They recounted the tale again. Becky's jaw dropped several times, and she covered her mouth when Grant described his attempt to stop the attack.

"You could have been killed," she said.

"What's the price of human life compared to a shrimp shack robbery?" Jackson said. "There must have been fifty bucks in that till."

"What was I supposed to do, let them go?"

"Yeah. Dead people don't make great witnesses. Except on *Ghost Whisperer*. *Medium*, maybe."

"So how'd you get out of there?" Becky asked. "Did the SWAT team come?"

Jackson explained his part in ending the hostage situation, with a few snarky comments from Grant thrown in. Becky was amazed, and Jackson played it up as much as possible. Grant rolled his eyes.

"I'm surprised the police let you go already," she said when they were finished.

"They had to rush out to a . . . what's a Code 10 anyhow?" Jackson asked Grant.

"In California it's a bomb threat."

"Bomb threat?" Becky asked.

"Yeah, over in Waianae."

"Busy day."

The evening's emcee announced that dinner would be served in fifteen minutes. Becky excused herself to go call her dad again, and Jackson and Grant went to find their parents.

"You seem a little sour," Jackson said.

"You're a little cavalier about all of this," Grant said.

"Dude, we put the kibosh on a robbery. I've earned a night of cavalierity." He leaned over. "Besides, it plays well with the ladies."

Grant rolled his eyes.

"Jealous?"

"Would I tell you if I was?"

Jackson smirked.

They found their parents by the hors d'oeuvres. When Hannah Douglas saw her sons, she embraced them both tightly.

"I take it Dad told you," Jackson said, noting his mom's cloudy expression. She didn't have the wrinkled brow of her husband, but her normally sweet face was drawing darkness from wide, brown eyes.

"You could have gotten yourself killed," she said, touching Grant's cheek. "Don't you ever do that again."

"I told you," Jackson said.

"Better get used to it, dear," David said. "A police officer can't avoid danger."

"He could learn how to tackle better," Jackson said.

"And you, smarting off to those robbers. You're lucky they didn't shoot you."

It was Grant's turn to smirk as Hannah chided her firstborn.

"Those for us?" Jackson asked, nodding at leis in her hand.

Hannah's face quickly transformed into a radiant smile. She tucked blond hair behind her ears. "Blue and yellow for you," she said, donning a handmade lei around Grant's neck. "It was a close as they had to UCLA blue."

"Thanks."

Hannah turned to Jackson, his lei the cardinal and gold of USC. He bowed his head as she slipped it on, then inspected the flower necklace. "Not bad, Mom."

David nudged his wife. "They're setting up tables, dear. If we want a good seat, we should get in line."

"Good seat?" Jackson asked.

"It's dinner theater, remember?" Hannah asked.

Jackson's shoulders slumped. "Dude, you were right. That shrimp shack floor wasn't so bad."

"You coming?" David asked.

"I'm going to grab some more pineapple," Jackson said. "And that punch. Where was that?"

David pointed it out and led Hannah toward the main grass area where dozens of white folding tables and slat-backed chairs were being arranged. Grant went with Jackson to the appetizer line.

"Now you seem a little sour," he said. "Relax, enjoy Hawaii."

"'Physician, heal thyself,' very nice." Jackson shrugged as he picked over the dregs of the fruit. "I don't know, it's end-of-vacation blues."

"At least we had a blast," Grant said.

Jackson shrugged again.

"What, you didn't have a great time?"

"I did. Just not as a great as I was hoping."

"I told you, making out with Evangeline Lilly under a waterfall was not going to happen."

"Mmm. Still."

"Volcanoes, surfing, the USS *Arizona*—what more could you want?"

"Nothing, dude," Jackson said with a nod. "It was great. But now . . . it's over."

"Not yet," Grant said. "Still one more night of fun. Come on."

Less excited about the luau pomp and pageantry than his brother, Jackson followed along. They joined their parents at a table close to the grassy stage and waited for the buffet tables to be rolled out.

"What's the matter with you two?" Hannah asked, looking from David to Jackson.

"Hmm?" David asked. "I'm just thinking."

"About what?"

"How ravishing you look, of course."

She made a fake smile, but Jackson could tell she appreciated the compliment, such as it was.

"You depressed about the end of vacation like Jack here?" Grant asked.

"No. I'm just thinking about your afternoon. It doesn't add up."

"How so?"

"If Jack's right, and his gut usually is, it begs the question of why that girl was trying to keep the robbers at the shrimp stand."

"Maybe she's a Five-0 recruit trying to prove herself," Jackson said with a glance at his brother.

"Or a wannabe Sherlock Holmes," Grant countered.

"It's odd," David said.

"Don't forget the bomb threat over in Waianae," Jackson added.

"Bomb threat?"

"It got called in just after our little situation ended."

"Waianae," David said, his musing frown returning. "All the way across the island."

"The whole police force must have been out," Hannah said, the end of her sentence interrupted by David's cell phone.

He unclipped it and studied the display. "Admiral Sullivan," he announced.

"Your old C.O.?" Jackson asked.

"Doesn't he know we're on vacation?" Hannah asked.

David nodded.

"What's he want?" Grant asked, frowning.

"I don't think his phone has psychic abilities," Jackson said out the side of his mouth.

"Whatever it is, it can wait," David said. "After all, we are still on vacation, right?"

As if to answer, the emcee called for everyone's attention and announced that it was time for the *imu* ceremony, meaning dinner was about to be served. David smiled and clapped his hands together, and all talk of the oddities of the day was put aside.

Chapter Twelve

4:34 p.m.

SNAPPER'S WAS LITTLE more than a beach bar, not half as fancy as the downstairs at Cameron's. Flimsy umbrellas flapped over blocky wooden tables and wicker chairs that rested at odd angles in the loose sand. The bar was under a roof, as were a few tables and corner booths on either side of the flattened-U-shaped bar. It looked as if one good storm would sweep the place to Compton.

Jackson had spent the twenty-some-odd-minute drive from campus trying to plan his entrance strategy. Slapping the P.I. license on the table and grilling Landon wasn't likely to get results, and might also cast a bit of a pall on Landon and Gina's date. He decided to play it by ear, which in this case, meant casually walking up to the bar.

"Hey, buddy, what can I get you?"

He had to be Landon's dad. Same oval eyes, oval face, strong jaw, projecting ears. He was dressed in khakis and a Hawaiian shirt, unbuttoned far enough to reveal a graying, hairy chest and leathery, well-tanned skin. A faded Dodgers ball cap was tipped back on his head, where the hair was thinning and graying too.

"I'm on the clock, so I'd better make it a soda," Jackson answered. "You got Pepsi?"

"Regular or diet?"

"Regular. Cherry if you got it."

Landon's dad turned around, filled a glass to the brim and then some, and slid it across the counter to Jackson. "On the clock, huh?"

"Claims adjustor," Jackson said. "I'm supposed to meet a guy. Wrecked his boat."

"You're meeting him here?"

Jackson nodded and took a gulp of his soda.

"What kind of boat, a canoe?" Landon's dad asked, and then guffawed and slapped the counter. Jackson laughed along with him.

"Well, make yourself comfortable. You want to see a menu, you let me know. Name's Larry."

"Jackson."

Larry washed glasses and Jackson worked the Pepsi. The only other guy at Snapper's was a either a bookie or a low-rate lawyer sitting in the back booth, wearing an old suit, papers spread out around him. There was no sign of Landon.

Larry turned the radio above the bar from Van Halen to Journey and hummed along. He then wiped down the bar, stopping when he got to Jackson. "Your guy late?"

"He said four-thirty, five." Jackson shrugged.

Larry put out a bowl of pretzels. "So what'd this guy do to his boat?"

That was a good question. Jackson went for the standby he'd heard a few times before. "Crashed it into the pier at twenty knots."

"Drunk?"

"He says not. Says the throttle jammed."

Larry laughed again, then smiled in the direction of the beach. "Hey, boys."

Jackson turned a casual glance to see Landon and another guy trudging toward the bar. The other guy was Hispanic with a small round head atop a wiry frame. Like Landon, he was dressed in jeans and a polo shirt. But whereas Landon sported an aloof grin, his face was expressionless.

"Dad," Landon said, taking a barstool a few down from Jackson. His friend sat on the other side.

"What's good?" Larry asked.

"Killing time."

"Beer?"

"The usual."

"Enrique?"

His reply was too soft for Jackson to hear, so he continued on the Pepsi and pretzels, hoping for some sort of opening.

Larry served the boys two beers and they chatted about the Dodgers, some woman Larry had been dating, and sailing. That brought Larry's attention to Jackson. "No show yet, huh?" he asked, turning his way.

"Yeah, I can wait. I get paid whether he shows or not."

Larry grinned. "Top her off?"

Jackson slid the glass to Larry, who took it to the fountain. "This guy's waiting on some knucklehead who drives his boat into the dock, drunk as a skunk, and wants insurance to pay it. Says the throttle was stuck . . . at twenty knots."

Larry guffawed. Landon grinned. Enrique lifted his beer.

"Reminds me of the night your pops and I had to outrun the *federales* off of Ensenada," Larry said, looking at Enrique.

"Which time was that?" Landon asked.

"We went down one weekend in February, just looking for some warm weather and some warm girls," Larry said with an ear-to-ear grin. "And we found both. We spent thirty-six hours drinking rum and eating bad burritos. I was too sick to stand and Javy was so drunk he couldn't see straight."

"That sounds like Pop," Enrique said.

Larry turned to include Jackson in the conversation. "We had this thirty-foot cruiser, an old piece of junk, and Javy tried to outrun them straight out to sea. Thought he was going to beat 'em to Japan. They circled around him, and he turned her back to shore, kept dodging all the way to land." He paused to chuckle. "He said he was . . . he said he was doing evasive maneuvers, but I knew he was so far gone he couldn't have kept her straight in the Panama Canal."

Larry returned Jackson's soda. "I'm down below, puking up everything I ever ate, and I pop my head up just in time to see Javy plow straight into the beach." He threatened to crack up laughing. "Best part was, we nearly trampled this old *señor* and *señorita* out for a romantic moonlit stroll. You should . . . you should've seen the look on their faces. I remember it to this day!"

"How long'd you get?" Enrique asked.

Larry finished chortling. "Overnight. We had a case of some local brew down below we bribed 'em with. How it survived hitting the beach at top speed I'll never know. It nearly killed us."

A man and woman came in off the beach and took a table on the sand, and Larry went to tend to them. Landon mumbled something to Enrique about needing waitresses, and Enrique muttered a vulgar comment back.

Then Landon turned to Jackson. "You're waiting for this guy who crashed his boat?"

Jackson nodded.

"Insurance?"

Jackson nodded again.

"What firm?"

"Bauer & Bauer." They were a legitimate firm in L.A. where Jackson had worked for a year and a half. And they were big enough that even if Landon worked there himself, he wouldn't know Jackson didn't any longer.

"No kidding," Landon said. "You know Jamie Kelso?"

Oddly enough, Jackson did. "Yeah."

"I dated her kid sister last year."

"Small world." Except that Landon apparently dated a relative of just about everybody in Southern California.

Larry returned and popped the tops on two bottles of beer. He delivered them to the man and woman and reassumed his place behind the bar. "I think your boy stood you up."

"I think so," Jackson answered, wondering what excuse could keep him at the bar. He munched a few pretzels. Maybe no excuse was needed. "So why were the *federales* after you?"

"We had familiar faces."

Jackson looked from Larry to his son to Enrique. "Familiar?"

"It wasn't our first time to Ensenada," Larry said, filling a glass of iced tea for himself. "Javy and I had grown to be something of celebrities down there."

Jackson was intrigued. "For what?"

107

"Importing."

Landon sniffed heavily several times.

"Drugs?"

Larry reached for the bowl of pretzels and took a handful. "A lot of things," he said, popping several and washing them down with half the glass of tea. "We'd run people who wanted to get out of the U.S., or occasionally into it. We ferried supplies—"

Landon sniffed again.

Larry waved him off. "I won't lie, there were some drugs. It was the '80s, we were young and crazy. But we had some good times."

"Where'd you and Javy team up?"

"Believe it or not, med school."

"What?"

"Hey now, don't act so surprised," Larry said with a grin. He palmed more pretzels. "I dropped out after a semester, but his daddy was pretty good," he said, jerking his thumb at Enrique.

"Until he dropped out too," Enrique added.

"He was still good. He used to make good money fixing people up on the side."

"On the side?"

"Yeah, you know, black market sort of a thing." Larry chuckled. "I remember this one time, we were taking a couple of shady dudes down to Mexico. Shady dudes—they were drug runners, and we knew it. But we agreed to run 'em, and they show up at the dock fresh out of a firefight with the police. Back in '86, maybe you heard about it."

"I was four."

"Maybe not. Anyhow, I'm half-sober, trying to avoid the Coast Guard and get us to Mexico, we got a monsoon coming in from Guam, and here's Javy down below stitching this old boy up."

"That takes skill," Landon said.

"Yeah, and guts. His buddy's standing over you with a gun. One wrong move . . ." Larry clicked to simulate a gunshot. "And if you don't fix him up, he'll kill you too."

"You ever consider staying in school?" Landon asked.

"What, and miss all the fun? Besides, the pay was pretty good. We each made a grand for our trouble and got to spend a week in this little place on the Baja. Purest blue ocean, nobody paying us any mind. It was a week of cold *cervezas* and hot *señoritas*!"

"Is that where Ricky came from?" Landon asked with a sly grin.

"No, man, I was the byproduct of 'The Revolution.'"

Larry laughed, but looked to Enrique to tell the story while he refilled his tea.

"Pop puts this entire town in a complete uproar because of their curfew," Enrique said. "He gets them to march on the little police station, throwing bottles and shoes and everything."

"How come I never hear about this one?" Landon asked.

"I wasn't there," Larry said. "I was with your mother."

"Which time?"

Larry scratched his head. "The second."

"What happened?" Jackson asked, leaning in to see Enrique.

"The whole town's going nuts, and they had to call in the Mexican National Guard or whatever to put down this uprising. Dad got three months in jail before finally getting out on bail."

"Who bailed him out?" Jackson asked, looking at Larry.

"Ma," Enrique answered. "She was the police captain's daughter."

Larry chuckled. "Alice and I were on the outs again, and I was about to go down and look for Javy, and he shows up with a pretty little Mexican girl and claims they're married. And he's now an outlaw in half of Mexico too." The chuckle turned to a roar. "Several months later, little Ricky comes along."

"Kept the two of you from ending up in a real prison," Landon said. "Or dead."

Larry nodded. "Probably. Thank your mother next time you see her, will you, Ricky."

"Yeah, sure." He huffed. "She still regrets the day she fell for Pop. Starts cursing and naming saints and threatening to move mountains."

All four had a brief laugh. Then Enrique clanked his empty bottle on the counter. "We should get going, man."

"Big plans tonight?" Larry asked.

"I hope so," Landon answered with a wink.

"He's got himself an intellectual from Cal," Enrique said, "and I've got a brunette with legs up to here."

"Intellectual?" Larry asked. "From Berkeley?"

"She's a social welfare major," Landon said. "We met in a chat room, and she's visiting relatives."

"Perfect," Enrique said. "No lasting repercussions. You ready?"

Landon peeled off some bills and placed them on the counter.

"What are you doing?" Larry asked.

"See ya, Dad." Landon said. He turned to Jackson, offering a handshake. "Nice meeting you, Jackson."

"Same here."

Enrique extended his hand as well. Apparently listening to Larry's stories of drug-running, beer-swilling, and skirt-chasing had qualified them as friends. As they shook, Jackson noticed a long, elegant tattoo on the inside of Enrique's arm, featuring Spanish script. *El Curador.* Son of a drug runner, maybe? It was one of several tats on Enrique's arms and the side of his neck that Jackson observed as he passed. To each his own.

"Behave yourselves tonight," Larry called as the duo left.

Enrique turned back and merely winked.

Larry wiped the bar where Landon and Enrique had been sitting. "Another Pepsi, or you want to move on to the hard stuff?" he asked.

"I think I'd better move on, period," Jackson said, reaching for his wallet. He settled his tab and thanked Larry. "This was more fun that assessing boat damage anyhow."

"You take care," Larry said.

Jackson nodded and left with a smile. He reached his car just in time to see Landon and Enrique race off down Ocean Drive in a black Dodge Caliber. Landon drove a Neon, so Jackson figured the car was Enrique's. Not a bad set of wheels.

Jackson got into the Granada, acclimated himself to the leather seats again, and pulled out his cell phone. As he exited the parking lot, he punched in Connie's number.

"Jackson, we were starting to wonder."

"Hey, Connie. Is Gina there?"

"She's in the pool. Just a second."

Jackson heard a door slide open, heard Connie holler that it was him, and then heard a swishing of water. "Hello," Gina said a moment later.

"Hi, Gina."

"What's the verdict?"

"I guess it depends," Jackson said. "If you're looking for a good time, Landon's probably going to give it to you. If you're thinking about a long-term relationship, you may want to think again."

"Long-term relationship. Why do you say that?"

"I talked to people, checked him out on Facebook, met him and his dad."

"You met him!"

"Yeah."

"Well, how is he? Did he say anything about tonight?"

"He mentioned you."

"He did! What'd he say? Did—Wait, did you tell him—"

"Relax, Gina. He thinks I'm just a guy at a bar."

"Okay. What else?"

Jackson took a deep breath. "This morning you said that you'd had bad experiences with men."

"Yeah. You think he's a bad experience?"

"I think he's looking for a party, not to meet the future Mrs. Brower tonight."

"I'm not planning on marrying the guy," she answered. "It's a first date."

"Okay. Just so you know."

"So that's it? No record or anything?"

"Not that I could find," Jackson said. He sighed. "He seems like a nice guy."

"Great!" She lowered the phone, and Jackson could hear her hollering to Diane and Connie. Then her voice was clear again. "Thank you, Jackson."

He hesitated. She was happy with a guy who would promise a party, not potential. He shook his head. "You're welcome, Gina."

"I'll make sure Aunt Connie pays you like she said."

"Please do. What time are you meeting him?"

"Seven. Ooh, I'd better get going. Thanks again, Jackson."

"Sure. Have a good time."

He closed his phone and sat back in his seat, waiting at a light. It went against the grain to recommend Gina date a guy who made Shawn Hunter and his two-week rule look like Mr. Dependable. Sure, Landon was a nice guy, but that didn't mean he was interested in anything more than scoring some casual sex and moving on to the next female who grabbed his eye. Problem was, Gina seemed satisfied with that.

Jackson took a deep breath. He'd done what they asked. He'd investigated Landon. He wasn't a criminal, didn't appear to be a sicko or a pervert, and he got pretty fair reviews from everyone but Barney. He was what he was. Gina had the facts, and he doubted a speech about premarital promiscuity would have any effect on her. He just hoped that if things went predictably, Gina wouldn't get hurt.

Connie would never forgive him if she did.

Chapter Thirteen

5:23 p.m.

JACKSON DROVE ALONG the coast, through Hawthorne and El Segundo, past the Chevron Refinery and LAX, and toward his grandpa Leroy's place in Marina del Rey. For the first time since waking up, he had plenty of time to himself with no distractions, and he remembered what day it was. Jackson forced himself to think about other things.

That led to replaying his two cases. He was convinced that if there were any deep, dark secrets about Landon, he would have at least sniffed them. Being a drinker and a partier, while not earning a recommendation in Jackson's book, lumped him in with an awful lot of college guys. Jackson again reminded himself that it was Gina's decision.

Then there was Shay and the wooden idols she was delivering for her brother. The nagging returned, humming a slightly different tune. It was starting to get annoying, and Jackson put his investigative abilities to work. He called Maggie.

"Hey," she answered with surprise in her voice.

"Hey. How was the interview?"

"Ugh. The kid didn't look at me the entire time."

"Whispering into his lap?"

"Reading D through F in the Encyclopedia. His parents were nice, but I'm going to be reaching to hit my word count."

"That's too bad."

"You didn't call just to ask 'how was work, honey?' did you?"

"No. I'm wondering if you could do me one more favor."

"What kind of favor? I've got a cold Coors in the fridge and Penguins-Rangers DVRed."

"What game?"

"Four. Two-one, New York. Want to watch?"

"No, I've got dinner with Grandpa. You and Sid the Kid have a good time."

"The favor?" Maggie asked.

"Shay, the girl I'm working for, said something about her parents dying a few years back. Car accident. I assume it would have made the papers."

"What are you looking for?"

"Anything."

"You don't believe her?"

"I do. I just . . . I don't know. Something's off here, Maggie. Maybe this is it."

"I can run a check."

"Name's Carmichael. Her brother's Blake. Not sure on the folks, but they're rich if that matters."

"Yeah, we file obits in order of wealth of the deceased."

"Just inject that appealing wit of yours into your article and you'll be fine."

"I'll call you."

"Thanks, Maggie. I—"

"You owe me, I know. Enjoy your dinner."

"Bye."

Jackson returned the phone to his pocket and concentrated on ignoring the nagging. Whatever it was, it could wait until tomorrow. He had more important things going on.

Leroy's houseboat was a forty-eight footer docked off Bora Bora Way, one of seven streets that extended on peninsulas into the harbor. There was no bridge over the mouth of the harbor, which combined with the outlet of the Ballona Creek as it emptied into the ocean, so Jackson was forced to drive around the harbor to access Bora Bora Way from the west. As he drove toward the end of the peninsula where Leroy's boat was moored, he passed rows and rows of boats on the left and apartment complexes and condos on the right. For those who didn't live on their boat.

Jackson parked in a small lot at the end of the peninsula, got out, and sauntered toward Leroy's houseboat, named *Marsha* in honor of his late wife. Leroy had bought it second-hand, fixed it up, done some remodeling on the interior, and tinkered with the engine. At present, it was questionable if it would survive any long, open water voyages, but at least it lived up to half its name, serving as an ample home for Leroy.

The boat was a double-decker, with a living room, kitchen, and one and a half bedrooms—along with fore and aft decks—on the lower level. Up top was the helm and more deck space, partly covered, but mostly open. It was a nice place to sit and enjoy an evening, especially if the grill was smoking, as it was tonight.

As Jackson neared the boat, Leroy appeared over the railing. "I was wondering if you'd show up."

"Am I late?"

"Thought maybe you'd blown off your old grandfather."

"Are you kidding? And buy my own steak?"

Leroy grinned and waved Jackson up. He boarded at the stern and took the spiral staircase up to the top deck where Leroy was standing beside an old grill. The smell of charcoal drifted past Jackson in a wave of smoke, making him salivate. Pretzels at Snapper's had not been very sustaining.

"Hey, bud. Happy birthday."

"Thanks, Grandpa," Jackson said, giving his grandfather a hug.

"Cream sodas in the cooler," Leroy said, nodding at a blue Coleman against the railing. Jackson followed his nod and retrieved a freezing cold can of A&W Cream Soda. On a good night, he had been known to throw back three or four cans, and Leroy was prepared.

Jackson popped the top, took a long, refreshing swig, and then straddled one of the chaise lounge chairs on the deck. It was a beautiful late afternoon, with warm sun, a nice breeze, and the promise of a good steak. Jackson drank it all in. Then he surveyed his grandfather as he prepared the grill.

Leroy Douglas had aged well. His body was still strong and still relatively straight. As usual, his tall frame was clad in jeans and a plain T-shirt. Occasionally Leroy threw on a polo or a sweatshirt, but not often. His short, dark brown hair was graying, but not much for a man three-quarters of a century old. The blue eyes Jackson had inherited still sparkled, and his rounded oval face still broke into grins that made the resemblance between the two of them striking.

Leroy had been born in the small town of Blythe, California, just a few miles from the Arizona border. His father, Jackson's great-grandfather, had fought in World War II, serving two tours of duty in the European theater. He had earned both the Purple Heart and Silver Star and had returned to Blythe to a hero's welcome. He had died six months later due to complications from his war injuries.

As a result, Leroy had grown up in relative poverty. He had felt the calling to the ministry and, after marrying Marsha Donne in the spring of '57, he became a full-time preacher. The marriage lasted forty years, his time in the pulpit, fifty. Leroy had never been rich materially—although he and Marsha had made it just fine—but had gained immense wealth spiritually. Almost as much as he cherished his friendship, Jackson valued Leroy's sage spiritual knowledge and counsel. Especially of late.

"So how you been, kiddo?" Leroy asked after spreading out the coals. He brushed his hands on his jeans.

"I'm hanging in there."

Leroy nodded.

Jackson took another swig of soda. "How about you, Gramps?"

"I'm still kicking, so not bad. A little cabin fever." He went to the cooler and pulled out a soda of his own, shaking the ice off it. "I've been toying with the idea of trying to fix the old lady up. Really get her going."

"Going as in open water going?"

"Um-hmm."

"Is that even possible?"

Leroy shrugged. "Worth a try. If nothing else, it'll give me something to do 'fore my brain and body turn to oatmeal."

"I don't think you have to worry about that."

Leroy straddled a chair opposite Jackson and slowly lowered himself onto it. He took a long drink of soda, and sat back. "Well, we've made it a year, bud."

Jackson looked down.

"They say it's the worst," Leroy said.

"They're right."

Leroy tapped Jackson's knee with his can. "Hey. That means it'll get better."

"It'd have to."

He waited for Jackson to look up. "Hasn't it?"

"Gotten better? No. Time doesn't heal all wounds. Time just adds more stuff jostling for endorphins."

"When you say 'stuff' . . ."

Jackson briefly thought of the Scotch. "Don't worry, not that kind of stuff."

"You know, your grandma used to complain that my sermons were too obvious, too on the nose. But I told her that sometimes the choir needed a little preachin' to."

Jackson looked up with a wry smile. "Go ahead."

"A year ago, I didn't know how I could ever go on. I was praying for strength and for grace but not understanding how I could ever get it—how the void in my life could ever be filled." He shook his head. "And I still don't. I just know that the peace that surpasses all understanding does just that. Not always, kiddo, but enough that I'm able to get by. Enough that I don't dread going to bed each night knowing it will just lead to another morning."

Jackson squinted into the sun descending toward the ocean.

Leroy continued. "If I may poke a little, you been trying that . . . praying—asking for peace?"

Jackson swallowed. Twice.

"You know at first, the pain was so raw that it just consumed me," Jackson said. "I couldn't do anything." He looked his grandfather in the eyes. "One night after work, I drove up into the mountains, off of Mulholland, and for about five minutes, I seriously considered driving off the edge of a cliff. Who knows, maybe I was just being dramatic. All I know is I wanted the pain to stop, any way I could make it.

"Then after the arrest, I started to realize the pain wasn't going to go away. I thought about Mom and Dad, about what they would think if I killed myself or blew my brain on crack. I couldn't do it, but I couldn't just move on like everybody always says. How are you supposed to move on when your life is decimated?"

Leroy looked him in the eye but said nothing.

"So I did everything I could to block it all out of my mind. I tried to resume a normal life, fill up my time with distractions—anything to keep from thinking about what happened."

"You said 'at first.' What about now?"

"The same. I'm still trying to stay distracted."

Leroy nodded. "You didn't answer my original question."

"Do I pray?" Jackson took a deep breath. "No, not too much. Every time I pray, it's just another reminder. It's like I'm in a constant tug-of-war, trying to keep the thoughts and memories from spilling out of my subconscious. If I let the rope slacken for just a second, I get dragged into the mud."

Leroy tipped his can up and drank slowly from it, his Adam's apple bulging with each gulp. Then he set it down and met Jackson's eyes. He hesitated for almost a minute, as if searching for just the right tidbit of wisdom.

"Do you pray . . . otherwise?"

Jackson looked down with a shake of his head. "Not very often. I . . ."

Leroy placed a warm hand on Jackson's shoulder. "I can't tell you how to grieve, bud. And I won't tell you to pray to get the miracle drug 'peace' either. But I will tell you, fifty-nine years of experience talking, that things won't improve if you're just walking parallel with God." He nodded, clapped his hands on his knees, and got up. "Gotta check the steaks."

Jackson used the break to drain his soda.

Leroy was right. He'd been feeling convicted for a long time about not praying enough, not maintaining the connection and the close relationship with his Heavenly Father. Fear that prayer would cause the dam to overflow was part of the reason, but it was also a convenient excuse. He knew God was good, that He wasn't to blame for what had happened, that He was the ultimate Comforter. But knowing and experiencing were two very different things. Not that that was God's fault.

"You're right, you know," Leroy said as he returned from the grill. "Time doesn't heal. But time allows for the healing to take place. Time is just another of the tools God can use."

Jackson nodded.

"Your grandma never really gave me advice," Leroy said. "Not in so many words. She just nibbled around the edge until I got the point. Well, I'm not that subtle, so I'll risk being pushy. You need to pray, kiddo. If not for peace, then just in general."

Head down, Jackson nodded.

"And if you can't, I'll pray for you until you're able to."

Jackson eventually looked up. "You don't give up, do you, Grandpa?"

"Not when I believe in somebody, no."

Jackson smiled and got up to get another can of soda.

"And it's not your fault, either."

Jackson stopped as if he'd hit a wall. He turned to face his grandpa. "Why do you say that?"

"Because I know you, bud. You're blaming yourself. But that's not how things work. Sometimes there's nobody to blame, there's no one at fault. God causes some things to happen; allows others. Whatever the case, He's got a reason."

"I know."

"I know you do. Like I said, sometimes the choir needs a little preaching." He sat back. "Sometimes the pastor does too," he said with a chuckle. "Shoot, with a little more preaching I might have turned out all right."

"You're more than all right, Grandpa. Without you, I know I wouldn't have made it."

"Same here, bud. Same here."

*   *   *

7:19 p.m.

THE STEAKS were perfect—brown and crispy on the outside, pinkish and tender inside. Leroy's homemade potato wedges and grilled corn on the cob accompanied the steaks—all washed down with more cream sodas.

Leroy and Jackson ate slowly, savoring the meal, the evening atmosphere atop the boat, and happy memories. For a brief while, Jackson was able to think back on the past without the dam of pain and sorrow bursting or overflowing. As he carried the dirty dishes down and into the kitchen, he shot a quick thank you heavenward, feeling like a blind man who had been allowed to open his eyes for a few minutes. Sure, the blindness would return. But maybe, just maybe, the sight would return again too.

Jackson climbed back to the deck, opened another cream soda, and sat down beside his grandpa. The marina was quiet and peaceful until Leroy flipped on a small transistor radio and set it on the table. The dulcet tones of Vin Scully describing Dodger baseball, live from PETCO Park in San Diego, crackled through the salty sea air. They took Jackson back to warm evenings on Leroy and Marsha's porch, when the legendary broadcaster had to battle to be heard over the crickets in the nearby fields. Jackson and Leroy would sit for hours at a time, until well after dark, listening to Dodger games over the same radio. The memory brought with it a sweet kind of sadness, something akin to nostalgia.

CCR began singing from Jackson's pocket. "I'll just be a minute," he said, leaning back to reach for his phone.

Leroy waved. "Take your time."

"Hey, Maggie."

"Am I interrupting dinner?"

"Just Scully and the Dodgers. How's your game going?"

"Second intermission, 1-1."

"What's up?"

"I checked out your girl Carmichael, like you asked."

"Yeah?"

"Name's nowhere in the obits. Or her brother. I went back five years. Eleven dead Carmichaels in Los Angeles and Orange Counties. None with survivors matching Shay or Blake, in name, age, sex, whatever."

"Hmm."

"Did she say they're from here?"

"No, I don't think so. No, just that she lives in Beverly Hills. I got the feeling she hasn't moved though, from their house I mean."

"Well, I don't know what to tell you," Maggie said. "It's not exactly proof she's lying."

"No, but it sure isn't proof she isn't either."

"Anything else you need to know?"

"If there is, I'll call."

"Say hi to your grandpa."

"Will do. See ya, Maggie."

"So long."

Jackson clapped his phone shut. "Sorry. Maggie says hey."

"Maggie . . ." Leroy said. "Forgive me, I'm getting old and senile."

"The reporter. Brown hair, tan."

"Right. And Samantha's the blond girl, the nurse."

Jackson grinned. "Yeah. And that reminds me, I'm supposed to call her. She's taking me for dessert later."

Leroy chuckled as Jackson dialed. He stood up and paced toward the starboard railing. Sam answered on the third ring.

"Hey, it's me," he said.

"Jackson, hi."

"Sorry I didn't call sooner."

"No, it's fine. Are you at your grandpa's?"

"Yeah, we just finished dinner."

"Are you still in the mood for dessert?" she asked. Her voice contained the least bit of hopefulness, and it warmed Jackson's heart.

"Yeah," he answered. "How does ice cream at the pier sound?"

"Sure. Whatever you'd like. When should I meet you?"

"Don't. I'll pick you up. Eight-fifteen?"

"Sure."

"See you in a bit," he said and closed the phone again.

Leroy's grin was wider as Jackson sat back down. "You still dating them both?" he asked.

"Sort of. It's casual."

"'Casual' meaning you haven't been busted yet?"

"I've got nothing to be busted for, Gramps. I haven't given either of them my class ring."

"Yeah. Do either of them know what you're doing?"

Jackson shrugged. "Have I told them, 'By the way, I'm also dating so-and-so'? No."

"Shoot," Leroy said, chuckling some more.

"Hey, for all I know they're seeing other people. I told you, it's casual. It's hardly even dating."

"They had a different name for that when I was growing up," Leroy said. "Philandering."

"Yeah, they also thought it was sinful to go to the movies or play cards when you were growing up."

Leroy continued to laugh. "I just want to be there to see it when one of them finds out." He scratched his head. "On second thought, I don't think I do."

"They aren't going to find out. I'm careful."

"You had better be."

"Besides, it's not serious with either one of them. I wouldn't do that."

"Um-hmm. I'm going to miss you when you move to Utah."

Jackson rolled his eyes.

"So what'd Maggie want, anyhow?"

Jackson took a swig of soda and launched into yet another explanation of his cases, giving his grandpa a thorough recap of the day's events. Leroy nearly choked when he heard about bribing Chrissy with *Wicked* tickets. And he agreed that Shay's story seemed to be missing a piece somewhere. Like Jackson, he wasn't sure what that piece was.

They sat on the deck until dusk, watching the sun slide behind the nearby apartment buildings and into the Pacific. Vin Scully did more talking than the two of them combined, but it didn't hinder their communion. They were grandfather and grandson, side by side, just like old times, as if all really was right with the world.

At eight o'clock, after the home half of the second produced a pair of hits but no runs, Jackson announced he'd better be going. "Thanks for dinner, Grandpa."

"Anytime, bud."

"And for the talk."

Leroy cupped Jackson's head in both of his rough, aged hands. "You're going to make it, kiddo. We both are. There's not a doubt in my mind."

They embraced, and Jackson thanked him again before heading for the stairs. The harbor was still quiet, and Jackson's clunking footfalls on the metal staircase seemed to echo across the water. He stopped for a moment, still able to hear Scully's cadence over the transistor up top. Closing his eyes, he could almost hear the crickets too.

Chapter Fourteen

8:14 p.m.

SAMANTHA MACRANEY LIVED in a modern apartment building on Princeton Street in eastern Santa Monica. It was a fifteen-minute drive from Marina del Rey, and as Jackson pulled to the curb in front of her building, the last vestiges of daylight were quickly vanishing in the west. Even so, the air was still warm and comfortable, with a gentle breeze blowing in from the ocean. It was perfect.

Before getting out of the car, Jackson quickly turned off the ringer on his phone (no need for Sam to ask him why his phone was playing "Bad Moon Rising" halfway through dessert) and slipped it back into his pocket. Then he strolled across the lawn to her front door. Sam's was a second-floor apartment with a door on the first level, and Jackson rang the bell and jammed his hands into his pockets to wait.

Sam opened the door almost immediately, a beatific smile on her face. "Hi."

"Hey," Jackson greeted, returning the smile. It was hard not to.

Standing five and a half feet tall, perfectly proportioned, Sam was a bombshell who didn't think she was a bombshell. Sun-enriched golden hair, tonight in a low, loose ponytail. Vivacious blue eyes that regarded Jackson with a mixture of allure and amusement. A gumdrop nose and small, perfect ears, tonight without earrings.

As usual, Sam was dressed simply but attractively, wearing a white, knee-length skirt with a pastel yellow blouse and a three-quarter sleeve denim jacket. An All-American girl. She was barefoot, one foot on its toes behind the other as she rested ever so gently with her right hand on the doorknob.

"I've got to grab my purse and shoes," she said. "Come on up?"

Jackson nodded and followed her inside, up a U-shaped flight of carpeted stairs. The stairway opened into Sam's living room, which in turn was open to the kitchen and dining room. A vaulted ceiling was home to a pair of skylight windows that let in extra sun and gave the living room an airy feel during the daytime. Now, lamps at either end of the room provided the only glow in the cozy apartment.

"Have a seat," Sam said. "I'll just be a second." She floated into the hallway leading to her bedroom, and Jackson dropped onto Sam's loveseat. Made for a night of vegging in front of the TV, the couch was incredibly receptive to a human posterior, Jackson's especially. It was tempting to suggest they forget dessert.

Sam returned wearing a pair of white slides, her purse over her shoulder. In her hands, she held a small, gift-wrapped package which she extended to Jackson. "This is for you. Happy birthday."

"Thanks, Sam."

It was a book. He could tell before opening it because of the size and shape, and almost before even seeing it because it came from Sam. The question was, which book?

She sat down next to him as he removed the bow and peeled back the paper. Then he smiled.

Out of the Blue, by Orel Hershiser.

"I saw it a while back at a book sale," she said, "and I remember you talking about him. You haven't read it, have you?"

"A long time ago," Jackson answered, flipping it over to look at the back cover.

"Oh. I'm sorry. I—"

He stopped her by taking her hand and giving it a quick squeeze. "Thanks, Sam."

"You like it?"

"Yeah. Orel was my hero until I was . . . He still is my hero. Yeah, I like it."

She smiled and leaned over for a quick hug and another, "Happy birthday." Jackson caught a whiff of something flowery, something that hadn't been there when she came to the door. Perfume.

"Ready to go?" Sam asked.

Jackson nodded as he got up and followed her downstairs.

"How was your dinner with your grandpa?" she asked as she locked her door. They started across the lawn to the car.

"Good," Jackson answered with a slight bob of his head. "Good," he said again, more to himself than to her. As much as he enjoyed steak dinners and time spent with his grandpa, he had also been sort of dreading this particular "anniversary" dinner. But it had been far more therapeutic than painful.

Jackson opened Sam's car door for her, waited for her skirt to clear the doorway, and then closed the door as gently as was possible. After thirty-five years, the passenger door needed a good shove in order to latch.

"So I've been thinking," he said as he started the car. He pulled out into the street. "The pier will probably be pretty crowded, and noisy." He looked her way. "What would you say to ice cream and a walk on the beach instead?"

"Mmm, yeah."

He nodded and turned back to the road.

"I hope I didn't rush you and your grandpa," Sam said as Jackson turned onto Colorado Avenue. It would lead them straight to the famed Santa Monica Pier. "I'm working four straight four-to-four shifts this week."

"Four a.m.? That's when I turn over."

"Four's when I work. I'm getting up at three."

He made a face. "You want to get the ice cream to go?"

She shook her head slightly. "No."

Parking at the pier could be a mess at peak times, but tonight there was plenty of space. Jackson and Sam quickly made their way onto the pier and to Pacific Park, the two-acre amusement park of motion picture fame. As usual, the park was a hubbub of activity, with its rides, midway games, and aromatic carnival-quality cuisine. Jackson's inner teenager begged to come out, to take a ride on the West Coaster, share a tuft of cotton candy or a bag of popcorn, and win Sam a stuffed animal at the bottle toss. He kept it at bay as they found the first place that sold ice cream cones.

"What'll it be?" Sam asked, reaching into her purse as they moved to the front of the line.

They both selected rocky road—he two scoops, she one—both in waffle cones. The steak was just settling in Jackson's stomach, but the ice cream beckoned.

"Thanks, Sam," he said, taking his waffle cone from the vendor and starting to lick.

"You're welcome." She returned the change to her purse and took her cone too.

"This is kind of weird," Jackson said, "having people treat me all day."

"All day?"

Oops.

He covered with a slow lick of rocky road. "Yeah. You. Grandpa with dinner. Reggie offered me lunch."

"You are a busy man."

"Yeah." The crowd around them made it hard for him to hear Sam's soft voice, and he reached out a hand to guide her to a more quiet part of the park as he briefly explained how his morning had started. Sam was naturally inquisitive, but he hoped that she wouldn't want a lot of details. He was getting sick of repeating the same story to everyone. She paid close attention while nursing her cone, but when he was finished, she just smiled at him.

"Should we take a walk?" she asked, her face lit by the flickering lights of the resplendent Pacific Ferris Wheel. Jackson was sure he had seen this in a movie.

"Sure."

They backtracked to the parking lot, and took the stairs down to the beach. In the daytime, the wide swath of sand would be covered with sunbathers, volleyball players, and people watchers. At night, the crowds were greatly diminished, and Jackson and Sam had a hundred feet of empty sand on either side of them.

"I forgot to tell you who I saw today," Jackson said as they meandered down the beach.

"Who's that?"

"Emmanuelle Delacroix."

"You saw her? Where?"

"At her house. I checked out some of her paintings."

127

"What were you doing at Emmanuelle Delacroix's house?"

Jackson hadn't gone into many specifics of the case earlier, and he told Sam just enough now to work in the visit to Delacroix's mansion.

"Is she snooty?" Sam asked when he was finished. "I always pictured her as terribly snooty."

"Not terribly," Jackson said. "Maybe a little eccentric."

"All artists are eccentric," Sam said, and took a lick of her ice cream.

Eccentricity. Was that why Jackson's inner voice kept nagging him about Delacroix? Was it just bugged by eccentricities? Somehow, he didn't think so.

They walked quietly for a while, both working on their cones. Slowly, the noise from the pier drifted away with the breeze, replaced by the steady crashing of waves and the caws of circling gulls. Sam broke the silence.

"Hey, Jackson."

He looked at her. She looked at the sand.

"I'm sorry about . . . this morning."

He frowned. "Sorry about what?"

"On the phone, I didn't mean to sound like I was checking up on you."

"It's okay."

"No it's not. I don't want you to think that I don't trust you, Jackson, or anything like that. I just . . . I know you know that I'm here, so I won't bother you anymore." She winced. "I'm bothering you now."

Jackson stopped and turned to face her. "You're not bothering me, Sam. I actually kind of like it."

Her shoulders dropped. "Really?"

"Yes. Trust me, you're not a bother."

The beautiful, blissful smile that had adorned her face when she first opened her apartment door returned. Jackson enjoyed it for a moment, then dropped his eyes to her hand, which cradled her ice cream cone. His was almost gone; her ice cream was still above the cone line, and melting fast. A thin trickle of chocolate had made its way over her knuckles and onto the back of her hand.

"You're dripping," Jackson said. He lifted her hand, wiped the ice cream with his finger, and licked it off.

Sam pulled a face of mock concern at the drips and went to work on the cone. Once she caught up, they started walking again.

"The fact is, Sam, I need you checking in on me once in a while. You're pretty much the only one who does."

"You have your grandpa, Reggie."

"Yeah, but that's different. You're a woman."

"Thanks for noticing."

"You know what I mean. A guy needs a female voice in his head every once in a while."

One that wasn't a touch husky.

Up on the beach, some guy was plucking away at his guitar, playing something slow and sad and perfect for the occasion. A jogger going north met them, his panting and violent footfalls on the sand creating a rhythm that was washed out by the waves. Then all was still again.

"I dug out the old photo albums last night," Jackson said, his cone finished.

Sam looked up.

"I spent a couple hours just reliving the old days. Our trip to the Grand Canyon, the last Christmas with Mom's side before Grandpa and Grandma died, Grant his first day on the force. It was almost like it was all real."

"That's a good step," Sam said quietly.

"I don't know about that. Kind of like taking a bulldozer to a dam. Part of me wants to unleash the entire flood—and I almost did last night. But the other half is fighting to keep it boxed up."

"Maybe it needs to come out."

"I tried that for the first few months. That didn't work either."

Sam said nothing. Instead she switched her cone to the hand that also held her sandals and then reached with her free hand and took hold of his, giving it a squeeze. She didn't let go, and they continued to make their way slowly down the empty beach. Past the third lifeguard station, Sam suddenly shrieked.

She dropped his hand and her sandals, and began wiping dripping ice cream from the hand holding the cone. It was a losing battle. "Help!"

"Just shove it in."

Sam eyed the cone for a second, then thrust it up at Jackson. He opened his mouth just in time for her to push it into his mouth. He leaned forward and sucked in, trying to keep the runny ice cream from dripping all over. He mostly succeeded.

"Um meht yuh," he said, then chewed and swallowed.

"It'd never fit," she answered, licking off several of her fingers. She made a face. "Sticky."

"There's plenty of water."

Still frowning, she squinted at him. Then she turned and jogged toward the water a hundred feet away. Even jogging in sand, she moved gracefully.

She reached the water's edge and braced herself for the first wave. When the second came, she bent down and rinsed her hands in the surf. Shaking them dry, she slowly made her way back to Jackson. She stopped in front of him and squinted again.

"What?"

She reached up with a cold finger and wiped below the corner of his mouth. "You dripped."

He nodded, and for a moment, their eyes locked. Even in the relative darkness, her azure eyes were wide and gleaming. Her smile was equally bright, and Jackson resisted the urge to pull her into a long, warm embrace.

Instead, he broke eye contact and looked back toward the pier. "We should get going, before it gets too late."

Sam stared at him for a moment longer before nodding. She bent to pick up her sandals, and they started leisurely for the pier, the iconic Ferris wheel and the famous Looff Hippodrome standing out on the horizon.

"So," Jackson said, "it works both ways. I haven't checked up on you in a while either."

"There isn't much to check on," Sam answered. "I'm working, reading, swimming when I can. I'm going back home the first weekend in June."

"Yeah?"

"Um-hmm. And Steve and I are talking about a hiking-slash-camping trip in Oregon or Washington sometime later this summer."

"Really?"

"Well, he's doing most of the talking."

"You don't want to go?"

"It's not that. But he'll want to kill his own food, catch rainwater, track bears, sleep under the stars. I'd prefer an all-weather tent and some canned food."

"He's a *Man vs. Wild* kind of a guy, huh?"

"Something like that."

"So how'd you end up in L.A. when your whole family's in Frisco anyway?"

"I got into UCLA," she said with a shrug.

"Yeah, but you could work anywhere."

"Maybe, but the hospital offered me a full-time position. Besides, sometimes a little distance is nice."

Jackson said nothing. Distance was all he knew anymore.

They walked the rest of the way in silence, Jackson fighting thoughts about his family, about Sam and Maggie, about life in general. When they reached the parking lot, Sam stopped and looked down at her feet. They were still covered in semi-wet sand, and she stooped to start brushing.

"Here," Jackson said, bending down. "Hop on."

She hesitated, but he took her arm and wrapped it around his neck, and before she could protest, lifted her onto his back. Her skirt was long enough and loose enough that it wasn't unladylike, and as he hoisted her a little higher onto his back, she wrapped her arms around him and leaned her cheek in close to his, her smile nearly squeaking with delight.

Such behavior was common for pier-goers, Jackson figured, so he thought nothing of his teenagerishness. Besides, Sam was twice as mature as he was, and she certainly wasn't objecting.

When they reached the Granada, Jackson swung around and set Sam down on the hood. "Wait here."

She smiled with uncertainty as he headed for the trunk. "What are you doing?"

He stuck his head out around the open trunk and had to smile at the picture of Sam sitting on the hood, feet dangling, ankles crossed, perplexity on her face, with the glitz of commotion of the amusement park behind her. It was the kind of picture a guy didn't need a camera for.

"Just a second," he said, digging through half-empty oil cartons and assorted tools. He found an old towel and brought it around the car to her. "Here, use this."

She took the towel. "Jackson, it has oil stains on it."

"Right, oil *stains*. Meaning they won't rub off."

Sam wrinkled her nose, but then accepted the towel. With a cross look at Jackson that was anything but sincere, she began to wipe the sand off her feet. He leaned against the passenger door and drank in the atmosphere. The more good memories he made, the less room there would be in his head for bad ones, right?

Sam finished and snapped the towel into Jackson's chest. She swung her legs over the edge of the car while he returned the towel and closed the trunk. When he returned, she was still sitting there beside his antenna, smiling adorably.

"Three o'clock comes early," Jackson said.

"Yeah."

He extended a hand, and she took it as she slid off the car. He held it until she was seated in the car, then closed the door behind her. As he walked around to his side, he eyed all the lights and sights of the pier one last time. The music and sirens and playful screams carried through the night air, all lighthearted and carefree. Jackson longed for it all to envelop him, but even if it did, he knew it would be superficial and fleeting.

With a sigh, he opened his door and got into the car. The air was stuffy inside compared to out on the beach, and even after all the years, the car still smelled like leather.

"Something wrong?" Sam asked.

"No," he said with another sigh. She put her hand on his knee, and he rolled his head to look at her. "You know what they say about alcoholics, how even after you quit, you're still an alcoholic. It never leaves you?"

"Yeah."

"That's how it is. Everything can be going great, I finally feel like maybe I'm making progress, and then it flares up again."

"Now?"

He shrugged. "To a small degree. Nine times out of ten I can manage it, but that one . . ." He shook his head. "I'm always going to be an alcoholic. That's just the way it is."

Sam grabbed his hand and held it in both of hers, looking him in the eye. "I refuse to believe that, Jackson. You're forgetting that Jesus is the Great Physician. And His healing isn't limited to physical infirmities. Spiritual and emotional ones too. You can never say never."

It wasn't preachy, just softly spoken, strong conviction.

"You sound like Grandpa."

Sam smiled, lifting his hand up in hers. "And I won't stop praying for you, Jackson."

"Good."

She slowly released his hand. "I suppose . . ."

"Yeah."

Jackson reached into his pocket for his keys, and with one last glance at Sam, started the car.

Neither spoke on the drive back to her apartment, both content to be together in the silence, enjoying the warm summer air blowing in through Jackson's window. When they reached her apartment, he eased to the curb and cut the motor. "I'll walk you to the door."

He opened her car door and reached a hand to help her. Still barefoot, she stepped over the curb and into the grass, dangling her sandals in her free hand. With a few fingers, she still held loosely to Jackson's hand as they walked across the lawn. They were halfway to the door when the underground sprinkler system suddenly sprang to life.

Sam's shriek pierced the night, echoing over the whir and hiss of the sprinklers. She dropped Jackson's hand and took off running for the safety of her sidewalk. With a grin, he followed, catching up to her in the doorway. She had escaped with a light misting; he had several squirt lines across his side and back, and suddenly the night air felt a little cool.

"You're soaked," she said, touching the wet fabric on his side.

"It'll dry."

"Agh, and I'm a mess," she said, wiping damp, loose hair off her cheek.

"You are far from a mess," Jackson said, tucking another strand behind her ear. He held his hand on her cheek for just a second, long enough for her to raise her eyes to his. "Thanks for dessert, Sam." He leaned forward and kissed her forehead.

Sam opened her eyes as he backed away, a calm smile stretched across her face. She reached down into her purse for her keys, opened the door, and turned back to face him. "I have off all weekend," she said. "You want to do something?"

First Reggie, then Maggie, now Sam. It was going to be a busy weekend.

He squinted at her. "What kind of something?"

"I don't know. Whatever."

"'Whatever' sounds good. I'll give you a call."

"Okay."

"Night, Sam."

"Good night, Jackson."

With one last smile, she slipped behind the door and eased it shut.

Jackson took the long way around the sprinklers back to his car. Before pulling away from the curb, he took out his phone and checked to see if he had any messages. Two, both from Shay. He merged onto the street and listened to the first.

"Jackson, it's Shay. Where are you? Call me right away, okay? Bye."

It was dated eight-thirty. He thumbed to the second message, from nine-fifteen.

"It's me again. Where are you? It's urgent. I'll try your house. Call me if you get this!"

Jackson headed north toward Sunset Boulevard, the quickest way back to Pacific Palisades. He was about to call Shay back when he saw another incoming call. It was her again.

"Hey, it's me," he said.

"Where are you?"

"Out. Where are you?"

"I'm at your house. Jackson, we need to make the third delivery tonight."

"What?"

"Ten p.m. tonight, not ten a.m. tomorrow."

That was the urgent, right away message? That some nutjob collector needed his wooden idol tonight?

Jackson sighed, loudly enough to transmit through the phone. "I'm on my way."

"Hurry."

"Yeah. Where's this last delivery?"

"Um, some place off of Laurel Canyon."

"I'll be there in ten minutes."

"Hurry!" Shay said again, and Jackson closed his phone. He should have told her to meet him at Cameron's, and he should have called Reggie to see if he was still around to let them into the safe. But at the moment, he really didn't care. Being half an hour late wasn't going to kill anybody.

Jackson rounded the famous Riviera Country Club and took the "backdoor" into Pacific Palisades. Ridgeline Drive emptied onto Sunset, and as he turned onto his home street, he was nearly sideswiped by a silver van. Who in Pacific Palisades drove a van? Who period drove a van anymore?

A block later, a kid in a Dodge Viper came flying out of a driveway, and Jackson had to slam on his brakes to avoid a crash. A Viper. That was more like it.

Jackson made it the final two blocks unscathed and swung the Granada into the driveway. Shay's convertible was parked on the road, unoccupied. Jackson quickly got out and approached the front door, expecting to find Shay fuming on his stoop. She wasn't there either. He shrugged. Knowing her, she had probably found a way inside and was looking for a low-fat snack. In his fridge, good luck.

Jackson let himself in and flipped on the light. "Shay, you in here?"

The only response came from the clock on the living room wall, ticking steadily.

"Shay?" He hollered once upstairs, in case she had gone there in search of a bathroom. The house was dark, so he doubted she had come in. He headed through the living room to the dining room and to his small deck. It was also empty.

For a moment, he toyed with the idea of pretending she hadn't called and going to bed. But with a sigh, he hopped the deck railing and walked around the north side of the house, around the garage, and back to Shay's car. Still empty.

So, like, where was she?

Chapter Fifteen

9:56 p.m.

FROM THE BACKYARD, Jackson heard loud voices and laughing. The ladies DiMarco. Shay couldn't be with them. One look at Connie's outfit would make her nauseous.

Jackson trudged around the south side of the house, completing the circuit. The laughing grew louder as he approached Connie's deck. She and Diane were lounged next to the pool, cocktails in hand, staring out at the lights of the valley.

"Drive you ladies home?" he asked.

"Oh dear!" Connie said, turning around in—and nearly falling out of—her chair. "Jackson," she said slowly as recognition hit. "Join us. Diane made bananana daiq-daiquiris. They're fantastata-fantastic."

"Thanks, but I'll pass."

Diane drained the last of her cocktail. "So how is your party?"

"Huh?"

"Don't be shy, Jack-Jackson," Connie said. "We're all adults here."

"What are you talking about?"

"The date you had over tonight. Is that the other case you were talking about?" she asked with a snort. "I see why you were hesitant this morning."

More laughing.

"A date?" Jackson asked. "You saw a girl at my place?"

Connie shook her head while still sipping her drink. "We just heard her."

"Sounds like you two are having quite a time," Diane added.

"Why, what'd you hear?"

Diane laughed some more. What was in those daiquiris?

"Don't worry," Connie said. "It wasn't that loud."

Sometime he would have to set them straight, but not until he figured out about what. He dropped to a squat, hoping that being at eye level might help them focus. "What did you hear?"

"It really wasn't anything," Diane said. "We heard her shrieking a little, yelling your name. We figured you two were horsing around."

"How long ago?"

"Five minutes maybe. I don't know." Diane sat up. "Why, was she the one who sped out of here?"

"Sped out?"

"Somebody tore out of here like one of the Ander-Andrettis," Diane said. "You guys weren't having a fight, were you? I'm sorry, we thought you were just having a good time."

"No, don't . . ." Jackson started to wave them off. He stopped when he thought of the van. Shay had been "shrieking a little" and yelling his name. Could what sounded like romantic horseplay to a couple of half-drunk ladies have been something more sinister, like a kidnapping?

Suddenly Jackson's stomach hurt. He had shrugged off all of Shay's concerns, figuring nobody could get that upset about some woodcarvings. Broken-into hotel rooms and stolen idols had seemed ridiculous that morning, as had Shay's fears of being followed or attacked. Now, not so much.

"What is it?" Diane asked.

"Nothing. I have to go. Thanks."

"Jackson," Connie said, raising her empty glass. "Gina called." She hiccupped.

Diane picked up the narrative. "She said to thank you. She's going out on some doctor's boat. She's very excited."

"A doctor? Landon's a sociology major."

"I think they're double dating."

So Enrique was a doctor? That would explain the expensive car. His dad had gone to medical school. Maybe he'd passed on the doctor gene.

Jackson shrugged internally. Who knew whose boat they were on, or how accurate Connie and Diane's story was. For all they knew, Gina was inside watching *Grey's Anatomy* reruns, her doctor McDreamy.

"And we're stuck here with cheap booze," Connie said. They both started laughing again, and Jackson left them to it and hurried back to his house. He dug out his cell and quickly called Shay.

"Hi, it's Shay! Sorry you missed me."

"Shay, it's Jackson. Call me."

He clapped the phone shut and ran through the house, making sure Shay wasn't there. He stopped on the stairway landing, looking up at darkness. If someone had come for Shay, was it possible they were still in the house? If they knew Shay was delivering the idols, there was a good chance they knew Jackson was involved. It didn't track, why they would drive off with Shay instead of waiting for him too. Maybe the van was just a van and Shay's disappearance had another explanation. Or maybe whoever had taken her didn't need Jackson, just needed him out of the way. Or maybe they had left somebody behind to take care of him. One thing was sure, if Shay had been kidnapped, he didn't have time to mess around.

Jackson climbed to the top of the stairs and did a quick sweep. Nothing. He stopped in the middle of his bedroom, trying to figure out what to do next. If Shay was in the van, she had a ten-minute head start. There was no way he could catch her. Unless . . .

Jackson whipped out his phone and quickly dialed Mouse.

"Hello." It was Pam.

"I need to talk to Mouse."

"Who is this?"

"Jackson."

"What do you want?"

"Pam! Now!"

"All right, all right, don't get huffy." She set the phone down, and he heard her holler for Mouse. He headed down to the garage while waiting for Mouse to put down his controller and come to the phone.

"Hey."

"Mouse, it's me."

"What's up?"

"Is there any way you can hack into Caltrans' system."

"What?"

"I need to track a van that was heading east on Sunset."

"Are you serious?"

"Deadly, man. Can you pull up their traffic cameras?"

There was a pause. "Yeah, I could do it I think. Might take some time."

"Get started. I'm coming over."

He closed the phone before Mouse could answer. Grabbing a high-power flashlight from the garage, he headed out and surveyed the property, looking for any signs that Shay or anyone else had been there. It hadn't rained in at least a week, and the ground was hard and dry. There were no footprints, no drag marks, no signs of a struggle. It wasn't surprising. It wouldn't take much to kidnap a girl Shay's size. One guy with fireman's training could handle her easily.

But to risk being seen by the neighbors, especially when two of them were out on the deck? Granted, they had probably been singing show tunes or something, but it was still nervy. Somebody wanted Shay badly. But because of the idols? It just didn't make sense, and as Jackson made one last circle of the house, he tried to think of an alternate explanation. None occurred to him.

Then he saw it. On the ground by one of several poplar trees at the northern edge of his property. Picked up by the edge of his flashlight beam was a periwinkle blue platform flip-flop. With sequins. He squatted down to pick it up, at the same time eyeing the surrounding ground for any other signs of what had taken place. There was nothing but the flip-flop.

Jackson dialed Mouse's number again.

"Hello."

"Pam, can I talk to Mouse again?"

She didn't answer this time, just set the phone down and hollered.

"Yeah?" Mouse said a moment later.

"How you coming?" Jackson asked.

"It's doable. I just want to know how careful I should be."

"What do you mean?"

"This sort of thing can leave a trail. I don't want it coming back to bite me, but if it's life or death . . ."

Jackson took a deep breath. "I think my client was kidnapped."

"By Brower?"

"No, another client. I saw a van racing out of the neighborhood, and I think she's in it."

"Okay. I'll leave a few dummy trails, but I'll be quick."

"Thanks, man. I'm headed out now."

"I think Pam's going out, so just come on in."

"Right. See ya."

Jackson closed the phone and tossed both the flashlight and the flip-flop onto the front seat of the Granada. Then he hurried inside and back up to his room, trying Shay's cell one more time. He got her voicemail again and snapped his phone shut.

Jackson's bedroom doubled as his office—an office that contained a desk, a few filing cabinets, and a bookcase. Jackson ransacked the pencil drawer of his desk, looking for the key that was somewhere near the back. He found it and used it to open a small lockbox buried in the back of his walk-in closet. From the lockbox he pulled out a Glock 19 pistol and quickly checked that the fifteen-round magazine was full. He closed the lid, then on second thought, grabbed a spare magazine just to be safe.

He also grabbed a black sweatshirt from the top shelf, tucked the gun into the back of his jeans, and headed downstairs. His clock said it was twelve minutes after ten. Shay had been gone at least twenty minutes. As he got into the car and backed out of the driveway, he did so with the realization that it was likely already too late.

Chapter Sixteen

10:27 p.m.

THE GUN WASN'T for Mouse's neighborhood, although after dark, it could have been.

Jackson spent the drive over going through everything Shay had told him, trying to trigger the nagging feeling he'd had all day in the hopes that he could come up with some clue as to who had taken her and why. But of course, now the nagging was silent, and all he had was the same inconclusive set of facts.

Jackson knocked but let himself in and found the living room, kitchen, and dining area completely dark. He knew immediately that Pam was gone; otherwise the TV would have been on. The only light came from down the hall, from Mouse's room, and Jackson hurried toward it.

Mouse was at his desk, rocking in place as usual. His hands flew from the mouse and keyboard in front of him to the keypad of the laptop on his left, his eyes sometimes following the hands, sometimes not. A bag of Gardetto's sat next to a one liter of Mountain Dew on the shelf to his right beside a three-inch thick coding book. He had everything at arm's reach.

"How's it going?" Jackson asked.

"Almost there," Mouse said without turning to acknowledge him. "The firewall's tricky."

Jackson pulled over the spare chair and sat down.

"I should have the feed come up on the laptop in a few minutes," he said. "You want to tell me exactly what we're looking for."

"A silver van," Jackson said. "Nearly ran me off the road turning left onto Sunset from Ridgeline."

"No idea where it was going?"

"Not in the least."

142

"What time?"

"Ten till ten."

Mouse pecked away at the keyboard, then turned expectantly to the laptop. The screen blinked, then went black. Then white letters blipped across the top. Access Not Granted.

"Junk." He typed some more.

"Where's Pam?"

"Clark."

"They're on again?"

"Apparently." Mouse turned toward the laptop again. Another blink, then the same message. Access Not Granted.

"Junk." His fingers raced over the keyboard. He turned again. The screen blinked twice, and then a menu appeared.

"We in?" Jackson asked.

"Almost." Mouse continued hammering away at the keys. "You call the police?"

Jackson sat back in his chair. "No. All I have is a flip-flop."

"A flip-flop? Hers?"

"Yeah. At my house."

"There," Mouse said. He reached for his bottle of Mountain Dew, unscrewed the cap, and with it in his hand, pointed at the laptop screen. "That's a map of L.A." He clicked on his computer and the map zoomed, close enough that roads distinguished themselves. "Dots are traffic lights in their current state. Red, green, no yellow, I don't know why. Gray border means there's a cam at the intersection."

"Okay."

"Tell me where you want to go. Whatever I put in here comes out on that screen."

"What's the first camera east of Ridgeline on Sunset?"

"Allenford."

"Go there."

Mouse zoomed in and clicked, and a moment later an empty black box filled most of the laptop screen. It blipped, and then the empty area was replaced by shot of the intersection of Sunset and Allenford.

"That current?" Jackson asked.

"Yeah. What time you want?"

Jackson dug out his phone and looked at his call log. "She called me at nine-forty-six. Let's start there."

Mouse typed the info in on his keyboard and the image momentarily disappeared. When it came back, the clock superimposed on the bottom corner read 09:46:00.

"Why's it sunny?" Mouse asked.

"Military time," Jackson answered.

"Duh." Mouse typed again, and after another blip, the clock displayed 19:46:00.

"Twelve and nine's twenty-one."

"Yeah." Mouse typed one last time and 21:46:00 appeared on the screen. He pressed another button to start the footage and they watched a stream of cars flow through the intersection.

"This thing have a fast forward?"

A couple of taps quadrupled the speed. Vehicles now shot past the camera as the time on the clock raced by.

"Stop!" Jackson yelled. "Go back."

Mouse rewound the footage a few seconds.

"There."

Mouse paused the image of a silver van barreling through the intersection.

"That it?" Mouse asked.

"Yeah, that's it. Can you blow it up?"

"Give me a minute. You sure? Lot of silver vans."

"In the Palisades, at this hour? No. No back windows, same model, same color. This is it."

Mouse shrugged and went to work. Jackson strummed his fingers on the desk while Mouse tapped away at his keyboard. The image on the laptop doubled in size.

"Is that it?" Jackson asked.

"Just going to get grainier."

"Can you enhance it?"

"I'm not *CSI*."

Jackson squinted, hoping to peer through the windshield and see the driver. It was no use. "Okay, what's the next intersection?"

"The 405."

"Let's do it."

"Time?"

"Whatever this is right now."

Mouse entered the info, and a few seconds later the next camera came up on the laptop screen. They waited five fast-forwarded minutes and the van passed by, still moving east.

"You have the other side of the highway?" Jackson asked. "See if he went north."

More typing, then another camera. The van continued on Sunset.

Jackson sat back in his chair. "If he was going north or south he'd have taken the 405, and he would have taken it to get to I-10 if he were going east. He must be going somewhere in West L.A."

"Unless he's trying to throw you off the trail."

"He doesn't know I'm on the trail, and if he was being surreptitious, he wouldn't still be on Sunset."

"Surrep-what?"

Jackson shook him off.

"So what's next?"

"Next intersection," Jackson said, and they went through the process again. Cameras at Beverly Glen, Coldwater Canyon, and Highland all showed the van passing farther east on Sunset.

"Where are you going?" Jackson asked quietly. Then to Mouse: "Next street."

Mouse glanced at the clock display in the corner of his screen. "We've been in the system a while."

"Is that a problem?"

"Shorter's better."

"What's next, Vine?"

Mouse answered by typing and bringing up the camera. They waited almost a minute, and then the van zoomed through the intersection. Jackson looked at the clock in the bottom corner of the laptop. 10:40. He looked at the time on the last camera images. 22:17:47. He was over twenty minutes behind the van and still didn't know where it was going. Time was ticking on Shay.

"Skip ahead. See if they got on the 101."

Mouse obeyed, but cameras on each side of the Hollywood Freeway showed the van continuing east.

"Sunset's going to dip down into downtown," Jackson said. "Why didn't they get on the 10?"

Mouse shrugged, passing through several more cameras. With each, he seemed to grow more nervous. "Silver Lake Boulevard," he announced. "We get to the 110, I'm done."

Jackson took a deep breath and eyed both clocks again. After several frames passed by, the van appeared. Then it turned.

Jackson rose out of his seat. "Silver Lake?"

Mouse nodded.

"You got a camera north?"

"One second."

Mouse tapped some more and pulled up the traffic camera at Silver Lake and Glendale. He and Jackson waited as nearly five minutes elapsed on the camera clock. No van.

"He got off before Glendale," Jackson said, hopping up. "Can you get me a street map of the area."

"Can I get out of here?"

"Hang on just a sec."

Mouse began to rock a little faster as he accessed a map of Silver Lake. Jackson leaned in to see the screen clearly. "Do me a favor," he said, pulling out his phone. "Check here . . . here and here, see if they came out the other side."

"What makes you think they went east?"

"They would have turned on Griffith Park otherwise."

"They could've taken I-10. Who knows where they're going."

"It's a guess. Check those three and you can get out."

Mouse got busy and Jackson dialed Reggie's number. He answered on the fourth ring. "What's up?"

"Hey, you free?"

"No, man, I'm on duty tonight. We're short a waitress and cook, and I still have paperwork due for tomorrow. Why, what you need?"

"A long story. I'll call you later."

"Man, I'm gonna be in bed later, man."

"Yeah." Jackson snapped the phone shut. "Anything?"

"Not yet," Mouse answered.

"I'm out of here. Stay by the phone?"

"Yeah, sure. Hey, where are you going?"

"Shay's in that van, and not with Lewis and Fuller."

"Be careful."

"Yeah," Jackson called over his shoulder, already on his way out. As he jogged to the car, he took Leroy's advice.

Lord, help me out on this one. I don't know what I'm getting into.

Somehow, he got the feeling he didn't know how right he was.

The quickest way to Silver Lake was on the Santa Monica Freeway, I-10. It again raised the question why the van had stayed on Sunset, but it was a question that would have to go unanswered. Jackson raced along ten miles faster than the speed limit, fast enough to shave time, not fast enough to get a ticket that would cost him money and time.

He called Mouse. "Anything?"

"No, he turned off before Hyperion and never came out. Not past any of the cams anyhow."

"You got an aerial photo?"

"I can." Jackson heard him pecking at the keyboard. "What am I looking for?"

"Anything to suggest where this van might have gone."

"What, like a rooftop sign advertising van parking?"

"Come on, Mouse, a girl's life's at stake."

"Yeah, yeah. Um . . ."

Jackson waited several long seconds.

"Where are you?" Mouse asked.

"Just past Crenshaw."

"So what, like five minutes out?"

"At least."

"Let me look around," Mouse said. "I'll call you back."

As he drove, Jackson tried to think of what he would do assuming he found the van. It depended where it was, and what or who he found with it. He also reviewed Shay's story yet again, trying to figure out what he could be missing and whether that something could be vital in finding her. Whatever it was, it wasn't waving flags anymore.

Jackson exited the freeway at Silver Lake Boulevard. When he crossed Sunset, he began surveying the neighborhood, looking for any signs of the silver van. There were none, just lots of tightly packed houses, any one of which could hide a van in the garage.

"Come on, Mouse."

He was about to start randomly driving up and down streets when the James Bond theme sounded from his phone.

"Yeah?"

"I found a couple of options. There's a couple of big mansions close to the reservoir. You know, a van, deliveries maybe?"

"What else?"

"There's a bunch of commercial buildings along Sunset."

"He would have stayed on Sunset then."

"They go back a couple blocks."

"What kind of commercial buildings?"

"I don't know. Stores or something. Try Lacey Drive. This one looks like a warehouse."

"I'll check it out. Anything else?"

"Not much to look for, dude."

"Okay. Lacey Drive?"

"Yeah, second right."

He spotted the street and hung a right. "I'm on Lacey."

"Three blocks, then the warehouse-looking thing is on your right."

Jackson drove without speaking. Three blocks east on Lacey Drive he saw what, to Mouse's credit, looked like a warehouse.

"Mouse, I see it. Big brown building?"

"I don't know. The roof's white?"

"Yeah, I don't see—"

"What is it?"

Jackson resisted the urge to step on the brakes and kept driving several more blocks before turning onto a shady, residential street.

"Jack, what is it?"

"It's there. Parked in the alley."

"The van? You sure?"

"Yeah. I gotta go, man."

Chapter Seventeen

11:06 p.m.

FEELING LIKE FLAVOR Flav or Lil Wayne, Jackson donned his black hoodie, tucked his gun—safety on—into the front of his jeans, and started on foot toward the warehouse. The extra ammo magazine was in his pocket, the bullets tingling as he thought of what he might be about to do. He'd had the gun for over a year, but had never fired it, other than at target practice. He'd never even brandished it. Now . . .

He had plenty of trees to help him stay undetected as he approached the warehouse. It was on the corner of Lacey Drive and a narrow side street that ran south but not north off Lacey. That provided another advantage as Jackson could stay in the shadows on the north side of the street and not have to cross over open pavement. At least not for surveillance.

He stopped at the end of the side street, looking at the side of the warehouse. From this angle, it appeared abandoned. Several of the windows were boarded up, the paint was chipped and fading, and the bushes along the side of the building were wild and untrimmed. A few blocks away, a building would never stand a chance of remaining in such poor condition—the locals would demand it be taken down. The locals on the north side of Lacey Drive either didn't care or didn't have enough clout.

Jackson inched farther along, hoping the neighborhood watch captain was already asleep. The front of the warehouse was equally rundown. The few windows in the office were dark, the door was barred, and the small parking lot in front of the building was cracked and overgrown with weeds. The only sign of life was the silver van parked in the alley between the warehouse and the adjacent building. It was backed in, hidden in the shadows, with nothing to suggest that it would be leaving anytime soon.

At first.

Then, as Jackson watched from the darkest section of the sidewalk, he saw movement. For just a moment, the darkness on the passenger side of the van split and became two shades of black. Just that quickly it was still again, but Jackson was sure it wasn't the light—or lack thereof—playing tricks with him.

The warehouse had a sentry.

Going in the front was out, and the windows on the side were too high up for access. The alley was out too, unless he could get the guard out of the way. And at the moment, that wasn't an option.

Slinking at first, then jogging, Jackson returned to his car and drove a block south. He passed by the warehouse's south side and saw a loading dock, another barred door, and more signs of neglect. No guard, and no means of access. Then he saw a hunched over man shuffling along the sidewalk and had an idea. He pulled to the curb.

Leaning over, Jackson rolled down the passenger window. The man never looked up as he walked within several feet of the car. "Hey," Jackson called. No response. He raised his voice. "Hey!"

The man glanced at him, then bent his head down again and kept walking. Jackson opened his door and reached for his wallet. "Ten bucks."

The guy slowed and looked over his shoulder.

"I'll give you ten bucks to talk to me." He held up a ten-spot, then extended it outward. After a moment's hesitation, the guy turned and trudged toward him. Jackson inched forward, keeping the money extended. The guy looked from the cash to Jackson's eyes several times, then timidly reached out with dirty fingers. They matched his jacket, his gray-yellow beard, his mangy hair, and his too-small stocking cap. His shoes were Nikes, mismatched, but reasonably new. The jeans weren't so fortunate.

"It's yours," Jackson said. "No strings."

One more look, then the guy grabbed the bill and stuffed it into the pocket of his coat.

"I'll give you twenty more if you do me a favor."

The man opened his mouth just far enough to reveal at least a dozen yellow teeth. "What favor?"

"Go down to the next street here, hang a left, then go left on Lacey, past that warehouse."

Dark, deep-set eyes focused on Jackson without comprehension.

"Walk west on Lacey, and when you get to the alley, cause a commotion."

The guy stared some more.

"Just make some noise. Sing, kick a bottle, do whatever," Jackson said, doubting that a hobo stereotype was going to offend the guy. "Make some noise for sixty seconds and then do whatever you want. The money's yours."

More staring.

"Will you do it?"

Uncertainty played across the guy's features. Was this some joke? Another guy having some fun with a homeless man? Was there a catch?

Jackson reached slowly for his wallet and withdrew his only twenty. It would go on Shay's expense tab, if she lived to pay him. He extended the twenty. "Here you go. Help me out?"

The man took the money, then nodded slightly. "Walk 'round the warehouse, make some noise in front of the alley?"

"That's all. Then go on your way."

He nodded, turned, and trudged away, looking over his shoulder only once. Jackson closed his car door and waited, wondering if the guy would come through or if he had just shelled out thirty bucks for nothing.

Jackson saw the man turn onto the side street, which was a good sign. He waited another minute and then crept back east toward the south end of the alley. He hurried under the yellow glow of the only streetlight in the area, then along the edge of the adjacent building. A furniture store, maybe. Whatever it was, it looked abandoned too. This wasn't the Silver Lake Jackson knew.

He waited, daring one peek into the alley. Fifty feet away, he saw the back of the silver van, but no movement. He leaned back, retrieved his gun, and clicked off the safety. Then he said a quick prayer for the homeless man, hoping that he hadn't just gotten him killed.

The night was quiet, except for the traffic a few blocks over on Sunset. Then he heard the sound of aluminum scraping concrete. The guy had found a can to kick.

Jackson dropped to his knees and tensed, waiting. He peered around the corner of the building again and froze as a car approached from the west. He tried to blend into the wall, and the car kept going with no signs that anyone in it had seen him. When the noise died away, Jackson heard a new sound. Singing. Sort of.

Bless his heart, the homeless man was singing "On the Road Again." It was slow and mournful, and quite pathetic, his voice sounding more like Scott Stapp than Willie Nelson. But between lines of the chorus, Jackson realized it was working. He heard footsteps, weak scuffs on the pavement. He risked one more peek into the alley and saw a separation of shadows again. The sentry was investigating. It was the opening Jackson needed.

He darted around the corner, covering the ground between the end of the alley and the back of the van in seconds, quietly, hopefully unseen. Then he crouched down by the back bumper and waited, trying to still his breathing so he could hear everything.

Ten seconds passed. Then ten more. He heard the scuffling again. The sentry was returning.

Jackson tensed as the footfalls sounded on the passenger side of the van. They stopped, and he heard a slight squeak as the guard rested against the side of the van. Jackson waited a minute, long enough to know the man was remaining in place. Gun in hand, he felt on the ground for a small pebble or piece of trash—something to make a little noise. He found a rock and skipped it across the concrete toward the warehouse. It wasn't much, but was enough of a noise to get the guard's attention.

Jackson heard the van squeak again, followed by more footfalls as the guard moved toward the back of the van. Jackson waited, and when he saw a leg, he struck. Dropping onto his backside, he swung his left leg, swiping at the man's Achilles. The man fell backwards, and Jackson retracted his leg and jumped to his feet, gun drawn. He surged forward, ready to shoot if necessary.

It wasn't. The guard had cracked his head when he fell, and was already on the verge of unconsciousness. Jackson dropped to his knee, grabbed the guard by the collar, and slammed his head against the side of the van. His body recoiled and slumped around the back tire.

Jackson quickly frisked him, finding a knife and a gun. The knife wasn't a cute little Swiss Army knife but a military-grade weapon. Jackson tossed it aside. The gun was a nine millimeter like his, and he took it along, just in case.

Taking a deep breath, Jackson surveyed his options. There was a door just a few feet in front of the van, metal, likely as not locked. But it was worth a try.

His own gun still drawn, Jackson reached for the door handle. The good news was it opened. The bad news was it creaked like the Munsters' front door.

Jackson ducked inside and squatted down, looking all around for signs that he had been detected and waiting for his eyes to adjust to the darkness. It only took a few seconds to recognize that he was in the heart of the warehouse, looking at the ends of rows and rows of massive storage shelves, each fifteen to twenty feet high. Parked a little ways to his right was a forklift. There was nothing but blackness down the corridor to the left.

Knowing anyone in the warehouse would have heard the creak of the door, Jackson shuffled across the concrete floor and took shelter in between the rows of shelving. Seconds later, he heard a single set of footsteps coming his way. He waited until a dark figure approached, the darkness making it impossible to discern anything but a general shape.

Jackson watched, his own gun drawn, still in his crouch, as the man stood in place for a few seconds, listening. He reached for a small flashlight, playing it first on the door. Seeing it was closed, he turned the beam on the forklift and down the side corridor, then toward Jackson.

"Freeze," Jackson said, rising halfway. He leveled the gun at the man, who in turn aimed his flashlight into Jackson's eyes.

"Drop it," Jackson said.

He did, and everything went dark. Before Jackson could react, his hands were kicked toward the shelves, knocking the gun loose. Still half crouched, Jackson lost his balance and fell over backwards and to the side, bumping his head on the edge of a wood pallet in the process.

That was the least of his worries. While the man had been shining his flashlight at the forklift, Jackson had spotted a gun in his other hand.

Knowing a shot was coming, Jackson rolled over, farther down the aisle. An instant later, a bullet bit into the concrete where he had just been.

Jackson rolled twice more as two more shots spit into the concrete and a pallet. Jackson reached for the guard's gun, still tucked into the back of his pants, doing a somersault into the middle of the aisle while he grabbed it. As he rolled, he clicked off the safety, and came up on his back, feet up in the air. Between his legs, he aimed at the blur of blackness that was moving. He squeezed the trigger.

Jackson had no idea how many shots he fired. He just kept pulling the trigger, varying his aim up and down, left and right, shooting anything inside the V formed by his outstretched legs.

Finally, he stopped. Slowly, shakily, he got to his knees and then his feet. His shots still echoed through the warehouse, which otherwise had gone eerily silent again. It was still dark, except for a small ray of light cast by the flashlight that was now rolling back and forth on the floor. The glow reflected off smoke hanging in the air and illuminated a growing puddle of blood on the concrete.

Gun still drawn, arm shaking, Jackson bent for the flashlight and confirmed his suspicions.

The man was dead.

At least half a dozen bullets had hit their mark, from the heart to the neck to the arm.

Jackson fell back to his knees. He wanted to throw up as a flood of emotions coursed through his body. Adrenaline. Disgust. Pride. Fear. Shock.

He had just killed a man. He had done it to save his own bacon, and that gun-pulling-while-somersaulting trick had been downright Bond-ish.

But he had just killed a man.

Chapter Eighteen

11:23 p.m.

THERE WASN'T TIME to process all the ramifications. Stifling his emotions—and his dinner—Jackson forced his mind back to business. There were probably others in the warehouse, and he had to be prepared.

He quickly checked the magazine in the gun. Four bullets. His own gun had a full magazine, and he retrieved it from the floor. Discarding the guard's gun, he picked up the dead guy's, found it had almost a full magazine, and tucked it into his jeans. Then he contemplated his next move.

In the aisle, he was a sitting duck with no clue where an attack could come from. A quick sweep with the flashlight revealed that the shelves were stacked floor to ceiling with pallets holding large cardboard boxes and wooden crates. It looked like computer equipment, shells for desktop computers, servers, maybe a few monitors. The shelves weren't scalable and there was no place in them to hide. So Jackson decided to get away from the body, the first place the next wave of attackers would look.

He headed for the back of the warehouse, hoping to clear that half from any threats. He ducked into each of three aisles, briefly shining his light between the shelves, gun aimed just over the beam. All were clear and he reached the back of the warehouse unharmed.

Jackson stopped to listen. All was quiet except for his heavy breathing.

Or was it?

Holding his breath, Jackson thought he made out the slightest of scuffing noises. Maybe footfalls; maybe his imagination. There was no flashlight approaching this time and negligible ambient light in the warehouse.

The scuffing, if it was real, had stopped. His back to the end of the last row of shelving, Jackson chanced a peek around the corner, down the back corridor of the warehouse. He saw nothing, just vague blackness.

Then the noise resumed. A little louder. A little closer.

Jackson turned his head back and forth, trying to determine which direction it was coming from. He felt like a gazelle in the bush, hiding in the tall grass, listening to an approaching leopard padding his way. Only unlike for the gazelle, making a mad dash across the Serengeti wasn't an option. Gazelles didn't have to worry about rescuing pretty Valley Girls.

The scuffing was coming from the far side, from where Jackson had entered the warehouse. And it wasn't scuffing anymore. It was distinct footfalls. Muffled, but distinct.

Jackson waited and listened, his back still to the end of the row of shelving. The footfalls grew louder, still barely audible. They stopped for a moment, then resumed, now clearly emanating from the back corridor of the warehouse. The leopard was getting closer.

Remembering his last foray into hand-to-hand combat, Jackson inched around the corner into the aisle, leaving a buffer of stacked computer parts between him and the hunter. He stopped and listened again and heard very slow footsteps. The leopard was searching, methodically.

Jackson needed a strategy. He couldn't just creep through a dark warehouse all night. He needed to find a way to turn this game of cat-and-mouse in his favor. He just hoped there was only one cat. If not, creeping could lead him right into—

Jackson's thoughts ended when a pallet above his head exploded.

He jumped and turned to see a thin space between boxes on his left, and he dove forward as another shot fired behind him. He squeezed one shot into the shelves, hoping his attacker would recoil a little. Then he took off down the aisle. As he rounded the corner, he fired two more shots for cover and literally dove into the next aisle.

Panting, Jackson popped to his feet. Adrenaline and fear fought evenly for control of his brain. He listened for a second and heard nothing, so he continued back the way he had just come. Zig-zagging through the warehouse could not be the solution, but it was better than duking—or shooting—it out with a man he couldn't see.

Expecting to be shot from the blackness in front of him at any second, Jackson heard a slight scuff from behind. Without looking, he fired a shot over his shoulder. He made one step right, fired behind him again, then dove back left to the shelter of the shelves.

He waited for a second and then darted another row up. He turned into the original aisle, the one where he had killed the first man, and as quietly as possible, hurried toward the west end of the warehouse, toward the forklift. And toward the door.

For a second, he thought about leaving, crashing through the door and making a mad rush to his Granada or the safety of the trees. But he couldn't leave Shay.

Pulling up at the end of the aisle, he listened again. Nothing.

One thing he figured, there was only one man hunting him. If there were two, he would have been shot from behind by now. No, this was a game of chess with nothing but two kings remaining on the board. Unlike chess, there were no draws, and the life-or-death game would continue until someone made a mistake.

Or tricked the other guy.

Jackson reached for the gun in his jeans, the gun that had belonged to the guy he had killed. Standing next to the forklift, he heaved it down the side corridor, toward the corner of the warehouse. He crouched behind the forklift, took the flashlight still clutched in his left hand, and switched it on, muffling the beam against his leg.

He waited until he was sure he heard footsteps of the man investigating the noise the gun had made clattering on the concrete floor. Left-handed, Jackson bowled the flashlight along the floor toward the gun and the man. As soon as it left his hand, Jackson leveled his gun over the console of the forklift. The flashlight spun and rolled, but it also illuminated just enough of the man for Jackson to take aim.

Shielded largely by the forklift, he took three quick shots, then ducked in delayed reaction to a shot that had been fired wildly in his direction. But there were no more. Jackson wasn't sure about the first and third, but his second shot had clearly found its mark. The man had slumped to the floor without making any sort of move toward one of the aisles.

Jackson emerged from behind the forklift and hurried to the man, his gun drawn and ready. But there was no need. He was down and out.

The second killing was masked by so much adrenaline that it didn't even register with Jackson's psyche. Jackson grabbed the man's gun, the gun he had thrown, and the flashlight. Then he set out to find Shay, well aware that there still might be others in the warehouse. He doubted they would keep coming at him one by one like bad computer AI, but he wasn't going to be caught with his guard down.

He reached the front of the warehouse and took stock of the situation. A wall ran from side to side, about ten feet in height, separating the warehouse from what Jackson presumed were offices. There were two doors, one in the middle of the wall, and one halfway between the first and the near corner. He picked the closest first. Gun ready, he grabbed the knob and pushed it open.

Light flashed in Jackson's eyes and he instinctively dropped to a crouch. His brain quickly processed three pieces of information. One, the room was maybe fifteen by twenty, with a desk, some filing cabinets, and a few wood chairs. Two, Shay was seated in the middle of the room, duct taped to one of those chairs. Three, a black guy stood beside her, his hand reaching for his groin, where the handle of a gun stuck out of baggy black jeans.

"Hands up," Jackson said.

The guy looked at him with wild, nervous eyes. His hand shook.

Jackson blinked a glance at Shay. She wasn't in the line of fire.

"Don't," Jackson said, rising slightly, settling in a firing stance. "Don't!"

The man's hand wrapped around the handle of the gun, and Jackson fired. The bullet tore into the man's right shoulder and he spun backwards, falling to the ground with a cry of pain. Jackson hurried toward him, and as the guy rolled over, he kicked the gun from his hand.

"Move and I kill you," Jackson said. "You have another weapon?"

Biting his lip, the guy managed a shake of the head.

"How many of you are there?"

He said nothing, obviously in pain.

"Four?" Jackson asked.

A slight nod.

"Counting the guard outside?"

Another nod.

"Don't move," Jackson said. Then he stepped back and knelt in front of Shay.

She was still in her pink polo, but the jean shorts had been replaced with actual jeans. One blue flip-flop hung partially around a foot that was duct taped—as was the other—to the leg of the chair. Her arms were behind her back, bound to the chair frame as well. Another piece of duct tape had been roughly applied to her mouth, catching several strands of loose blond hair in the process.

Shay's eyes were puffy, it appeared from crying, and the hair that wasn't caught in the duct tape was messy and, in places, damp with sweat. The makeup was smudged, the necklace gone, and one of her earring backs had fallen out, leaving the earring dangling in her ear.

But the worst damage was the cut on her cheek, over the bone, directly underneath the left eye. It was a clean cut, an inch long, not terribly deep. But it had bled down onto the duct tape and down the side of her chin and neck, starting to stain her shirt.

"It's going to be okay," Jackson said, stroking her other cheek. As gently as possible, he peeled back the duct tape, taking extra care under the cut.

"Let's get you out of here, okay."

"Jackson . . ."

"It's okay. It's okay."

He reached around her to peel the duct tape holding her arms, at the same time peeking at his last shooting victim. He was still writhing in pain, but not moving otherwise.

"Does it need stitches?" Shay asked as he worked on untying her ankles.

Jackson looked at the cut again and shook his head. "No, it's not even bleeding anymore. I don't think it's very deep. It's . . ."

"What?"

He eyed the cut. It was smooth, as if done by a knife, and straight. But there were several points along the inch-long gash that were slightly uneven. Almost as if . . .

"Did they cut you multiple times?"

Shay nodded. Jackson nearly put a few more slugs into the guy in the corner.

"Did they hurt you . . . any other way?"

"No. No, I'm fine. Can we get out of here?"

He yanked the last piece of tape from around her ankles. "One second." Jackson hurried around her and bent down by the injured man. He dug through his pockets, pulled out a wallet, and quickly sorted through it. He found a California driver's license in the name of Dwayne Mickens, but that was it as far as identification. He tossed it in the corner and took Shay's hand. "Let's go."

"What about me?" Mickens whined.

"Flesh wound. Come on."

Shay took his hand and stood up, then wobbled.

"Here," Jackson said, bending down. "Climb on."

"I can walk."

He shook his head. "Climb on."

Shay reluctantly wrapped her arms around Jackson's neck, pinching his waist with her knees and thighs as he stood up. He was surprised—for her size, she was heavier than he had expected. The opposite of Sam, who was even lighter than she looked.

He froze for just a second.

A few hours ago, he had been lightheartedly carrying Sam across the parking lot at the Santa Monica Pier. He could taste the ice cream on his tongue, smell the perfume she had donned while retrieving his present. Now he was preparing to cart Shay across the carnage of an abandoned warehouse. Carnage he had created.

Leaving Mickens whimpering in pain, Jackson carried Shay back toward the door. He set her down by the forklift. "Wait here just a second."

"What's going on?"

"I need to find out who these guys were."

Making eye contact, he nodded, hoping she found it assuring. Then he rushed over to his first victim and quickly searched him for ID. Nothing.

After checking on Shay and making sure Mickens hadn't recovered and appeared at the end of the corridor with a Gat, he raced down to the end of the warehouse and searched the second victim. He found a driver's license

161

with the name Lewis Varden, Jr. and some cash. He left everything with the body and went back to Shay.

"One more second," he said, opening the door and peeking outside. The guard was where Jackson had left him, slumped by the back wheel of the van.

"Okay," Jackson said. He wiped down the two guns and the flashlight with his shirt and left them both behind, taking just his gun. With one more look down the hall to make sure Mickens wasn't stirring, he clicked the safety of his gun on and turned to Shay. "Climb on."

This time Shay didn't resist, but again wrapped her arms around his neck. Jackson hoisted her up, nearly faltering. The adrenaline was rushing out of his body, leaving him weak. He ignored the onrushing fatigue and forced himself to walk through the door, down the alley, and along the sidewalk toward the car.

Holding onto Shay with his free hand, he stuck the gun into his jeans and reached for his cell phone with the other. He dialed 9-1-1 and told them there had been a shooting, gave the address as best he knew it, and asked them to send an ambulance.

When he reached the Granada, he set Shay down and opened the door for her. "It's okay," he said, touching her arm. "You're safe now."

She nodded and sat down.

Jackson closed the door behind her and took one last look back at the warehouse. All was still. As he rounded the car, he called Mouse.

"Yeah?"

"Mouse, it's me. I got her."

"You're okay?"

"Yeah," Jackson said as he opened his door. "Yeah, we're out."

Chapter Nineteen

11:32 p.m.

"YOU HAVE ANY idea who those guys were?" Jackson asked as he drove. "What they wanted?"

Shay shook her head, at the same time feeling the cut with her fingers.

"Hurt bad?" Jackson asked.

"I'll live."

Half a block ahead, Jackson spied an all-night convenience store. He whipped into the parking lot as a police car raced in the other direction. He parked in the first row in front of the entrance and turned off the engine. "Wait here. I'll be back in a couple of minutes."

She nodded and he got out.

The store was mostly deserted, and Jackson ran up and down the aisles. A hundred thoughts flashed through his head: Shay's body being dragged from his property, a knife slicing her cheek, her screaming in pain as they tortured her. He saw himself unloading his gun through the crosshair formed by his legs—more clearly than when it had happened in real life—him killing the second man, and him plugging Mickens. He fantasized about not questioning Mickens, but unloading another magazine into his body.

Then he saw a pregnant woman buying ice cream, just before he ran her over.

Muttering an apology, he turned the corner and leaned against the shelf. It was all he could do not to throw up. He took several slow, deep breaths and forced himself to focus.

He started walking again, under control this time. He turned down an aisle containing everything from antacids to toilet paper. He grabbed a roll of paper towels, a tube of antibiotic ointment, some pain relievers, and two bottles of water. The bored clerk didn't even blink at the combination, stuffing the items into a plastic bag and returning Jackson's change without so much as a word.

Bag in hand, Jackson returned to the car.

Shay was gone.

Jackson dropped the bag, instantly on alert, looking every direction. How could someone have followed him? Was it the guard by the van? Had he woken up and tailed them? Jackson should have shot the tires. Or the guard.

Jerking his head in every direction, Jackson saw nothing. He turned to look in the glass windows of the store. No sign of her there, but she could have come in while he was in the aisle. To use the bathroom maybe?

Leaving the bag, he hurried back inside, where the clerk had his face in a magazine.

"Did a short blond girl come in here recently?" Jackson asked. "Pink shirt, pretty? Looked like she just came from a *Saw* shoot."

The clerk shrugged, and grunted something that sounded like a "No." Jackson scanned each of the aisles. There was no sign of her. He returned to the parking lot and ran out to the sidewalk. He looked north and south, knowing that if the van had come back and taken her, it would be long gone. But he looked up and down the street nonetheless.

Glancing right a second time, he saw her in the parking lot of the gas station on the corner. At a payphone. He sighed and took off running.

Shay was holding the phone receiver in one hand, staring at the dialing instructions on the stand.

"What are you doing?"

She jumped and turned. "I need to make a call."

"To who?"

She hesitated. "Blake."

"What's going on, Shay? Who were those guys?"

"I don't know."

"What happened?"

"I need to make a call."

"You tell me what happened, then you make the call."

164

She sighed. "They grabbed me from your place. I was waiting for you."

"Then what?"

"They threw me in the back of the van and taped my hands and feet. We drove for maybe forty-five minutes, to the warehouse."

"Then what?"

"They took me to that room and . . ."

"And what?"

"They hit me a few times, and then one of them cut my cheek."

"Why?"

"I don't know," she said, on the verge of tears.

"They never said what they wanted, who they were?"

"They wanted the idols."

"They said that?"

"Isn't it obvious?"

"No, Shay, it isn't. What is obvious is that something isn't right here. Those guys didn't strike me as the type interested in woodcarvings. I don't think they risked a kidnapping in Pacific Palisades, drove you across town, and slit your cheek over woodcarvings. If I didn't know better, I'd think you had messed up somebody's drug deal or something."

Shay's lip trembled.

Jackson stepped back. "No . . . No . . ." He shook his head. "This is about drugs, isn't it?"

She bit down on her lip.

"This is about drugs. Not your little wooden idols. It's about drugs!" Jackson turned around and paced a few steps away. "Oh man!"

He turned back toward Shay. "Now it all makes sense—why these deliveries are so important, why people are so secretive about it, why you didn't want me around. Let me guess, they had to test the blow, make sure it was legit?"

Shay barely nodded.

"That's why the idols are so light. They're hollow. You're smuggling the drugs inside the carvings. That's who your brother works for, isn't it? Some big-time dealer. Or is the brother all a front too?"

"No. Blake's real."

"So what'd you do, deal on somebody else's turf. Is that what this is about? Now I've shot three of them and you got me messed up in this?" He waved a finger. "I'm out of here. Find your own way wherever it is you want to go."

"Jackson, wait."

For some reason, he did.

"It's not what you think," she said.

"It's not?"

"No. You're right, they are drugs. They're Blake's. They're his deliveries."

"So where is this brother of yours?"

"He's . . . he's probably dead. That's why I need to call."

"Call who? What are you talking about?"

Shay gulped back tears and took a deep breath. "After Mom and Dad died, Blake started doing drugs. He got messed up with this gang, the Grays. He called me this morning and said he was in some sort of trouble, that I had to make these deliveries or they'd kill him."

"Why?"

"I don't know. He just said I had to do it. I panicked. I didn't know what to do. I called you."

"Out of a thousand P.I.s," he muttered. "What an idiot I was."

"You have to help me," she said. "If you don't, they'll kill Blake."

Jackson shook his head. "Don't put that on me. He's the one who started using, who got hooked up with a gang. I've already risked my life, already killed two people. Killed two people, Shay! I shot them!" He shook his head. "I'm not about to get in the middle of some gang initiation or punishment or whatever this is. I'm out."

"So that's it, huh? You're just going to let him die?"

"Look, I'm sorry about your brother. Really, I am. But I'm not putting my butt on the line to save some druggie from his dealer."

"Some druggie? You know, I'm not just a stupid blonde, Jackson. I checked you out before I hired you. In case you forgot, you were a druggie too."

"No. No! No, I smoked one joint. One joint, once."

"So what, because he got addicted and you didn't, your life's too good to save his?"

"Addictions aren't accidents, Shay."

"Is that going to help you sleep tonight?"

Jackson shook his head and turned away again.

Shay grabbed his arm. "Please! Blake made a mistake. He's an idiot. But they're going to kill him, Jackson. Unless we make the deliveries." She dropped his arm and put her hand over her mouth and nose. "If they haven't already."

Jackson brushed his hand through his hair. There were so many reasons to just leave, not the least of which was that dealing drugs was a serious crime. But when Jackson looked into Shay's eyes, he saw something there. An innocence, behind the lies and the pleas for help committing a felony. He sighed.

"We just have to make the final delivery?" he asked.

"Yes. But I have to call Blake's . . . boss."

"Figueroa?"

She shook her head. "His name's Sanders. I have to tell him what happened."

Jackson hesitated, not sure himself what had happened. "They take your purse?" he asked.

Shay nodded.

"Use mine." He handed his cell to her, and she offered him a brief smile in return. What a sucker he was.

Shay dialed and held the phone close to her ear. Waiting, she bit her lip. Then perked up.

"It's Shay. . . . I know, I know." She looked at Jackson. "I . . . had a problem . . . No, I still have it! I'll make the delivery, like, right away. . . . Please, don't hurt Blake. . . . Right away. . . . Totally, for sure."

She closed the phone and handed it back to Jackson. "Thank you."

He didn't answer, still wondering if maybe he was being snowed.

They started back to the car. "Tell me everything," he said. "Who are these Grays, how long has Blake been with them, what does he do? Everything you know."

167

She shrugged. "You haven't heard of the Grays? You're a P.I."

"The name's familiar. Believe it or not, I don't take a lot of mob cases either."

"I don't know much," she said with another shrug. "They're a gang. He joined up about six months ago, I think."

"And now they have him making deliveries?"

She nodded.

"So why you? Why is his life on the line?"

"I don't know. He just called me and said I had to make the deliveries. He said the drugs were in his safe deposit box. He granted me access after Mom and Dad died."

"Were the idols your idea?"

"No. That's how the Grays deliver their drugs, apparently."

"No Figueroa, no Tahitian warlords, no modern-day Indiana Jones?"

Shay shook her head.

Jackson did too. "I should have known. Fifty grand for a piece of gnarled wood." He looked her in the eye. "Anything else I should know? Anything else you're not telling me?"

Shay looked down. "No."

He opened the driver's side door for her.

"I'm driving?"

"No, I'm going to clean your cut." He nodded at the bag, still on the ground by the door.

"We don't have time. It's not that ba—"

Jackson cranked the side mirror so she could see her face. The cut had dried, but the entire left side of her face and neck were streaked with bloodstains, except where the duct tape had been. The hair that had been perfect that morning and afternoon was clumped and disheveled, and the eyes were still puffy and red.

Shay looked appropriately shocked.

"Does it hurt?" Jackson asked as he reached into the shopping bag. "You want some Tylenol?"

"No. I'm fine."

"You sure."

"Yes."

Jackson reached for the roll of paper towels and the bottles of water. He handed one to Shay.

"What's this for?"

"Drinking."

"Oh."

He opened the other and poured a small amount onto a balled up tuft of paper towel. "I'll be as gentle as I can."

She nodded and he began dabbing, first wiping the fading stains off her neck, jaw, and cheek. Shay winced as he neared the actual cut, but didn't complain.

"So you have no idea who those guys were?" Jackson asked as he worked. She shook her head.

"They didn't say what they wanted? They just started cutting you?"

She looked down. "I think . . . I think they were working up to it."

Jackson gently lifted her chin. "Do you have any idea where the Grays operate? Where their territory is?"

"No. Blake lives in Hawthorne. Maybe it's close to there."

"I'm guessing," Jackson said. "Hold tight." He dabbed around the cut with a clean paper towel. Shay winced with a sharp intake of breath, but again said nothing.

"If I had to bet, I'd say one of our deliveries was on somebody else's turf. They probably intended to rough you up and send a message to this Sanders guy."

"Good thing you found me."

"You have no idea."

"How did you?"

"I have a buddy who hacked into Caltrans. We tracked the van on traffic cameras."

"You hacked . . . You knew about the van?"

"I met it as I turned onto my street."

"You saw me inside?"

He shook his head and reached for the tube of antibiotic ointment. "I put two and two together. This will sting."

169

Squeezing a small glob onto his finger, Jackson began daubing the cut with the ointment. "These deliveries—was Blake originally supposed to make them?"

"I don't know." Wince. "Maybe."

Jackson capped the tube and put everything back into the bag except the bottle of water. That he kept, tossing the bag into the backseat and helping Shay stand up.

"Don't I need a Band-Aid or something?"

"I don't think so. It's not bleeding, and you don't have to worry about getting dirty. The open air's good for it."

She frowned but didn't argue.

Jackson nodded. "Let's go."

Chapter Twenty

11:46 p.m.

"WHY DID YOU ask about Blake and the deliveries?" Shay asked when they were back on the road.

"If we did deliver on somebody else's turf, the first person to know it other than them would be Sanders." Jackson shrugged. "We don't know what your brother did to tick him off. Maybe these original deliveries were supposed to be in another gang's territory."

"Wait . . . you think he wanted Blake to get caught?"

"It's possible." Jackson pulled out his phone.

"Who are you calling?"

"Reggie. Your drugs are in his safe. What is it, anyhow? Coke? Heroin?"

"I . . . I don't know. It's white, powdery."

Jackson nodded as he put the phone to his ear.

"Are you going to tell him?" she asked.

"No. Not yet."

Reggie picked up his cell on the fourth ring. He was still at Cameron's, having just finished up for the night. He agreed to wait for Jackson and Shay to get there. Jackson promised they'd be there by midnight and closed the phone. He stepped on the gas.

"Are you mad at me?" Shay asked.

"Yep."

"What else could I have done? I knew Blake was messed up in all of this. I wanted protection."

"You could have told me the truth."

"And you would have hung up on me."

"Yeah, probably."

"So what was I supposed to do?"

Jackson didn't answer, concentrating instead on the empty freeway. Something about all this still smelled bad. But unless he just dropped Shay, he would have to try to wade through it.

"Where was the crash?" he asked.

"Huh?"

"You said your parents died in a car crash? In L.A.?"

She turned her head. "No, in San Jose."

"Why San Jose."

"Daddy was there. On business."

Jackson nodded. "But they lived in L.A., in Beverly Hills?"

"Yeah. Is something wrong?"

"No."

They drove silently for several minutes without even looking at each other.

"Delacroix," Jackson said.

"What?"

"Emmanuelle Delacroix, the painter lady. I knew there was something about her."

Shay shook her head in confusion.

"She mysteriously disappeared a couple of years ago, for about six weeks. Nobody knew why, but one of the popular guesses was that she was in rehab."

"For what?"

"Guesses again, but snow was the leading vote-getter."

"Snow?"

"Cocaine. Like what's probably in that idol."

"Oh."

"Nose candy, freebase, booger sugar."

"And you just remembered this now?" Shay asked.

"I knew there was something about her, but it just clicked. Explains why she was on the list." He sat back. "Although . . ."

"What?"

"If this guy Sanders was sending Blake to make some deliveries on another gang's turf to punish him or test him or whatever, I wouldn't think he'd pick somebody famous for one of the deliveries."

"So?"

"So, I have no idea. But something's still not right with all of this."

Shay had no response to that, so they finished the drive again in silence.

The parking lot at Cameron's was almost empty. The kitchen stopped serving at eleven, but it was usually midnight before the last patrons left. Staff sometimes didn't get out until one, but aside from Reggie's big, black Hummer H3, the only other car in the lot was a beat-up sedan. Waiter wheels.

Reggie met them at the front door and showed them down to his office. "Kind of late to be delivering blocks of wood, ain't it?" he asked as he opened the safe. "Hey, what happened to your face?"

"It's a long story, Reg," Jackson said. He grabbed one of the two idols and turned it slowly in his hand. "What's the secret?" he asked, looking at the bottom of the carving. "How does it open?"

"I don't know," Shay answered.

"Open?" Reggie asked. "For what?"

Shay shot Jackson a look, imploring him to silence.

"That's a long story too. We'd better get going."

"You sure everything's all right, man? You come in here at midnight dressed like a mugger, she's got a gash on her cheek, and now you want to tap into these babies?"

Jackson glanced back at Shay before answering. "Yeah, we're all right."

Reggie nodded. "All right, bro. It's your show. Hey, man, what'd you want earlier?"

"Nothing. Thanks for waiting up."

Reggie dismissed him with a wave. "Be careful."

Back in the car, Jackson turned to Shay. "Okay, where to? You said Laurel Canyon."

"Yeah. The address was in my purse."

Jackson closed his eyes.

"What are you doing?"

"Shut up a minute." He kept his eyes closed, trying to remember the piece of paper Shay had showed him that morning. "Nine-seventy-two Green Summit Road?"

"Yeah. How'd you do that?"

"Superpowers. There's a map in the glove. Tell me you can read maps, Shay."

She didn't answer but went for the glove compartment as he started the car.

Green Summit Road was in a small subdivision off of Laurel Canyon, not far from the famed Mulholland Drive. Shay could indeed read a map, and by twelve-fifteen, they were driving down Green Summit Road, looking for the right address.

"Is that it?" Jackson asked, letting off the gas pedal and pointing up to a mansion on the left. It was set back from the road at least a hundred feet, with a spacious lawn and elegant trees lining the property. If he had to deliver drugs in the middle of the night, this was the neighborhood he wanted to do it in.

"Keep going," Shay said as he reached for the brakes.

"What?"

"Keep going!"

"Okay," he said, pushing down on the gas instead.

"Did you see that car back there?" Shay asked.

He glanced in his mirror. "Maroon Crown Vic?"

She nodded.

"What about it?"

"Undercover cops."

"How do you know?"

"I've, like, seen TV. That is totally a cop car."

Jackson sighed. Cops anticipating the delivery. Great, now in addition to having vengeful gang members trying to keep them from marking up their territory, he and Shay also had to dodge a couple of narcs. No problem.

"Well, we can't just show up at this hour," he said. "Not with you looking like that, not with the drugs on us. And certainly not in this car. It screams gangbanger."

"So what?" she asked. "We can't delay. They might kill Blake."

"When you talked to Sanders did he say if he had talked to the buyer? You were supposed to be here at ten originally. Does he know you're coming now?"

"Yeah, he said they'd spoken."

"Okay. Then I'll sneak in the back."

"How?"

"It's pretty rural out here, and pretty dark. If we park on the next street over, I can cross the yards and come up on the house from the back. The cops will never see me."

"You?" Shay asked.

"Yes."

"But I'm supposed to make the deliveries."

"And you hired me to help. Either we do it my way, or I drop you and the idols off, give you a quarter to call Sanders, and split? Take your pick."

Shay huffed.

"It's dark, it's mountainous, there's probably rattlesnakes and cougars prowling around. And besides, I need you for the decoy."

"Decoy?"

"Yeah. After I get out, you go back and act like you're lost. Get the cops attention while I sneak in the back way. They saw the car, but I don't think they could have seen who was driving or how many people were inside. Just make up a good story and it'll make sense."

She nodded.

"And come up with a story for why you have a cut on your face."

She nodded again.

Jackson pulled to the curb on the next street over, roughly parallel to 972 Green Summit Road. He'd have to cover about a hundred yards.

"After you leave the cops, come back here and wait for me," he said, taking the tote with the idols from her. "We'll call Sanders as soon as I get back, and he can confirm the delivery."

"Okay."

"Don't worry. This will work."

She nodded yet again.

He pointed to his cheek. "You figure out what you're going to tell the cops?"

"I'll, like, say I'm an actress or something. I can be on the way to a shoot."

"At midnight?"

Shay shrugged.

"Driving a '76 Granada?"

"It can be my, like, first gig."

Shay must have been feeling better, Jackson realized. Her Valspeak was coming back.

"I think we'd be better off saying you fell down the stairs," he said as he opened his door. "By the time you drive back around, I should be there. Don't stay any longer than you need to with the cops."

"Right."

He swung the door closed as she climbed into the driver's seat. He waited until she pulled away from the curb, then surveyed his surroundings. The terrain was dark, with a rocky outcropping across the street and strands and groves of trees splashed between residential properties. Most of the houses had gates barring the driveway, some with lights shining on the gate or address plate, some without. Most were far enough away from the road and from each other that Jackson could easily slip through the neighborhood unseen.

He hoped.

Darting through the darkness, he crossed the street and ran between two houses, then turned to his right, through a small thicket of underbrush and pines. He continued along the back of one property until he came to what he had calculated as the backyard of 972 Green Summit Road. He stopped for a second, again taking in his surroundings. There were two big oak trees in the opposite back corner and one immediately to his left. The house was dark except for light coming through two windows under the tree to his left and another light streaming through a pair of sliding glass doors, illuminating the back porch.

Jackson had taken two steps when he heard a growl. A pair of growls he saw as he turned to his left. He spotted two sets of incredibly white teeth that were visible even in the darkness. Rottweilers.

They charged. He ran.

Jackson reached the first tree to his right and shimmied up it. The hounds yapped at his heels, but he managed to grab a low branch and pull himself up before they got any flesh.

He climbed higher as the growling turned to barking, barking that would surely wake the owner of 972 Green Summit Road. And the cops parked out front. And the cops at every precinct in town.

That's when Jackson realized he had dropped the idols during his flight to the tree.

Chapter Twenty-One

Tuesday, May 15
12:29 a.m.

JACKSON WATCHED IN amazement and dread from his little canopy in the tree.

The porch light came on and a big silhouette emerged through the sliding glass doors. It belonged to a male, tall and husky, with a voice like thunder.

"Marcus, Howie, shut up!"

As the man stepped into the light, Jackson could see he wore a pair of black shorts and a light-colored sweatshirt. He held something in his hand, a mug maybe. And he was even huskier than Jackson had thought at first.

"What are you barking at?" the man growled with a tinge of a Texan accent.

Jackson thought he was far enough up to be hidden, at least until Husky aimed a flashlight at the tree. But to be safe, he tried to back farther into the branch he was sitting on/leaning against.

Marcus and Howie continued to bark, and Husky ambled off the porch and into the lawn. He stopped at the bottom of the tree and craned his neck. After gazing upward for a few seconds, he turned around. "If that's just a squirrel, I'm going to tan your hides!"

Tan your hides? Who was this guy, Yosemite Sam? And who named a Rottweiler Marcus? Or Howie? A Raiders fan, maybe?

"Get back inside," Husky said as he returned to the porch. The dogs started to follow but stopped as a commotion came from the side of the house. Two men ran into the yard, flashlights in hand. Marcus and Howie turned to them, snarling.

Before anyone had a chance to react, Shay came around the other side of the house. "Tyson, Jeremy, get back here!" She ran over to the dogs while Husky and the two men watched in astonishment.

Shay grabbed both of the dogs by their collars. Remarkably, they allowed themselves to be dragged backwards.

"What's going on here?" Husky asked.

"I'm so sorry," Shay said. "I don't know why they ran off like this. Come on!"

"Wait a minute!"

"These are your dogs, ma'am?" one of the men asked.

"Hey, who are you guys?" Husky asked. "What's going on?"

"Sir, I'm Detective Woodson. This is Detective Salinas. We heard the dogs and saw them chasing a man through your yard."

"A man?" Husky asked. "Is that what's up in that tree?"

"We can find out," Woodson said, turning his light toward Jackson's hiding spot.

"Hold on. Y'all investigate dogs chasing people? Is that what my tax dollars are going for?"

"We were conducting another investigation," Woodson replied.

"Sir," Salinas asked, "can we look in your tree?"

Jackson tightened. What explanation could he have for being in the tree? And why was Shay claiming to own Marcus and Howie/Tyson and Jeremy? And what about the idols, still lying in the tote in the middle of the lawn?

He decided to be proactive and began climbing down the tree. Immediately, a pair of flashlights lit the way.

"Keep those hounds back, Shay. You want to lower that light?"

"Sir, who are you?" Woodson asked.

"What are you doing in my tree?" Husky asked.

"Sorry about that, but those stupid dogs started after me." Safely on the ground, Jackson turned to Shay. "How many times do I have to tell you to keep those mongrels locked up!"

"Sir," Woodson interjected. "Who are you, and what were you doing in that tree?"

"I am the poor slob who married her sister," Jackson said. "And I was in this tree because of those two brutes."

"Tyson, Jeremy, stay."

At Shay's commands, the Rottweilers quieted the growling that had intensified ever since Jackson alighted from the tree.

"Will someone tell me what on earth is going on?" Husky asked.

"Be happy to," Jackson answered. "After Tess and I split, she moved in with Shay and the brothers Cujo here. Well, when she left, she took half my stuff with her. And since Tess won't return my calls," he said with a glare at Shay, as if it were her fault, "I stopped by to pick up a few things. I didn't expect to be run off like an intruder at a junkyard." He turned to Shay again. "You Sanders women are possessive, you know that!"

Jackson turned to Husky, hoping that dropping the name Sanders had clued him in. It at least gave him something to think about, judging by the fact that he took a step back, out of the conversation.

"Ma'am, do you live around here?" Woodson asked.

"On the next street over, Allen Park."

"Address?"

"Nine-four-seven."

Salinas wrote it down.

"Is what he said true?" Woodson asked. "Was he over tonight?"

"I was actually sleeping, so I don't know. But judging by the way Tyson and Jeremy are all worked up, I'd say so."

"And he is your sister's ex-husband?"

"Emphasize the 'ex' please."

And then it happened. For no other reason than being bored with his partner asking all the questions, Detective Salinas let his flashlight beam wander across the lawn and onto the tote bag.

"Is that what you were after?" he asked.

Jackson nodded. "Dropped it when the Baskervilles came after me." He started for the bag, but Salinas raised his flashlight beam like a laser.

"Hold on, sir. I'll get it."

"Suit yourself."

"I'm really sorry about this," Shay said to Husky. "I hope they didn't wake you."

"N-no. No, I was just having a nightcap," he said, holding up his mug.

Salinas returned with the tote and started to open it.

"Do you mind?" Jackson asked. "That's sort of private."

Salinas hesitated. "Is there a reason you don't want me to look in here?"

"Yeah. It's my stuff. Same reason I don't want anybody else to see it either. Same reason I didn't want my ex keeping it for three weeks after I told her I wanted it back."

"May I ask what's inside?"

"Sure, but I'm not telling."

Salinas looked at Woodson. Jackson looked at Shay. Marcus and Howie looked at Husky.

"Can I have my bag back?"

Woodson took a few steps forward. "Ma'am, is your sister home?"

"Um, no. Why?"

"Can you verify that these items belong to your brother-in-law?"

"Ex-brother-in-law," Jackson and Shay said simultaneously.

Shay took the bag, then very cutely, asked to borrow Salinas' flashlight. He handed it to her, and she peered into the bag. With disgust, she snapped off the light and closed the bag. "These? These are what you came over for, some stupid old high school bowling trophies?" She turned to the officers. "Yeah, they're his all right. Take them. I'm sure if Tess knew they were still in the house, she'd have thrown them out."

"Ma'am, are you all right?"

"Yeah."

Woodson raised his flashlight. "Your cheek, there's a cut."

"Oh," Shay said with a smile. "That would be Tyson. He gets a little rough sometimes. He's still just a pup. It's really just a scratch."

Woodson and Salinas again looked at each other. They were obviously uncomfortable with the situation, and if they were worth their powdered donuts, knew they were being conned. But they didn't have much recourse. Other than dragging everyone in for questioning and impounding the idols, which of course would lead to massive jail time for Jackson. He decided to push the issue while the detectives were indecisive.

"Can I have the bag?" he asked.

Salinas checked with Woodson for consent and handed the bag to Jackson. He clutched it firmly in his hands.

"I take it you have a car in the neighborhood?" Woodson asked.

"At her house."

"Ma'am, are you comfortable with him returning to your house?"

"Hey, I want to get out of here as quick as I can," Jackson said. "Don't worry about me."

"He'll be fine," Shay said. "He won't try anything. His lawyer's a real bozo."

"All right." Woodson turned to Husky. "Sorry to disturb you, sir."

"No trouble."

"Come on boys," Shay said, pulling at the dogs' collars. "Let's get you home."

To Jackson's surprise, they followed her around the side of the house toward the street.

"Maybe you should come this way," Woodson said. "Better than retracing your steps through the neighbors' yards. It is late, and these are private residences. We can give you a lift if need be."

"Yeah," Jackson said. He looked up at Husky. "Actually, you think I could trouble you for a drink of water or something? Running from those hounds can make a guy thirsty."

Husky nodded. "Yeah, sure."

Woodson and Salinas exchanged glances. The wool was sliding over their eyes, and Jackson was afraid they'd change their minds.

"We'll be headed out," Woodson said after leveling stern gazes at Jackson and Husky. "Sorry again for the trouble."

Husky nodded, and he and Jackson watched them leave. When they rounded the corner of the house, Husky and Jackson exchanged glances. Husky's eyes then dropped to the bag in Jackson's hand. "You want to come on in?"

Jackson nodded. "Yeah."

He followed him through the sliding glass doors and into a lavish, rustically decorated dining room. Husky closed the doors behind them and drew the blinds. Jackson stood anxiously, worrying about Shay. How was she controlling the dogs? Would the cops just let her go, without following her to make sure she returned to 947 Allen Park Drive? Was there even a 947 Allen Park Drive? And what would she do with Marcus and Howie?

"You were supposed to be here three hours ago," Husky said.

"Sorry, we ran into a snafu. You weren't supposed to have vice sitting out front."

"Cops are watching the neighbors down the street. Rumor is they have a meth lab."

"It takes all kinds."

Husky didn't laugh. "What's your friend going to do with my dogs anyhow?"

"I'm not sure. Right now, they're probably soiling the backseat of my car."

"She must be good with animals," Husky said, pulling out a chair. He nodded for Jackson to take a seat across from him, which he did. "Marcus and Howie don't take to many folks."

"I noticed."

"Yeah, sorry. I let 'em out to pee. Usually they don't find anyone to chase at this hour."

Jackson shrugged, anxious to get the exchange over with.

"Okay, let's get to it."

Jackson set the tote on the table and slid it across to Husky. He wasted no time reaching into it and pulling out the carvings. There was no surprise on his face, no questions asked. He simply turned the idol over in his hands. Then he twisted at the base, and pulled off the bottom of the idol like the cap on a can of Pringles.

Out fell two little bags of white powder.

Cocaine.

"Y'all don't mind if I test it, do you?"

Jackson shook his head. "Knock yourself out."

183

Husky got up from the table, walked into the kitchen, and returned with a knife at least twice as large as was necessary. It was practically a cleaver.

He slit the end of one of the bags and inserted the point of the knife into the opening, pulling out a tiny trace of the powder. He dabbed it with his finger, lifted the finger to his mouth, and ran it along the inside of his lip, against the gum. Just like the guys on TV always did. Jackson hoped it was the good stuff.

After a moment, Husky set down the knife and sat back. "Okay. We're good. But tell Sanders we need to work out a new delivery method."

"You got that right."

"Now I just need my dogs."

"Well, I'm hoping my friend is parked one street over with Snoopy and Spike. If so, and if the coast is clear, she can walk them back."

Husky nodded. "I'll wait up."

Jackson met his eyes. "I'll go check on her right now."

Another nod as Jackson stood up. "That was quick thinking out there. Nice work."

"Yeah, you too." He almost felt like shaking hands with the man, like they were buddies now. User and supplier.

Before Jackson left, Husky went to the front of the house and checked to make sure the Crown Victoria was gone. It was, and he let Jackson out via the sliding glass doors in back. Jackson wasted no time, dashing through the yard and to the relative safety of the scrub behind Husky's neighbor's house. It was anyone's guess where Woodson and Salinas had gone, and all he needed was for them to be circling the neighborhood and find him slinking through the weeds.

He emerged on Allen Park Drive and found the street quiet. Better yet, he saw the Granada parked two houses down, and he hurried to check on Shay. She was waiting with a very patient Marcus and Howie. That was until they saw Jackson. Then they began to snarl.

"Quiet," Shay said over her shoulder, and immediately they lowered their heads in shame.

"Hey, Sis," Jackson said. "Nice going back there."

Shay grinned. "Thanks."

"How'd you know to come in like that?"

"I was driving by, like we planned, and I saw the cops going around the far side of the house."

"So you decided to join the party?"

"I figured something had gone wrong and . . . If it was your brother?"

Jackson nodded and shook off the invading thought. "Speaking of cops," he said, "any sign of Sonny and Rico?"

"No, the street's quiet. So did you make the delivery?"

"Yeah. It's legit, by the way. We're now drug traffickers."

"We've been drug traffickers since ten-thirty this morning," she replied, no happier about it than he was.

"Well, Hoss wants Adam and Little Joe back. I'd take them, but I'd come back with a pair of stubs."

"I can do it," Shay said.

"All right. He'll be waiting by the back porch. You see anything suspicious, release the hounds and double time it back here. Got it?"

"Got it."

Jackson stood back as Shay coaxed Marcus and Howie out of the backseat. He watched until she disappeared in the void between houses, and then inspected the backseat of the car. Hairy, it was otherwise clean. The smell was another factor.

Jackson anxiously waited out the minutes. Woodson and Salinas had to have seen Shay get into the car with the dogs, and even if they didn't remember it from earlier, they wouldn't forget it now. And there couldn't be many red Granadas in the neighborhood. The sooner they were far away, the better.

While Husky was fetching the knife to test the cocaine, Jackson had noticed a grandfather clock in the living room. It had read twenty till one. It now dawned on Jackson that it was no longer his birthday. He had survived. The Scotch was untouched. He hadn't drunk himself into a coma or driven off a cliff or anything dramatic. Maybe, just maybe, there was a chance he could live a reasonably normal life after all.

Dealing drugs. Killing gangsters. Dodging cops all the while. Normal indeed.

Shay returned, minus the Rottweilers, and slid into the seat next to Jackson.

"Let's get out of here," he said.

"Can I have your phone? To call Sanders?"

He fished it from his pocket, and while she dialed, he started the car and headed for home. With any luck, this guy Sanders and the Grays would let her brother go, he would get into rehab and clean up his life, Jackson would never see either of them again, and he wouldn't have to answer for the lives he'd taken, either to the police or to some gang lord.

"Hi, it's Shay."

Jackson snapped his head to the side to follow her conversation.

"Yeah, just now. It took longer than I thought because there were cops there. . . . Yeah, they were, like, undercover." Jackson heard Sanders swear, and Shay moved the phone from her ear. She had to interrupt him to continue. "No, it's okay. They totally didn't know. It just took us longer. . . . I am. Trust me. Call him and see. . . . Can I talk to Blake? . . . But you—"

Jackson turned his head. Shay looked panicked. "I, um, lost my phone . . . I borrowed it . . ."

After a short pause, she lowered the phone.

"What happened?" Jackson asked.

"He said he would call back after confirming the delivery."

"What about Blake?"

She shook her head. "He didn't say."

Before he knew it, Jackson had reached out and taken Shay's hand in his. "It'll be okay."

"You don't know that."

No, he didn't. Gang leaders were low on the scale of trustworthiness. Sanders had nothing to gain by letting Blake go. But somehow, Jackson had to keep Shay's hopes up as long as they had a chance.

He dropped her hand. "Did he say how long till he calls back?"

"No. Just to keep the phone."

"Okay," Jackson said. "So now we wait."

Chapter Twenty-Two

1:14 a.m.

SANDERS CALLED JUST as Jackson was pulling into his driveway. The neighborhood was quiet. Then again, it was quarter after one in the morning. Shay's convertible was right where she had left it. Next door at Connie's, the party had died down. It was fifty-fifty if Gina had come home.

Shay still had the phone on her lap, and as Jackson killed the engine, she answered it.

"Hello? . . . Like, duh. . . . Sorry. . . . Hahn Park? That's, like, in half an hour. . . . Yes. . . . Yes. . . . I will. . . . "

"What'd he say?" Jackson asked as soon as she closed the phone.

"I'm supposed to go to Hahn Park at quarter till two. Alone."

"The park? What part? It's huge."

"He said there was a pull-off on the dirt road just south of the water tower, near the TV tower."

Jackson nodded.

"We'd better get going," Shay said.

"I want some answers first."

"Answers? To what?"

"To questions that have been bugging me all day."

"Jackson, this is not the time."

"I can be at Hahn Park in twenty minutes. We have time."

Shay huffed. "What do you want to know?"

"For starters, how you knew that was a cop car in front of the Hulk's."

"I told you, I watch TV."

"*The Simple Life* doesn't count. And how about the fact that you just conveniently hired me, a person with a past you could manipulate?"

187

"I told you, I'm not stupid, Jackson."

"No, I don't think you are. Running in to rescue me from the dogs, playing it cool with the cops. And I didn't take you for a Rottweiler charmer, either."

"So you just assume because I'm perky and pretty that I must be an airhead, is that it? That I can't possibly have any talents or any brains?"

"No. I assumed you were an airhead because you acted like one all day. Now all of the sudden you're observant, bold, quick on your feet."

Shay looked away.

"And what happened to your accent?"

"What?" she asked softly, still looking out the window.

"You so totally have, like, stopped talking like you're so totally from, like, the Valley."

Shay lowered her head, but didn't face Jackson.

"If Blake really is your brother, and his life really is on the line, don't you think you should tell me everything—tell me the truth?"

Her voice was so soft it was almost indistinguishable. "Blake's not my brother."

"Who is he?"

"My partner."

"Your partner?"

Shay nodded slightly, still facing away from Jackson.

"You mean you guys are dating or something?"

"No, I mean he's my partner. We're cops. Undercover."

Jackson let that sink in for a moment. That's how she had recognized Woodson and Salinas as cops. That's how she had checked him out as a private eye. That's how she had known how to react at Husky's house when things were going sideways.

"You're a cop?" he repeated.

She nodded and turned her head. "I'm sor—"

Jackson shoved open his door and got out of the car. He paced several steps away, to the edge of the driveway. He heard Shay open her door and get out too.

"I'm sorry, Jackson."

He turned around. "Sorry? I could have been killed tonight! You've got me delivering drugs, lying to cops, getting mixed up with half the gangs in L.A., and you're sorry! I've had it. Get out of here!"

"Blake's life really is in danger."

"A lot of lives are in danger," he said. "Now including mine, thanks to you!"

She started to walk around the car, but Jackson put up a hand.

"Stay where you are."

"What?"

"I've never hit a girl before, but if you come over here, that might change."

"Jackson."

"Don't 'Jackson' me. Just go."

Staring him down, she walked around the car, stopping inches in front of him. "You want to hit me, fine. Hit me."

He was tempted.

"I'm sorry I lied to you, but I did what I thought I had to do."

"You thought playing Elle Woods gave you a better chance than telling it to me straight?"

"It's not that simple, Jackson."

"Why not?"

"Because it's not. It's complicated. And I'll explain everything—the truth, I promise. But can I do it while we're on the way to the park?"

Jackson shook his head. "I'm not going to the park."

"Why? Because of pride? Because I lied? A man's life hangs in the balance. What difference does it make what his name is or who I am? And he's not a druggie, Jackson. He's one of L.A.'s finest."

"Then why aren't you talking to L.A.'s finest right now?"

"It's a long story. Please, Jackson."

He clenched his jaw, gritting his teeth. Shay had the power to seduce him with her vibrant, vulnerable blue eyes. She (whatever her name really was) could also do it by staring with those same eyes, steely and strong, and now seemingly a shade darker blue.

Dropping his head, Jackson muttered his assent. "Let's go."

"We should take my car. He'll be suspicious if I show up in this."

"How you going to start your car? Weren't your keys in your purse?"

"There's a spare set attached under the bumper."

She quickly retrieved the keys and they got into her convertible. Shay took the wheel and tore off, likely waking half of Pacific Palisades in the process.

"I take it you know how to get there?" Jackson asked.

"GPS. Unless you know a quicker route."

"Take Sunset to Chautauqua to the PCH. Then take the freeway to La Cienega."

"Roger."

Jackson sat back into his seat, letting the tension of the day drain out of him. Or trying to let it, rather. It wouldn't go.

"Shay" brushed hair out of her face, not with the delicate flip of several fingers she had used earlier, but by raking her hand through her blond locks. She looked different too. She still was dressed like a model for Claire's, still had makeup on the cheek Jackson hadn't washed, and still was naturally beautiful. But gone was the Valley Girl façade. It was as if her mask had crumbled, revealing the hard-nosed, stone-faced cop underneath. If Jackson could be so bold as to judge the book by its cover.

They turned onto Chautauqua.

"So, Shay, what's your real name?"

"Ashley."

"Ashley," he repeated. "And Blake?"

"Detective Dylan O'Brien."

"You said you'd explain everything," Jackson said. "Go for it."

"Should we maybe come up with a plan first? They said for me to come alone. We should figure out how we want to play this? I think—"

"No, I want the story first."

"But—"

"No buts. We may not have to worry about how to play it because you may end up playing alone. Spill."

Ashley sighed. "LAPD's known for a while that the Grays have been dealing all kinds of drugs, but they've had no hard evidence. They run a major auto parts business, but that appears to be on the level. And they've got fingers in a lot of pies, but we've got nothing we can make stick. Anyhow, last fall LAPD made the decision to try to put a mole inside the Grays. They picked Dylan. We're talking deep cover here, Jackson. *Point Break*. It took him till Christmas just to get his foot in the door. DED was almost ready to pull the plug."

"DED?"

"Drug Enforcement Division." She looked at him, raising her eyebrow at the seriousness of the situation. "As Dylan's partner, I'm the go-between. This isn't cute nine-to-five work. He became Blake Carmichael, a spoiled kid who took a turn for the worse after his parents died."

"Go on."

"Dylan couldn't just drive back to HQ and give a report, so he would call me. I was his kid sister, his only friend in the world. I had the alias all set, practiced being all Shay-ey, bought these stupid clothes and nail polish and everything. But I was never supposed to get involved. At worst, one of Sanders' thugs might talk to me on the phone or tap our conversations. But we had codes worked out. We were prepared."

"What went wrong?"

"DED got impatient. Three months went by, with Dylan feeding them a steady diet of info through me, and they wanted to call it quits again. They said they'd gotten everything out of him that they could, that they would need to do a lot more groundwork before they could take Sanders and the Grays down."

She shook her head in disgust. "Dylan argued that he should stay in place, serve as a mole through the whole operation. He was committed, long term. He had done too much work to quit, knowing that once he was out, the odds of ever getting to Sanders were slim. They went back and forth—through me—for several weeks. Then somebody at DED floated the idea that Dylan had turned. You know, gotten in too deep. They worried that he didn't want to leave because he was enjoying the perks of being part of the Grays."

"Drugs?"

"Cocaine. He's been using for six months, as little as possible, but he had to be convincing."

"Is that . . . sanctioned?"

Ashley made eye contact. "Officially, no. But he had authorization."

Jackson nodded. "Is it possible? That he turned?"

"Absolutely not! Dylan is the best police officer I know. He's one of the best people I know! There's no way."

"You said he was on coke for six months. That changes a—"

"No, Jackson! Not a chance!"

"Okay." He sat back and shrugged. "So what happened next?"

Ashley took a deep breath. "DED gave him an ultimatum. Get out, or we cut you off."

"Seems harsh."

"It was. And Dylan chose to stay. I don't know, maybe he didn't think they meant it. But he was convinced he was doing important work, that with him inside, we had a chance to get Sanders."

"And DED cut him off?"

She nodded. "They ordered me out, assigned me to desk duty until Dylan came out of cover. I didn't know what to think. I trust Dylan with my life, but I have to obey orders. I told him, best I could, what was happening, and told him he could still call me in an emergency. That was late last month. I didn't hear from again until last night. Well, Sunday night."

"What'd he say?"

"Not much. I'm pretty sure they were listening. But he said there were three deliveries that he was supposed to make, and didn't, and Sanders was going to kill him unless I made them for him. I was still in character, as his sister. Apparently Sanders bought it and was willing to let me try to save Dylan. That much is true."

"Are you sure?"

"Am I sure what?"

"That Sanders bought it. Are you sure he doesn't know Dylan's a cop?"

"Dylan never would have called me if he thought Sanders knew. He wouldn't risk it."

Jackson nodded. "When he called you, did you go to DED?"

"No. I thought about it, but they've cut ties with him after he called their bluff. They're convinced now that he's turned. I don't think they'd do anything anyhow, except maybe give me more grief so that I couldn't help Dylan. I'm his only chance, Jackson. We are."

"So why me?" Jackson asked. "Why'd you have to hire a private eye?"

"Look at me. I'm five-five and a buck-ten soaking wet. This is my first undercover role, and I'm the equivalent of Woman Number Three. Talking on the phone like a drip is one thing. Making deliveries is another."

"You needed muscle?"

Ashley nodded.

"And you picked me? There's got to be a gorilla-for-sale firm somewhere?"

"I did some checking, Jackson. Your arrest is public record, you know."

"And what, you wanted somebody who was part of the drug culture or something?"

"I wanted somebody who might understand. Who wouldn't drop me if they found out the truth."

He looked out the window, then back at her. "So why not the truth? Why'd you have to keep up the persona?"

"Because for all I know, Sanders has had people watching me all day. He thought Blake Carmichael had a Beverly Hills sister named Shay. I had to play the role. I figured it would be easier if I played it for everyone."

Jackson shook his head. "And you didn't think after you were kidnapped and tortured that maybe it was time to own up?"

"Nothing changed, Jackson. Sanders could still be watching me. For all I know, he's watching us now."

"So who were those guys at the warehouse? Any idea?"

Ashley shook her head. "Your guess is as good as mine. I don't know any more than I've told you. This time." She turned her head, dipping it slightly, her smile a mixture of puppy and provocateur.

Jackson looked away, determined to make a decision uninfluenced by her eyes.

"What do you say?" There was a hint of gravel in her voice as she asked it, reminding him just a little of the way Maggie pleaded to get her way. And like with Maggie, he ultimately capitulated.

"Okay," he said. "But if I find out that you so much as mispronounced a word of what you just told me, I will drive you over to Sanders' crib and duct tape you and your badge to his front door, got it?"

She smiled undaunted. "Got it."

Chapter Twenty-Three

1:33 a.m.

"FIRST THING," JACKSON said, "we need to know exactly where we're going. Can I have my phone?"

Ashley retrieved it from her pocket and handed it to him, and he calculated the odds of Mouse still being awake. One-thirty wasn't late if he was into a video game. With Pam gone, it was likely.

Six rings. Then, "Yeah?"

"Mouse, you still awake?"

"Mmm."

"I need one more favor, pal."

He groaned. "I'm not hacking into anything."

"I just need a satellite feed."

"Like Google satellite feed or NASA?"

"Google will be fine," Jackson replied. "I need to know the layout of Hahn Park."

"Give me a minute."

"No problem."

"So what are you and your lady friend up to?" Mouse asked.

"Dealing drugs."

"Funny."

"You got the map?"

"Coming up right now," Mouse answered. "Okay, what do you need to know?"

"We're supposed to find a dirt road that goes past a water tower."

"Give me a minute," Mouse repeated. "Okay, yeah, here it is."

"Then there's a pull-off south of the water tower, by a TV tower or something."

"Yeah, about a hundred yards."

"Okay, what's around it?"

"Nothing, man. Just grass on the east, some trees across the road on the west."

"How far are the trees from the road?"

"From the road, not far. From the pull-off, probably twenty, twenty-five yards."

"Agh. Okay, how do we get there?"

"Quickest way is probably the entrance off of La Cienega," Mouse answered. "Follow that around until you get to a stand of TV towers. It's your second right. And . . . there might be a gate."

"Might?"

"It shows up on one angle, not the other."

"Great. How far is this pull-off from the edge of the park?"

"Couple hundred yards, at least, to the east side. Farther south."

"Okay. Thanks."

"Yeah, man. Should I take the cordless to bed?"

"Night, Mouse."

Jackson closed the phone.

"Well?" Ashley asked.

"One of three things happens when we get there," Jackson said. "A, they're really going to let Dylan go, in which case he'll be there, but probably nobody else. They wouldn't risk getting caught. B, no one will be there, and they're just making sure you follow directions before they actually release him to you somewhere else. Or C, it's a trap, and we probably get shot."

Ashley processed for a minute. "Okay, we should—"

"Nope," Jackson said. "We do it my way."

"Did you forget I'm a police officer?"

"Did you forget?" he asked. "You're the one who hired me, so that means we do it my way or I walk. And by the way, I've changed my billing policy. This is officially day two."

"Okay then, what's your plan?"

Jackson held up his gun, checking the ammo. He had used nine bullets in the warehouse, leaving him six and the extra magazine. Not much if he was going up against a gang, no doubt armed to the teeth. But it was all he had. He shouldn't have discarded the extra guns at the warehouse.

"Well?" she asked.

"You got a lot of junk in your trunk?"

"Excuse me?"

Jackson gestured with his thumb. "Of the car. Is it empty?"

"Yeah, mostly. Why?"

"Because I don't know where else to hide. I could get out before we get to the rendezvous and hide in the trees, but if something comes up and you have to leave in a hurry, I'm stuck in the trees. Plus, they'll likely be watching us anyhow."

"So what can you do in the trunk?"

"This thing have an inside release lever?"

"I don't know."

"Pull over."

"What?"

"Pull over," Jackson said. "I want to check it out."

"We don't have time. Besides, you can get in through the backseat. It folds down."

Jackson unbuckled his seatbelt, reclined the seat, and climbed into the cramped backseat of the convertible. It took him a moment to find the loop that pulled the left half of the backseat downward, enabling him to climb into the trunk.

"Any chance you've got a light in here?" Jackson asked.

"Um, yeah. There's a flashlight in the glove." Ashley reached over and opened the glove compartment, then handed a tiny penlight back to Jackson. With it, he crawled into the trunk. It was tight, but he was able to fit and look around. And sure enough, there was an inside release latch for the trunk.

Jackson reached back for his gun, which he had left on the seat. Then he began hammering at one of Ashley's taillights until it came loose. Grabbing the wires, he pulled the broken light out and twisted his body so that he was positioned to look out the opening. Almost immediately, he was nearly blinded by the headlights of a passing car.

"Okay, we're set," he said, climbing back to the seat. It wasn't a big opening, but it would give him some vision and a better chance to hear anything that was said. It also wasn't an ideal plan, but given the time constraints and the geography of their meeting place, it was about all he could come up with. At least he would be with Ashley.

Jackson remained in back, leaning forward as she drove. "So what's this Sanders guy look like?" he asked.

"He's tall, well built. Light brown skin, short black hair, usually a goatee. Narrow, narrow eyes."

"So he looks like every other thug in L.A."

"I guess."

"You know anybody else in the gang?"

"Just Sanders."

La Cienega Boulevard was the first exit east on I-10, and less than two minutes after taking it, they arrived at the entrance to Hahn Park.

Covering over three hundred acres in the center of the city, the Kenneth Hahn State Recreation Area boasted walking trails, sports courts, picnic areas, and magnificent views of downtown Los Angeles and the Pacific Ocean. Lakes stocked with trout and catfish, a Japanese garden, and four playgrounds made the park a welcome attraction for all ages. During the day. At night, it was home to foxes, skunks, raccoons, and apparently drug runners.

"Just keep following this road for a while," Jackson said, hunched down in the backseat so he could just see over the dashboard. Ashley's headlights cut an eerie glow through an otherwise dark park. Gangsters aside, Jackson was sure they weren't the only humans in the park, but he didn't want to know about the other recreators either.

After a minute, they turned almost due east. Up ahead on the left side of the road, several metal towers loomed over the treetops. "You think one of them is the TV tower?" Ashley asked.

"No, I don't think so. Mouse said we'd have to take our second right."

Moments later they spied a pair of roads running south. The first was paved and straight, leading past what looked like maintenance buildings. The second was paved for a short while, long enough for a parking lot to loop around to the side. Then the road turned to a dirt path.

"The yellow brick road," Jackson said. He scrunched a little farther down. "You see a gate?"

"Yeah," Ashley answered. "But it's open."

"Wonderful. Either they're negligent on security or somebody else is already here."

The path ran nearly parallel to the paved road for several hundred yards. When both roads reached a large white water tower on the right-hand side, the paved road turned sharply west, while the dirt path veered slightly east. Not long later, Ashley's headlights swept over an open field of grass. Cutting into the field was a dirt turnout that rejoined the path a hundred or so feet down.

"There's a car," Ashley said. "Black, four-door. Oldsmobile maybe."

"Take the turnout," Jackson said, "and stop in front of their car. Don't look my way, and don't get out of the car until you see Dylan."

She nodded.

"If you hear any shots or if I come out of the trunk, drop to the ground and stay there, got it?"

"Got it."

"We'll make it, Ashley."

That was all he had time to say before scrambling back into the trunk and pulling the seat back into place. Alone in the dark, he clicked the safety on his gun off and waited. He heard two car doors open and close. Then all was quiet. He waited some more.

A sudden tap made Jackson jump. He realized it was knuckles rapping on Ashley's window, and he strained to hear what came next.

"Where's Blake?" Ashley asked.

"In the Olds," a man answered.

"Can I see him?"

"Yeah. Get out the car, shorty."

"Not until I see Blake."

The man said something, but Jackson couldn't make it out. He didn't like where this was going already. If the Grays were going to turn Dylan over, they'd turn him over. Push him out of a car and run. This wasn't an exchange;

Ashley had nothing to offer them. There was no reason for her to get out of the car to come see Dylan, unless these guys were up to something.

"Look, a'ight, I ain't bringing him to you till you get out the car."

"And I am not getting out until I see my brother."

There was more talking that Jackson couldn't make out, and then he heard the man's voice again. "Last chance."

Ashley didn't respond, and Jackson willed his ears to hear something. A car door opened, then closed softly. Had she gotten out?

Jackson tensed, waiting for any sign that he should come out of the trunk. He moved his head close to the popped out taillight, hoping to catch some additional sounds. There was nothing.

The seconds ticked by. Finally he heard voices again. Two men, it sounded like. One approached, his voice rising. Jackson couldn't make out the words, and then the voices stopped. A moment later, the car door opened and closed again.

Was Ashley back? Jackson realized then that they should have worked out an all clear signal.

The car started and made a reverse Y-turn. It was the right speed for Ashley—or rather Shay—but Jackson was worried. There had only been one door opening and closing. If Ashley was the driver, Dylan wasn't with her. And if Ashley wasn't the driver, who was and where was she?

Jackson turned so that he could look out the taillight hole. He saw headlights following them as they bounced along the dirt path and turned onto the main park road. They left much quicker than they had come in, and soon were headed south on La Cienega.

Not the way they had come.

Jackson thought about risking a peek. It was dark, and there was a good chance the driver—if it wasn't Ashley—wouldn't spot him. But if he was spotted, it could be trouble. Maybe Ashley was in the other car, forced to ride with one of Sanders' thugs to Dylan's location while somebody else drove her car. Unlikely, but Jackson didn't want to take the chance.

In minutes, they were on the freeway, still going south. Jackson heard a jet pass overhead and deduced they were just east of LAX. A pair of headlights had remained behind them, but Jackson wasn't sure if it was the Oldsmobile or some other car that had gotten in line when they merged onto La Cienega. Whoever it was, they were keeping a steady pace.

After several minutes of flying down the freeway, Jackson again weighed his options. He could burst through the backseat, gun drawn, and demand answers from whoever was driving. Or he could wait and let things play out. Since he didn't know what he was up against, or where Ashley was and whose custody she was in, he settled on the latter. If and when they got somewhere, still having the element of surprise would work in his favor.

And so he rode for what he guessed was fifteen minutes, all on the freeway. Finally, the car began to slow. It made a few quick turns, and Jackson concluded they had left the interstate. Peeks out the back weren't much help, other than to inform him that they were now alone. The tail car had dropped off. And wherever they were, it was deserted. They were still in town, but Jackson guessed an industrial sector. Close to the port, perhaps?

They coasted to a stop, and Jackson thought he heard a door open. He tensed, his gun again at the ready. His thumb went to the safety, which he had turned back on when they started moving. Now, in an instant, he could flip it off and be ready to shoot whatever came at him.

But nothing did. First the motor revved, then the car shot forward with a jolt. Jackson had a sinking feeling in his stomach, one that quickly increased when the car crashed into something. Whatever it was, it only slowed the car for an instant. Then the vehicle was airborne.

Jackson braced himself, knowing what was coming next.

The car flew through the air for several seconds and landed with a soft thud. Jackson's body was hurled toward the front end of the trunk, and he was saved from losing consciousness only because he had protected his head with his arms.

Pain seared through his elbows, shoulders, hips, and knees. But it paled in comparison to the fear that hit him with the same force as the crashing car.

As water started to rush in through the hole where the taillight had once been, Jackson felt the car beginning to sink at a forty-five-degree angle, front first. He was right, they had taken the freeway to the docks. And he was pretty sure that Ashley's car had just been driven off a pier into the Pacific Ocean.

*   *   *

Five years ago . . .
Friday, May 25
7:27 p.m.

"ARE YOU still fretting over this afternoon?" Hannah asked. The theater part of dinner theater was at intermission—the stage having gone dark except for a few flickering tiki torches—and David and Grant were back at the buffet line getting seconds.

"No," Jackson said, although it had nagged at him from time to time. "Just thinking about home."

"Do you have to work Monday?"

"Eight a.m."

"Hard coming back from vacations, isn't it?"

"Worse than going is good sometimes, I think."

"Best advice," Hannah said, leaning forward, "is just get back to your routine as quickly as possible. It's a fine line between fondly remembering and hanging on."

Jackson winced.

"Too corny?" she asked.

"No, your lei's in your barbecue sauce."

Hannah made a face as she sat back and inspected the lei. Then she lifted it to her mouth and licked the sauce off in a cute way only his mom could.

Jackson took a long pull on his iced tea and sat back as he set the glass down. "I don't know. It's just been like this has been the be all-end all to look forward to, and now that it's over . . . what's next? Grant has his dream career ahead of him, and you and dad have a Navy retirement villa in South Florida, I'm sure."

"Hey," Hannah said with mock affront. "That's a ways off."

"For me, it's just back to the grind."

"We'll go on vacation again," Hannah said.

"Sure. Except how much longer until Grant has his own family that he goes on vacation with? Then I just tag along with the two of you on empty-nester cruises?"

"Absolutely not," David said, pulling back his chair and sliding up to the table. His plate was piled full again.

"Honey, they're going to charge you extra on the flight tomorrow."

"That's only for luggage." He draped his napkin over his lap. "Your near-death experience trigger a midlife crisis, Son?"

"I'm just kind of tired of not knowing where my life is going," Jackson answered.

"Finally, you've caught up to the rest of us," Grant said as he sat down.

"Is there anyone else eavesdropping over my shoulder?"

"Yeah, but they don't seem too interested."

"Grant," Hannah scolded.

He shrugged and started on a pork rib.

"You know there is another option," Hannah said.

"What's that?"

"You could start a family of your own."

Grant looked up.

"We've already got you married off to some bossy lady sergeant," Jackson said. "And I'm not exactly ready for a family."

"Here, here," Grant said.

"I'm not just screwing around for screwing around's sake," Jackson said. "Some of us aren't blessed with a life calling straight out of the womb."

"Don't rush it, sweetie. Keep praying, keep obeying, and God will show you His will."

"Yeah."

"There's always the Navy," David said, dabbing his mouth with his napkin.

"Tried that once."

"That was the Army. The Navy's a whole different world."

"Stop recruiting, David," Hannah said. "One son in the line of danger is enough."

Grant smiled. "Maybe you could be a librarian, Jack, or a secretary or something."

"I'll let you all decide my fate," Jackson said, scooting back from the table. "I'm going to get some more to eat before Kamehameha's revenge starts."

"Not so bad, is it?" Grant asked.

"No. In fact, I don't think we'd have even needed to stop for tacos," Jackson said with a smirk. He wore it all the way to the buffet line, and was about to start piling *huli-huli* chicken onto his plate when he felt a tap on the shoulder. He turned to see Becky.

"Hey," he said, smiling immediately. It faded when he saw her frown. "Still not get a hold of your dad?"

"No, and I'm getting worried. I'm actually catching a ride back with the Halvorsens." Chet and Shirley, an older couple from Missouri, had been on several of the same excursions as Becky and the Douglas family. He was an old windbag with a bad accent, and Jackson didn't envy her the ride.

"That's why I came, to say goodbye."

Jackson set down his plate and met her baby blues for a second. "It was nice knowing you," he said.

"Yeah, you too."

"I'll look for you on election day."

"Yeah, right."

"If you're ever in San Diego, we'll meet up for some air hockey."

"And if you're ever in Topeka . . ." She shook her head. "Why would you be in Topeka?"

They both smiled for a moment and made eye contact again. It was the look of two people who had struck up a friendship, who given time might have struck up something more, but who would likely never see each other again. It was *Casablanca*, two ships in the night, blah, blah, blah. Jackson felt like a teenager leaving summer camp.

He took a mental snapshot of Becky—her mischievous eyes and playful smile, confident but smooth jaw line, and golden hair swept across bare shoulders by the island breeze. The last waning orange and pink rays of daylight created a beautiful backdrop, and the soft glow of tiki torches and gentle strains of the string quartet playing dinner music made it a moment he wouldn't soon forget.

So too did Becky when she reached out and gave him a quick hug. It was their first physical interaction, other than a playful slap on the shoulder or a fist bump during *NBA Jam* in the arcade, and it made Jackson wish for more than just a vacation encounter. But such was life.

"Where's Grant?" Becky asked when they separated a second later.

Jackson pointed him out at the table.

Becky raised her eyebrows. "Guess that's it."

"Yeah. I'm sure your dad's all right."

She nodded. "Thanks."

"Take care," Jackson said.

"You too."

He held up a hand to wave as she turned to leave. He stood and watched her through the crowd until she reached the table. She said a few words to Grant, hugged him too, and then was gone.

The drums started again, announcing intermission was over. Jackson picked up his plate and returned to the buffet line. But he found his appetite was gone. Childish as it may have been, he missed Becky, and saying goodbye to her was just adding to his post-vacation doldrums. Plus, snatches of their conversation were coming back to him.

"I can't get a hold of Dad," she said.

"He's not here?"

"Senator Dennis had a last-minute schedule change."

"Still, I thought he'd have time to return my call by now," she said.

"When'd you last talk to him?"

"Little before four."

"I'm surprised the police let you go already," she said when they were finished.

"They had to rush out to a . . . what's a Code 10 anyhow?" Jackson asked Grant.

"In California, it's a bomb threat."

"Bomb threat?" Becky asked.

"Yeah, over in Waianae."

"Busy day."

Jackson scooped some chicken and a few ribs onto his plate and headed back to the table as the second half of the play began. He stopped in his tracks, remembering his parents' words:

"Waianae . . . All the way across the island."

"The whole police force must have been out."

Suddenly it made sense.

A purposefully botched robbery that became a hostage situation, thanks in part to one of the hostages. A bomb threat on the other side of the island at almost the same time, the combined crimes diverting the majority of Oahu's police force away from Honolulu. A U.S. senator about to embark on a presidential campaign making a last-minute schedule change. One of his primary aides going silent and not returning his daughter's phone calls and texts. And David's old Naval Intelligence C.O. calling him in the middle of a family vacation in Hawaii.

Jackson hurried to the table and dropped his plate. He scooted his chair close to his father's. "I think I know what's going on."

David slowly turned away from the stage. "What's that? Going on with what?"

"Everything today."

Hannah and Grant had also turned their attention to Jackson.

"I think something's happened to Senator Dennis."

Chapter Twenty-Four

2:17 a.m.

LETTING THINGS PLAY out, then, had been a mistake. Maybe too had been the decision to hide in the trunk to begin with. Jackson should have done a stop, drop, and roll out of the car when Ashley turned onto the dirt road at the park and hidden in the trees. What, if anything, he could have done was unknown, but at least he wouldn't be sinking toward the bottom of the ocean.

At impact, Jackson had dropped the gun. Now he felt it under his back. At least it hadn't discharged. More importantly, his flailing hand had felt the flashlight. But as the car twisted and floated downward, it rolled away from his fingers and into the water that was quickly rising in the trunk. The more that came in, the heavier the car got, the faster the car sunk, and the more water came in. Jackson had to hurry.

Contorting his body in the small trunk, Jackson delved his hand into the water, feeling around for the flashlight. The seconds were agonizing as he groped blindly through the water, still being jostled as the car settled deeper into the ocean. When the water was almost to his chin, Jackson's fingers finally grabbed hold of the light. Despite being wet, it clicked on, and Jackson quickly found the inside release mechanism for the trunk.

He tucked his gun into the back of his jeans, pushed the flashlight into his pocket, and took a deep breath. Then he readied himself for the deluge that would come as soon as the trunk opened.

With one hand, Jackson took hold of the release and pulled on the small tab. With the other, he pushed upward on the trunk, fighting against the force of the water. He lost.

The trunk opened, but gallons of murky ocean water came pouring in, knocking Jackson backward. His head cracked against the rim of the trunk, and his last thought was that he was going to pass out and never wake up. His life was over. Just a few more moments until . . .

Except he didn't pass out.

Somehow he remained conscious, and after several seconds, the cobwebs cleared. The trunk was open, held so by the water that had quickly filled every void. Jackson forced himself up, wriggled through the opening, and used his rudimentary swimming skills to kick toward the surface. His shoes, heavy jeans, and baggy sweatshirt all slowed him down, and he wondered if he had become disoriented underwater. Maybe he was swimming sideways until his breath gave out and he really did die.

But the water grew slightly clearer. The dark of night was lighter than the dark of the ocean floor, and Jackson realized he was going to reach the surface. He was going to make it.

With fire in his lungs, Jackson burst through the surface, inhaling wonderful salt air. He bobbed in the water for a few seconds, breathing deeply before trying to gain his bearings.

Ahead and to the right were rows and rows of shipping containers, brought in by road and rail and waiting to be shipped to ports unknown. And having just been shipped from said ports. The tall cranes that loaded and unloaded the containers blinked in the night, as did the distant lights of Los Angeles and its many suburbs. Giant cargo ships created dark masses where light should have been, and the sounds of forklifts and tugs and the cranes sounded even in the middle of the night. The port never slept.

More shipping containers were stacked to Jackson's left as well, as far as he could see. Behind him, a thin strip of land extended into the harbor, creating more dock space and separating the water Jackson had plunged into from the Pacific Ocean. A thin channel led in or out of this part of the harbor, one of many such sections at the port.

Directly ahead of him, the wharf was less than a hundred feet away, but Jackson found he had to swim several hundred yards to find a place where he could get out of the water. He scaled a rock jetty and stood, dripping and panting in front of thousands of blue, red, and orange container boxes.

A forklift rumbled past, the driver either not seeing Jackson standing there or not caring. At two-thirty in the morning, he was probably half-asleep and held up by gooey coffee. Jackson couldn't blame him.

He took a moment to take stock of himself. He was alive, bruised in a few places, and had a knot forming in the back of his head, but was otherwise unhurt. He still had the flashlight, and it still worked. The Glock would be fine, and Jackson double-checked that the safety was on and that the gun was hidden under his clothes. Next he reached for his cell phone, which had survived the journey in his pocket. He had thought of using it while in the trunk, and probably should have called someone—Mouse, Reggie, the cops—to give them his location as best he knew it. Now it was too late. The phone was waterlogged and useless.

Jackson still had his wallet and the four dollars he hadn't spent bribing winos and buying first aid supplies for Ashley. But payphones, if he could find one, didn't take soggy dollar bills.

They did take change, and Jackson had been given several coins at the convenience store where he had tended to Ashley's cut. He dug into his pocket and pulled out a quarter and two pennies. The quarter would work, and Jackson set out to find a payphone somewhere amidst the crates and containers. If payphones still existed.

As he walked, he wondered what had happened to Ashley. For a moment, he panicked, thinking that maybe she had been in the car too, tied up and tossed in the backseat and now at the bottom of the sea. That didn't wash. He had only heard one car door open and close before leaving Hahn Park. Besides, drowning by submersion off a pier wasn't really gangster style for execution. They were ditching the car. If they wanted to kill Ashley, they could do that much more simply.

So was that what this was—the Grays tying up loose ends? Had they bated Ashley into coming to the park just so they could get her and get rid of her? And what about Dylan? What had he done to put his life in danger, to necessitate Ashley delivering drugs in exchange for his life? Was Sanders offering Dylan a potential out through Ashley, or just manipulating them to get his snow delivered? And was Dylan even alive anymore? For that matter, was Ashley?

Jackson couldn't let himself think that way. He had to hope they were both still alive and concentrate on finding them. And he couldn't do that on foot at the Port of Los Angeles.

After ten minutes of wandering, he finally found a parking lot, and in the corner of the lot, a payphone. The phonebook had been torn out of the phone stand and the cord was peeled and bare in places. But when he lifted the phone off the hook and deposited his quarter, Jackson heard a dial tone.

He called Reggie, who picked up just before his voicemail.

"Yeah."

"Reg, it's me."

"J? What's up?"

"I need a ride, man."

"Where you at?"

"The port. I'm in some parking lot, looking at the Desmond Bridge."

"You all right?"

"More or less. But Ashley—Shay's in trouble."

"I'll be there ASAP, man. Where should I meet you?"

"Uh . . . The Des is on Ocean, so just get off Ocean by the port, west of the bridge. I'll find you."

"Okay, man. I'm out."

Jackson hung up the phone. It had to be getting close to three o'clock. That meant it had been an hour since he and Ashley had parted ways at the park. Finding her was not going to be easy. He could try having Mouse hack into Caltrans again to trace an Oldsmobile that had appeared on La Cienega around two. But it had been dangerous getting into their system once. Twice would be pushing it, even if Mouse agreed to try.

He could call the police, and maybe should have already. But what would he tell them? Your potentially rogue undercover cop is in trouble, and so is your semi-rogue undercover cop's contact, and I have no idea where either of them are. Help me? It wasn't the best of options either.

Jackson set out toward Ocean Boulevard. It would take Reggie close to half an hour to get there, even if he sped. Which he probably would. At any rate, it would be a while. As Jackson walked toward the street to wait, he went over everything again.

First, he worked through Ashley's story, just checking to make sure it computed. She and Dylan were undercover, he more so than her. LAPD's Drug Enforcement Division wanted to pull the plug on his sting operation, but thinking he was close to bringing down Sanders and the Grays, he had insisted on remaining in deep cover. DED broke off contact with him, essentially leaving him to freelance, and stuck Ashley behind a desk where, conceivably, she couldn't get in the way.

And then Dylan had done something to make Sanders angry. He hadn't made the three deliveries—why not?—and Ashley had been forced to make them to save his life. Or was that just a story Sanders had fed her through Dylan? She claimed Dylan would never have called her if he had known Sanders was onto him. So maybe Sanders wasn't. Or maybe he was and Dylan didn't know. Or maybe a green cop in her first undercover role was confused about how things were supposed to go down.

Even if Dylan's cover was still safe, how was Ashley making his deliveries supposed to square him with Sanders and earn his freedom? Drug dealers weren't known for their sweet forgiveness, for letting bygones be bygones.

Not that it seemed to matter anymore. Each new development made it seem more and more like Sanders had no intentions of ever releasing Dylan. Big surprise. Jackson kicked himself for ever buying into that possibility in the first place. They never should have gone to Hahn Park. Then again, his day was full of never should have's.

Jackson reached Seaside Boulevard, connected to Ocean Boulevard by a looping exit that reversed traffic coming over the Desmond Bridge. It made as much sense to wait for Reggie there as anywhere.

Sitting down by the curb, Jackson took out his phone and played with it, hoping it was salvageable. He pried the cover off, shook it in the air in an attempt to dry it, and removed the SIM card and battery and reconnected them.

Still dead.

"Come on!" He smacked the phone against his palm, hard enough to sting. "Piece of junk." He stood up and repeatedly pushed the power button, harder and harder, but the phone refused to turn on. Another smack, and a few more pushes. "Turn on, you stupid piece of crap!"

The phone was unresponsive.

With a final growl, Jackson slammed the phone to the ground. It clattered against the curb, the cover cracked and split, and little phone parts spilled out onto the pavement. For good measure, Jackson gave what was left of his phone a kick into the street.

He sagged back down onto the curb and dropped his head into his hands. And he cried.

The torrent that had been kept at bay by adrenaline and activity came flooding out. He was no longer just a private eye with baggage.

He was now a drug dealer.

And a killer.

Twice over.

The victims were gangbangers, sure. But they had souls. Souls that had been ushered into eternity, and not on the cool side. Evil as they may have been, it was still a sobering thought. Especially since he had been the usher.

And it had all happened so quickly. Taking the life of another human being should be the result of a long, contemplative process. The path should be clearly marked, lined with warning signs and red flags so that only the most convicted of their cause or the most depraved could possibly continue into the abyss. The legal system allowed for months and months of appeals and employed numerous safeguards to make sure no criminals were put to death unjustly. Serial killers didn't just kill; they tortured cats, fantasized about hurting women, or had extreme fascinations with death before turning into complete sociopaths. Even soldiers thrust into battle spent months ahead of time in boot camp, preparing for that moment.

But Jackson had gone from dude to killer in a matter of minutes. At nine-thirty, he had been playing with Sam, lighthearted and carefree. Two hours later, he had hunted down and killed two men.

Even worse, the thought had been in his heart much earlier. He had grabbed the gun, not as a prop, not thinking merely of self-defense. He'd left his house prepared to do whatever he had to.

Since the day he'd bought his gun, Jackson had known that taking a life was a possibility. It was the reason he bought a gun and not a Taser. It was just part of being a private investigator. But he had never given it serious thought. Not when he'd purchased the Glock, not when he took his gun-safety course, and not when he'd impressed himself by hitting bull's eyes at target practice.

Now it was serious.

Jackson stood and paced, letting the night air dry his tears and cool his face.

"Forgive me, Lord," he prayed aloud. "Forgive me."

That brought fresh tears to his eyes, and he wiped them with his sweatshirt sleeve.

Deep inside, he knew that the killings had been justified, at least as much as any killings could be. It wasn't legal or heavenly retribution that scared him most. It was something he'd heard several times before, from soldiers, policemen, and criminals on TV.

Killing got easier.

A horn diverted Jackson's attention, and he turned, expecting to see Reggie pulling to the curb. It was a case of mistaken right-of-way coming out of the loop and didn't concern him.

Jackson sat back down and decided to focus on Ashley. He could cope with all the ramifications of killing two people later. He had little if any time to find her, and no leads to go on. So maybe there was something he already knew that could provide him some answers.

Something with the three deliveries, maybe? The locations were similar— West Hollywood, Beverly Hills, and Hollywood Hills West. All affluent neighborhoods. And thus all wealthy clients. A handicapped minimalist, a famous artist with a history of (alleged) drug use, and a giant Texan with a pair of brutish dogs. No apparent connection there. The times, maybe? Eleven, two, and ten.

Jackson sat upright. Ashley had originally told him ten the next morning. Was that an honest mistake or part of her scheme? It didn't make sense as a scheme. So had she been mistaken or had the timeline changed? And how had she found out about the correct time? For that matter, what difference did it make when the drop-offs were made? Was there something to the specific times other than dealer-buyer peculiarity?

There was too much still unanswered, and Jackson was getting a headache. A repercussion—or concussion—from cracking his head one too many times. He took a deep breath, hoping some salt air would clear his thoughts. It didn't.

Jackson looked up and spotted Reggie's black H3 as it hit the loop. He removed his black hoodie. Dodger blue, even when soaked, was a little brighter than black. Then again, he was the only dude standing along the side of the road, looking half-drowned. He shouldn't be hard to spot.

The Hummer coasted to a stop in front of Jackson and the passenger door opened before he could grab it. "What happened to you, man?" Reggie asked, leaning back to his side of the vehicle.

"I thought I'd cool off while waiting, take a dip," Jackson answered as he climbed into the front seat.

"Don't drip all over. Where we headed?"

"I don't know. North."

Reggie shifted into drive and stepped on the gas. "You want to tell me what's going on?"

Jackson did, starting with the call he had received from Ashley after dropping Sam off.

"Man, she got kidnapped?"

Jackson nodded.

"That why you called earlier? Man, why you didn't say anything?"

"You were busy," Jackson answered. He continued to recount his night, from tracing the van to following it to Silver Lake to the shootout in the warehouse and his rescue of Ashley.

"Dang," Reggie said, rubbing his head. "What you gettin' into, man?"

"That ain't the half of it, brother. While I was playing Nurse Nightingale, she runs off and tries to make a phone call to some guy named Sanders who's got her brother and will kill him if we don't make the third delivery."

"Sanders. Why's that ring a bell?"

"Because he runs the Grays."

Reggie's head whipped to the side. "The Grays? Are you serious, man? Man, you're lucky you ain't dead."

"Don't I know it." He continued explaining how Ashley had told him the truth about the idols and coaxed him to continue helping her. He told Reggie about outwitting the cops to make the final delivery, and about Sanders' instructions to meet at Hahn Park. And then that Ashley had told him the truth again, about being a cop.

"A cop? That chick's a cop?"

"Yeah. Her name's Ashley."

"And the dude's not her brother?"

"Partner."

"And this is what, the third version of the truth?"

"Or so."

Reggie shook his head. "And you're still working for her? Man, what you won't do for a pretty face."

"She's my client, Reg. And she's in trouble. Lying or not, I owe her."

"That's where you're wrong, bro. Once the client lies, they're out."

Jackson shrugged.

"How'd you end up at the port?"

Jackson explained the rest of the night to Reggie, concluding by glancing at the dashboard clock. 3:05.

"It's been an hour and a half. We've got to find her."

Reggie nodded. "All right, chief. So what we do?"

Chapter Twenty-Five

3:06 a.m.

JACKSON WATCHED THE city roll by in a blur out his window. Reggie's question was a good one. What should they do? They were nearing ninety minutes since he—and presumably Ashley—had left Hahn Park, he going south in the back of her trunk, and she going . . . somewhere. By now she and her captors could have disappeared into any ghetto in Los Angeles, vanished into the California countryside, or hopped a plane for Rio.

"Maybe we should call the cops," Jackson said. "Tell them everything that's happened."

Reggie nodded.

"But if Ashley didn't think they would help her then," Jackson continued, "why would they help us now?"

"Because they didn't know this Dylan dude was in trouble. Now that his neck's on the line, their stance might change."

"Yeah, but all we have is what Ashley told me, and now she's gone. And she's gone because she was working with Dylan, which they had forbidden her to do. And what could they do? What evidence is there that we don't have? Forensics going to go to the park and find her based on tire treads?"

"They might have the lowdown on the Grays."

"Yeah, but no new evidence to act on. If they had anything before, they would have acted on it. It's just Ashley's word."

"Man, are you even sure she's telling you the truth? I mean, she already lied to you twice?"

"Yeah, she's telling the truth," Jackson said with a nod. "I think."

Reggie switched lanes to pass a dump truck. "What's it hurt to call them?" he asked.

Jackson mulled for a second. "I guess nothing."

Reggie grabbed his phone out of a cubby in the dash and tossed it to Jackson. It was a flip phone, similar to his own, and he opened it and paused. "You think I should call 9-1-1 or try to get a hold of DED?"

"At this hour?"

"Right." Jackson tapped the phone keypad three times and waited.

"Nine-one-one Emergency Response." It was a woman, her voice urgent and yet calm.

"Yeah, I need to report a kidnapping."

"Who was kidnapped?"

"A police officer named Ashley . . . uh, I don't know her last name. I know she was working undercover out of the DED."

"How do you know her?"

"She hired me. I'm a private investigator."

Reggie looked over, then back at the road.

"Tell me what happened," the woman said. Jackson did, as briefly as possible. He and Ashley had gone to Hahn Park to meet with the Grays, per instructions, to get Dylan back. He hid in the trunk and was driven away. Ashley was gone.

"Are you sure she's gone, sir?" the woman asked. "Have you checked the park where you last saw her?"

"No, but she wouldn't still be there."

"So you haven't checked her last known whereabouts."

"No."

"Have you checked her home, tried contacting her?"

"I don't know where she lives and she lost her phone earlier."

There was a pause on the other end of the line. Confusion? Uncertainty? Disbelief?

"Sir, you said she was part of an undercover operation?"

"That's right."

"I'm going to transfer you to LAPD," the woman said. "If there's an official operation in progress, we don't want to interfere with it."

"Fine," Jackson said. "Just hurry, please."

Reggie looked up as Jackson lowered the phone from his mouth. "What's up?"

"They're transferring me to LAPD."

Reggie rolled his eyes.

Jackson waited for close to a minute before a male voice came on the line. "Los Angeles Police Department."

Jackson quickly explained why he was calling and was just as quickly put on hold. He was transferred to a tip line, then to an automated system when he explained that he wasn't calling to report seeing any of the FBI's most wanted at the corner grocery. Finally, he reached a husky-voiced guy at DED.

"Sergeant Locker."

"Sergeant, I'm calling about Dylan O'Brien."

"What about him?"

"I've been working with his partner Ashley in an effort to find him."

"Who is this?"

"My name's Jackson Douglas. I'm a private investigator." He could hear fingers racing across a keyboard.

"What do you want?"

"Ashley's been kidnapped."

"Kidnapped?"

"That's right." He once again explained what he knew, how he knew it, and what had transpired over the last few hours. He left out the parts about delivering drugs, figuring it wasn't relevant at the time. Not relevant enough to end him up in jail again.

"You think the Grays have Larson?" Locker asked.

"Larson?"

"Detective Larson. Ashley."

"Yes, sir. She told me you all shut the investigation down, but she wanted to help her partner."

Locker groaned.

"Anyhow, they've got her now too."

"Where?" the sergeant asked.

"I have no idea. That's why I'm calling, so you can find her."

"We'll look into it."

"Look into it? I thought you all were supposed to have each other's back. Shouldn't you be turning the town upside down to find two of your own?"

"Don't lecture me on protocol, Douglas. I don't know how you're messed up in all this, but Larson and O'Brien are acting on their own. We'll take care of it."

The phone clicked before Jackson could get another word in. Not that he had any more to say. He closed Reggie's phone and put it back in the cubby. "Well, that went pretty well."

"You got a better destination for me?" Reggie asked. They were passing the airport, nearing I-10.

"Your place or mine," Jackson said.

"What's next?"

"I don't know. What do you know about the Grays?"

"Not a lot. I think they were originally known as the SDF gang."

"SDF?"

"Yeah. That was before my time here, though."

Jackson nodded. "They have a sworn enemy? Bloods to their Crips or something?"

Reggie shrugged. "I don't know." He continued north on the 405. "We'll go to your place so you can change. Besides, if she happens to get free, that's where she'd go."

"No, she'd call my phone," Jackson said. "Or what's left of it. You probably can't buy a plain old phone anymore. You have to get something with a keypad and Bluetooth this or that and a camera with a telephoto lens the size of a peanut built into it, don't you?"

Reggie scratched his head. "Why do you ask about the Grays' enemy?"

"I've been thinking. Those guys at the warehouse grabbed Sh—Ashley from my place. It wouldn't make sense for the Grays to take her—not before she could make the final delivery."

"Unless they didn't want it made."

"A faction in the group?"

"Maybe. Why would some other gang grab her?"

"I don't know, unless she was making deliveries on their turf. If Dylan-slash-Blake was originally supposed to make the deliveries, maybe they were a test of some kind. Could he get through enemy lines. Else it was a setup all along."

Reggie shrugged.

"Don't suppose you happen to know who owns Beverly Hills, Hollywood, that area."

"I don't stay up like I should, man."

Jackson fought the thought that came into his head, then reached for Reggie's phone.

"Who you callin' now?"

"A source." He dialed from memory and waited and hoped. His call went to voicemail, so he hung up and tried again. After the third ring, a very sleepy, even deeper than usual voice answered.

"Hello."

"Hey, your Rangers pull it out?"

"Jackson?"

"Sorry to wake you."

"What . . ." He heard rustling. "What time is . . . three-twenty-five?"

"I need your help, Maggie. It can't wait."

Her voice carried attentiveness now. "What is it?" And still some grogginess.

"What do you know about gangs?"

"You've got to be kidding me."

"I'm not, Maggie. Ashley—I mean, Shay, the girl I was working for—she's been kidnapped."

"The princess?"

"Yeah."

More rustling. "What's that got to do with gangs?"

"I think the Grays were behind it. You know them?"

"Um . . . yeah, a little. They make the news."

"What can you tell me?"

"At three-thirty in the morning, not much. Ow!" She swore and Jackson backed the phone away from his ear.

"Dresser?" he asked.

"Doorpost."

"You awake now."

"What do you want, Douglas?"

Yep, she was awake. "Everything you know about the Grays. And any rival of theirs. And who controls Bel Air to Hollywood."

"I don't know much," she said. "I don't hear the gritty details."

"Anything's more than we know."

"We?"

"Reggie."

"Right." She sighed. "The Grays were founded in the early '90s by Tone Sanders, some punk from Compton. Back then they were known as the SDFs."

"SDFs?"

"San Diego Freeway. It ran through the heart of their territory, from the mountains down to the 105."

"Clever bunch. Why the name change?"

Jackson heard cabinets opening and closing. "Sanders is half black, half white and was able to attract both races into the gang. He kept the peace, and they earned the name Grays."

"Black mixed with white."

"Right." Now she was running water.

"Okay, so what do they do?" Jackson asked.

"Mostly put on plays for the elderly. What do you think? Drugs, drugs, drugs, some prostitution, grand theft, more drugs."

Jackson nodded. "What about auto parts?"

"Sure, and they probably own a few Laundromats too. But the real dough comes from drugs."

"They got any rivals? Sanders have an enemy?"

"Besides every cop in the city?" she asked.

"Besides."

"The Silvaz."

"The Silvaz?" he repeated.

"Yeah, with a Z." He could hear a coffee pot starting to grumble. "Formed by a guy named Pace and some cat who calls himself Shaq. They split off from the Grays when Sanders bagged Pace's girl."

"Isn't that how it always starts?"

"Shaq started to emerge as the leader of the Silvaz," Maggie continued. "He and Sanders had been pals, but they were always at odds—over race and culture, drug money, whatever. The Silvaz aren't anywhere as big or powerful as the Grays, but they do all right. They cater to a different group, to more exclusive clients."

"What if the Grays started to move in on those clients?"

"It'd get ugly, fast. But the Grays don't want to start anything, because they have the upper hand. They're bigger, cover more territory, have more connections and more manpower. Why risk it? And the Silvaz aren't strong enough to take the Grays down and don't want to try until they know they can. So, they exist in peace and stay out of each other's turf."

"I wish you knew more about this stuff, Maggie."

"I wish you did so I didn't get calls at three-thirty in the morning. You know, when I told you to call me tonight, I meant at a decent hour."

Jackson grinned. "So where are the Silvaz based? Where's home?"

"Originally, Silver Lake. That's why they call themselves Silvaz. And because silver is a more refined version of gray. Cute, huh?"

"Silver Lake?" Jackson repeated.

"Yeah, why?"

"That's where they took Ashley. Some warehouse off of Sunset and Silver Lake Boulevard."

"I thought you said the Grays had her."

"They do, now. Somebody else took her earlier."

"Kidnapped by two gangs in one night?"

"Yeah, well. What else you got?" he asked.

"The Silvaz split off in '98, maybe early '99. The fun started in '03. Rumors that Pace was making time with Shaq's girl. Then Shaq's sister gets pregnant."

"Let me guess. Pace?"

"Yeah. There was already a power struggle in the works, but this put it over the top. Until Shaq had Pace killed."

"Really?"

"That was the word on the street, although nobody could prove anything. There was a small revolt, but Shaq kept things together. He's been running things ever since."

"The Silvaz deal in Beverly Hills, West Hollywood, up into the mountains?"

"Probably," she said. "Don't tell me you're caught in a turf war?"

"I don't know what I'm in." Jackson gave her a few more details as Reggie turned onto Ridgeline Drive.

"What did the police say?" Maggie asked.

"Little. It's up to us to find her, and we have no ideas where to start. I don't suppose you happen to know where to find this guy Sanders?"

"Check the sewer."

"Know anybody who does know?"

"No. My sources generally run a little different than that."

"Yeah. Hey, any chance you can find out who those guys were at the warehouse? Were they taken to a hospital, a morgue, something? Maybe we can link them to one of the two gangs."

"What good will that do?"

"It's more information," Jackson said as Reggie parked behind his Granada in the driveway "Anything helps."

"Now that I'm up, sure. I'll call you back."

"Call Reggie. My phone's out of commission."

"Sure. This number?"

"Yeah. Thanks, Maggie."

"Right."

He closed his phone and he and Reggie got out. Jackson checked to make sure that the neighborhood was still quiet, that nobody was waiting behind the trees to grab or cap him. They made it inside and he quickly filled Reggie in on the other half of his conversation with Maggie. Then he left him to ponder what it all meant while he changed into some dry clothes—a pair of jeans and a long-sleeved tee. He rejoined Reggie in the kitchen, where he was digging through Jackson's refrigerator for a late night snack. They found some leftover slices of pizza, some bread, and some not yet spoiled ham. In two minutes, they were stuffing their faces.

Reggie's phone chirped. "Maggie," he said, tossing it to Jackson.

"What you got?"

"You're quite the marksman."

He winced.

"Two DOAs—a Lewis Varden, Jr. and a Ray Hullinger—and another guy with a bullet in his shoulder—Dwayne Mickens." Jackson heard her take a drink of coffee.

"No fourth guy?" he asked.

"You killed another?"

"Just concussed him."

"No mention."

"What do we know about these guys, anything?"

"Nothing else's reported, but the name Varden rang a bell, so I checked him out. He has a couple of priors, including a drug charge back in the day. Undercover cops busted him and a guy named Freddie Pace."

"Shaq's old partner?"

"Bingo. There's your Silvaz tie-in."

"Unless Varden and Pace were tight and he went the other way in the split. Maybe he's working against the Silvaz now."

"That was almost ten years ago, Jackson."

"Yeah." He looked at Reggie, who was plowing into his sandwich while trying to follow the conversation. "This guy Shaq, you said he and Sanders were pals?" Jackson asked.

"Yeah, way back when."

"Think he might know where to find him?"

"Maybe, but you'd have to find him first too. Same dead end there. These guys don't want to be real accessible."

"Yeah, I suppose."

"Sorry, Jack. I just don't have the connections."

"Yeah." He sighed. "Thanks a lot Maggie. I ow—I'll pay you back, promise."

"I'll hold you to it."

Despite the circumstances, Jackson couldn't help smiling at the tone in her voice as he closed the phone. He again caught Reggie up.

"So, not to be a broken record, man, but what we gonna do?"

Jackson crashed onto his couch, wanting badly to forget Ashley and Dylan and Los Angeles gangs and just go to bed right then and there. Now that he was dry and warm and not in imminent danger, his body was ready to give in. He forced himself to sit up.

"Okay, Sanders has Ashley."

"Are you sure?" Reggie asked, now on a piece of cold pizza.

"Sure enough. If he doesn't, we're not even to square one, so we might as well forget it."

Reggie bobbed his head in agreement.

"And we have no idea where to find him, and we aren't getting any help from the police either. Somehow, either because they kidnapped Ashley because she was on their turf or because Freddie Pace and Lewis Varden were tight back in the day or whatever—somehow, the Silvaz are mixed up in this too."

"Right."

"Let's follow the hunch that, for whatever reason, the Grays had Dylan and thus Ashley making deliveries in Silvaz territory, or to Silvaz clients."

"Okay."

"So the Silvaz grab Ashley, intending to send a message, not having any idea who she is or what's going on."

Reggie nodded as he stuffed the folded crust into his mouth.

"Which means the Silvaz and Grays are still at odds, and Shaq, if he knew where Sanders was, would want nothing more than to let that cat out of the bag."

"Maybe. But how you going to find Shaq, and how you going to get him to talk to you after you put slugs into three of his peeps?"

"A, then B," Jackson said. He waved the phone. "May I?"

"I'll send you the bill."

Jackson dialed Maggie again. "Still up, I hope?" he asked.

"I started the day. What is it?"

"Any word on where they took this Mickens guy, the one who survived?"

"What hospital? No. Why?"

"It doesn't matter."

"Jackson. Are you going to do something stupid?"

"We'll see."

"Jackson."

He paused.

"Is Reggie with you?"

"Yeah."

"Put him on the phone."

"What?"

"Put him on."

Jackson sighed and handed the phone to Reggie. "She wants to talk to you."

It didn't last long.

"Well?" Jackson asked as Reggie squeezed the phone shut.

"She said not to let you do anything stupid."

Jackson nodded.

"You going to do something stupid, man?"

"Just another phone call."

Reggie tossed him the phone. "I'm gonna see what else is in that fridge."

He left and Jackson punched in Sam's number.

"Hello?" Properly puzzled for ten to four.

"Sam, it's me."

"Jackson? What's going on?"

"I need a favor."

"I'm on my way out the door. Work, remember?"

"I do. I'll be quick. Long story short, I need to know which hospital a shooting victim was taken to. Can you find that out?"

"What's going on? Are you okay?"

"I'm fine, but I have a client who's in trouble. The vic's name is Dwayne Mickens. He was shot over in Silver Lake around midnight. I need to know where he is, and I need to talk to him if I can."

She was quiet for just a second. "I'll make some calls and call you back."

He thanked her, telling her to call Reggie's cell instead of his. Reggie had returned with a bag of chips, and they sat side by side, munching and waiting in silence. It took Sam all of five minutes to return the call from her car.

"Dwayne Mickens, twenty-four, single gunshot wound to the right shoulder?"

"Sounds right," Jackson replied.

"He's at Hollywood Presbyterian Medical Center over on Vermont and Sunset."

"Can we talk to him?"

"Probably not."

"Are there any strings you can pull?"

She paused.

"Please, Sam. I wouldn't ask if it weren't an emergency."

"I'll be at work in five minutes," she answered. "I'll see what I can do."

"Thanks, Sam. I appreciate it."

He closed the phone and tapped Reggie's knee. "Let's roll."

"Where to, man?"

"Hollywood Prez."

"You get in to see Mickens?"

"I will. And if not, I've got a backup plan."

Chapter Twenty-Six

4:14 a.m.

JACKSON AND REGGIE were almost to the hospital when Sam called back. Jackson had taken possession of Reggie's phone and he answered before the first chirp was finished.

"Yeah?"

"Jackson, you're in."

"Thanks, Sam. I knew you could do it."

"I know a lady at HPMC and I told her the gist of what you told me. Mickens just came out of surgery about an hour ago; he's in recovery right now. She said she would let you, and only you, see him, and only for a few minutes."

"That's all I'll need."

"Ask for Joanne at the front desk."

"Will do. Thanks, Sam."

"Jackson, whatever you're into, be careful."

"I will."

"Call me later, let me know everything's okay. Late night shootings have me a little worried."

"I will. Don't worry, I'll be fine."

"Bye, Jackson."

"Bye." He snapped the phone shut. "We're in. Well, I'm in."

"How you gonna get this Mickens guy to roll over on Shaq?"

"Depends. If the nurse leaves us alone, I sit on his shoulder."

Reggie nodded. "She buy that 'I'll be fine' business?"

"Seemed to."

He shook his head. "Suppose the nurse don't leave you alone. Think you can appeal to his sweet side?"

228

"I'll have to," Jackson answered.

Joanne met them at the front desk. She was tall and plump, with bright splotches of makeup that stood out on round cheeks and clashed with her purple hospital scrubs. The hair fit the body, big and coiffed and prematurely graying. Her stern gaze practically scared Reggie into a waiting room seat before she admitted Jackson to follow her.

"Sam says you're a private investigator," she said as they walked down the quiet hallway.

"That's right."

"And this man is involved in one of your cases."

"Yeah."

"And you need information from him that's life and death?"

"I believe so."

"Mr. Mickens just came out of surgery at three o'clock," Joanne said. "He needs rest, so I can't permit you much time with him."

"I appreciate that. I just need to know who he's working for."

Joanne stopped dead. "Nobody ever answers that one."

"It's all how you ask," Jackson said with a smile. He had a feeling sitting on Mickens' shoulder was out.

"I don't like this idea," Joanne said. "I never would have agreed to it if not for Sam. Just remember that."

"Trust me, Joanne, I wouldn't do anything to taint her reputation. A few hours ago, a young woman was kidnapped, and the only way I can find her is by talking to Dwayne Mickens."

Joanne searched his face for truth, then nodded. "This way."

She led him to what felt like the far end of the hospital, to the next to the last room on the left of a long hallway. She peeked inside, then turned back and motioned for Jackson to enter. "I'll be right outside the door," she said.

"Thank you, Joanne."

He stood at the foot of Mickens' bed as she quickly checked something on a machine and left. He looked down at the man he had shot some five hours prior. He was naked above the waist, with a large bandage on his right shoulder and a sling holding it in place. And he was awake.

"Who are you?" he asked in a hoarse voice.

"You don't recognize me?" Jackson asked.

The reply was faint, and Jackson was afraid Mickens was drifting out of consciousness. He walked over and knelt down beside him. He whispered.

"I'm the guy who shot you five hours ago in a warehouse over in Silver Lake."

Mickens turned his eyes.

"And I'm the guy who is going to put the bullet right back into your shoulder with my bare hands if you don't cooperate."

"Nurse," Mickens called feebly. Jackson coughed to cover him. Then again. He put up his hand.

"Listen to me. I need to know who you were working for and where I can find him."

Mickens didn't cry out, but he looked at Jackson with a mixture of fear, anger, and defiance. Mostly fear.

"Hey, man, just tell me what I want, and I'll leave you alone. You can make a full recovery and can go back to dealin' dope and cappin' brothers, all right?"

Mickens shook his head slightly. "I . . . I ain't afraid of you."

"Who's your boss?"

Nothing.

"Is it Shaq? You working for Shaq?"

The voice said nothing, but the eyes screamed an affirmative.

Jackson leaned a little closer. "Well Shaq ain't here, is he?" he asked, barely audible. "And he never has to know. I just need to know where I can find him. I'm not going to bring the cops in or try to take him down. I just need to talk to him . . . to get to someone else."

"He'll . . . he'll kill you."

"Maybe. Where is he?"

Mickens shook his head again. "No. He'll kill me if he finds out I told you."

Jackson looked away for a moment. The equipment at Mickens' bedside beeped and hummed and lit up the otherwise darkened room. Jackson leaned in even closer.

"I'm going to find him. One way or the other. But if I don't find him very, very soon, I am going to be very, very upset when I do. And if I'm upset when I find him, I am going to tell him you sold him out. Who you think he's going to believe, you or me, when I'm standing there in front of him?"

Mickens closed his eyes and turned his head.

Jackson grabbed his jaw and turned the head back. He saw a red flag by the side of the road, but disregarded it. "That girl you had tonight, the one you and your boys were torturing, is going to die if I don't find Shaq. And if she dies, if she's hurt, a lot of people are going to suffer, and you are one of them. You hear me? I don't play by the rules. I will hunt you down, and make you beg for Shaq! Where is he?"

Joanne popped around the corner. "What are you doing?"

"Where is he!" Jackson asked louder, squeezing Mickens' jaw.

Mickens jerked his head away, and before Joanne could get there, Jackson punched Mickens' injured shoulder with his free hand. Lightly, but it still caused him to recoil and howl with pain.

"Get away from him!" Joanne yelled. "Annie, call security!"

Jackson raised his fist, threatening to strike again. "Where is Shaq!"

Mickens cried out. "Sil-Silver L-Lake." He moaned. "A p-place on Keilor Drive. 1710 Keilor Drive."

Jackson unclenched his fist. "Thanks."

He turned around just as Joanne grabbed him and tugged him toward the doorway. "What do you think you're doing! This man was just shot!"

"Yeah, I know. I'm the one who pegged him."

Her eyes widened. "And you had the gall to have Sam—"

"Sam has no idea what I did," Jackson answered. "This isn't her fault. And for the record, I shot him to keep him from torturing a girl whose life is now in danger."

Joanne tuned him out, pushing him into the hallway. She turned her head. "Phil. Phil, watch this man. I'm calling the police."

Jackson turned to see a tall, young, handsome, very muscular security guard hurrying his way. He was the kind of guy who would make girls' knees buckle, and he was having the same affect on Jackson for different reasons.

Phil looked at Joanne, then eyed Jackson. "What's going on?"

"He just assaulted a patient," Joanne answered.

"I told you—"

"Come with me," Phil said.

"Where?" Jackson asked.

"We have patients trying to sleep here," Phil replied. "Let's handle this elsewhere."

"There's nothing to handle. You all don't seem to get this."

"Sir, please come with me."

Jackson put up his hands and let Phil march him down the hall and into a small workroom while Joanne threatened to call the cops again.

"You want to tell me what's going on?" Phil asked.

Jackson paced to the end of the small room, to a shelf lined with copy paper, then turned around. "Yeah. Five hours ago, I shot that guy to keep him from killing a young lady named Ashley. Now her life's in danger again, and he had the information I needed to find her."

"Have you called the police?" Phil asked.

"Yeah."

"And?"

Jackson shook his head. "They're not cooperating."

"I see."

"Look, I get that you're just doing your job, Phil. But I've got to get out of here. You seem like a decent guy, and I'd hate to have to use my Brazilian jiu-jitsu on you. What do you say you just let me go?"

"Brazilian jiu-jitsu?"

"Yeah."

Phil smiled. "I'm a level four black belt. Bring it on."

Jackson stared him down for a moment before slumping his shoulders. "I fold." He paced back to the copy paper. "So what's the deal, we going to play Cowboys and Indians for a while?"

"I believe Joanne is going to call the police. You assaulted an injured man."

"An injured man who was dealing drugs! Who kidnapped a girl! To save her life!"

"Why don't we let the police decide and handle that?"

Jackson sighed. "What about a bribe? I have four dollars."

Phil smiled.

Jackson considered a surprise bull rush attack. It would probably leave him unconscious on the floor with elbows and knees that bent the wrong way. Meanwhile, the seconds ticked by, and Ashley was long out of time.

"Level four, huh?"

"That's right."

"So what are you doing here? Four a.m., shouldn't you be at an underground fight club busting heads for Benjamins or something?"

Phil smiled again. "Only on weekends."

Jackson considered the possibility that Phil was serious. No, with a face like that, why risk it? There were better ways to make money.

"Can I make a phone call?"

"What for?"

"To let my buddy know to go save the girl's life, since I clearly can't."

"Do you have a phone?"

"Not on me, no. I thought I could use one here, and you can snap my neck if I say the wrong word."

Phil mulled on it for a moment. "Come with me."

The crack in the wall.

Jackson left the room with Phil close behind. "Where we headed?"

"Nurses' station on the left. There's a phone there you ca—"

Looking over his shoulder as Phil answered, Jackson saw a slight gap and made a break for it. Phil reached to grab him, was an inch too late, and pitched forward as Jackson sprinted down the hallway. Phil chased after him, his long strides quickly making up ground. Jackson ran like mad, hoping he could remember which series of hallways to take. He and Joanne had made several turns.

Rounding the corner, Jackson saw the lobby up ahead. He started shouting. "Reg, let's go! Let's go!"

By the time he reached the front desk, Reggie was on his feet, a curious look on his face. But he wasn't running.

"Reg-gie! Let's go!"

Jackson slowed, waiting for Reggie to join him. He saw his big friend's eyes widen, and turned to look behind him. Phil was closing quickly, ready to unleash his best Bruce Lee impersonation on Jackson. Then Reggie charged.

Reliving his days as an All-Conference defensive end, Reggie intercepted Phil just before he could reach Jackson. Lowering his shoulder, he crashed into Phil's chest, stopping him cold and dropping him like a Big 12 quarterback. Phil fell, and Reggie fell on top of him.

Black Belt, meet Sack Master.

Reggie got up. Phil did not. The nurse behind the desk dropped her jaw and the phone she had been holding to her ear. Two patients in the waiting room watched with equal shock. Jackson resisted the urge to slap Reggie's head and start woofing like a defensive back. Instead he grabbed his friend's arm and pulled him toward the door. They hurried across the parking lot and were buckling themselves into Reggie's Hummer when the first police cruiser turned into the lot.

"Ready to roll, big man?" Jackson asked.

Reggie let out a deep breath and turned the ignition. Calm and easy, he backed out of the stall and made for the exit. "Where to?"

"Silver Lake," Jackson said. "Maybe we'd better go the speed limit."

Chapter Twenty-Seven

4:36 a.m.

"WE CLEAR?" REGGIE asked.

Jackson faced backwards to make sure no one was following them down Sunset Boulevard. He turned around. "Clear. Man, if you had tackled like that, the Chargers might have kept you on."

"I was protecting you, man. Maybe I missed my calling. Maybe I should've been an offensive lineman."

"What you just did's illegal on offense, dude."

"Are we in trouble?"

"Probably, yeah. Although I think they were too stunned to see what car we got into."

Reggie winced. "I hope that dude's all right. I didn't mean to hurt him."

"He's a black belt; I'm sure his sensei tossed him around for kicks in the early days." Jackson punched Reggie's shoulder. "That was huge, bro."

He turned his head. "Man, you need to calm down. I thought you was going to throw the bones in there or something."

Jackson settled into his seat. "You're right. We've got to focus on Shaq."

"Yeah, you got a plan? You can't just waltz into his crib, man. Especially since you shot up four of his dudes."

"I only shot three. I just smashed the other's head into a van."

"So, you got a plan?"

Jackson exhaled. "Not as of yet."

Reggie took one hand off the steering wheel and massaged the top of his head.

"Hey, suppose I'm just some dude off the street," Jackson said. "Any chance Shaq tells me where to find Sanders?"

"Naw, he tells you to get lost, in not so nice words. You ain't got nothing to offer him, man. Why should he give you the time of day?"

"Maggie said it. The Silvaz aren't strong enough to take down the Grays. What if I change the status quo?"

"Yeah, and how you gonna do that?"

"I don't know exactly. But if I can con Shaq into thinking I do, I've got a chance."

"Sounds like suicide to me."

"Yeah, well, we'll see."

Within five minutes, they were in Silver Lake, looking for Keilor Drive and Shaq's house. It didn't take long to find it. Keilor Drive ended in a cul-de-sac, at the end of which was a driveway leading to a gate. Beyond the gate was a small community. Shaq's crib.

"All right, J, what's the word?"

"You wait here. Give me . . . fifteen minutes, then call in the Marines."

"You going in there alone?"

"Yeah. I'll talk to Shaq, man to Diesel."

Reggie extended a relaxed hand. "I hope you know what you're doing."

Jackson clasped the hand. "I hope so too, Hoss."

"You're on the clock."

Silver Lake was deathly quiet as Jackson got out. Sunrise was at least an hour away, and there was no sign of it yet on the eastern horizon.

At quarter till five in the morning, Jackson had no idea what he would find at Shaq's house. Did gangsters stay up late partying or getting high or enjoying their harems? Would Shaq even be home, or out cutting a deal or making it rain at a club? And was there any chance of Jackson getting in even if he was home?

He had thought about trying to sneak in. But he didn't have spy gear and would probably just get caught anyhow. He decided to cut out the middleman. Besides, time was not on his side.

Just like rich non-gangsters, Shaq had an intercom mounted on the gate. Jackson, surreally, rang the buzzer. It elicited no response, so he pushed the button three or four times, then held it for twenty seconds.

"Yeah, who is it?"

"I need to see Shaq," Jackson answered.

"Shaq, man," the voice answered with a laugh. "Man, Shaq's gone. This is Kobe's town, now, bro."

"Not that Shaq. The one that lives here."

The voice huffed. "Man, what you—"

"Tell him I have information about the guy who wasted two of his thugs tonight."

There was no answer, just a click. A minute passed, and Jackson looked to see where Reggie had parked the van. Facing away, ready to take off down the street at a moment's notice.

While he waited, Jackson asked himself again what was he doing here? Ashley had lied to him twice, and she and Dylan had brought this on themselves. They were cops. Undercover cops, no less. They knew the risks even when they were following proper protocol. Good intentions aside, they had gone rogue. Ashley had involved Jackson, and here he was, quarter to five in the morning, knocking on the door of one of the baddest dudes in L.A. Why?

The intercom clicked again. "Hang tight, man."

So Jackson hung, glancing back at Reggie's Hummer several times. The temptation to run away was strong, but he stood his ground until two men emerged from the darkness on the other side of the iron gate. One of them manually unlocked the gate and swung it open. Jackson stepped through the opening, and the guy closed the gate behind him.

"Shaq's sleeping," one of them said gruffly. "Talk to us."

Jackson nodded his understanding, then shook his head. "Not a chance."

They looked at each other. And smiled. Then the quiet one sucker-punched Jackson in the jaw. He reeled backwards and tumbled into the gate, banging his head for good measure and stumbling to the ground. Both men moved in, pummeling him in the stomach, ribs, chest, and head. After a minute of the onslaught, Jackson gave in and succumbed to unconsciousness.

When he awoke, it was to a pungent odor that caused his head to jerk. That hurt.

He was on the ground, a hard floor, on hands and knees. His stomach ached, his ribs burned, and he tasted blood in two places in his mouth. He was also pretty sure one eye was swelling, but then again, the room was poorly lit. A cellar, it appeared, judging by the cold concrete floor and shapeless walls. A cellar or a tomb.

A hand grabbed the back of Jackson's hair, pulling him back so that he sat on his knees. The lights seemed to grow brighter, and he realized a man was standing in front of him.

Check that, a monster.

He was tall and large. Not fat, considering the height. Just big. His skin was pitch black, in stark contrast to the extra large white T-shirt he wore. Black sweatpants. Nikes. His head was bald while a neatly trimmed beard hugged his jaw line. The eyes and mouth were empty shapes until he stepped close enough that Jackson wanted to tremble. He managed not to.

"Nobody kicks in my door in the middle of the night," the man said. The voice was a growl, deep and raspy. Actually sounded a little like the real Shaq.

"I rang the buzzer," Jackson said.

"What you want?"

He took a few deep breaths. "Not to get killed until I tell you part two."

"What's part one?"

"I'm the one who killed your men tonight at the warehouse."

Shaq flinched but didn't strike. Jackson expected the deathblow to come from behind anyway, but a look from Shaq sheathed it. For the moment.

"I'm here to offer you a deal."

Shaq laughed. Deep and throaty. Then the smile vanished. He grabbed Jackson's shirt and pulled him to his feet. "I could snap your neck."

"Yeah. But then I couldn't make the deal."

"You'd better talk fast," he said, letting go of the shirt.

"I want the girl. Sanders has her and I don't know where to find him."

"And you think I'll tell you?"

"I was hoping."

Shaq started to laugh, but turned angry instead. Interposing several choice words, he asked, "Why would I do that?"

"Because I'm willing to do you a favor."

Shaq stared at him again.

"Tell me where Sanders is," Jackson said, "and I'll take him down."

Shaq's boys chuckled.

"You'll take him down?"

"That's right."

Shaq's stare continued. So did Jackson.

"I know the deal. The Grays are bigger than you, they own more territory, make more dough." He hoped, at least, that last part was true. "With Sanders out of the picture, you have an opening. I killed two of your guys, so I owe you. Taking out your rival has to mean more than giving me an address."

"And how's a little piece of crap like you going to get to Sanders?"

"I took out four of your guys earlier," Jackson said. "And I got in to see you."

"That's different."

"What have you got to lose? Five minutes ago, two of your boys were dead and you had nobody to blame for it. If I walk out of here and never so much as touch Sanders, you're right where you were. But if I take him down, you win the lottery."

Shaq leaned back, pursing his gigantic lips. "I want collateral."

"Great, I've got four bucks in my wallet."

Shaq nodded and one of his goons roughly grabbed Jackson. Another removed his wallet. He tossed it to Shaq, who took a few steps back and rifled through it. He pulled out the four dollars, held them up, then crumpled them into a ball and tossed them to the floor.

"You should know my Visa has a low limit," Jackson said.

Shaq withdrew Jackson's driver's license and held it to the light. "Ridgeline Drive, Pacific Palisades." He jammed it back into the wallet. "How about this, white boy: you don't deliver, and Ima send my boys to your house to collect?"

"And if I do, you never send anyone to my house?"

"You put a cap in Sanders' dome, and I'll leave you alone."

239

"What if I get him sent to San Quentin, life no parole?"

Shaq showed a row of very nice white teeth, interspersed with gold. "No, no, no. G, tell him how it is."

One of his minions stepped forward. His mouth appeared to be wired shut, and sounded like it when he spoke. "Yuz duzzent killz dat O.G., weeza killz yuz, maaan!" He gestured with his hands as he spoke, as if karate chopping a midget.

Shaq took a step closer. "A bullet in his head, or a bullet in yours. Yo' choice, man."

Jackson tipped his head. "All right then. I kill Sanders, we're good?"

"Yeah," Shaq said with a chuckle. "You kill Sanders, we straight." He came closer to deliver his threat. "But if this some kind of trick, you can't put up, you miss and hit him in the neck instead and he just paralyzed . . ." Shaq tapped the side of Jackson's head with his finger. "Got it, homes?"

Jackson nodded.

Shaq smiled again. "I gotta give it to you, dawg, you sure got 'em to come in here and try to make a deal with me."

"I'm very persuasive."

Shaq huffed. "I ain't give you one chance of taking Sanders out. But I learned tonight that some my boys a little soft. You'll make good practice, 'specially if you know it's comin'."

Jackson kept his mouth shut while Shaq raked him with his eyes. The big man nodded, and Jackson turned to see his minions leaving. When the door closed, Shaq spoke.

"Sanders has a club in Santa Monica, off Olympic on Grainger. It's his base of operations, with a front as an auto parts warehouse or something."

"His hideout is a in a club disguised as a warehouse?"

"Yeah, man. Word is, he got some sort of underground palace there or something. It's tight, man. He's sealed up. You'll never get in."

"That his only place?"

Shaq laughed. "Man, you are white. Naw, it ain't his only place."

"So what if he isn't there?"

The laugh turned to a grin. "Then you'd better run, white boy. You had better run!"

Jackson nodded. "This warehouse/club have an address?"

"I don't know, man. The 1900 block of Grainger."

"Yeah, well, thanks."

"There's one more thing, man."

"What's that?"

Shaq drilled him in the gut with an iron fist. "That's for Dwayne."

A left cross knocked Jackson backwards. Shaq grabbed him to keep him from falling. "That's for Ray."

He let go of Jackson's shirt, then blasted him with a right hook. "And that's . . ."

Jackson later assumed it was for Lewis Varden, Jr. At the time, he was busy blacking out again.

Chapter Twenty-Eight

5:05 a.m.

ANOTHER HULKING BLACK guy picked Jackson up off the pavement. His impulse was to lash out, but he couldn't command his arms and hands to obey anyhow. All he could do was stiffen and try to jerk out of the man's grasp.

"Whoa, man, easy. Whoa. It's me."

Struggling to stay balanced on one knee, Jackson realized the hulking black guy was Reggie. He dropped to all fours again, trying to catch up on breath. Everything hurt—his stomach, his ribs, his head most of all. He had an aching jaw, a puffy eye, and a very fat lip. And perhaps a concussion. His brain felt like it had been in a vice that had fallen off a cliff.

"Man, you all right?" Reggie asked.

"Wh . . . where are we?"

"On the sidewalk, bro. They threw you out the gate like Jazz, man."

Jackson turned and sat down, resting his arms on his knees. He lifted his head slowly. "I got it."

"What, Sanders' place?"

Even Jackson's slight nod sent tremors of pain through his head.

"What is it?" Reggie asked.

"I have no idea."

"Man, let's get out of here." Reggie pulled a reluctant Jackson to his feet and helped him to the Hummer, parked a dozen yards around the cul-de-sac.

"Just don't take me back to the hospital," Jackson mumbled as he climbed into the passenger seat. "I don't need another run-in with *Walker, Texas Ranger*."

"I think you need a hot shower and warm bed," Reggie said as he headed around to his side.

Jackson massaged his temples and cheeks, trying to bring himself around. He remembered Ashley and that woke him up. He had a location. An iffy one, but a location.

"Grainger," he said when Reggie got in. "Off of Olympic, in Santa Monica. Sanders owns a warehouse that doubles as a nightclub and triples as his secret pad."

"Off."

"Huh?"

"That's the name of the club," Reggie said. "Off."

"Off what?"

"Off the record, for one thing. Off the books. Mostly, it refers to the style of entertainment."

Jackson nodded. "Man, how do you know about this place?"

"I hear things," Reggie answered. "And it is off the record too, man. Word of mouth only, secret access. This isn't just some underground rave."

"Well, it was all Shaq gave me. That and Parkinson's."

"He did that himself, not his goons?"

"They took turns." Jackson touched a particularly ginger spot on the back of his head.

"So how'd you get him to give you Sanders' location, anyway?" Reggie asked.

"Simple. I kill Sanders or Shaq kills me."

Reggie looked over. "For real?"

Jackson made the mistake of nodding again.

"You really gonna ice this guy?"

"Let's just find him first."

Reggie turned onto Glendale. "There something you ain't telling me, man?"

"Like?"

"Like why you're going to the mattresses like this's your sister or something? The girl get to you that much?"

"I don't know," Jackson said. "I owe her."

"You sure you ain't trying to pay back the world for what's happened to you?"

Jackson turned his head. Reggie's words were rumble strips on the road to killing. Flashing red lights. Buzzers.

"You have me confused with a suicide bomber named Achmed," Jackson said. "I'm trying to save a lady's life, that's it. He's a crack dealer, Reg. The lowest of the low. I'm doing the world a favor."

"You can justify it that easy?"

"When it's him or me, yeah. And if I go down, so do Ashley and Blake-slash-Dylan-slash-Whatever his name is."

"You want to maybe call Five-0 instead?"

"That wasn't part of the deal."

"You want to see this thing through with Sanders, all right. But while you're hunting him down, who's gonna rescue the girl?"

"They aren't going to listen to me anyhow."

"Now you know where she is," Reggie said. "And where they can find Sanders."

Jackson reached for the phone in the cubby. "Why not. They've been so accommodating so far." He dialed LAPD, wiped some blood on his sleeve while he waited, then asked to speak to Sergeant Locker. He held until Reggie hit the freeway.

"Sergeant Locker."

"Hey, Sarge, how'd you like to rescue Larson and O'Brien?"

"Douglas?"

"Yeah."

"I thought I told you to let us handle this."

"And you were doing such a great job, too. Listen, Mac, do whatever you want, all right. But I know where Sanders is, where Larson and probably O'Brien are, and where, I'm guessing, there's enough snow to stage Winter X. Not to mention evidence of other illegalities. You want a scoop or not?"

Locker paused for a few seconds. "What are you talking about?"

"There's a warehouse in Santa Monica, off of Gr—"

"Grainger, yeah we know. It's legit."

"You also know about the underground gentlemen's club there?"

Locker's silence told Jackson he did not.

"Or that this warehouse/club is where Sanders hangs out in a little subterranean lair? That he smuggles these drugs to his buyers from this warehouse? In little wooden idols, not mufflers and tire rims?"

Locker had swallowed his tongue.

"And from what I hear, this place is pretty secure. Better call SWAT."

"How do you know this?"

"A little birdie told me. You think I'm jerking your chain, that I got nothing better to do at five in the morning than crank call you?"

"How do you know Larson and O'Brien are there?"

"The birdie was chatty. Look, Sarge, I'm going to be there in fifteen minutes. If you're not, I guess I'll assume you're not coming. Good luck explaining that one to the next of kin."

This time he hung up on Locker.

"Happy?" he asked Reggie.

"Happier than he probably is."

"Yeah, well."

"So tell me this, All-Star, if SWAT shows up and steals the show, how you gonna plug Sanders?"

"It was your idea to call them."

"I'm just making sure you're thinking, man. Suppose they don't show? Then what you gonna do? Just knock on the front door?"

Jackson shrugged again. "I guess I'll have to work more of my charm."

It was still a little early for rush hour traffic, and Reggie made good time getting across town on the Santa Monica Freeway. He took it all the way into Santa Monica, to Cloverfield Boulevard, then doubled back a few blocks on Olympic. Jackson spotted the street sign first.

"There. Grainger."

"Turn?"

"Yeah, check it out."

Reggie made the right onto Grainger Avenue, which quickly dead-ended in a cul-de-sac short of the freeway. There was a salvage yard on the right, boxed in by eight-foot-high aluminum walls. On the left were a factory that fronted on Olympic and a brick warehouse that faced Grainger. Jackson didn't need to see the address to know it was Sanders' warehouse. It was the only building on the street.

Beyond the warehouse were a loading dock and a tiny parking lot opening directly into the cul-de-sac. A thin row of trees separated the lot from the freeway and the buildings on the next street over.

"That it?" Reggie asked.

"Has to be," Jackson said. "Just turn around like you're lost."

Reggie obeyed, going to the end of the cul-de-sac and returning to Olympic. Jackson surveyed everything a second time as they passed. A narrow alley ran between the warehouse and the factory and possibly connected to an alley behind the warehouse too. But it was too dark to tell.

"Now what?" Reggie asked at the stop sign.

"Right," Jackson said. "Take the next street, see if we can see what's going on from the back side."

Reggie nodded. "Looked pretty standard to me."

"Shaq said his crib and the club were underground. The warehouse is probably legit on the surface."

Singler Street was the next street east, and Reggie made a right past an oil storage facility on the corner of Olympic and Singler. South of the storage facility was a parking garage and then a building housing a dime store and a hole-in-the-wall restaurant, both of which were dark, possibly abandoned. A small parking lot on the south side of the building ran under the freeway, access to it blocked from the warehouse parking lot by more trees and underbrush. The foliage stretched from under the freeway to the edge of the parking garage, with no alleys between any of the buildings and no line of sight to the warehouse.

Reggie looked over at Jackson, not needing to ask another, "Now what?"

"Loop back. See if you can get in that parking garage."

Singler was quiet, and Reggie made a U-turn under the freeway. A moment later, he hung a left into the parking garage entrance. He stopped almost immediately. A yellow gate, blaring the word "closed" in big black letters, barred their path.

"No ticket thingy?" Jackson asked.

Reggie shook his head.

246

"Park on the street," Jackson said. "We can walk in and see what the warehouse looks like from this side."

There was no parking on the street, so despite Jackson's protest that this was hardly the time to worry about parking violations, Reggie drove past the combination dime store and restaurant and parked in the adjacent lot. He and Jackson got out and quickly hiked back toward the garage. Dawn was half an hour away and the sky was beginning to lighten. But this little corner of Los Angeles was still plenty dark, and it appeared that the two of them were the only humans stirring in the neighborhood.

"This club, Off," Jackson said as they turned and walked up the down ramp of the parking garage. "You happen to know its hours?"

"Not sure it keeps regular hours, man. More of a 'by invitation' sort of a place. Special parties."

Jackson nodded as Reggie let out a low whistle.

"What?"

"Get a load of these cars, J."

A third of the stalls were occupied, more as they neared a stairwell in the northwest corner. The cars ranged from bulky SUVs to sports cars and coupes. They were bright and shiny, all of them new, none of them cheap.

"The Grays deal in auto parts," Jackson said. "Maybe this is their shed."

"Or showroom, man. In either case, they've probably got eyes on us."

"Great."

The garage was only three stories tall, and they climbed to the top. It was open to the sky, with only a small cubby that housed a stairwell poking up above the surface.

"No cars up here, man," Reggie said.

"Good thing no lights either," Jackson said. He frowned. "Why's the stairwell here?"

Reggie frowned. "You'd expect it by the street."

"Yeah." Jackson shrugged, and led the way to the western wall of the garage. He and Reggie crouched down. They were slightly south of and across an alley from the warehouse, maybe twenty feet away from the edge of its gently sloped tin roof. The warehouse was dark, as it should be at five-thirty on a Tuesday morning. The windows were all black, and the only door

Jackson saw was by the loading dock on the near left corner. A pair of windows on the second floor had been boarded up, and if Jackson's eyes and the dim lighting weren't playing tricks on him, a doorway on the first floor had been filled in with bricks. There was no access from the alley.

From atop the garage, they also had a clear view of the parking lot. A lone semi-trailer sat in the far corner, a delivery truck was parked next to the warehouse, and a dumpster rested on three wheels in the left corner of the lot. That was it. No cars—especially no black Oldsmobiles. No guards or bouncers on duty. Nothing to indicate that anyone was even there. Then again, the parking garage housed at least two dozen vehicles.

"What do you say, J?"

Jackson didn't answer. After a day and night of flying by the seat of his pants and making split-second decisions and outwitting police and gangbangers, he had nothing. He was beaten, exhausted, and stymied.

"I guess Locker isn't coming," he said at last.

Reggie shook his head. "It's your call, dude. I'm right there with you, man."

"No. This one's mine," Jackson said, taking a deep breath. He turned and started back down toward ground level.

"What are you going to do?" Reggie asked. "There's no way you can get in there by yourself, man."

"I'll just channel my inner Sam Fisher." He shrugged. "I have no other choice."

"Let me go with you."

"No chance. You won't fit in through the ducts."

"I ain't playin' with you, man."

"Neither am I, Hoss. This is a suicide mission. No need in getting two of us killed."

"No need getting one of us killed. You can still opt out."

"And spend the rest of my life running from Shaq? No thanks."

"Better than taking a clip to the chest, ain't it?"

Jackson shrugged.

Reggie sighed in submission. "You want me to cover you from up top?"

"No, stay in the car. If I come out of there, I'm going to need a fast getaway. If I don't, then somebody has to call the cops. Maybe they'll come to the rescue of a civilian."

Reggie nodded. "Where do you want me parked?"

"Right where you are," Jackson said. "We'll come running through the trees."

They emerged from the parking garage on the sidewalk and strode to the Hummer. Jackson retrieved his Glock and the extra magazine. He sighed and leaned back against the side of the door.

"You sure, man?"

"Yeah. Look, if something happens, tell Grandpa . . . tell him . . ." Jackson shook his head. "I don't know what to tell him. Just take care of him, all right?"

"Absolutely, brother." Reggie extended his fist. Jackson tapped it and turned to go.

The trees that separated them from the warehouse parking lot provided good cover, and Jackson was able to get within fifty feet of the loading dock while remaining hidden. Crouched in the underbrush, he paused at the edge of the trees to gather himself.

Lord, I don't know what I'm doing. I don't even know what to ask. Just . . . help.

Taking a deep breath to summon his courage, Jackson started forward. One step and he stopped. Movement to the left had caught his eye, and he quickly dropped to the ground, trying to still his breathing. He watched as first one dark form, then another, then a third appeared from the trees next to the freeway.

Jackson followed them carefully as they took up positions behind the dumpster and the unhitched semi-trailer. He peered across the parking lot and across Grainger to the salvage yard. At first he saw nothing, but then noticed a slight discontinuity in the shadows by the wall. There were two more figures there.

It hit him. SWAT. Locker had come through!

Jackson froze in the underbrush, waiting. For all he knew, more black-clad figures were sneaking through the trees behind him. Even if they weren't, he didn't want to risk being seen by those crossing the parking lot. He lay on his belly for several minutes, watching as the figures crept across the lot and hugged the wall of the warehouse. There weren't enough of them, and where was the battering ram? Or that freaky thing Colin Farrell's character invented to pull down walls?

The figures against the wall waited. So did Jackson. A moment later, he heard a loud grumbling, and headlights swept across the parking lot. At first he thought it was Reggie's Hummer, but he realized this vehicle was much larger. A hybrid SUV and Monster truck.

All pretenses of secrecy aside, it barreled into the parking lot, the beams of the headlights passing right over Jackson as he remained prone on the ground. It turned again and backed in toward the loading dock, stopping just feet from the concrete barrier. Four men jumped out, suited in black. They dragged something out of the back of the vehicle and lugged it up the steps to the loading bay door. A battering ram.

The door came down in seconds, and suddenly the area teemed with SWAT officers. They scurried into the warehouse, and Jackson retreated to update Reggie. He found him behind the wheel, eyes closed, head slightly bowed. Praying.

"Dude!" Jackson said and Reggie looked up.

"J, what's up?"

"SWAT's here, man. They just broke into the warehouse."

"What?"

"Come on!"

Jackson and Reggie hurried back into the trees and they both dropped to the ground in the underbrush at the edge of the warehouse parking lot. It was empty, save for the SWAT truck.

But the silence and stillness didn't last long. Three police cruisers, lights flashing, whipped into the parking lot and a dozen uniformed officers scrambled out of the cars. They began setting up barricades and taking shelter behind the cars, weapons drawn. From down the alley behind the building, Jackson saw more lights, suggesting the police had the other side covered too.

"Maybe we better get out of here," Reggie said. "Before they show up on our tail."

"I can't man," Jackson said. "I've got business to take care of."

"Man, are you serious? You can't just kill a guy with cops everywhere, even if he is the baddest drug dealer in the city."

"It's him or me, man. Dawg eat dawg, you know?"

"Man, you've spent too much time with these hoods, man."

Gunfire interrupted their debate. A few quick bursts, followed by silence.

Jackson and Reggie waited, along with the cops in the parking lot, who had been joined by reinforcements. Locker had called in everyone short of the 4th Army.

More gunfire erupted in several brief barrages. Then one last, long salvo, followed by a fleeting final pop, and the night was eerily silent again.

The silence only lasted a moment. Sirens began wailing in the pre-dawn stillness. The cops in the parking lot held their positions, guns drawn, ready to unleash a volley of bullets if the wrong people came out of the broken-down loading bay door. Their wait was less than a minute.

"All clear!" a SWAT officer announced from the doorway, and as if on cue, more chaos erupted. Ambulances roared into the lot, followed by more police cruisers and another SWAT vehicle. Sirens blared, and the officers waiting behind their cars began talking into and being squawked at by their walkie-talkies. Large floodlights were quickly erected and aimed at the side of the warehouse as dozens of officers ran into the building and the first SWAT officers began filing out.

They brought with them gang members. Some were handcuffed and uninjured. Others had minor wounds. A SWAT officer helped a limping comrade out of the building. EMTs scurried into the building and came out with several victims on gurneys, none of them appearing to be lawmen.

Jackson and Reggie watched it all from the trees and scrub. Ten minutes after the last shot sounded, there was still no sign of Ashley, Dylan, or Sanders (unless Ashley's description had been way off). And the hubbub was starting to die down.

"I need to get in there," Jackson said.

"What?"

"Something's not right. I need to check it out."

"You got a plan?"

"As a matter of fact, I do."

Chapter Twenty-Nine

5:51 a.m.

JACKSON LED THE way back to Reggie's Hummer. He opened the door and began rifling around in the storage compartment built into the door.

"What do you need?" Reggie asked.

"You got any old coffee cups in here?"

"What?"

"Coffee cup. Doesn't need to be clean."

"Yeah, I think so." Reggie opened the back door and began digging. He emerged a moment later with an empty Starbucks cup. "This do?"

"Perfect," Jackson said. He set it on the seat, exchanging it for the police badge he had pulled out of the door compartment.

"Where did you get that?" Reggie asked.

"It's Grant's," Jackson said, clipping it onto his jeans.

"What was it doing in my door?"

"I grabbed it when we stopped back at home. Thought I might need it to bribe my way in to see Mickens. The Bauer approach seemed better."

"You just going to walk in there and act like you a cop?"

Jackson checked his appearance in the mirror. A little rough, thanks to Shaq and his thugs, but not as bad as it felt. He nodded at Reggie. "Exactly right, partner."

"Uh, I ain't got a shield, bro."

"You won't need one. You're the strong, silent type. Come on."

They started back into the trees again. "Follow my lead," Jackson said.

"Whatever you say, man."

Carrying the empty coffee cup in his hand, Jackson stopped at the edge of the trees and waited until it was clear. When no one was looking, he stepped out into the parking lot and strode straight for the loading dock door. He didn't have to look to know Reggie was on his six.

"Who are you?" a SWAT officer manning the doorway asked.

Jackson lifted his shirt to reveal the badge. "Douglas. This is Switzer. Locker told us to get down here. He inside?"

"Not sure," the man replied. "You're detectives?"

"Been working a sting on Tone Sanders for six months, and now I hear some cowboy P.I. just screwed everything up."

"If Locker's inside, he's through there," the officer said. "Careful, it's a mess."

"Thanks." Jackson nodded and pushed through. Emergency lighting revealed racks and racks of auto parts, neatly arranged and stored—except for a rack on the far wall that had fallen to the floor, scattering pieces all over the concrete floor. Jackson followed the destruction to an open stairway leading down. Two EMTs carrying a stretcher appeared at the bottom of the stairs, and Jackson and Reggie stood aside to let them pass.

"Switzer?" Reggie asked.

"Thought you'd like that."

"I hope you know what you're doing."

"Strong and silent," Jackson said as he started down the stairs. With his shirt tucked behind his badge, Jackson passed by another SWAT officer on the landing. He casually took a drink of air from his cup as he and Reggie turned the corner. The auto parts in the basement were not so neatly arranged. At least, not anymore.

Several shelves were tipped completely over. A few more were leaning against the wall or against other shelves. Everything from mufflers and exhaust pipes to pieces for which Jackson couldn't imagine a place on a vehicle were on the floor. Some were in boxes, most weren't. And bullet holes had made Swiss cheese of everything.

To Jackson's left, a concrete wall ran north and south. A medic was helping a fallen SWAT officer who sat slumped against the wall. He appeared to be okay. Two more EMTs were trying to revive a fallen gangster a little farther along the wall. He appeared very un-okay. Half a dozen officers were milling around, talking, inspecting, doing whatever they did. None of them paid more than a passing glance at Jackson and Reggie.

Jackson took a risk. "Sergeant Locker!"

Heads turned; nobody responded. Grounds to keep moving.

"This just a half basement, you think?" Jackson asked.

"No," Reggie said, nodding toward the corner. A doorway was cut into the concrete wall, presumably leading to the east half of the basement. Ignoring the cops who were ignoring them, Jackson took another fake drink and moved to the opening. The doorway became a small hallway with two doors—one marked "Storage" and one marked "Restroom"—on the right, and a steel door straight ahead. It was open, purple and pink light emanating from the other side, and Jackson and Reggie continued onward.

"Pilgrims in an unholy land," Jackson muttered as they stepped into the dark room. The faint light coming from under a bar and from recesses in the ceiling illuminated just enough for Jackson to recognize the place as Sanders' underground club.

The room was L-shaped, spreading around behind the restrooms and storage room. The bar extended from the inside elbow of the L and branched off into each wing, in the process wrapping around what Jackson deemed a runway. The walls were lined with private booths and secluded little alcoves where drug deals could be struck and sealed, off-the-book bets could be placed, and terrorist activities could be planned. Mirrors on the ceiling, the walls, and the surface of the bar reflected everything.

"Like a little house of horrors," Jackson said.

"I never did like carnivals, man."

Jackson turned his attention to the outside corner of the L where a large mirror cut the corner. Three officers—the only other people in the club— stood clustered around the middle panel of the mirror, and Jackson approached them slowly, making sure none of them had sergeant's stripes.

"Any of you all seen Sergeant Locker?" Jackson asked.

The one nearest to him turned. "No. You are?"

"Douglas." Jackson feigned a swig. "This is Switzer. Locker called us in." He nodded at the mirror. "Any sign of Sanders?"

"None."

Jackson crossed his arms and stuck his tongue into his cheek, his contemplative detective face. "How many of his people were here?"

"Seven," the man answered. "Two dead, five wounded."

"All males?"

"That's right."

Jackson nodded at the mirror. "We know if there's anything behind this?"

"The middle panel's actually a door," a second officer volunteered. "It's locked."

"We assume it's two-way and that's the office behind it," the first officer said. "Kitchen's back that way, along with a . . . dressing room."

Jackson had another belt of not coffee and ruminated some more. He nodded at Reggie. "Hey, B, hand me that stool, will you?"

Reggie raised an eyebrow but slid a barstool to Jackson. He hefted it into his arms, nodded an "excuse me" at the three officers, and swung it, seat first, at the mirror.

The mirror shattered into a million pieces, and the officers quickly drew their weapons. One of them shone a flashlight into the revealed space. It was a simple triangular room, concrete floor, concrete walls. It was empty except for another door in the corner.

"I heard a knock-knock joke like this once," Jackson said. "Ends with a green gorilla." He approached the door, made of solid steel and firmly locked. A keypad in the door appeared to be the only means of entry. No handle, no knob, no external hinges.

Jackson turned to the officer who had done most of the speaking. "You want to get somebody down here to open that door?"

"Yes, sir."

The officer left the room and his comrades stepped outside into the club. Jackson paced to the corner, hand over his mouth. Now what? The room behind the door had to be Sanders' private palace. But was he even there? Were Ashley and Dylan? Had Shaq set Jackson up? If so, did the kill-or-be-killed rule still apply with purposely faulty intelligence? And how long until somebody figured out Jackson wasn't a detective?

"You all right, J?"

"Yeah," Jackson said. "I just . . ." Something caught his eye, and he stooped to the ground.

"What you find?" Reggie asked.

"I don't know." Jackson picked up a shiny item and played it between his fingers. He stood. "It's a sequin. Like from a flip-flop."

"They were here."

"Yeah. And we need . . ."

"What?"

Jackson closed his eyes.

"What is it?" Reggie asked.

"This doesn't make sense."

"What?"

"Come on."

"Where we going?"

Jackson was already out of the room, leaving the two officers in his wake. With Reggie on his tail, they hurried through the club, out the hallway, and back into the other half of the basement. Several officers still remained in the subterranean warehouse, as did the paramedics working on the fallen gangster. Jackson rushed past them all and back up the steps.

"You want to fill me in, J?" Reggie asked, climbing behind him.

"You're Sanders, the cops come, you just retreat farther and farther into your building?"

"I got any alternatives?"

"No, and that's my point. It's a nice door, but it isn't exactly Helm's Deep. This is more of a Robert Neville ending."

"What are you getting at?"

They broke into open air, unhindered by any officers. Jackson hurried into the trees and along the side of the parking garage, back toward Singler Street. "Look at this neighborhood," he said over his shoulder. "Old factories, warehouses, dive buildings. So why's the parking garage look like a staging ground for *The Fast and the Furious*?"

"Don't know," Reggie answered.

"I'm a bad-to-the-bone gangster with an off-the-record club and a private crib underground, I'm going to have a backdoor out of there."

"To the garage?"

"I'm guessing the foundation of the garage is actually a basement."

"Sanders' lair."

"Uh-huh. With stairs leading up to a garage full of getaway cars and an exit onto another street."

"If that's true, man, he's long gone."

Jackson stopped at the sidewalk. "Unless you were right and he's got a camera in there." He nodded across the street, where a black and white was just leaving. Singler Street was clear. Jackson turned to Reggie. "And now he makes his move."

Reggie rubbed the top of his head and sighed.

"You got your sidearm, Switzer?"

"In the Hummer, Detective."

"Hurry."

Reggie was gone less than two minutes, in which time Jackson took a position by the front support column of the garage. All was quiet.

"What's the plan?" Reggie asked when he returned, his Sig P220 in hand.

"This is the only exit. We move in."

"What if they see us?"

"Then they retreat toward the cops. Works for me."

Reggie nodded. "Your lead."

They started up the ramp, moving from car to car for cover. Not knowing where a camera might be concealed, they concerned themselves more with not giving a potential gunman an easy target.

Reaching the top of the ramp, they stopped, hiding behind a navy SUV. Directly ahead of them, in the northwest corner of the garage, was the stairwell. There was no sign of movement, and no cameras stood out as Jackson surveyed the scene.

Reggie looked at Jackson for a cue. He responded by nodding at the stairwell. They crept over to it, and while Reggie covered him, Jackson eased the door open, careful not to let it squeak. It was only an inch ajar when a clang echoed up the shaft. It was followed by footsteps, and Jackson looked at Reggie with wide eyes.

"Let's go," Reggie mouthed.

Jackson quietly shut the door and they hurried to take cover behind a concrete barrier that separated the aisles of the garage. Jackson readied his weapon and looked toward Reggie. He motioned to get his attention and made a phone gesture with his hand. Reggie reached into his pocket and slid the phone to him.

Jackson held the phone down as he opened it and quickly punched in 9-1-1. It was all he had time for before the door burst open. He jerked his head up to peek over the concrete wall.

The first man through the door matched Ashley's description of Tone Sanders perfectly. Tall, muscular, light brown skin, buzzed black hair, a goatee, and eyes that were barely more than slits. He was followed closely by a hulking white guy and then a consortium of thugs, dragging with them a man and a woman.

Ashley and, Jackson assumed, Dylan.

Jackson caught Reggie's eye to make sure he knew who they were looking at, then signaled to make sure his friend was ready. He nodded.

Shielded by the roof of a Lexus parked on the other side of the wall, Jackson popped to his feet. He had Sanders in his sights. "Don't move, homes."

Everyone moved. Sanders whirled and dropped to the ground as Jackson squeezed two shots over his head. His other thugs crouched down while reaching for weapons. Ashley and Dylan just went to the ground.

The shots came flying from across the garage, and Jackson and Reggie both ducked behind the concrete barrier. The barrage was intense, and Jackson was content to let Sanders' men shoot themselves empty. But he wasn't going to let them use the spray of bullets as cover to get back into the stairwell or to a getaway vehicle.

Still crouched, he hopped around Reggie and poked his head up a few feet to his right, behind the cover of a support column. Through the side and rear window of an SUV, he had a line on one of Sanders' goons, and he took

258

it, blasting two shots that felled the man. It drew intense fire Jackson's way, and he ducked down again.

Reggie, meanwhile, had scooted to his left. Raising his head and arms above the barrier, he squeezed off four shots. When he dropped down again, he indicated he had taken out another man. There had been at least four, plus Sanders. Maybe five. But the odds were evening.

Jackson motioned for Reggie to switch places with him, and then instructed his pal to draw fire. Reggie did, and Jackson used the opportunity to hop the ledge. He crouched behind an old Camaro and took aim. One bullet just missed Sanders shoulder, but another caught one of his thugs in the chest. He slumped.

Jackson was out of bullets and quickly expelled the empty magazine, replacing it with the spare in his back pocket. At the same time, a scuffle broke out as Dylan tried to wrest the gun away from another of Sanders' men. The man managed to crack Dylan on the head, loosening his grip on his hand and the gun. But before he could turn the gun on Dylan, Reggie pumped four shots into his chest.

Jackson scooted around the Camaro and entrenched himself between it and the SUV. Sanders and his remaining compatriot had grabbed Ashley and were headed for the southwest corner of the garage. They covered themselves with a volley of bullets, and Jackson could only crouch and hide until it was over.

He heard the click of an empty gun and spun up over the trunk of the Camaro. Sanders' man was reloading, and Jackson put three slugs in his chest and abdomen. Reggie had crossed the barrier too and taken up a position behind the SUV. They watched as Ashley momentarily escaped Sanders' grip. But before she could get out of their line of fire, he grabbed her by the hair, pulled her back, and placed his gun to her jaw. He began backing toward a dark Ford Mustang.

At the same time, two more men burst through the door atop the stairwell. Bullets whizzed over Jackson's head as he fell to the concrete floor behind the Camaro. Several shots spat into the hood of the SUV, and Jackson saw Reggie go down. He rolled onto his back. "Hoss?"

"Yeah!"

Jackson turned and aimed behind the back wheels of the Camaro. He saw a leg and fired. His target fell, and Jackson climbed to a crouch. He heard several more shots and raised his head just in time to see the second man go down.

"J!" Reggie hollered.

"Yeah," Jackson answered, turning around to see Sanders slam the trunk of the Mustang on Ashley. Jackson stood and fired, two bullets that found their mark in Sanders' shoulder. He staggered, but somehow managed to get down and into the drivers' side of the car.

"She's in the trunk!" Jackson yelled before Reggie could fire. The Mustang backed up, keeping the trunk in Jackson's line. It stopped, and with a squeal of tires, headed for the exit ramp.

Jackson leaped over the hood of the Camaro and jumped back over the barrier. He raced after the car, and as Sanders made the corner leading to the exit, Jackson managed to squeeze off two more shots toward the front of the car.

They missed, and with more burned rubber, Sanders was gone, down the ramp to freedom.

Chapter Thirty

REGGIE'S PHONE LAY on the floor a few feet away, and Jackson scooped it up.

"Hello? Hello? I'm at the shootout on Grainger and Olympic. We've got a mess of people down and Sanders has escaped in a navy Mustang. He's on Singler Road with a hostage in the trunk. Repeat, Tone Sanders is in a navy Mustang with a hostage in the trunk."

Jackson clapped the phone shut and jumped the barrier again. Of Sanders' seven men, four were dead, one was as good as dead, and two others were seriously wounded. Reggie appeared fine, and nodded before Jackson could ask. Dylan was another story.

His face was bloodied and bruised and his clothes were covered with blood. Some of it was fresh, some of it old; some had dripped and some had soaked through. He looked the part of a man who had been tortured, and Jackson figured he had been compromised as an undercover cop. Maybe before Ashley had ever come to him for help.

More than that, Dylan looked as if he hadn't slept in days. His eyes were red and glazed, and Jackson wondered what kind of drugs they had been pumping into him. Or he had been pumping into himself.

But despite his wounds, Dylan wasn't ready to quit fighting. He was on his feet, looking for a weapon. He picked a Glock off a dead man and searched for a full magazine. Then he headed for the nearest car, a red Firebird. The door was locked, and instead of trying for another car, he smashed the window with his elbow. Unlocking the door, he crawled down onto the floor and began digging for wires.

Jackson looked at Reggie. "You okay here?"

He nodded.

"Stay with these guys, wait for the cops. I'm going with him." Jackson hurried around to the passenger side of the Firebird and broke the window with the butt of his gun. By the time he got the door open, Dylan had the car started.

"What are you doing?" Dylan asked.

"Same as you, pal. You okay to drive?"

"Watch me."

Jackson slid into the seat and buckled his seatbelt as Dylan put the car in gear. They raced around the parking garage, scraping bottom as they descended to street level. Dylan pushed the accelerator, knocking off his mirror on the corner of the garage and spinning sideways as he turned south onto Singler Road.

"You sure they went this way?" Jackson asked.

"Singler leads to Pico, the quickest way to the freeway."

"Then where?"

"I don't know, man. Who are you?"

"A private eye. Ashley hired me."

"What?"

"To help save you."

Dylan glanced at him for a second. He whipped the car onto northbound Pico Boulevard. "Nice work."

Jackson wasn't sure if the remark was sarcastic or not, so he let it go. "Any idea where Sanders might go?"

"Yeah, either a place up in Brentwood or one down in Torrance."

"What about a hospital? I hit him twice in the shoulder."

"Good?"

"I'm surprised he's still up."

They went under the freeway again, Dylan made a hard right back under the freeway a third time, and then veered equally sharply to the left, onto the ramp. He stomped the gas pedal to the floor.

"Sanders won't go to the hospital, man." Dylan winced. "He'll . . . find somebody to do it quiet. No records, you know?"

"Okay, any idea who?"

"Not a clue," Dylan said, wincing again as he looked over his shoulder. Traffic was picking up on I-10, and Jackson kept his eyes peeled for any navy cars. Then he realized he still had Reggie's phone in his pocket. He fished it out.

"You're a cop. Who should I call?"

"Here," Dylan said. He took the phone, swerving into the middle lane as he dialed. "Locker, it's O'Brien. I'm in pursuit of Sanders and Larson on I-10 eastbound. Driving a navy Mustang. . . . No. . . . I've been with him six months, Marty . . . I don't know. North or south on the SDF. . . . Right."

Dylan closed the phone and tossed it back to Jackson.

"So, north or south?" Jackson asked.

"There's more options south," Dylan said. "South."

They took the ramp leading onto I-405 southbound, and Dylan pressed the accelerator over eighty. Jackson got a lump in his stomach, realizing that if Sanders and Ashley had gone a different direction, they were now getting farther away twice as fast. But this was a shot in the dark anyhow.

"You sure you pegged him good?" Dylan asked. He had to yell against the wind rushing in through the broken windows.

"Yeah, two to the left shoulder. He's got to be leaking bad."

Dylan swore and stared at the freeway ahead of him, as if willing the navy Mustang to appear. Jackson cast a quick glance at his new partner. If not for the drugs and the beating, he would have been a handsome guy. Tall, strong, blond hair, blue eyes, chiseled features. He wondered if maybe there was more than partner loyalty between Dylan and Ashley. It would explain her desperate moves throughout the past twenty-four hours, and the intensity on his face now.

Jackson returned his eyes to the freeway. He saw semis, old pickups, Beemers and Benzes, and a hatchback loaded with luggage and UCLA bumper stickers, but no Mustangs.

UCLA.

It gave Jackson an idea and he picked up the phone. He just hoped Sam had her cell with her and was free to answer it.

"Hi, it's Sam. I can't take your call right now, so please leave me a message. Thanks, and have a great day."

He disconnected and quickly dialed Information.

"What city?"

"Santa Monica."

"Pardon?"

"San-ta Mon-i-ca!" he said, shouting to be heard over the roar of the wind.

"Name?"

"Uh, the UCLA Medical Center."

"One moment."

Dylan glanced his way again. "What are you doing?"

"Playing a wildcard."

The operator came back and gave him the number, and at his request, connected Jackson with the hospital. He had to wait four rings for an answer, and then asked for Sam, saying it was an emergency.

They were nearing the Marina Freeway interchange when she came to the phone. "This is Sam," she said, anxiety in her voice.

"Sam, it's me. I need your help again."

"Why, what now? Where are you?"

"Long story, but do you know of any black market doctors?"

"What?"

"Something off the record, if a guy got shot but couldn't go to the E.R.?"

"Why couldn't he go to the E.R.?" The anxiety was back. "What's going on, Jackson?"

"We're chasing a guy who's been shot twice, and he can't risk being seen at a hospital. Any idea where he'd go?"

"Maybe a clinic? Who's we?"

"You know of any clinics that take that kind of customer?"

Dylan shook his head. "No clinic, man."

"Not a clinic, Sam. Anything else?"

"I've heard a name a couple of times in the E.R." she said. "*El Curador.*"

Jackson sat up. "*El Curador?* You sure?"

"Yeah. I don't know anything about him, or even if it is a him. For that matter, I don't know if he's what you're looking for. It's a guess."

"Thanks, Sam."

Jackson closed the phone.

Dylan looked over. "A name?"

"*El Curador*," Jackson answered. "You know Spanish?"

"Yeah. It means 'The Healer.'"

Jackson's brain accelerated into hyperdrive.

"What? What's going on?" Dylan asked.

El Curador. The Healer. The name, perhaps, of an off-the-books doctor. Also the wording on the tattoo Jackson had seen earlier on Enrique's arm. Enrique, whose dad Javy had made a living operating on drug dealers and running them by boat to Mexico. Like father, like son?

"You got something or not?" Dylan asked.

"Sanders, he ever talk about Mexico?"

"What?"

"He ever talk about going to Mexico—a contingency plan or anything?"

"No, man. He . . . He has a cousin—a second cousin, maybe—outside of Tijuana. Why?"

"Because I think that's where he's going."

"What? How?"

"Give me a sec." Jackson opened the phone again and dialed Connie's number. "Connie, it's Jackson."

She swore in Italian. "Jackson, what do you want?"

"I need to talk to Gina. Is she there?"

"Gina?"

"Connie, it's urgent. Please!"

"All right, all right. Let me check."

He heard her get out of bed, mumbling to herself in a mixture of English and Italian. He wished it were all in Italian. She knocked on a door, and he heard her talking to Diane. He knew the answer before she came back on the phone.

"No, she didn't come in."

265

"What's her cell number?"

"What? What's going on, Jac—"

"Connie, it's an emergency! I need Gina's cell number."

He heard her talking to Diane again. Then he heard Diane's voice, and a moment later, Connie repeated a number to Jackson. He quickly memorized it, thanked her, and before she could ask any more questions, disconnected the call. Immediately, he punched in Gina's number.

"Hello," she answered sleepily.

He was relieved she picked up the phone. "Gina, it's Jackson. Where are you?"

"I'm . . . ugh . . . I'm . . . I think I'm on a boat."

"You think?"

"Yeah." She groaned again. "Yeah, I'm on . . . Landon's friend's boat."

"Enrique?"

"Yeah, how—"

"Do you know where he is?"

"Who, Enrique?"

"Yeah."

"No. Up top, at least last night."

"Where are you on the boat?"

"What's going on, Jackson? What time is it?"

"Early. This is important, Gina. Are you in the cabin?"

"Is that the bedroom?"

"Yes," Jackson answered.

"Then yes."

"Is anyone with you?"

"No. Landon was."

"Are you moving?"

"No, I'm just laying here."

"The boat, Gina. Is the boat moving?" Jackson asked, looking at Dylan and asking for patience with his eyes.

"Um . . . yeah."

"Where'd you go last night?"

"What?"

"On the boat. Where did you go?"

"Just out. Nowhere."

"Is there a window in the cabin?" Jackson asked.

"Yeah."

"I need you to get up and see if you recognize anything."

"What is going on?"

"Gina, it's an emergency. Please, just trust me."

She groaned and mumbled to herself, but Jackson heard her moving around. "There's land," she reported. "Ugh, what time is it?"

"Do you recognize anything, any buildings?"

"No, it looks like there's . . . a river ahead maybe?"

"What side of the boat are you on?"

"What?"

"What side of the boat are you on?"

"I don't know, portside or something."

"Right or left."

Gina groaned again. "Right."

"Do you see airplanes up in the sky?"

"What?"

"Are there planes up in the sky, out the window? Lights in the sky, maybe?"

"Um . . . yeah, I think so. Yeah, there's one right there, an actual plane."

"A jet?"

"Yeah."

"LAX," Jackson said. "Marina del Rey."

"What?" Dylan asked.

Jackson lowered the phone. "He's going to Marina del Rey."

Dylan swore, then jerked the car into the right lane. He hit the horn and nearly ran over a two-door in front of him.

"Gina, lock the door to the cabin and stay where you are no matter what."

"What's going on, Jackson?"

"Just trust me. Stay below deck, no matter what, you got it?"

"Y-yeah. What's going on?"

"It's complicated. But I'll be there soon."

Dylan floored the accelerator as he swerved onto the edge of the road and shot past several cars and onto the exit ramp. "You sure about this?"

"Sort of," Jackson said, punching in 9-1-1 for the fourth time that night. He explained the situation as briefly as possible to the operator and closed the phone.

"Sort of?" Dylan said. "What's that mean?"

Jackson expelled the magazine from his gun and counted. He had six remaining bullets, plus one in the chamber. He reloaded and turned to Dylan.

"We'll find out."

Chapter Thirty-One

6:16 a.m.

A BRILLIANT MORNING had dawned over the Los Angeles Basin. Thin wisps of clouds hung over the Santa Ana Mountains east of the city, reflecting the vibrant orange light of the rising sun off one another and displaying it across the sky. It was breathtaking.

And unsettling. Almost as if with the vanishing darkness, any chance of tracking down Ashley had vanished too.

But Jackson had a lead, he hoped. Once again, he opened Reggie's cell, counting that his grandpa would be up or close to it by dawn.

"Hello?"

"Grandpa."

"Jackson. Good grief, kiddo, it's barely morning."

"I need a favor. Can you tell me if there's a boat coming into the harbor?"

"What?"

"A nice-sized cruiser, coming in. Check discreetly."

Leroy paused for a moment. "Do I want to know what's going on?"

"Even if you did, there isn't time to explain."

"Hold on, I'll check." There was a slight commotion, then the mumbling of a seventy-five-year-old man. "I expected this sort of thing when I was in the pulpit, you know. Calls at all hours of the night, weird requests."

"Come on, Gramps, you're usually making lunch by now."

"Har, har."

A door opened and closed.

"Okay, what am I looking for?"

"Any boat coming into the harbor."

269

"Yeah, there's one. White, looks like a forty-footer or so. Nice, too."

"You see anybody onboard?"

"No . . . just the name. E-L . . . Curator?"

"*El Curador.* That's the one."

Dylan looked over, a brief glance as he made a mad dash across town, swerving around traffic, racing through yellow and red lights, using the horn instead of a turn signal. "What, he's there?"

"He will be."

"Where are you?" Leroy asked. "Sounds like a jet running into a herd of geese."

"I'm coming to you," Jackson said. "Keep an eye on the boat, will you? Let me know where she goes?"

"Hey, whatever you say, bud."

Jackson lowered the phone from his mouth, waiting anxiously for Dylan to get them to the harbor and for Leroy to tell him where to go. There were eight different channels where a boat could dock in the harbor, three on the east side and five on the west. Plus a handful of other docks and moors.

"Jack."

"Yeah?"

"He's headed between Bali and Mindanao. He's turning in, looks like to Mindanao."

"Thanks, Gramps." Jackson closed the phone and relayed the news to Dylan. "East side."

Dylan answered by hanging a hard right, tires screeching, horns around him blaring.

"There's going to be at least one more innocent on the boat," Jackson said. "A girl. Probably two."

"You want to tell me what's going on?"

"A girl I know is on a boat called *El Curador.* She's with a guy I know, who has a tattoo on his arm."

"*El Curador.*"

"Right. The Healer. Same name as the supposed black market doctor my friend knows."

"You're connected," Dylan said, whipping left.

"P.I." Jackson turned the safety off on his gun as he saw they were nearing the harbor.

Dylan turned left again, onto Lincoln Boulevard. Ironically, it led them right past the Centinela Freeman Regional Medical Center. Bali Way was the first right. Mindanao was the second, and Dylan took it on the sides of two wheels.

Jackson scanned the water for any sign of *El Curador*.

"You see it?" Dylan asked.

"No. Keep going."

Dylan took that as a cue to step on the gas, and they shot forward at breakneck speed. They passed rows of mostly empty parking spaces, beyond which were rows and rows of docked boats. A supper club momentarily blocked their view, and then Jackson saw it. Parked across parts of three spaces next to the dock was a navy Ford Mustang, trunk open.

Leaving plenty of rubber on the road, Dylan stomped on the brakes. Jackson nearly hit the dash, and was out of his seat in a second. Dylan beat him out of the car and to the Mustang. The trunk was empty. The driver's seat was covered in blood, and there were drops of it around the car.

"He's hurt bad," Dylan said, looking around. Jackson joined him and soon spotted *El Curador* at the end of the dock. A dark-skinned man was helping two people onboard, an injured man and a blond woman. Sanders and Ashley. The guy helping them was Enrique.

Dylan took aim and sailed a warning shot over their heads. All three ducked down onto the deck of the boat, which immediately began backing away from the dock. Jackson and Dylan sprinted in pursuit. They had to pull up short, Jackson literally sliding on the deck to stop himself from skidding into the water.

Dylan swore as the boat backed farther into the harbor.

"Come on!" Jackson yelled as he got to his feet. They raced back to the car. "It'll take him a while to get up to speed! We can circle around on Fiji and catch him!"

Dylan dove behind the wheel, and Jackson had to grab onto the passenger door and get in as Dylan stepped on the gas. He took the circle at the end of Mindanao on two wheels, accelerating more as he headed back to the east. Jackson got on the phone again.

"Hello?"

"Grandpa, that boat is coming back out of the channel. I need you to block it."

"What?"

"Just get out into the channel and do anything to slow it down. And keep your head down!"

To his credit, Leroy didn't ask questions. "If this baby sinks, I'm moving in with you," he said, already scrambling. Jackson left him to the task of getting his large houseboat out into the channel and concentrated on keeping an eye on *El Curador*. He also dialed 9-1-1 again and told the dispatcher to send the cops, the Coast Guard, and the U.S. Navy toward Marina del Rey. If Sanders and Ashley reached the open water, there would be nothing he and Dylan could do.

Dylan had clearly taught Ashley how to drive, or vice versa. He tore around the corner onto Admiralty Way, coaxing every last ounce of energy out of the Firebird. He hung another right onto Fiji Way, following it around the southeastern side of the harbor. Along the way, they caught up with and surpassed *El Curador*, which was chugging steadily toward the mouth of the harbor. Jackson kept an eye out, looking for any sign of Sanders aboveboard. But he was nowhere to be seen, almost assuredly down below, now with a harem of hostages.

Jackson counted off in his head. Sanders. Enrique. Landon. Ashley. Gina. Probably Enrique's date. He turned to Dylan. "Don't shoot any of the girls unless they're packing."

Dylan answered with stone-cold intensity, coasting to a stop in the circle at the end of Fiji Way. Jackson got out and circled around to Dylan's side of the car, where the pair of them crouched down to watch the scene unfold.

El Curador was gaining speed and making its way toward the open ocean. But Leroy had managed to get *Marsha* started and edged out from the dock. It would be close.

Jackson spotted Landon atop the bridge and saw him physically startle as Leroy maneuvered the houseboat into his path. Landon slowed, then turned and gunned his engine in an effort to get around the houseboat. But old *Marsha* had a little giddyup in her getalong too, and she continued to force Landon wider. Both boats drew closer, veering farther and farther to the near edge of the channel, threatening to crash into one of the many docks that lined the shore. Jackson got up.

"Where you going, man?" Dylan asked.

"For a swim."

Jackson took several deep breaths, trying to time things perfectly. He took off sprinting, turning onto the longest of the docks and making a beeline for the nose of *El Curador*. He planted his foot on the edge of the last plank of wood and pushed off the corner, soaring through the air like Mike Powell as Leroy forced Landon so wide that he almost brushed against the dock.

With a thud that nearly broke bones and that threatened to knock the wind out of him, Jackson collided with the bow of *El Curador*. Hanging on for dear life, he managed to swing one leg up onto the railing and pull himself aboard. Almost immediately, Landon cut power, coasting around *Marsha* and farther into the channel.

Jackson had climbed onto the stern, in a small seating area next to the galley, or kitchen. In front of him, steps led up to Landon on the bridge and down to the cabin. Jackson rolled to his feet and came up in a crouch, reaching for his gun. He was too late.

Sanders appeared in the cabin stairway, gun drawn in his right hand, his left shoulder sagging and bleeding profusely. His face was gray and his eyes wide. How he was still conscious Jackson had no idea. And at the moment, no concern.

Jackson dived to the side as several shots spit into the deck of the boat. He rolled behind the galley counter and looked up to see a small fire extinguisher attached to the side of the counter. He ripped it off the hook, pulled the tab, and began spraying in the general direction of Sanders.

Foam and steam mixed, creating a blinding fog. Jackson peeked around the counter, heard a few shots, and ducked down again. He dove left and sprayed from that side of the counter, hoping to draw more fire. And hoping said fire didn't hit the engine and blow up the entire boat. He also hoped Leroy had taken cover on his houseboat, which floated fifty feet to stern.

While Sanders was momentarily distracted, Jackson scampered around the right side of the counter and popped to his feet. He unleashed another spray of foam while running in the general direction of Sanders. When he saw him through the mist, he swung the fire extinguisher, aiming for the gangster's head. He missed, connecting instead with his shoulder. His left shoulder. His bleeding shoulder.

Sanders' howl of pain woke the valley. He fell to the deck, and Jackson slipped in the foam. He slid once before rising to his feet, again reaching for his gun. Somehow, despite the pain, Sanders had risen, his gun still in hand.

Like in the movies, the mist in the air seemed to separate, giving Jackson a clear view of his target. He squeezed the trigger, and felt the small kick as his Glock discharged.

One pull of the trigger.

Two almost simultaneous shots.

Jackson looked down to see where he had been hit, but he was clean. He looked back up as Sanders slumped to the deck, the gun falling from his lifeless hand. Jackson turned his eyes to the shore where Dylan stood, gun drawn, still slightly crouched as he aimed toward the boat.

So if Shaq wanted to split hairs, maybe Jackson hadn't been the one to kill Sanders.

Jackson approached the fallen drug dealer, kicked the gun away, and made sure he was indeed dead.

As a doornail.

Jackson whipped around as someone dashed up from the cabin. Enrique. He made no effort to attack Jackson, instead diving off the side of the boat and into the water.

Jackson ran to the railing, then turned his gun up to Landon, who had watched it all from the bridge. Jackson wasn't sure if he was a threat and should be watched, or if he should go down to check on the girls instead, or if he should keep an eye on Enrique. So he did all three, sort of.

Landon stayed put. Jackson hollered down into the cabin. Enrique swam toward Leroy's houseboat and warranted all of Jackson's attention.

He trained his gun on him, ready to fire. Then Leroy emerged on the front deck of the boat, just as Enrique reached for it.

Jackson wanted to scream. He wanted to stop time, pull a *Matrix* and whip around to a different angle so he could take out Enrique without risking hitting his grandpa. Instead, he was forced to watch as time ticked by in agonizingly slow seconds. Did Enrique have a gun? Would he hurt Leroy or just try to avoid him? Was there anything Jackson could do?

His worries were for nothing. Leroy had come prepared. With a frying pan.

He allowed Enrique to climb halfway onto the boat, exposing his head. Then Leroy teed him up like a hanging Barry Zito curveball. The clang echoed through the morning, rousing the deep-sleepers who hadn't been wakened by Sanders' earlier bellow.

Enrique slipped into the water.

Leroy twirled the frying pan in his hand, then blew over the top of it.

Jackson whirled around and turned the gun on Landon. He raised his hands and cooperated by slowly coming down the stairs.

"It was Enrique's idea, man. I had no say."

"You carrying?"

"No. No, man."

Jackson believed him. "Why don't you go bob for your friend?"

Landon looked at him in disbelief for a moment, then plunged overboard.

"Keep an eye on him, Cool Hand," Jackson said to Leroy. He twirled the frying pan again.

Dylan paddled up to the side of the boat. Jackson reached a hand to help him over the side. "Nice shooting, pardner."

Dylan nodded and led the way down below. Still cautious, he kicked open the cabin door.

Three girls screamed in alarm. Ashley, none the worse for wear. Gina, perhaps slightly so. And a dark-haired, dark-skinned girl who appeared calmest of all. Enrique's date. She was probably used to sordid undertakings.

Ashley's scream turned to delight and she jumped into Dylan's arms, wrapping him in a giant hug. Then she pulled back and immediately began to fuss and worry about his appearance, asking if he was okay, scolding him for his heroics, and so forth. Gina, who had taken the time to dress in jeans and a black baby doll top, gave Jackson a quick hug, and then held onto his arm and shoulder. He embraced her loosely, trying to imagine recent events from her perspective.

"It's okay," he said. "You're okay now."

When she let go after a moment, he hurried back up top to make sure Leroy wasn't having any trouble with Landon and Enrique. Landon had rescued his pal and was backpedaling in the water while holding onto him. Enrique appeared to be regaining consciousness, and Jackson kept his gun at the ready, just in case.

All at once, everyone arrived. The police. The Coast Guard. More police. A news crew. Curious bystanders, including a few in boats. Still more police.

Jackson held up his gun, shouting information to the officers, who quickly figured out what was going on. A Coast Guard cruiser ran up next to *El Curador* and several officers came aboard. More fished Landon and Enrique out of the water. Jackson checked in with the guy in charge, then swam over to the houseboat to check on his grandpa.

"You okay?" Jackson asked, giving him a huge, wet hug.

"Yeah, I'm fine. You want to explain what's going on here?"

Jackson nodded. "Yeah, but first holster that frying pan."

Chapter Thirty-Two

7:20 a.m.

TUESDAY MORNING WAS in full swing by the time Jackson finally arrived home. The last hour had been a circus.

First, the police and Coast Guard had sorted everything out, both at the harbor and back at Sanders' warehouse in Santa Monica. Jackson had given at least three recountings of his night, drawing incredulous looks all around. Fortunately, Ashley and Dylan had been around to corroborate his story.

Jackson had also explained that he was the one responsible for the shootings at the warehouse in Silver Lake, as well as for the incident at Hollywood Presbyterian. Desperate times called for desperate measures, he reasoned, and the authorities had largely agreed. He would need to give a detailed statement later, undergo some further questioning, and be available to fill in any details that proved necessary, but it looked like he would be off the hook. Plugging gangbangers wasn't the heinous crime it seemed. Or felt like.

Jackson also had been thanked profusely by Gina, Ashley, and Dylan. Shortly after everything played out aboard *El Curador*, Dylan had collapsed from exhaustion, pain, and withdrawal. But first he had offered Jackson a firm handshake and thanks for saving his and Ashley's lives. She had wrapped Jackson in a tight hug, assuring him that she was okay. She had come through the night unscathed, aside from the gash on her cheek; Dylan had borne the brunt of the Grays' beatings.

Ashley had thanked Jackson for helping her, staying with her despite her lies, and not giving up. She had also fussed a little over his battle wounds, which were nothing compared to Dylan's, but had suddenly hurt twice as much as they had all night. She had hugged him again, then went to tend to

Dylan, who had the full attention of the medics. They had been late to the scene, but had showed up in full force.

Lastly, Jackson had been reunited with Reggie, who had gotten word from the cops in Santa Monica that things were unfolding at the marina. He had hurried over as soon as he could and had become the fifth person to get an explanation from Jackson. He had also given him a lift back home, with a quick stop at McDonald's to grab half a dozen breakfast sandwiches.

"You sure you're okay?" he asked as Jackson got out of the Hummer at his place.

"I'll live, I guess. Thanks for everything, man."

"Don't mention it, bro."

They clasped hands and Reggie told Jackson to call if he needed anything.

"Yeah. I'll talk to you when I wake up Thursday."

"Right on, man."

Jackson turned toward the house.

"Hey! You did good today, J."

"Yeah, great."

"You did what had to be done, man."

Jackson looked over his shoulder and sighed. "Yeah."

Reggie waved and drove off, leaving Jackson alone in the driveway. He stood for a minute, trying to gather the strength to make it inside. The birds in his and Connie's trees chirped back and forth to one another, oblivious to the violence and mayhem that had unfolded. Above, the sky was brilliant blue, free of clouds or the typical marine layer. And the same breeze that had blown in off the ocean on Monday was kicking up again this morning. Serene, beautiful, the kind of day that made a person glad to be alive.

Usually.

Jackson turned and trudged inside, wanting nothing but unconsciousness and lots of it. One foot after the other, he made it upstairs, peeled off his clothes, and fell into bed. He was out in two minutes.

*   *   *

Five years ago . . .
Friday, May 25
11:07 p.m.

JACKSON SAT sprawled on his bed, surfing channels. KITV had preempted *Nightline* for more coverage from the Royal Honolulu Hotel, and Jackson dropped the remote onto his comforter. A male reporter gave the same speech Jackson had seen him give an hour ago, one that had been echoed by correspondents from all of the other networks.

Grant emerged from the bathroom, changed into a pair of mesh shorts and an old UCLA basketball jersey, so worn that Ed O'Bannon's number 31 was almost completely faded away. He tousled his hair. "Anything new?"

"No. They're out of facts." Jackson clicked off the TV and swung his legs off the bed. He stood and walked to the sliding glass door, unlocked it, and stepped out onto the balcony. A warm, tropical breeze rushed over him and back into the hotel room. The air was so salty he could taste it.

The same breeze ruffled the fronds of countless palm trees below him. Towering into blue sky during daylight hours, they seemed to spread a shroud over the hotel compound at night, almost completely obscuring the old-fashioned lampposts that lit the square known as "Central Park." Surrounded on three sides by six separate villas that constituted the Royal Honolulu Hotel, Central Park covered several acres of lush paradise. Comprised of a bubbling stream, a koi pond, a small aquarium of sea turtles, and dozens upon dozens of species of Hawaiian flora, the garden was a perfect place to relax. Several gazebos had been tucked into secluded corners of the park, and the hotel's three swimming pools were practically hidden amongst the foliage.

Except tonight.

Tonight, the pale blue—tinged with reddish-brown—water of the far pool stood out because of the police tape encircling it. The tape also cordoned off some of the surrounding foliage and a path leading to the nearest villa, which had been evacuated. Unlike most nights, when the park and pools played host to romantic strolls and moonlight swims—or daily recaps with a cute girl—tonight there wasn't a soul around.

That didn't include the reporters, most of whom probably didn't have souls anyway. They had been clustered in a corner of the driveway where telephoto zooms could just make out the edge of the pool. Lights from their setups created a ghastly contrast to the quiet, subdued, oddly peaceful setting in the park.

Grant quietly appeared beside Jackson. They stood for several minutes, just listening to the breeze and the caws of some distant native bird.

"You all right?" Grant finally asked.

"Yeah, sure." Jackson sighed. "I should have figured this out sooner."

"How could you have?"

He shrugged.

"Even if you had, it would have been too late," Grant said.

"Yeah."

"This was a well-planned, perfectly executed, precise attack. There was nothing anybody could have done."

Jackson turned his head. "Why again are you becoming a cop?"

Grant let the question drift off into the wind. "We should get to bed," he said.

Jackson wasn't ready. He leaned against the balcony railing with his hand. "I can't stop thinking about Becky. What must have been going through her mind when she got back here and saw everything? The crowd, the police, the bodies."

"Yeah."

"It had to be terrifying, thinking her dad was dead. If that was Mom or Dad . . ."

"How was she when you talked to her?"

"In shock, I think. Like everybody else. I don't know. Relieved."

Grant nodded.

"You know, this still doesn't make sense," Jackson said, turning to face his brother. "Why would cold-blooded assassins leave everybody but the senator alive?"

"Maybe they weren't that cold-blooded."

"They dragged his body from his room and threw him in the pool, Grant. They were sending a message to somebody." Jackson shook his head. "You do that, in the middle of the day when there are people—kids!—around the pool, but you take care not to kill any of his aides or bodyguards?"

Grant shrugged.

"And who uses blowguns anyhow?"

Another shrug.

"And how can it be that nobody saw anything at four-thirty in the afternoon but 'guys in black that looked like ninjas,'" he said, quoting one of the witnesses whose interview had played over and over on the local TV stations that night.

"These guys were pros, Jack. This wasn't some crazy with a sawed-off shotgun. They probably got in without anyone seeing them, dumped him in the pool for whatever reason, and were gone just that quickly."

"And why Dennis?"

Grant shrugged again.

"Why in Hawaii? Why here, at the hotel, with theoretical witnesses? Why tonight?"

"And why the pool?" Grant said. "What message is that sending that leaving him in his bathtub wouldn't?"

"Exactly."

Grant shook his head. "I guess that's the way it goes sometimes, Jack. Sometimes you never know the whys."

Jackson sighed. "Some memory to take with us, huh?"

"Worse for Becky."

"My last image of her was supposed to be a kiss at sunset, not consoling her while she watched her father regain consciousness."

Grant raised his eyebrows. "Wait a second? A kiss?"

Jackson smiled. "I said 'supposed to be.'" He winked as he turned inside. Grant followed him, locking the balcony door behind them. Jackson tried to push the crazy events of the night out of his mind as he brushed his teeth. But thinking about a five-hour flight, jetlag, and returning to work didn't do much for his psyche.

A soft knock sounded on the door as Jackson emerged from the bathroom. He looked at Grant, then opened the door connecting their room to David and Hannah's.

"Hey, Dad."

"Thought you boys might still be up. Have a minute?"

"Yeah," Grant said from the bed.

David slipped into the room and eased the door shut. "Crazy day, huh?"

"Shrimp shack robbery, luau, senator's assassination," Jackson said. "Yeah, I'd say."

"Have you been watching the news?"

"Yeah, but it hasn't changed in two hours."

"Hmm." The frown returned as David leaned back against the entertainment center. "Anyhow, with everything that's gone on, I didn't get a chance to tell you how proud I am of the two of you."

"Proud?" Jackson asked.

"For what you did this afternoon. You showed a lot of courage and a lot of smarts."

"Wasn't enough, I'm afraid."

David pursed his lips. "You did what you could."

"And if I hadn't," Grant said, "maybe the police could have responded here in time. I just played right into their hands."

"From what I hear, the killers were long gone before the authorities were even notified. The robbery and bomb threat were just precautions, distractions."

"Still."

"Still nothing," David said. "You can only control what you can control. And that's what you boys did. You were thrown into a dangerous situation and you reacted. Your methods certainly balanced the spectrum, but you got the job done. Without you, two more criminals would be at large, and who knows what might have happened to the hostages."

"Thanks, Dad," Jackson said.

"You know, your mother and I have always been proud of you, especially as we've watched you mature into young men. Today just sort of brings it into focus. And reminds me that life is short. So I just wanted to tell you how much we both love you and how proud we are of who you are. You guys are the real deal."

"We get it honest," Jackson said.

Grant nodded his agreement.

David smiled humbly. "You mind if we have a prayer?"

"Not at all," Grant said.

David nodded, then bowed his head. "Heavenly Father, I thank You for my two boys. Thank You for the character You've instilled in them. Thank You for protecting them this afternoon. I pray for Senator Dennis's family and friends as they grieve, and for the others involved in this tragedy. And I pray that You would bring Senator Dennis's killers to justice in Your time.

"I thank You for the time You've given us with one another here in Hawaii. Please guard our journey home tomorrow. In Jesus' name . . . Amen."

The entertainment center creaked softly as David stood up. "You boys get some sleep," he said.

David returned to his room, and Jackson closed the door behind him.

"He's right, you know," Grant said.

"Yeah, what's that?"

"You did good today."

"Yeah?"

"Yeah."

Jackson nodded. "You too, dude. All kidding aside, you're going to make a great cop."

"Thanks, bro."

"I mean, you were a sidearm, a nightstick, and a partner away from nailing that dude today."

Grant shook his head as he pulled back his covers and crawled under them. Jackson killed the lights and did likewise.

"You could be my partner," Grant said.

"Huh?"

"Join the force. A couple of brothers laying down the law on the streets of L.A.?"

"Pitch it to Fox," Jackson said.

"I'm serious, Jack. You should think about it."

"I'm not sure blues and a shield are for me."

"Wrong side of the law?"

"Funny." He yawned. "Besides, I think we've got a better script if you're the by-the-book cop and I'm the wisecracking P.I. who always gets the girl."

"So it's a comedy now."

"Except for your scenes."

He could almost hear Grant smile.

"But seriously, Jack, all earlier kidding aside, whatever you do, I'm here for you. And so are Mom and Dad."

"I know, bro."

*   *   *

7:26 a.m.

SOMETHING WAS beeping or ringing, and as Jackson opened his eyes, he determined it was his phone.

That wasn't possible. His cell phone was waterlogged, and he didn't have a landline.

Then he realized it was the doorbell.

Jackson buried his head under the pillow and nearly drifted off again before the doorbell sounded once more. His was the only doorbell in the world that rang louder when pressed harder and more frequently. With a growl, Jackson rolled out of bed.

He found his jeans and the Dodgers tee he had started the day before in. They were still wet, but a reasonable covering. He nearly fell as he stumbled down the stairs and jerked the front door open.

It was Connie, waking him at seven-thirty for the second day in a row.

But this time, for the first time, she didn't speak. She didn't care that his clothes were wet and rumpled or that he looked like a mugging victim. She just lunged into the house and engulfed him in a great big Italian hug.

Finally, she uttered her first words.

"Thank you."

He closed his eyes and sighed. "You're welcome, Connie."

Chapter Thirty-Three

Tuesday, May 22
11:26 a.m.

THE DRIVE ALONG the Malibu coastline never disappointed, and Jackson took his time, enjoying the views right and left. The rugged Santa Monica Mountains—wilderness interspersed with luxurious communities—were on one side and the untamed Pacific was on the other. Above it all, a sky free of smog was an even more vivid blue than usual. Monday's cool rain had moved out, and the air was again warm and comfortable.

Malibu Colony Drive ran parallel to the coast, just off of the PCH and just west of Malibu Lagoon State Beach. The two-lane road was lined with cramped houses of every shape, size, and style. None of them had yards, half backing onto the beach, half onto the backwaters of the lagoon or a private golf course.

Dr. Zachary's was the latter, a two-story box-shaped bungalow that doubled as his office. Jackson arrived a few minutes early, parked in one of three stalls outside the front door, and took a deep breath of salt air before entering.

Alaina, the perky secretary, was in her normal place behind the desk, typing away furiously. The small waiting room was empty, and after Jackson checked in with Alaina, he sat down and thumbed through an old issue of *Field & Stream*. The same old issue he had thumbed through on his last visit. He sighed and dropped it back on the table.

This was the point in time when he usually tensed up, waiting for Zachary to finish with his ten-thirty. This time, however, Jackson was relaxed. Maybe it was the weather, although it was almost always good. Maybe it was the fact that he had cheated death eighteen times a week ago, and other than a few sore ribs and some fading scars, was none the worse the wear for it. Or maybe it was the fact that Connie had ensured he wouldn't have to cook for the rest of the month. Up to several times a day, she had been bringing over casseroles and pastries and desserts and whatever she felt like making next— all of it delicious. In her eyes, he had saved Gina's life. Maybe so. And maybe this would cause her to give up dating complete strangers for a few weeks. Maybe not. Either way, she was back in Berkeley, Diane was back in Sacramento, and once Connie ran out of recipes to try, things would return to normal.

The office door opened and a very timid, very thin man walked out. He smiled at Alaina, looked uncertainly at Jackson, and then strode directly for the door. Alaina raised one eyebrow at Jackson. "You can go in now."

He nodded, and with a deep breath, rose and entered Zachary's office. There were two chairs and a bookcase on the left, the obligatory psychiatrist's couch on the right, and Zachary's wooden glider in the middle. It was framed on either side by double-hung windows that looked out at the lagoon.

Beyond the couch on the right was another door, leading to Zachary's private study. As Jackson closed the door to the waiting room behind him, Zachary emerged from the study.

Furman T. Zachary, Ph.D., had to be seen to be believed. He was freakishly tall, or at least appeared so because he was so thin and gaunt. His skin was pasty white, his hair dark black with a few hints of gray over the temples. It was pulled back into a tight, short ponytail and held by a rubber band, knotted twice. His face was long and narrow, the nose more so, the ears too. His well-trimmed goatee matched the hair in blackness, except under each corner of his mouth, where it was gray.

From the neck up, he looked like a white version of Snoop Dogg.

The similarities ended there. Zachary wore brown tweed pants that somehow were too long for him, hiding cheapie sandals that were today worn with navy socks. An off-white dress shirt was covered by a tan vest, complete with beads, two of which were navy to match the socks. He wore more bracelets than Tim Tebow, some of them in the Lance Armstrong "Live Strong" fashion, some of them plain string, one having red, white, black, green, and yellow beads. Jackson was pretty sure he had made one just like it one summer at Vacation Bible School. The multitude of bracelets maybe accounted for Zachary's incredibly long arms. They hung practically to his knees.

He carried two legal pads in his left hand and a cup of hot tea in his right. His wide eyes widened a little more when he saw Jackson and he nodded a greeting. Then he nodded at the couch. "Have a seat."

As had become his custom, Jackson prostrated himself on the sofa, head facing the doctor's chair and the two windows. The supine position had nothing to do with whatever psychological vulnerability Freud would have given it. Laying down was just more comfortable than sitting.

Zachary took to his glider, set the mug of tea next to a pipe that he smoked when the conversations got muddy, and crossed his legs. "How are you today, Jackson?" he asked. The voice was deep and dry and rumbled through the room. It was even more powerful when it spoke softly.

"Pretty good, Zach," Jackson said. (Zachary insisted his patients call him Zach.) "Thanks for switching the appointment."

"You had a busy week," Zachary said, clicking his pen.

He didn't know the half of it. Tuesday morning, after Jackson had called to reschedule his appointment, he had been visited by someone from the DEA. The cops had called to question him for six more hours that afternoon and evening. Fortunately, his stint as Detective Douglas never came up. Wednesday he had slept until noon, when Connie had brought over the best lasagna Jackson had ever eaten. Then Ashley had stopped by to thank him again and let him know that Dylan was on his way to rehab.

They talked for several hours on his deck, going over everything that had happened Monday and into Tuesday while eating homemade cheese Danishes, courtesy of Connie. Ashley apologized for lying to Jackson, he apologized for going Jack Bauer on her, and she explained a little more of what had gone on behind the scenes.

The three deliveries had originally been assigned to Dylan, as a sort of test before Sanders "promoted" him. Dylan got greedy and thought he could make the deliveries with dummy drugs, keeping the real stuff as evidence. He was found out, with Sanders assuming he was stealing the drugs for his own use and not because he was a cop. Even so, he would likely have been killed if he hadn't somehow convinced Sanders to give him another chance. Enter Ashley. Dylan had called her, hating to put her in such a position, but also hating to lose any chance of catching Sanders. And hating to die.

Ashley still wasn't sure why there had been such a precise schedule for the deliveries. Maybe it was one of Sanders' peculiarities; maybe it was his clients. The confusion about the time of the third delivery had been her error from the beginning, she blushingly admitted. The 'dumb blonde' wasn't entirely an act, she said.

As for what had changed Sergeant Locker's mind about coming to her and Dylan's rescue, Ashley wasn't sure. Jackson had just gotten through to his more humane side, she reasoned. Whatever the cause, it had set a lot of things in motion. Combining Jackson's testimony with hers and Dylan's, LAPD had been granted warrants to investigate several suspected Grays hangouts in and around the city, and were close to having warrants to search for evidence of the drugs at the homes of the three delivery recipients. And, Ashley added, there was rumor around the department that Jackson was up for a commendation.

Before leaving, Ashley took Jackson's hand in a purely platonic way and said that if he ever needed anything to give her a call. Rumor also had it that she was in line for a promotion to Detective II, and having a friend on the force couldn't hurt. Jackson agreed. Rockford had Becker. The brothers Simon had Downtown Brown. Shawn Spencer had Juliet O'Hara. And Jackson, like totally, had Ashley.

Then had come the weekend.

Friday had been the Dodgers-Giants game with Maggie. L.A. had won 11-2, instigating a weekend sweep that propelled them to first place in the National League West. Three hours of burgers and recapping his adventures of the previous week had followed the game and been just as enjoyable.

Saturday, Jackson and Leroy had tinkered on *Marsha's* engine until it had become obvious they either needed parts or had no idea what they were doing. Jackson and Reggie had hung out that evening, and Jackson had stopped by Mouse's house for a few hours of killing video baddies late Saturday night.

Sunday, Jackson had been up in time for church, after which he had planned to play tennis with Sam. Sore ribs had forced him out, and they had returned to her apartment and cooked a four-course dinner before watching her all-time favorite movie, *The Maltese Falcon*. For an old black and white, it wasn't bad, schweetart.

Monday, Jackson had finally caught up on sleep and mentally prepared for his session with Dr. Zachary. Subconsciously—or maybe partially consciously—he had tried to decide which manner of deflection he would use. Humor, rabbit trails, downright standoffishness? All had been used before, and none had fooled Zachary. But the doctor never pushed, content to let Jackson bare his soul at his own pace. At a discounted hundred dollars per hour, why not?

"A busy week?" Jackson echoed. "Yeah, you could say that."

"And this all started last Monday?" Zachary asked.

"Yeah."

"Your birthday, correct?"

"That's right."

"Did you have time to celebrate?"

"Yeah, more or less." He recounted having lunch with Maggie, dinner with Leroy, dessert with Sam.

"That's more or less?"

Jackson smiled.

"What about . . . by yourself?"

The smile faded. "What do you mean?"

"I mean . . . birthdays are very introspective times, especially milestones like number thirty. People often like to reflect, ruminate . . ."

"You want to know if I thought about killing myself?"

"If you did, I would certainly like to know, but that's not what I'm asking."

"What are you asking?"

Zachary smiled. "I'm sure somewhere in the course of your day, you had a few moments to yourself. What was on your mind? What were you thinking about?"

Jackson looked down. "To tell you the truth, I didn't have a lot of free time. When I did, I was trying to figure out if my client was lying to me or how to save her life."

He looked up and saw Zachary nod. Unsatisfied, but unwilling to push.

Jackson lowered his head again. He had vowed not to be difficult this time, and reluctantly, he opened his mouth. "Sunday night, I, uh . . . I took out the family photo album for a few hours."

"Why?"

"I don't know."

Zachary nodded, the same look on his face.

Jackson sighed. "I guess . . . I wanted to be sad. I wanted to let the dam break, to let everything come out."

"Did it?"

"No."

"Why not?"

"Because I stopped it. I knew if I let it out, I would never get it back in."

"Is that a problem?"

"Last time it was all out, I ended up in jail and then in your office."

"Do you think things might have changed since then? That it might be different now?"

Jackson shrugged.

"Do you think there might ever be a time when it is different?"

Jackson answered with another shrug.

Zachary slowly traced his eyebrow with his index finger. "Let's explore this metaphor of yours, about the dam. You talked about not wanting the dam to break, not wanting all the water to rush out because you're afraid you won't be able to get it back in. But I don't think that's it—not entirely. I think you're afraid you're going to drown, that the water is going to crush you."

"Yeah, maybe."

"But if you don't let it out, it just keeps building and building, pressing against the dam until it cracks, the water rushes out, and you're . . . crushed.

It's no different except that you have to endure the pain and strain of holding that water back for days and weeks and years before it bursts."

Zachary leaned forward. "But what if it isn't all or nothing? What if instead of keeping it all held in or blowing the dam, we opened a sluice gate? Let out just a little water? Relieved some pressure?"

Jackson eyed the doctor.

"You'll still get wet," Zachary said, "but you won't drown, won't get crushed. If it's too much, we close the gate again. But maybe you'll be able to deal with a little bit of water not all at once. Your emotional river can drain without flooding, so to speak, and then, maybe, you can let a little more out."

Jackson actually sat up. "Okay, so how do I open a sluice gate in real life?"

"That . . . is what we have to determine."

"You're the Ph.D."

"And you're the Bureau of Reclamation. You control the dam. So you pick the gate to open and let out some water."

"Okay, can we stop the metaphors for just a minute? What do you want to know?"

"It's not about me learning things about you, Jackson. It's about you confronting things."

"So what do you want me to confront?"

Zachary leaned back and rocked. Then he lit his pipe.

Jackson made a face. "Uh-oh."

Zachary sat in the creaking chair for several minutes, exhaling thin curls of smoke. Then he stopped rocking. "As a private investigator, I assume you do background checks on your clients before you take their cases, correct?"

"Uh, yeah."

Usually.

"I don't. I want to know nothing about my patients before I meet them, because I want everything I know about them to be shaped by what they tell me. And by what they don't tell me—by the way they tell me or don't tell me. I've been trained, Jackson—all my life, not just for a few years while earning my degrees—to observe everything about a person. Where they look when they talk, how they sit, facial responses to questions, posture, and so on and so on. And I've learned quite a bit about you over these last eight or nine months. But what I haven't learned, is what's really at the root of your problems." He leaned forward. "What is the source of your pain?"

Jackson looked down.

"I haven't pushed," Zachary said, "because when I start to push, you start to pull back. Everyone does; it's only natural. And I'm not going to push you now; I'm just going to tell you what I think and let you decide where we go from there."

Zachary swallowed. "We've been removing water buckets at a time. And we can keep doing that if you want. But if you're ready, you can also open that sluice gate . . . relieve a little of the stress and tension, the pain that you've been feeling. You don't have to tell me everything, and if you find the water's rising too fast, we'll close it back up." He folded his hands. "It's entirely up to you."

Jackson looked at Zachary for several long minutes. The doctor continued to smoke. Jackson took a deep breath and sat back.

"Last year . . . on my birthday . . . I went to have dinner with my mom and dad, and my brother and his fiancée." He swallowed. "There was, uh . . . there was an explosion in the restaurant, and . . . Mom, Dad, and Grant were killed."

Zachary's wide eyes narrowed slightly, wrinkles forming on his cheeks. He was not writing anything, just looking and listening.

"I'm an old school kind of guy," Jackson continued. "My family meant more to me than anything in this world, and in an instant, they were gone." He leaned forward. "So part of me wants to blow the whole dam, to let the water out, so it will crush me and kill me and end this misery! Nothing is more terrifying than letting a little out at a time, to let it slowly eat away at me, because it's not just water—it's acid. With piranhas swimming around in it. And that's why I keep it locked up, keep it behind the dam, because even though I know you're right, that someday it's going to crack and come rushing out, every day that it doesn't is a day that is almost tolerable. And right now, tolerable is about all I can hope for."

Zachary sat back and rocked, smoked his pipe, and studied Jackson. Finally, he spoke.

"When we suffer the loss of a loved one, part of us dies too. The closer the relationship, the larger the part of us. And so, in one sense, you're right. All you can ever do is tolerate again, because part of you is gone. But at the same time, we do have to keep living. We do have to move on, as crass as that can sound. We don't 'get over it,' but we learn to cope."

"That sounds like tolerating."

"Maybe so. But in a sense, all of life this side of glory is tolerating. We all experience various degrees of sorrow and loss in our lives, and sadly, despite all you've gone through, you'll probably experience more pain in the future. I'm sure you experienced pain in the past. The choice that you face is whether you want to settle for merely tolerating or whether you want to cope? Do you want to tolerate, or do you want to go on, with part of you missing, but maximizing what of you is left?"

Jackson got up and paced. "This isn't just pain, Zach. This isn't just a setback. This is . . . this is crippling."

"No it isn't."

"How can you say that?"

"Because you are not crippled. You are still thinking, feeling, and deep inside, longing to be healed. Longing to have that pain go away. But I'm guessing, longing to hold onto that pain, because if you let it go, you lose a connection to your family."

"That's crazy."

"Human beings sometimes are crazy. We view any connection to someone we love—even pain—as valuable, and don't want to let it go or be free of it. Jackson, you're standing on a balance beam." He gestured with his hands, like they were a scale. "On one side of you is that dam—all that pent up pain and sadness. And it's a constant struggle to keep it from bursting open and crushing you. On the other side is that sluice gate, where you can let a little bit of it out. But you're also afraid to do that, because you don't want to lose that water—the connection you feel to your mother, father, and brother."

"So what do I do?" Jackson asked.

Zachary nodded. "Yes, what do you do? I don't want to scare you or pressure you, Jackson, but—and I'm speaking from years of experience again—nobody can hold the dam back forever."

Jackson sighed. Where had his good feelings gone? Wasn't his therapist supposed to make him feel better, not worse?

"And there's one more thing we're forgetting here, Jackson."

"What's that?"

"It rains from time to time. You're afraid of letting water out of the dam because you're afraid eventually, your reservoir will dry out. But it rains."

Jackson slowly wandered back to the couch and sat down. He rested his head in his hands for several long minutes, during which there was nothing but silence. When he finally lifted his head, Zachary was sitting perfectly still, watching and waiting.

"Rain?" Jackson asked.

"That's right."

"Okay, so what will the rain look like?"

Zachary shrugged. "It could be a multitude of things. Maybe a happy memory from your childhood. Maybe a new relationship. Maybe fostering an existing relationship. Maybe . . . exactly what you're doing right now. Letting out a little bit of that pain, letting just a trickle of water through the sluice gate. Grade school science, Jackson. Water from lakes and rivers evaporates into the sky and becomes rain again, sans piranhas."

Jackson smiled. "So that's it? I have to pour out my soul to you once a month?"

"No, you *can* pour out your soul to me. You also have your grandfather, your friends, other family. And don't forget, you have a Heavenly Father as well."

Jackson nodded.

"Why don't we do a rain dance," Zachary suggested after a moment. He reached for his pipe. "You spoke of Maggie and Sam. You had lunch and dessert with them on your birthday. Friends?"

Zachary changed gears like Ashley and Dylan.

"Yeah," Jackson answered.

"Just friends?"

Jackson smirked. "Sort of."

Zachary rubbed his eyebrow with his finger. "Let's explore . . . your relationship with them."

Jackson shrugged and laid back town, figuring it should be an easy way to finish their hour. He returned to his hedging and dodging routine, not ready to open every page of the book just yet. Besides, what did a single, forty-year-old guy with a ponytail and a rawhide vest know about romance?

At promptly twelve-thirty, Zachary stopped writing, closed the sheets of his notepad, and removed his pipe. He clapped his thighs and stood up. "You're doing quite well, Jackson," he said. "Better, I think, than you realize."

"Does our little breakthrough today mean we're done?"

"It's up to you."

"It is?"

"I think you're ready to make that decision. If you feel that there's nothing more to gain by our sessions, then you're probably right. If you think today was a good first step, then I don't think we should sit back down."

Jackson nodded and grinned. Then he offered Zachary his hand. "I'll see you next month."

Zachary shook his hand and nodded. "I look forward to it."

Jackson let himself out of the office, taking the time for once to return Alaina's perky smile. Outside, he paused and looked up into the bright blue sky, squinting against the afternoon sun.

And prayed for rain.

Acknowledgements

A SPECIAL THANKS to my wife Sierra for her love, support, and encouragement, and for letting me chase my dream. Thanks to my parents, Doug and Jean Birr, for their many efforts proofing my manuscript and for spurring me on and believing in me when I needed it most. Thanks to Mark Robinson for curtailing my excessive use of commas, and to Crystal Balint for adding another perspective to the proofing process. And thanks to Tiffani Robinson for being my editor, sounding board, and best friend. I couldn't have done this without you all.

To my readers, thanks for indulging my artistic license. It was used liberally. I did just enough research—hopefully—to create a realistic story and setting. Everything else is my imagination. Where fact and fiction intersect, I hope those who know better will excuse me.